THE
FORBIDDEN
GAME

FOR MORE TALES FROM THE DARKNESS
BY L.J. SMITH, DON'T MISS:

Night World 1:
Secret Vampire, Daughters of Darkness, Spellbinder

Night World 2:
Dark Angel, The Chosen, Soulmate

Night World 3:
Huntress, Black Dawn, Witchlight

Night World:
The Ultimate Fan Guide

Dark Visions:
The Strange Power, The Possessed, The Passion

The Night of the Solstice

Heart of Valor

AND COMING SOON, THE CONCLUSION
TO THE NIGHT WORLD SERIES:

Strange Fate

THE FORBIDDEN GAME

THE HUNTER · THE CHASE · THE KILL

L.J. SMITH

SIMON PULSE

New York London Toronto Sydney

SIMON PULSE

An imprint of Simon & Schuster Children's Publishing Division

1230 Avenue of the Americas, New York, NY 10020

This Simon Pulse paperback edition June 2010

The Hunter copyright © 1994 by Lisa J. Smith

The Chase copyright © 1994 by Lisa J. Smith

The Kill copyright © 1994 by Lisa J. Smith

All rights reserved, including the right of reproduction in whole or in part in any form.

SIMON PULSE and colophon are registered trademarks of Simon & Schuster, Inc.

For information about special discounts for bulk purchases, please contact Simon & Schuster Special Sales at 1-866-506-1949 or business@simonandschuster.com.

The Simon & Schuster Speakers Bureau can bring authors to your live event. For more information or to book an event contact the Simon & Schuster Speakers Bureau at 1-866-248-3049 or visit our website at www.simonspeakers.com.

Designed by Mike Rosamilia

The text of this book was set in Adobe Garamond.

Manufactured in the United States of America

2 4 6 8 10 9 7 5 3 1

Library of Congress Control Number 2009934857

ISBN 978-1-4169-8940-0

These titles were originally published individually by Pocket Books.

CONTENTS

THE HUNTER

For Peter, who has both feet firmly on the ground—
thank heavens!

With special thanks to John Divola, for lending some of his
extraordinary photographs to Zach.

CHAPTER 1

Jenny glanced back over her shoulder. They were still behind her, on the other side of the street but definitely following. They matched their pace to hers; when she slowed to pretend to look in a store window, they slowed, too.

There were two of them, one dressed in a black T-shirt and leather vest, with a black bandanna on his head, the other in a long flannel shirt, black-and-blue plaid, unbuttoned. Also unwashed. They both looked like trouble.

The game store was a few blocks ahead. Jenny quickened her pace a little. This wasn't the best neighborhood in town, and she'd come here specifically because she didn't want any of her friends to see her. She hadn't realized, though, that Eastman Avenue had gotten quite so rough. After the last riots the police had cleared things up, but many of the vandalized stores still had boarded windows, which gave Jenny a creeping feeling between her shoulder blades. They were like bandaged eyes turned toward her.

Not at all the place to be at dusk—but it wasn't dusk yet, Jenny told herself fiercely. If only those two guys would turn off onto another street. Her heart was beating unpleasantly hard. Maybe they *had* turned. . . .

She slowed again, her feet in their lace-up canvas Tretorns making no sound on the dirty sidewalk. From behind and to the left she heard the flat smack of running shoes and the clack of bootheels. The footsteps slowed.

They were still there.

Don't look back, she told herself. Think. You have to cross over at Joshua Street to get to the store—but that means crossing left, to *their* side of the street. Bad idea, Jenny. While you're crossing they can catch up to you.

All right, then, she'd turn off before that, she'd go right on this next street up here—what was it? Montevideo. She'd go right on Montevideo, and then she'd find a store to duck into, a place to hide until the two guys had passed by.

The Tower Records on the corner of Eastman and Montevideo was no longer in business. Too bad. Back straight, stubbornly pretending she was perfectly calm, Jenny walked by the darkened windows. She caught a glimpse of herself in one of them: a slender girl with hair that Michael had once said was the color of honey in sunlight. Her eyebrows were straight, like two decisive brush strokes, and her forest-green eyes were dark as pine needles and even more serious than usual. She looked worried.

She turned right at the cross street. As soon as she was out of sight of Eastman Avenue, she stopped and stood as still as a deer, backpack swinging from her hand, eyes desperately scanning Montevideo for cover.

Directly opposite her was a vacant lot and beside that a Thai restaurant, closed. Behind her the looming bulk of the record store presented a blank wall to the street all the way down to the park. No cover. Nowhere to hide.

Jenny's neck prickled and her little fingers began to tingle.

She turned toward Eastman and hugged the wall, tossing back her hair to listen.

Were those footsteps or just the sick thudding of her own heart?

She wished that Tom were with her.

But of course that was the whole point. Tom couldn't be with her, since it was his party she was shopping for.

It was supposed to have been a pool party. Jenny Thornton was known for her pool parties, and here in southern California late April was a perfectly reasonable time to have one. The temperature often hovered in the mid-seventies at night, and the Thornton pool glowed like a huge blue-green jewel in the backyard, giving off little wisps of steam from its surface. The perfect setting for an outdoor barbecue.

Then three days ago the cold snap had come . . . and Jenny's plans were ruined. Nobody except polar bears swam in this kind of weather.

She'd meant to rethink things, to come up with some other brilliant idea, but it had been one of *those* weeks. Summer's fourteen-year-old schnauzer had finally had to be put to sleep, and Summer had needed Jenny for moral support. Dee had taken a kung fu exam, and Jenny had gone to cheer her on. Audrey and Michael had had a fight, and Zach had had the flu. . . .

And then suddenly it had been Friday afternoon, with just hours to go before the party and everyone expecting something special—and *nothing* set up.

Fortunately an idea had come to her in the middle of computer applications class. A game. People gave murder mystery parties and Pictionary parties and things like that. Why not a game tonight? It would have to be a very special game, of course. Something chic enough for Audrey, sexy enough for Tom, and even scary, if possible, to keep Dee's interest. Something seven people could play at once.

Vague notions had run through Jenny's head of the only really exciting games she'd ever played as a child. Not the ones the adults arranged, but the kind you devised on your own once they were safely out of the house. Truth or dare and spin the bottle. Some combination of those two—only more sophisticated, of course, more suited to juniors in high school—would be ideal.

That was what had brought her to Eastman Avenue. She'd known perfectly well it wasn't the best neighborhood, but she'd figured that at least none of her friends would see her and find out about this last-minute scramble for entertainment. Jenny had gotten herself into this mess; she would get herself out of it.

Only now the mess was getting bigger than she'd bargained for.

She could definitely hear footsteps now. They sounded very close and were approaching quickly.

Jenny looked down Montevideo again, her mind taking in irrelevant details with obsessive precision. The record store wall was not truly blank after all. There was a mural on it, a mural of a street that looked much like Eastman Avenue before the riots. Strange—parts of the mural looked *real.* Like that storefront painted in the middle, the one with the sign Jenny couldn't quite make out. It had a door that looked real: The handle seemed three dimensional. In fact . . .

Startled, Jenny took a step toward it. The knob appeared to change shape as she moved, like any three-dimensional object. She looked more closely and found she could see the difference in texture between the wooden door and the painted concrete wall.

The door was real.

It couldn't be—but it was. There was a door stuck in the middle of the mural.

Why, Jenny didn't know. There wasn't time to wonder about it. Jenny needed to get off the street, and if this door was unlocked . . .

Impulsively she took hold of the knob.

It was cool as china and it turned in her hand. The door swung inward. Jenny could see a dimly lit room.

One instant of hesitation, then she stepped inside.

Just as she did, she consciously took in the sign above the door. It read: "More Games."

CHAPTER 2

There was a push-button lock on the inside door-knob, and Jenny depressed it. There were no windows looking out on Montevideo, of course, so she couldn't see whether the two guys had followed her. Still, she had a tremendous feeling of relief. No one was going to find her in here.

Then she thought, More Games? She had often seen signs reading "More Books" in the arty, shabby used bookstores around here, signs with an arrow pointing up a narrow staircase to another floor. But how could there be More Games when there hadn't been any games at all yet?

Just the fact that it happened to be a game store she'd stumbled onto was strange, but very convenient. She could do her shopping while she waited for the tough guys to go away. The owner would probably be glad to have her, with that mural camouflaging the door they couldn't do much business here.

As she looked around she saw just how strange the store really was. Even stranger than the usual odd shops around Eastman Avenue.

The room was lit by one small window and several old-fashioned lamps with stained-glass shades. There were shelves and tables and racks like any other store, but the objects on them were so exotic that Jenny felt as if she'd stepped into another world. Were they all games? They couldn't be. Jenny's mind filled suddenly with wild images from *The Arabian Nights,* images of foreign bazaars where anything—anything— might be sold. She stared around at the shelves in amazement.

God, what a weird chessboard. Triangular. Could anybody really play on a board like that? And there was another one, with strange, squat chessmen carved of rock crystal. It looked more than antique—it looked positively ancient.

So did a metalwork box covered with arabesques and inscriptions. It was made of brass or maybe bronze, decorated with gold and silver and Arabic writing. Whatever was in that box, Jenny knew she couldn't afford it.

Some of the games she could identify, like the mahogany mah-jongg table with ivory tiles spilled carelessly on the green felt top. Others, like a narrow enameled case crawling with hieroglyphics, and a red box embossed with a gold Star of David in a circle, she had never seen before. There were dice of every size and description: some twelve-sided, some shaped like pyramids, and some ordinary cubical ones made of odd materials. There were card decks fantastically colored like illuminated manuscripts.

Strangest of all, the weird antique things were intermixed with weird ultramodern things. A cork bulletin board on the back wall sported signs reading: "Flame." "Rant." "Rave." "Surf the Edge." "Cheap Thrills." Cyberpunk, Jenny thought, vaguely recognizing the terms. Maybe they sold computer games here, too. From a boom box on the counter came 120-beat-a-minute acid house music.

This, thought Jenny, is a very peculiar place.

It felt so—cut off—from everything outside. As if time didn't exist here, or ran differently somehow. Even the dusty sunlight slanting in that one window seemed wrong. Jenny would have sworn the light should have been coming from the other direction. A chill went through her.

You're mixed up, she told herself. Disoriented. And no wonder, after the day you've had—after the *week* you've had. Just concentrate on finding a game, if there's anything here that you can actually play.

There was another sign on the board, a sort of square:

```
W       E       L       C

O       M       E       T

O       M       Y       W

O       R       L       D
```

Jenny tilted her head, examining it. What did the letters say? Oh, of course, she had it now. *Welcome* . . .

"Can I help you?"

The voice spoke from right behind her. Jenny turned— and lost her breath.

Eyes. Blue eyes. Except that they weren't just blue, they were a shade Jenny couldn't describe. The only place she'd seen a blue like that was once when she'd happened to wake up at the precise instant of dawn. Then, between the window curtains, she'd glimpsed an unbelievable, luminous color, which had lasted only a second before fading to the ordinary blue of the sky.

No boy should have eyes as blue as that, and especially not surrounded by lashes so heavy they seemed to weigh his eyelids down. This boy had the most startling coloring she'd ever seen. His eyelashes were black, but his hair was white—true white, the color of frost or tendrils of mist. He was . . . well, beautiful. But in the most exotic, uncanny way imaginable, as if he'd just stepped in from another world. Jenny's reaction was instant, total, and absolutely terrifying. She forgot Tom's existence.

I didn't know people could look like that. Real people, I mean. Maybe he's not real. God, I've got to stop staring—

But she couldn't. She couldn't help herself. Those eyes were like the blue at the core of a flame. No—like a mile-deep lake set in a glacier. No . . .

The guy turned and went to the counter. The boom box clicked off. Silence roared in Jenny's ears.

"Can I help you?" he repeated, politely and indifferently.

Heat rose to Jenny's cheeks.

Ohmigod, what he must think of me.

The moment those eyes had turned away from her, she had come out of it, and now that he was farther away, she could look at him objectively. Not something from another world. Just a guy about her own age: lean, elegant, and with an unmistakable air of danger about him. His hair was white-blond, cropped close at the sides, long in back and so long over the forehead that it fell into his eyes. He was dressed all in black in a weird combination of cyberpunk and Byronic poet.

And he's still gorgeous, Jenny thought, but who cares? Honestly, you'd think I'd never seen a guy before. On Tom's birthday, too—

A flash of shame went through her. She'd better start her shopping or get out of here. The two alternatives seemed equally attractive—except that the tough guys might still be outside.

"I want to buy a game," she said, too loudly. "For a party— for my boyfriend."

He didn't even blink at the word *boyfriend*; in fact, he looked more laconic than ever. "Be my guest," he said. Then he seemed to rouse himself to make a sale. "Anything in particular?"

"Well . . ."

"How about Senet, the Egyptian Game of the Dead?" he said, nodding at the enameled case with the hieroglyphics. "Or the I-ching? Or maybe you'd like to cast the runes." He picked up a leather cup and shook it suggestively. There was a sound like rattling bones.

"No, nothing like that." Jenny was feeling distinctly unnerved. She couldn't put her finger on it, but something about this guy sent whispers of alarm through her blood. Maybe it was time to go.

"Well—there's always the ancient Tibetan game of goats and tigers." He gestured at a curiously carved bronze board with tiny figurines on it. "The fierce tigers, see, stalk the innocent little goats, and the innocent little goats try to run from the tigers. For two players."

"I—no." Was he making fun of her? There was something to the twist of his mouth that made Jenny think yes. With dignity she said, "I was looking for—just a game that a lot of people can play at once. Like Pictionary or Outburst," she added defiantly. "But since you don't seem to have anything like that in the store—"

"I see," he said. "That kind of game." Suddenly, looking at

her sideways, he smiled. The smile unnerved Jenny more than anything yet.

Definitely time to go, she thought. She didn't care whether the tough guys were still outside. "Thank you," she said with automatic politeness, and she turned to the door.

"Mystery," he said. His voice caught Jenny halfway across the room. She hesitated in spite of herself. What on earth did he mean?

"Danger. Seduction. Fear." Jenny turned back to face him, staring. There was something almost mesmerizing about his voice—it was full of elemental music, like water running over rock. "Secrets revealed. Desires unveiled." He smiled at her and pronounced the last word distinctly: "Temptation."

"What are you talking about?" she said, tensed to hit him or run if he took one step toward her.

He didn't. His eyes were as innocently blue as Nordic fjords. "The Game, of course. That's what you want, isn't it? Something . . . very special."

Something very special.

Exactly what she'd thought herself.

"I think," she said slowly, "that I'd better—"

"We do have something like that in stock," he said.

Now's your chance, she told herself when he disappeared through a door into the back room. You can just walk out of here. And she was *going* to leave, she was just about to go, when he appeared again.

"I think," he said, "that this is what you've been looking for."

She looked at what he was holding, then up at his face.

"You've got to be joking," she said.

The box was about the size and shape of a Monopoly game. It was white and glossy and there wasn't a single word, line, or figure printed on it.

A blank white box.

Jenny waited for the punch line.

There was something about it, though. The more she looked at that box, the more she felt . . .

"Could I see it?" she said. Touch it, was what she meant. For some reason she wanted to feel the weight of it in her hands, the sharpness of its corners in her palms. It was silly, but she did want to. She *really* wanted to.

The guy leaned back, tilting the box between his own hands, gazing at its glossy top. Jenny noticed that there wasn't a single fingerprint on the shiny finish, not so much as a smudge. She also noticed that his fingers were long and slender. And that he had a snake tattooed on his right wrist.

"Well . . ." he said. "I don't know. On second thought, I'm not sure I can sell it to you after all."

"Why *not*?"

"Because it really is special. Un-mundane. I can't let it go to just anybody, or for just any reason. Maybe if you explained what it was for. . . ."

Why, he's a tease, Jenny thought. Without in the least stopping being scared, or disturbed, or any of the other things she'd been since she'd come into this store, she started being amused as well. Wildly, inexplicably amused.

Maybe if I looked like him, was that gorgeous, I'd be a tease, too, she thought. She said seriously, "It's for a party tonight, for my boyfriend, Tom. He's seventeen today. Tomorrow night we'll have the big party—you know, with *everybody* invited, but tonight it's just our group. Our crowd."

He tilted his head to one side. Light flashed off the earring he was wearing—a dagger or a snake, Jenny couldn't tell which. "So?"

"So I need something for us to do. You can't just get seven people in a room, throw Doritos at them, and expect them to have a good time. I've screwed up massively by not getting organized until now—no real food, no decorations. And Tom—"

The guy tilted the box again. Jenny watched its surface turn milky, then bright, then milky again. It was almost hypnotic. "And Tom will care?" he said, as if not believing it.

Jenny felt defensive. "I don't know—he might be disappointed. He *deserves* better, you see," she added quickly. "He's—" Oh, how to explain Tom Locke? "He's—well, he's incredibly handsome, and by the end of this year he'll have lettered in three sports—"

"I get it."

"No, you don't," Jenny said, horrified. "He's not like that at all. Tom is *wonderful.* He's just—*so* wonderful that sometimes

19

it takes a little keeping up with him. And we've been together forever, and I love him, and I have since second grade. Okay?" Anger gave her courage, and she advanced a step toward the guy. "He is absolutely the best boyfriend in the world, and anybody who says he isn't—"

She stopped. The boy was holding out the box to her. Jenny hesitated, nonplussed.

"You can hold it if you want," he said gently.

"Okay," Jenny said, embarrassed, her vehemence fading. She took the glossy box gingerly between her palms—and forgot everything else. It was cool and just weighty enough to be intriguing. Something inside rattled slightly, mysteriously. There was a quality about it that Jenny couldn't describe, a sort of electric current that ran up her fingers as she held it.

"We're closing," the boy said briskly, with another of his arbitrary mood swings. "You gonna buy it?"

She was. She knew perfectly well anybody crazy enough to buy a box without looking inside it deserved whatever they got, but she didn't care. She wanted it, and she felt a strange reluctance to take the lid off and peek in. No matter what, this would make a great story to tell Tom and the others tonight. *"The craziest thing happened to me today. . . ."*

"How much?" she asked.

He went to the counter and hit a key on an antique-looking brass cash register. "Call it twenty."

Jenny paid. She noticed the cash drawer was full of odd-looking money all jumbled together: square coins, coins with holes in the center, crumpled bills in pastel colors. The wrongness of that cut into her pleasure in the box a little, and she felt another chill, like spiders walking on gooseflesh.

When she looked up, the boy was smiling at her.

"Enjoy," he said, and then his heavy lashes drooped as if at a private joke.

From somewhere a clock chimed the little unfinished tune that meant half past some hour. Jenny glanced down at her watch and stiffened in horror.

Seven-thirty—it couldn't be! There was no way she could have been in this store for over an hour, but it was true.

"Thank you; I have to go," she gasped distractedly, heading for the door. "Uh—see you later."

It was just a politeness, not meant to be answered, but he did answer. He murmured what sounded like "at nine" but undoubtedly was "that's fine" or something like that.

When she looked back, he was standing half in shadow, with the stained glass of a lamp throwing blue and purple stripes on his hair. For just a second she caught something in his eyes—a *hungry* look. A look completely at odds with the indifferent manner he'd worn while speaking to her. Like—a starving tiger about to go hunting. It shocked Jenny so much that her "goodbye" froze in her throat.

Then it was gone. The boy in black reached over and turned the acid house music on.

Terrific soundproofing, Jenny thought as the door closed behind her and the music was cut off. She gave herself a mental shake, throwing off the lingering image of those blue eyes. Now if she *ran* all the way home, she might just have time to throw some Cheez Whiz in the microwave and shove a handful of CDs in the player. Oh, God, what a day!

That was when she noticed the tough guys.

They were waiting for her across the street, hidden in the blue-gray shadows of dusk. Jenny saw them coming and felt a jolt to her stomach. Swiftly and automatically she stepped backward, reaching behind her for the doorknob. Where *was* it? And why was she so stupid today? She should have asked the guy in black if she could use the phone; she should have called Tom—or Dee— *Where was the knob?*

They were close enough that she could see that the one in the flannel shirt had bad skin. The one with the bandanna was grinning in a very creepy way. They were both coming toward her *and where was the freaking doorknob?* All she could feel behind her was cool, painted concrete.

Where is it where is it—

Throw the box at them, she thought, suddenly calm and clear. Throw it and run. Maybe they'll stop to investigate it. Her mind, utterly practical, ordered her hand to stop searching for a doorknob that wasn't there. Waste of time.

With both hands she lifted the white box to throw it. She wasn't sure exactly what happened next. Both guys stared at her and then—they turned around and started running.

Running. Flannels was in the lead, and Bandanna just a length behind him, and they were running like deer, with an animal grace and economy of motion. Fast.

And Jenny hadn't thrown the box after all.

My fingers . . . I didn't throw the box because I couldn't let go because my fingers . . .

Shut up, her mind told her. If you're dumb enough to care more about a box than about your own life, okay, but at least we don't have to dwell on the subject.

Walking quickly, sweatered arms cradling the box to her chest, she started for home.

She didn't turn around to see how she'd missed the door-knob with all her behind-the-back fumbling. At the time she simply forgot.

It was ten to eight when Jenny finally neared her street. The lighted living rooms in the houses she passed looked cozy. She was out in the chill dark.

Somewhere on the way home she'd started to have mis-givings about the game. Her mother always said she was too impulsive. Now she'd bought this—thing—without even knowing exactly what was inside. Even as she thought it, the box seemed to thrum slightly in her arms as if charged with hidden power.

Don't be silly. It's a box.

But those guys *ran,* something whispered in the back of her mind. Those guys were *spooked.*

As soon as she got home, she was going to check this game out. Examine it thoroughly.

A wind had sprung up and was moving the trees on Mariposa Street. Jenny lived in a sprawling ranch-style house set among those trees. As she approached it, something slunk furtively by the front doorway. A shadow—a small one.

Jenny felt a prickling at the back of her neck.

Then the shadow moved under the porch light and turned into the ugliest cat in America. Its fur was mottled gray and cream (like a case of mange, Michael said), and its left eye had a permanent squint. Jenny had taken it in a year ago, and it was still wild.

"Hey, Cosette," Jenny said, darting forward and petting the cat as relief swept through her. I'm really getting jumpy, she thought, scared by every little shadow.

Cosette put her ears back and growled like the possessed girl in *The Exorcist.* She didn't bite, though. Animals never bit Jenny.

Once in the front hallway Jenny sniffed suspiciously. Sesame oil? Her parents were supposed to be leaving for the weekend. If they'd changed their minds . . .

Alarmed, she dumped her backpack—and the white box—on the living room coffee table as she galloped to the kitchen.

"At last! We were beginning to think you weren't coming."

Jenny stared. The girl who'd spoken was wearing an army fatigue jacket and sitting on the counter, one incredibly long leg braced on Jenny's mother's blondwood kitchen table, the other dangling. Her hair was cropped so close to her head it looked like little nubs of black velvet on her skull. She was as beautiful as an African priestess, and she was grinning wickedly.

"Dee . . ." Jenny began.

The other inhabitant of the kitchen was wearing a black-and-white houndstooth-check jacket and Chanel earrings. Around her was spread a sea of utensils and ingredients: metal cleavers and ladles, eggs, a can of bamboo shoots, a bottle of rice wine. A wok was sizzling on the stove.

". . . and Audrey!" Jenny said. "What are you *doing* here?"

"Saving your butt," Audrey answered calmly.

"But—you're cooking!"

"Of course. Why shouldn't I cook? When Daddy was assigned to Hong Kong we had a chef who was like part of the family; he used to talk Cantonese to me while Daddy was working and Mother was at the beauty parlor. I loved him. Naturally I can cook."

While this speech was going on, Jenny was looking back and forth from one girl to the other. When it was over she burst into laughter, shaking her head. Of course. She should have known she couldn't fool these two. They must have seen that under her facade of self-confidence about the party she was frantic. They knew her far too well—and they'd come to

25

rescue her. Impulsively Jenny hugged each of them in turn.

"Since Tom loves Chinese, I decided to take care of the food," Audrey went on, dropping something dumplinglike into the wok. "But where have you been, hmm? Run into some kind of trouble?"

"Oh—no," Jenny said. If she explained what had happened, she'd just get yelled at for going into a bad neighborhood. Not by Dee, of course—Deirdre Eliade's recklessness was matched only by her somewhat skewed sense of humor—but by the ever-practical Audrey Myers. "I was just buying a game for tonight—but I don't know if we're going to need it after all."

"Why not?"

"Well . . ." Jenny didn't want to explain that, either. She didn't know *how* to explain it. She only knew she needed to look at that box before anyone else arrived. "It might be boring. So what are you making?" She peered into the wok to change the subject.

"Oh, just some *Mu shu rou* and a few *Hei jiao niu liu.*" Audrey was moving around the kitchen with her usual mannered grace, her tailored clothes unmarred by a single spot of grease. "That's stir-fried pork and spring rolls to you provincial types. Also fried rice and the trimmings."

"Pork," said Dee, taking a leisurely sip of Carbo Force, her favorite energy drink, "is death on wheels. You have to lift at the gym for a week to work off one pork chop."

"Tom loves it," Audrey said shortly. "And he looks all right."

Dee gave a maddening laugh, and hostility flashed across the room like lightning.

Jenny sighed. "Oh, get over it. Can't you call a truce for just one day in the year?"

"I don't *think* so," Audrey hummed, expertly fishing a spring roll out of the wok with chopsticks.

Dee's teeth flashed white in her night-dark face. "And ruin a perfect record?" she said.

"Look, I am not going to have Tom's party ruined—not even by my two best friends. Understand?"

"Oh, go to your room and become beautiful," Audrey said indulgently and picked up a cleaver.

The box, thought Jenny—but she did have to change her clothes. She'd better make it fast.

CHAPTER 3

In her room Jenny exchanged her crewneck sweater and jeans for a flowing cream-colored skirt, a tissue-linen blouse, and a beaded batik vest that glowed with hundreds of tiny golden threads.

Her eyes were drawn to a stuffed white rabbit on the dresser. The rabbit was holding a daisy with the words *I love you* emblazoned across its center. An Easter gift from Tom, a ridiculous thing, but one she knew she would keep forever. The fact that he wouldn't say the words in public just made this secret confession all the sweeter.

For as long as she could remember, she had been terribly in love with Tom. Whenever she thought of him, it was like a sudden quick ache, a sweetness almost too much to bear.

She felt it in various places in her body, but it was an emo-
tional thing, mainly, and centered in her chest. It had been that
way since second grade. Stuck around the frame of the mirror
were pictures of them together—at the sixth-grade Halloween
Hop (in costume), at the ninth-grade graduation dance, at the
junior prom two weeks ago, at the beach. They had been a
couple for so long that everyone thought of them as Tom-and-
Jenny, a single unit.

As always, the very image of Tom seemed to wrap a thin
blanket of comfort over her. This time, though, Jenny felt
something nagging at her underneath the comfort. Something
tugging at her to think about it.

The box again.

Okay, go look at it. Then think *party*.

She was dragging a brush through her hair when there was
a perfunctory tap at the door and Audrey came in.

"The spring rolls are finished and the stir-fry has to wait
till the last minute." Audrey's own hair, which she always wore
up, was glossy auburn, almost copper. Her eyes were chestnut
and just now narrowed in disapproval. "New skirt, I see," she
added. "A long one."

Jenny winced. Tom liked her in long skirts, especially the
soft and flowing kind. Audrey knew it and Jenny knew she
knew it. "So?" she said dangerously.

Audrey sighed. "Can't you see? You're letting him get too
sure of you."

"Audrey, please—"

"There's such a thing as being too good," Audrey said firmly. "Listen to me, because I *know*. Guys are weird, *n'est-ce pas*? You never want one to be that sure of you."

"Don't be ridiculous," Jenny began, then stopped. For some reason, for just a second, she thought of the guy at the game store. Eyes as blue as the core of a flame.

"I'm serious," Audrey was saying, her head tilted back to look at Jenny through spiky jet-black eyelashes that touched equally spiky copper bangs. "If a guy feels too secure, you lose his attention, he takes you for granted. Starts looking at other girls. You want to keep him off balance, never knowing what you'll do next."

"Like you do with Michael," Jenny said absently.

"Oh, Michael." Audrey made a dismissive gesture with exquisitely polished nails. "He's just keeping the seat warm until I decide who's next. He's a—a bookmark. But do you see what I'm saying? Even Dee thinks you give in to Tom too much."

"Dee?" Jenny raised her eyebrows ironically. "Dee thinks all guys are lying hounds. As boyfriends, anyway."

"True," said Audrey. "It's strange," she added thoughtfully, "how she can be so right about that and so wrong about everything else."

Jenny just made a wry face at her. Then she said, "You know, Audrey, maybe if *you* tried being nice first—"

"Hmm, maybe . . . when the devil goes ice-skating," Audrey said.

Jenny sighed. Audrey was the newcomer to their group; she'd moved to Vista Grande last year. All the others had known each other since elementary school, and Dee had known Jenny longest of all. When Audrey arrived, Dee had gotten—well, jealous. They'd been fighting ever since.

"Just try not to kill each other during the party," Jenny said. Deliberately she pulled her hair back—the way Tom liked it—and anchored its silkiness with an elastic band.

Then she smiled at Audrey and said, "Let's go back to the kitchen."

When they did they found that Michael and Zach had arrived—looking, as usual, as different as night and day.

Michael Cohen was shaped like a teddy bear, with dark hair as rumpled as his gray sweats and the eyes of a sarcastic spaniel. Zach Taylor had light hair pulled back in a casual ponytail, an intense beaky-nosed face, and eyes as gray as the winter sky.

"How's the flu?" Jenny said, kissing Zachary's cheek. She could do this safely because she'd been exposed to his germs all week, and besides, he was her cousin. Zach's gray eyes softened for just an instant, then went cool again. Jenny was never quite sure if Zach liked her or merely tolerated her the way he did everyone else.

"Hello, Michael," she said, giving him a pat instead of a kiss. The liquid spaniel eyes turned toward her.

"You know," Michael said, "sometimes I worry about us, about our whole generation. Do we know what we're doing? Are we any better than the Me Generation? What do we have to look forward to, except driving better cars than our parents? I mean, what is the *point*?"

"Hello, Michael," said Audrey.

"Hello, O light of my life. Is this an egg roll I see before me?" Michael said, reaching.

"Don't eat that. Put it back on the plate with the others and take it out to the living room."

"I live to serve," Michael said and departed.

God—the box, Jenny thought. Michael was the sort who would potter around the room reading your mail and opening your drawers in an absentminded way. Insatiably curious. She followed him.

Her stomach knotted at the sight of it, pristine and rectangular and gleaming on her mother's solid ponderosa pine coffee table. Jenny's mother had worked very hard with a very expensive decorator to make sure the living room looked "natural and inevitable and not at all arty." There were Navajo weavings and Hopi baskets on the walls, Zuni pots on the floor, and a Chimayo rug above the fireplace. Jenny wasn't allowed to touch any of them.

Calm down, she told herself. But even approaching the white box was strangely difficult. She picked it up and realized that her palms were sweaty enough to stick to it.

Thrummm. The current tingled through her fingers. The feeling of something wrong increased.

Oh, hell! I'll just throw the thing away, Jenny thought, surprised at the relief the idea brought. We'll play canasta.

Michael, munching spring rolls, was eyeing her with interest.

"What's that? A present?"

"No—just a game I bought, but I'm going to get rid of it. Michael, do you know how to play canasta?"

"Nope. So where's the sun bunny?"

"Not here yet—oh, that's probably her. Would you get the door?"

Michael just looked vaguely at the plate in his one hand and the roll in his other. Jenny ran to the hallway, still holding the box.

Summer Parker-Pearson was tiny, with thistledown hair and dimples you wanted to poke your fingers into. She was wearing a china blue shirtdress and shivering.

"It's freezing out here. How're we going to go swimming, Jenny?"

"We're not," Jenny said gently.

"Oh. Then why did I bring my bathing suit? Here's my present." She piled a shirt box wrapped in maroon paper on top of the white box Jenny was holding, added a small tote bag to the stack, and headed for the living room.

Jenny followed, put all the things on the coffee table, then pulled the white box from beneath them. *Thrum.* Summer was saying hello to Mike and Zach and Dee.

"Look," Jenny said, "if you guys will excuse me for a second—" She was cut off by the doorbell. This time she didn't want anybody else to answer it. "I'll get it."

Tom was on the doorstep.

He looked good. Of course, he always looked good to Jenny, but tonight he was especially handsome, really *devilishly* good-looking, with his dark brown hair neat and short and his smile faintly mocking. Tom wore simple clothes like other guys, but somehow he wore them differently. He could make a pair of Basic Jeans look as if they'd been tailored for him. Tonight he was wearing a teal T-shirt under a button-down shirt that was simply a beautiful blue, an intense color that reminded Jenny of something.

"Hi," Jenny said.

He grinned rakishly and held out an arm to her.

Jenny went willingly, as always, but she hung on to the box. "Tom, there's something I want to talk to you about, alone. It's hard to explain—"

"Oh, no, I'm getting 'Dear Johnned' on my birthday," he said loudly, arm still around her, leading her down the hallway to the living room.

"Quit it," Jenny said, exasperated. "Can you please be serious for a minute?"

Tom was clearly in no mood to be serious. He waltzed her

into the living room, where everyone but Audrey was sitting around laughing and talking. He ignored her protests, which were growing fainter anyway. Tom always made Jenny feel better, and it was hard to stay worried with him around. All her fears of shadows and thrumming boxes seemed faraway and childish.

Still, she felt a prickle of unease as he took the box from her, asking, "What's this? For me?"

"It's a game," Michael said, "about which Jenny's being very mysterious. She can't let go of it, apparently."

"I understand why," Tom said as he shook the box to hear the rattle. Jenny looked at him sharply. He didn't seem to be joking, or at least no more than usual, but how could you say that about a blank white box? Why should Tom look so deeply intrigued by it, shifting it in his hands eagerly?

There *is* something about it, Jenny thought, opening her mouth to speak. But just then her mother came in from the back of the house, fastening an earring and wafting perfume. Jenny shut her mouth again.

Mrs. Thornton had been blond like Jenny when she was young, but over the years her hair had darkened to a golden brown, honey-in-shadow tone. She smiled at everyone and said happy birthday to Tom. "Now, let me see," she said to Jenny, "Joey's out of the way at the Stensons', and we'll be back late Sunday, so everything should be ready for you."

Then, as Jenny's father appeared behind her with a small suitcase, she added earnestly, "Dear one, I know you're going to break *something.* Just don't let it be the R. C. Gorman vase, all right? It cost fifteen hundred dollars, and your father is deeply attached to it. Otherwise, clean up whatever you destroy and try to keep the roof on."

"If it comes off, we'll nail it back," Jenny promised, then kissed her mother's smooth Shalimar-scented cheek without embarrassment.

"Krazy Glue in the kitchen drawer," Jenny's father muttered in her ear as she kissed him in turn. "But watch out for the R. C. Gorman vase. Your mother would die."

"We won't go near it," Jenny said.

"And no . . ." Her father made a vague fiddling gesture with one hand. He was looking at Tom in a way that Jenny thought was what people meant when they said *askance.* He'd taken to looking like that at Tom lately.

"Daddy!"

"You know what I mean. Only the girls are staying the night, right?"

"Of course."

"Right." Her father pushed his wire-framed glasses higher on his nose, squared his shoulders, and looked at her mother. They both glanced around the living room one last time—as if to remember it—and then, like a pair of fatalistic soldiers, they turned and marched out the door.

"Don't have much faith in us, do they?" Michael said, looking after them.

"It's the first time I've had a party while they've been away for the weekend," said Jenny. "That they know about," she added thoughtfully.

When she looked back, Tom had the box open.

"Oh—" Jenny said. And that was all she said. Because Tom was lifting out sheets of thick, glossy tagboard, printed in colors so vibrant they glowed. Jenny saw doors and windows, a porch, a turret. Shingles.

"It's a dollhouse," said Summer. "No, I mean one of those paper thingies, like you get in the big flat books and cut out. A paper house."

Not a game, Jenny thought. And not dangerous. Just a kids' toy. She felt a wave of relaxation soften her, and when Audrey called from the kitchen that the food was ready, she went almost dreamily.

Tom was suitably surprised and impressed at the Chinese dinner, and the fact that Audrey was responsible for it.

"You can cook!"

"Of course I can cook. Why is it that everyone assumes I'm a mere social ornament?" She looked at him from under spiky lashes and smiled.

Tom smiled back, maintaining eye contact. Audrey kept flirting as she served him, smiling up at him, allowing her fingers to touch his as she handed him a plate. But when he moved away, she slanted a grim, significant glance at Jenny. *You see?* that glance said.

Jenny returned the look benevolently. Tom was always nice to other girls, and it didn't bother her. It didn't mean anything. She was feeling very pleased with the world as they all filled their plates and went back to the living room.

There was no formal dining. They all sat around the coffee table, some on leather footstools, some directly on the Mexican paver tiles. Jenny was surprised that the white box with the sheets of tagboard wasn't already put aside.

"You got some scissors?" asked Zach. "Actually, an X-Acto knife would be better. And a metal ruler, and glue."

Jenny stared at him. "You're going to *make* it?"

"Sure, why not? It looks like a good model."

"It's cute," Summer said and giggled.

"You've got to be kidding," Jenny said. "A paper house . . ." She looked around for support.

"It's a game," Dee said. "See, there are instructions on the back of the lid. Scary instructions." She shot a barbaric smile around the room. "I like them."

Michael, with bits of spring roll hanging out of his mouth, looked alarmed.

"But how can you play a *game* with a paper house?" Jenny felt her voice going weak again as she saw the way Tom was looking at her. The way only Tom could look—charming, persuasive, and tragic. It was all a put-on, but Jenny could never resist. "Oh, all right, you big baby," she said. "If you really want it. I should have gotten you a rattle and a pacifier, too." Shaking her head, she went off to fetch the scissors.

They put the model together as they ate, occasionally getting grease on the tagboard, gesturing with chopsticks. Tom supervised, naturally. Zach did a lot of the cutting; he'd had practice matting the photographs he took. Jenny watched his careful, clever fingers transform the flat sheets of paper into a three-foot-high Victorian house and was forced into admiration.

It had three floors and a turret and was open in front like a dollhouse. The roof was removable. Sheet after sheet had to be cut out to make all the chimneys and cornices and balconies and eaves, but no one got tired of working, and only Michael complained. Tom seemed delighted with the whole thing. Even Audrey, whom Jenny would have thought far too sophisticated to enjoy this, lent an experienced hand.

"Look, here's some furniture to put inside—are you done with the first floor, Zach? You see, this is the parlor, and here's a little parlor table. Gothic Revival, I think. Mother has one. I'll put it . . . here."

"Here's a sort of Oriental screen thing," Summer said. "I'll put it by the table for the dolls to look at."

"There aren't any dolls," said Jenny.

"Yes, there are," Dee said and grinned. She'd curled her long legs up and was reading the instructions to herself. "And they're *us*. It says we each get a paper doll for a playing piece, and we draw our own face on it, and then we move the pieces through the house, trying to get to the turret at the top. That's the game."

"You said it was scary," Tom objected.

"I didn't finish. It's a haunted house. You run into a different nightmare in every room while you're trying to get to the top. And you have to watch out for the Shadow Man."

"The *what*?" Jenny said.

"The Shadow Man. He's like the Sandman, only he brings you nightmares. He's lurking around inside, and if he catches you, he'll—well, listen. He'll 'bring to life your darkest fantasies and make you confess your most secret fears,'" she read with obvious enjoyment.

"All right!" said Tom.

"Oh, geez," said Michael.

"What kind of darkest fantasies?" said Summer.

Mystery, thought Jenny. Danger. Seduction. Fear. Secrets revealed. Desires unveiled.

Temptation.

"What's wrong with you, Thorny?" Tom said affectionately. "You're so nervous."

"It's just—I don't know if I like this game." Jenny looked up at him. "But you do, don't you?"

"Sure." His hazel eyes, brown flecked with green, were sparkling. "It's good for a laugh." Then he added, "Don't be scared. I'll protect you."

Jenny gave him a mock glare and leaned against him.

When she was away from Tom, the skin of her forearm missed him, and so did her shoulder and her side and her hip. The right side because she always sat on Tom's left.

"Go get some of Joey's crayons," Dee was ordering Summer. "We're going to need to draw a lot. Not just the paper dolls that are us; we're also supposed to draw our worst nightmare."

"Why?" said Michael unhappily.

"I told you. We have to face a different nightmare in every room. So we each draw one on a slip of paper and shuffle the papers and put them facedown on the floor of different rooms. Then when you get to a room, you can look at the slip and see what that person's nightmare is."

Tom wiped his fingers on his jeans and went to sit by Dee on the couch, bending his head over the instructions. Summer jumped up to get crayons from Jenny's little brother's room. Zach, ignoring the rest of them, was working silently. Zach didn't say anything unless he had something to say.

"I think I'm going to like this," Audrey said, judiciously placing furniture in the different rooms. She was humming a little, her polished nails gleaming, her hair shining copper under the track lighting.

"Here are the crayons, and I found some colored pencils, too," Summer said, returning with a Tupperware container. "Now we can all draw." She rummaged through the sheets of glossy tagboard left in the box, finally producing one printed with human outlines. The paper dolls.

They were all enjoying themselves. The game was a hit, the party a success. Jenny still felt cold inside.

She had to admit, though, that there was a certain satisfaction in cutting neatly along dotted lines. It brought back long-ago memories. Coloring the paper dolls was fun, too, the Crayola wax sliding richly onto the stiff matte tagboard.

But when it came to drawing on the rectangle of paper Summer gave her next, she stopped helplessly.

Draw a nightmare? Her worst nightmare? She couldn't.

Because the truth was that Jenny had a nightmare. Her own, personal, particular nightmare, based on something that had happened long ago . . . and she couldn't remember it. She could never remember it when she was awake.

The bad feeling was coming on, the one she sometimes got late at night. The scared feeling. Was she the only person in the world who woke up in the middle of the night sure that she'd discovered some awful secret—only, once she'd awakened, she couldn't remember what it was? Who felt sick with fear over something she couldn't remember?

A picture flickered through her mind. Her grandfather. Her mother's father. Thinning white hair, a kind face, tired, twinkling dark eyes. He had entertained her when she was five years old with souvenirs from far-off places and magic tricks that had seemed real to a child. His basement had been full of the most wonderful things. Until the day something had happened. . . .

That last horrible day . . .

The flicker died, and Jenny was glad. The only thing worse than not remembering was remembering. It was better to just leave the whole thing buried. The therapists had said differently at the time, but what did they know?

Anyway, she certainly couldn't draw it.

The others were all sketching assiduously. Tom and Dee were snickering together, using the lid of the game box as a desk. Summer was laughing, shaking back her soft light curls, drawing something with a lot of different colors. Zach was frowning over his nightmare, his face even more intense than usual; Audrey's eyebrows were arched in amusement.

"Where's green? I need lots of green," said Michael, hunting among the crayons.

"What for?" asked Audrey, eyes narrowed.

"Can't tell you. It's a secret."

Audrey turned her back on him, shielding her own paper.

"That's right, they're secrets," Dee agreed. "You don't get to see them until you reach the room they're in."

Nobody here could possibly have a secret from me, Jenny thought. Except Audrey, I've known them all forever. I know when they lost their first tooth and got their first bra. None of them could have a real secret—like mine.

If she had one, why not the others?

Jenny looked at Tom. Handsome Tom, headstrong and a little arrogant, as even Jenny had to admit, if only to herself. What was he drawing now?

"Mine needs green, too. And yellow," he said.

"Mine needs black," said Dee and chuckled.

"All right, done," Audrey said.

"Come on, Jenny," Tom said. "Aren't you finished yet?"

Jenny looked down at her paper. She had made a form-less doodle around the edges; the middle was blank. After an embarrassed moment with everyone's eyes on her, she turned the paper over and gave it to Dee. She would just have to explain later.

Dee shuffled all the slips and put them facedown in various rooms on the upper floors. "Now we put our paper dolls in the parlor downstairs," she said. "That's where we all start. And there should be a pile of game cards in the box, Summer, to tell us what to do and where to move. Put them in a stack on the table."

Summer did while Audrey fixed the paper dolls on their little plastic anchors and set them up in the parlor.

"We need just one more thing," Dee said. She paused dramatically and then said, "The Shadow Man."

"Here he is," Summer said, picking up the last sheet of stiff tagboard from the box. "I'll cut out his friends first—the Creeper and the Lurker." She did, then handed the figures to Audrey. The Creeper was a giant snake, the Lurker a bristling wolf. Their names were printed in blood-red calligraphy.

"Charming," Audrey said, snapping anchors on. "Any-where in particular I'm supposed to put them, Dee?"

"No, the cards will tell us when we meet them."

"Here's the Shadow Man. He can shadow me if he wants; I think he's cute," Summer said. Audrey took the paper doll from her, but as she did Jenny grabbed her wrist. Jenny couldn't speak. She couldn't breathe, actually.

It couldn't be—but it was. There was no question about it. The printed face that stared up at her was unmistakable.

It was the boy in black, the boy from the game store. The boy with the shocking blue eyes.

CHAPTER 4

Jenny felt as if a black riptide was trying to suck her underwater. It was him. The boy from the game store. Every detail of his face was reproduced perfectly, but it wasn't a photograph. It was a drawing, like the snake and the wolf. The boy's hair was colored silvery-white with blue shadows. The artist had even captured his dark eyelashes. The portrait was so lifelike it looked as if those eyes might blink at any minute, as if the tips might speak.

And it *radiated* menace. Danger.

"What's the matter?" Audrey was saying. Her face swam in and out of focus as Jenny looked up. Jenny's eyes fixed on the beauty mark just above Audrey's upper lip. Audrey's lips were moving, but it was a minute before Jenny could make sense of the words. "What's wrong, Jenny?"

What could Jenny say?

I know this guy. I saw him at the store. He's a real person, not some made-up character in a game. So . . .

So what? That's what they would ask her. What difference did it make? So the game must have been invented by some-body who knew the guy, and the guy had modeled for the picture. That would explain why the box was blank: Maybe it wasn't even a real, mass-produced game at all.

Or maybe the guy was crazy, had a fixation with this par-ticular game, and had bleached his hair and dressed up to look like the game character. Dungeons and Dragons, Jenny thought suddenly—people were supposed to get heavily into that, sometimes even go overboard. That's the answer.

At least, it was the answer somebody here tonight would give. Tom, maybe, because Jenny could tell he wanted to play, and once Tom made up his mind on anything, he was immov-able. Dee, because danger always kicked her. Zach, because the game involved art; or Summer, because she thought it was "cute." They all wanted to play.

A good hostess didn't get hysterical and ruin a party because she had shadows on the brain.

Jenny forced a smile.

"Nothing," she said, letting go of Audrey's wrist. "Sorry. I thought I recognized that picture. Silly, huh?"

"You been drinking the cough syrup again?" Michael inquired from the other side of the table.

"Are you all right, Thorny? Really?" Tom asked seriously. His green-flecked eyes searched hers, and Jenny felt her smile become more stable. She nodded. "Fine," she said firmly.

Tom got up and dimmed the track lighting.

"Hey," said Michael.

"We need it dark," Dee told them, "for this next part. The reading of the oath." She cut a glance at them, the whites of her eyes shining like smoky pearls.

"*What* oath?" Michael said warily.

"The Oath of the Game," Tom said. His voice was sinister. "It says here that we each have to swear that we're playing this game of our own free will, and that the game is real." Tom turned the lid of the box around for them to see. On the inside cover, above the printed instructions, was a large symbol. It was like a squared-off and inverted *U,* the two uneven horns of the letter pointing downward. It was deeply impressed in the cover and colored—as well as Jenny could tell in the dim light—rusty red.

I will not ruin this party, I will not ruin this party, Jenny thought. I *will not.*

Tom was reading from the instructions: "'There is a Shadow World, like our own but different, existing alongside ours but never touching. Some people call it the world of dreams, but it is as real as anything else' . . . and then it says that entering the Shadow World can be dangerous, so you play at your own risk." He grinned around the group. "Actually, it says that the game can be hazardous to your life. You have to swear you understand that."

"I don't know if I like this anymore," Summer said.

"Come on," said Dee. "Live dangerously. Make it happen."

"Well . . ." Summer was taking this seriously. She pushed soft light curls off her forehead and frowned. "Is it getting warm in here?"

"Oh, swear, already," said Michael. "Let's get this thing over with. I swear I understand that this game may kill me before I'm old enough to get a McJob like my brother Dave."

"Now you." Dee stretched out a black-spandex-covered leg to nudge Zachary. "Swear."

"I swear," Zach said in bored tones, his thin face unreadable, his gray eyes cool as ever.

Summer sighed, capitulating. "Me, too, then."

Audrey adjusted her houndstooth jacket. "Me, three," she said. "And what about *you,* Deirdre?"

"I was just about to, Aud. I swear to have a great time and kick the Shadow Dude's ass."

Tom had gotten up and was lurking over Jenny. "How about it, devil woman? I swear—do you?"

Normally Jenny would have jabbed an elbow upward into his ribs. At the moment all she could manage was a colorless smile. They all wanted to do it. She was the hostess. They were her guests.

Tom wanted it.

"I swear," she said and was embarrassed when her voice cracked.

Tom cheered and tossed the box lid in the air. Dee's foot flashed out, kicking it back toward him. It fell on the floor by Jenny.

You jerk, if you really cared about me, you'd care about how *I* felt, Jenny thought in a rare moment of anger toward Tom. Then she squelched the thought. It was his birthday. He deserved to be indulged.

Something about the box lid caught her eye. For just an instant the upside-down *U* looked as if it were printed in red foil. It had—flashed—Jenny thought. But of course it couldn't have.

Everyone was kneeling around the table.

"Okay," said Dee. "All the little dollies in the parlor? Then somebody's got to turn a card. Who wants to be first?"

Jenny, feeling that if she was going to do this she might as well do it thoroughly, reached out and took the top card. It was glossy white like the game box and felt slick between her fingers. She turned it over and read: "'You have gathered with your friends in this room to begin the Game.'"

There was a pause. Then Summer giggled.

"Sort of an anticlimax," Audrey murmured. "Who's next?"

"Me," said Tom. He leaned over Jenny and took a card. He read, "'Each of you has a secret you would rather die than reveal.'"

Jenny stirred uneasily. It was just coincidence, because these were preprinted cards. But it did sound almost as if someone were answering the question she'd thought of earlier.

"My turn," Summer said eagerly. She read, "'You hear the sound of footsteps from one of the rooms above.'" She frowned. "But there aren't any rooms above. This is a one-story house."

Tom chuckled. "You're forgetting yourself. We're not *in* this house. We're in *that* house."

Summer blinked, her large blue eyes traveling over the pastel, basket-adorned walls of the Thornton living room. Then she looked at the Victorian paper house, with the seven paper dolls neatly arranged in the parlor like a group of guests too polite to go home. "Oh!"

She was just putting the card back when they all heard the noise from above.

Footsteps.

A quick light patter, like a child running on a wooden floor.

Summer shrieked and looked in terror at the ceiling.

Dee jumped up, her dark eyes blazing. Audrey stiffened. Michael grabbed at her, and she smacked his hand away. Zach's face was turned up; even his ponytail seemed to be tense. But Tom burst into laughter.

"It's squirrels," he got out finally. "They run on the roof all the time, don't they, Jenny?"

Jenny's stomach was knotted. Her voice wavered slightly as she said, "Yes, but—"

"But nothing. Somebody else take a card," Tom said. Nobody did. "All right, I'll do it myself. This is for you, Mike." He flipped a card.

"'You go to the door to get some air, but it seems to be stuck,'" he read. He looked around at the group. "Oh, come on. It's a *game*. Here, look." He stood up in a fluid motion and went to the sliding glass door that looked out on Jenny's backyard. Jenny saw his fingers moving, flipping the locks on the handle. A sense of dread overwhelmed her.

"Tom, don't!" she said. Before she knew what she was doing, she jumped up and took his arm. If he didn't try the door—if he didn't *try* it—the card couldn't come true.

Tom was jerking at the handle, ignoring her. "There's something wrong with it—there must be another lock."

"It's stuck," Michael said. He ran a hand through his rumpled dark hair, an oddly helpless gesture.

"Don't be stupid," Audrey snapped.

Dee's sloe eyes were glittering. Her hand darted out and she took a card. "'None of the doors or windows in this house will open,'" she read.

Tom went on yanking furiously at the door. It wouldn't budge. Jenny caught his arm again. She was trembling all over with a sense of danger.

"Take another card," Zach said softly. There was something strange about his thin face—it was almost trancelike. Zombied out.

"No!" Jenny said.

Zachary was taking the card himself.

"No," said Jenny again. She had to stop this, but she couldn't let go of Tom. "Zach, don't read it."

"'You hear a clock strike nine,'" Zachary read softly.

"Jenny doesn't have any clocks that strike," Audrey said. She looked at Jenny sharply. "Do you? *Do you?*"

Jenny shook her head, her throat clogged. Every inch of her skin seemed to be raw, waiting. Listening.

Clear and sweet, the chimes rang out. The chimes of the clock at the game store, the clock she couldn't see. It seemed to be coming from far above. It began to strike the hour.

One. Two. Three. Four.

"Oh, God," Audrey said.

Five. Six. Seven.

At nine, Jenny thought. See you later—at nine.

Eight . . .

"Tom," Jenny whispered. The muscles in his arm were hard under her hand. Now, too late, he turned toward her.

Nine.

Then the wind came.

At first Jenny thought the riptide had gotten her. Then she thought it must be an earthquake. But all the time she had the sensation of air rushing by her, as if a hurricane had come in through the closed sliding glass door. A black, roaring hurricane that burned even as it froze. It hurt her like a physical thing, shaking her body and blinding her. She lost track of the room. The only thing real was the fistful of Tom's shirt she held.

Finally she lost track of that, too. The pain stopped for a while, and she just drifted.

She woke up on the floor.

It was like the only other time she'd ever fainted, when she and Joey had both been home sick with the flu. She'd jumped out of bed suddenly to tell him to turn down that stupid cartoon—and the next thing she knew she was waking up with her head in a wastebasket. Lying on the carpeted floor of her room, then, she had known that time had passed, without being sure how she knew it. This was the same.

Painfully Jenny lifted her head and blinked to bring the far wall into focus.

It didn't work. Something was wrong. The wall itself, which should have been pastel-colored and hung with weavings and baskets, was wrong. It was paneled with some dark wood, and an Oriental screen stood in front of it. Heavy velvet curtains obscured a window. A brass candlestick was attached to the wall. Jenny had never seen any of these things before.

Where am I?

The oldest question in the book, the biggest cliché. But she really didn't know. She didn't know where she was or how she had gotten there, but she knew that whatever was going on was all wrong. Was—beyond her experience.

Things like this didn't happen.

It had happened anyway.

The two ideas jostled in her mind. She was already disoriented, on the verge of panic. Now she began to shake, and she felt a swelling in her throat.

No. Start screaming now and you'll never stop, she told herself. Don't think about it. You don't have to deal with it. Just find Tom.

Tom. For the first time Jenny looked at the floor. They were all lying there, Zach with his blond ponytail streaming out behind him (on a moss-green carpet worked with cabbage roses, but don't think about that, don't think about that now), Summer with her light curls cradled protectively in her small arms, Audrey with her French twist coming loose. Dee's long legs were sprawled near the window, and Michael's stocky body was curled in a ball beside her. Tom was lying against the wall—where the sliding glass door should have been. As Jenny got up unsteadily and began moving toward him, he stirred.

"Tom? Are you okay?" She took his hand, and when his warm, strong fingers closed around hers, she felt better. He groaned and opened his eyes.

"Hell of a headache," he muttered. "What happened?"

"I don't know," Jenny said in a small, precise voice. She was still close to having hysterics. She hung on to his hand hard enough to bruise. "We're not in the living room anymore."

It was just the truth, and she had to say it. She needed to share it with someone, the way Summer had needed to share about her dog being put to sleep. But Tom scowled.

"Don't be stupid," he said, and Jenny felt the little needle stab she always did when he snapped at her. "We can't be anywhere else. Everything's fine."

All his good humor had vanished, along with the rakish charm of his smile. His neat brown hair was just slightly mussed, and his green-flecked eyes looked both dazed and angry.

He's defensive, Jenny realized. Scared that it's his fault. She tried to squeeze his hand, but he was getting up.

So were the others. Dee was rubbing the back of her neck, looking around with quick, alert movements. She reached down and pulled a groaning Michael to his feet. Audrey was standing, too, her hands automatically going to fix the combs in her auburn hair even as she stared at the room.

Summer was cowering by the spindly-legged table that had taken the place of Jenny's mother's coffee table. Only Zach didn't seem frightened. He was standing and his clear gray eyes were open, but his lips moved soundlessly and he looked— entranced. As if he were moving in a dream.

Nobody said a word. They all looked around stupidly, trying to make sense of their surroundings.

They were standing in a Victorian parlor, lushly carpeted,

furnished with Gothic Revival tables and chairs. A green lamp with a silk fringe hung from the ceiling. It looked like the perfect place for a seance.

Jenny *recognized* it.

She'd seen the pattern of the cabbage-rose carpet printed on tagboard. Zach had cut out the paneling with an X-Acto knife, and Audrey had put together that mahogany table.

They were in the paper house. It had come alive around them. They were *inside* it. . . .

Jenny's hands came slowly up to cover her mouth. Her heart had begun a deep, sick pounding.

"Oh, my God," Summer whispered. Then, with gathering force, "Oh, my God, oh, my *God*—"

Michael began to giggle hysterically.

"Shut up," Audrey said, breathing hard. "Both of you, shut up!"

Dee went to the wall and touched a candlestick, fingers dark against the bright brass. Then she reached up and stuck her fingers in the candle flame.

"Dee!" Tom rapped out.

"It's real," Dee said, looking at her fingertips. "It burns."

"Of course it's not real!" Audrey said. "This is all—some kind of illusion. Like virtual reality—"

Dee's eyes flashed. "It is *not* virtual reality. My mom's a computer expert—she knows what real VR is. Not the Pac-Man kind you get with video games. Even they can't do anything like this. Besides, where's the computer? Where's our helmets?" She smacked a flattened hand against the wall. "No, this is *real*."

Michael was feeling a chair, still half giggling. "So maybe it was some of Audrey's mushrooms. What were they called? Shiitake? Maybe it's a judgment on us."

"Take it easy, Mike," Tom said. He looked angry, which Jenny knew meant he was feeling uncertain. She watched him, all the while stroking the smooth mahogany of a tabletop. She felt the same compulsion that Dee and Michael obviously did—to *touch* things here. She kept expecting them to feel like cardboard, but they were real.

"Okay," Tom said, "we're *not* in the living room. We've been—moved somehow. Somebody's playing a joke on us. But we don't have to just stand around like idiots and take it."

"What do you suggest we do?" Audrey said acidly.

Tom strode over to the parlor doorway, which opened on a dim hall. "The guys can come with me and scout around; you girls stay here and keep your eyes open."

Dee threw him a scornful look, then turned narrowed eyes on "the guys." Michael was tapping on the walls, muttering, and Zach was just staring, the skin of his face drawn tight over bones. Jenny wanted to go to him, but she couldn't move.

"Good luck," Dee said to Tom. "Hurry back to protect us."

"Don't anybody leave," Summer said, her blue eyes wet.

"You protect *Jenny*," Tom snarled at Dee, thrusting his face close to hers. Jenny felt an instant of throbbing warmth, which was immediately swept away by coldness. How could anyone protect anyone here?

Dee crossed the room and put an arm, hard as a boy's, around Jenny's shoulders. "Right," she said.

"I think we should stay together," Michael said nervously.

"Oh, what's the *difference*?" Audrey said. "It's not really happening anyway. We're not here."

"Then what is it?" Summer asked, on the verge of hysteria. "Where are we?"

"In the Game."

The voice came from the corner of the room, from the shadow behind the Oriental screen. It was a voice that didn't belong to any of the group, but one that was familiar to Jenny. She'd only heard it once before, but she couldn't mistake it. Like water over rock, it was full of elemental music.

Every head turned.

The boy stepped out of the shadows.

He was just as beautiful as he had been in the store. But here, against the backdrop of this quaint and fussy room, he looked even more exotic. His hair shone in the dimness like white cat's fur or mountain snow. He was wearing a black vest that showed the smooth, hard muscles of his bare arms, and pants that looked like snakeskin. His eyes were heavy-lidded, shielded by long lashes. He was smiling.

Summer gasped. "The picture. The paper doll in the box. It's *him*—"

"The Shadow Man," Michael said hoarsely.

"Don't make me laugh," Tom said. Lip curled, he looked the apparition up and down. "Who the hell are you? What do you want?"

The boy in black took another step forward. Jenny could see the impossible daylight color of his eyes now, though he wasn't looking at her. His gaze swept over the others, and Jenny could see it affect them, like a wave of cold air that caused them to draw together. She could see each of them reacting as they looked into his face and saw—something there. Something that caused their eyes to go wide and suspicion to turn to fear.

"Why don't you call me Julian?"

"Is that your name?" Tom said, much more quietly.

"It's as good as anything else."

"Whoever you are, we're not scared of you," Dee said suddenly, letting go of Jenny and stepping toward. It sounded like the truth, as if Dee, anyway, was not afraid, and it seemed to encourage the others.

"We want to know what's going on," Tom said, loudly again.

"We haven't done anything to you. Please just let us go home," Summer added.

"You can't go home again," Zach murmured. It was the first time he'd spoken. He was wearing a strange half smile.

"Bud, you're in worse shape than I am," Michael told him in a low voice. Zach didn't answer.

Only Jenny stayed back, not moving, not speaking. Her sense of dread was getting stronger all the time. She was remembering a look like a starving tiger's.

"At least tell us what we're doing here," Audrey said.

"Playing the Game."

They all stared at him.

"You agreed to play. You read the rules."

"But—playing? What playing? You mean—"

"Don't talk to him about it, Mike," Tom interrupted. "We're not going to play his stupid game."

He's so scared, Jenny thought. He still thinks this is all his fault. But it isn't, Tom, it isn't. . . .

"I mean," the boy in black said to Michael, "that you all swore you were playing of your own free will and that you knew the Game was real. You invoked the rune Uruz." He sketched a shape in the air with his finger, an inverted *U*. Jenny noticed that the snake tattoo she'd seen on his wrist in the store had vanished. "You pierced the veil between the worlds."

Audrey laughed, a sharp false sound like glass shattering.

Michael breathed, "This is nuts."

Dee's expression said that she agreed. "What's a *rune*?"

Audrey opened her mouth, then shut it again tightly, shaking her head. Julian's lip quirked and he lowered his voice.

"It's magic," he said. "A mystical letter from an ancient alphabet. In this case designed to let you walk between the worlds. If you don't understand it, you shouldn't be messing with it."

"We didn't mean to mess with anything," Summer whispered. "It's all a mistake."

The fear in the room had heightened. Jenny could sense it like a yellow aura enveloping them all.

"No mistake. You chose to play the Game," the boy said again. "Now you play until you win—or I do."

"But *why*?" Summer said, almost sobbing. "What do you want from us?"

Julian smiled, then looked past her. Past all of them, to the one person who hadn't said a word since he'd entered the room. To Jenny.

"Every game has a prize," he said.

Jenny met the impossibly blue eyes and knew she'd been right.

They stood for a moment, looking at each other.

Julian's smile deepened. Tom looked back and forth between them. Understanding slowly dawned on his face.

"No . . ." he whispered.

"Every game has a prize," the boy repeated. "Winner take all."

"*No!*" Tom said and launched himself across the room.

CHAPTER 5

Tom lunged at the boy in black—and drew up short. His eyes were fixed on something at his feet. Jenny couldn't understand it—it was as if he saw something terrifying there on the carpet. He turned to get away from it and stopped. It was behind him, too. Slowly he backed up against the wall.

Jenny was staring at him in dismay. It was like watching one of the mimes out at Venice Beach. A very good mime—Jenny could tell that the things Tom was facing were small, that they were trying to climb up his legs, and that he was terribly afraid of them. But there was nothing on the carpet.

"Tom," she said in a thin voice and took a step.

"Don't come near me! They'll get you, too!"

It was awful. Tom, who was never afraid of anything, was cornered by empty air. His lips were drawn back from his teeth, his chest was heaving.

"What is it?" Summer whimpered.

The others were all staring in silence. Jenny whirled on the boy in black, who was leaning against the parlor wall and watching in amusement.

"What are you doing to him?"

"In the Game you have to face your nightmares. This is just a free sample of Tom's. No reason for the rest of you to be in on it."

Jenny faced Tom, drawing a deep breath. She took a step toward him.

"Stay back!" Tom said, sharp and frightened.

"Doesn't look like he's conquered it yet," Julian remarked.

Jenny stepped right into the midst of what Tom was staring at. She felt nothing but air around her bare ankles. She saw nothing. But Tom did—he yanked her to him, to the wall, falling down with her to his knees. He kicked out.

"Tom, don't! There's nothing there! Tom, *look* at me!"

His green-flecked eyes were wild. "Keep away from her. Keep back!" He was scuffing with his outstretched foot at the empty floor beside Jenny, trying to push something away. His mouth was quivering with disgust.

"Tom," she sobbed, shaking him. He didn't even glance at her. She buried her face in his shoulder, holding him with all her strength. Trying to will him sane again.

And then—her arms collapsed in on themselves. It was like one of those magician's tricks where the beautiful girl is hidden beneath a sheet—and then the sheet caves in and falls to the floor. Tom was there—Tom wasn't there. Like that. Jenny's embracing arms were empty.

She screamed.

And looked helplessly, wildly down at her hands, at her lap. At the floor. Tom couldn't be gone.

He was.

She looked behind her and saw that the others were, too.

Jenny's eyes darted to the dim hallway. It was empty. The curtains over the window were flat and still. But Dee was gone, and Audrey was gone, and Zach and Michael and Summer were all gone from the parlor. All five of them, without a sound. The way things vanish in dreams.

Please let it be a dream, Jenny thought. I've had enough, now. Please, I'm sorry; let it be a dream.

She was clutching the carpet so tensely that her fingernails were bending back. It hurt, and the pain didn't wake her up. Nothing changed. Her friends were still gone.

The boy in black was still there.

"Where did they go? What did you do with them?" she said. She was so dazed that it came out as a sort of insane calm.

Julian smiled whimsically. "They're upstairs, scattered around the house, waiting to face their nightmares. Waiting for you. You'll find them as you go through the Game."

"As *I* go?" Jenny said stupidly. "Look, you don't understand. I don't know what's—"

"You're the main player here, you know," he interrupted, gently chiding. "The door back to your world is at the top of the house, and it's open. If you can get to it, you can go. Bring your friends and they can leave, too."

Jenny's mind was still stuck on one thing. "Where's Tom? I want—"

"Your—Tom—is at the top." He pronounced the name as if it were something not mentioned in polite society. "I'll be giving him my *special* attention. You'll see him when you get there—if you get there."

"Look, please. I don't want to play any game." Jenny was still speaking as if this was all a mistake that would be cleared up somehow, as long as she stayed rational. As long as she avoided his eyes. "I don't know what you're thinking, but—"

He interrupted again. "And if you *don't* get there, then I win. And you stay here, with me."

"What do you mean—with you?" Jenny said sharply, jerked out of her courtesy.

He smiled. "I mean that you stay in this place, in my world. With me—as mine."

Jenny stared at him—and then she was on her feet, her composure shattering. "You're out of your mind!" she said. She would have lunged at him, herself, if she'd ever had any practice at violence.

"Careful, Jenny."

She stopped, frightened by what she sensed in him. Looking into his eyes, she saw something so alien, so terrifying, that she couldn't move. It was then, at last, that she *believed* what was happening. Full realization of what this boy had done, of everything that had happened tonight, crashed in on her. The young man standing before her, looking almost human, could do magic.

"Oh, God," she whispered.

All her violence had drained away, replaced by a fear older and deeper than anything she'd ever experienced. An old, old recognition. Something inside her knew him from a time when girls took skin bags to the river to get water, a time when panthers walked in the darkness outside mud huts. From a time before electric lights, before candles, when darkness was fended off with stone lamps. When darkness was the greatest danger of all.

Jenny looked at the boy standing beside her with his hair shining like moonlight. If Darkness had taken on a face and a voice, if the powers of night had gathered themselves together and formed themselves into a human being, they would have made something like this.

"Who are you?" whispered Jenny.

"Don't you know yet?"

Jenny shook her head.

"Never mind. You will, before the Game is over."

Jenny tried to regain her calm. "Look—let's just . . . You were at the game store."

"I was waiting for you."

"So this was all—set up? But why *me*? Why are you doing this to *me*?" Jenny could feel hysteria tugging at her again.

Then he said it. He was looking at her with eyes like the sky on a November morning, one corner of his mouth turned up. He spoke gravely and a little formally.

"Because," he said, "I've fallen in love with you."

Jenny stared at him.

"Surprised? You shouldn't be. I first saw you a long time ago—you were such a pretty little girl. As if there was sunshine all around you. Do you know the story of Hades?"

"What?" She didn't like this mercurial jumping from subject to subject.

"Hades," he said encouragingly, like someone helping her cram for a final. "Greek god of the Underworld. Ruler there. He lived in the world of shadows—and he was lonely. And then one day he looked up to the earth's surface and saw Persephone. Picking wildflowers, I think. Laughing. He fell in love with her on the spot. He wanted to make her his queen, but he knew perfectly well she wouldn't go with him willingly. So . . ."

"So?" Jenny got out.

"So he hitched his black horses to his chariot. And the earth split open in front of Persephone's feet. And her wildflowers fell to the ground."

68

"That's a story," Jenny said, trying to keep her voice steady. "A myth. There's no such person as Hades."

"Are you sure?" After a moment Julian went on: "Anyway, you're luckier than Persephone, Jenny. You have a chance to get away. I could just take you, but I'm giving you a chance." He looked at Jenny with eyes like liquid sapphires, wild exotic eyes. She couldn't speak, couldn't look away.

"Who are you?" she whispered again.

"Who do you want me to be? I love you, Jenny—I came from the World of Shadows to get you. I'll be anything you like, give you anything you want. Do you like jewels? Emeralds to match your eyes? Diamonds?" He reached outspread fingers toward her throat, not quite touching.

"What about clothes? A different outfit for every hour of the day, in colors you've never imagined. Pets? Have a marmoset, or a white tiger. Far-off places? You can lie in the sun at Cabo San Lucas or Côte d'Azur. Anything, Jenny. Just imagine."

Jenny covered her face with her hands. "You're *crazy*."

"I can make your wildest dreams come true. Literally. Ask me for something, something you thought you could never have. Quick; I may not make the offer again."

Jenny was almost sobbing. His voice, soft and insistent, made her feel as if she were falling. She had a terrifying desire to collapse in his arms.

"*Now*, Jenny, while we're still friends. Later, things won't be so pleasant. I don't want to hurt you, but I will if it's necessary. Save yourself a lot of pain and bother and let me make you happy now. Give in, yield to me. It's going to happen eventually, anyway."

The sensation of falling vanished. Jenny's head snapped up. "Oh, really?"

"I never lose."

Something was waking up in Jenny. Usually she got angry quickly and got over it as quickly, like a summer cloudburst. Now she felt the slow kindling of something different, a deliberate, steady fury that would burn a long time.

"Careful, Jenny," Julian said again softly.

"I will never give in to you," Jenny told him, equally soft. "I'll die first."

"It won't come to that, I hope. But other things might happen—once you start playing the Game, I can't change the rules. Your friends might suffer."

"What? How?"

He shook his head at her. "Jenny, Jenny. Don't you understand anything that's going on? They're all playing the Game. They agreed to take the risks. Now they'll have to take the consequences." He turned.

"No—wait!"

"It's too late, Jenny. I gave you a chance; you refused it. From now on we'll be playing the Game."

"But—"

"You can start with this riddle." Turning back, head tilted slightly, he recited:

"I am just two and two. I am hot. I am cold.
I'm the parent of numbers that cannot be told.
I'm a gift beyond measure, a matter of course,
And I'm yielded with pleasure—when taken by force."

Jenny shook her head. "That tells who *you* are?"

He laughed. "No, that tells what I want from you. Give me the answer, and I'll let one of your friends go."

Jenny pushed the riddle to the back of her mind. It didn't make any sense, and while Julian was in the room, it was impossible to concentrate on anything else but him.

In all this time he hadn't lost his whimsical good cheer, his charm. He was obviously loving this game, having a wonderful time.

"That's all," he said. "Let the Game begin. By the way, if you get hurt in these nightmares, you get hurt for real. If you die, you die. And I can tell you right off that one of you probably won't make it."

Jenny's head jerked up. "Who?"

"That would be telling. Let's just say that one of you probably doesn't have the strength to get through. Oh, and did I mention the time limit? The door in the turret—the door back to your own world—is going to close at dawn. Which tomorrow is at exactly six-eleven. If you can't get to it by then, you're stuck here—so don't waste your time. Here's something to remind you."

Far away but clear, an unseen clock chimed. Jenny turned toward the sound, counting unconsciously as it struck. Ten.

When she turned back, Julian was gone.

Jenny held herself motionless. There was no sound. The fringe on the green velvet lamp rippled slightly; otherwise the room was still.

For an instant just being alone was enough to panic her. She was by herself in a house that didn't exist.

No, don't freak. *Think.* You can look around now. Maybe there's a way out of here.

She went to the window, pulled the heavy peacock-blue curtain aside. Then she froze.

At first she simply stared, breath catching in her throat, feeling her eyes go wide like a deer's. Then she whipped the curtain back in place, jerking it past the closing point, pressing it against the window with her hands. She could hardly make herself let go of the velvety material, but she did, and then she backed away quickly. She didn't want to see outside again.

A landscape of elemental terror. Like something out of the Ice Age—as painted by a mad impressionist. A blizzard with huge ungainly shapes lumbering through it. Blue and green flashes like lightning giving glimpses of deformed creatures crawling over icy ground. Twisted pinnacles of rock corkscrewing up toward a blank white sky.

She wouldn't survive a minute out there.

When the devil goes ice-skating, Jenny thought. So what if Hell's already frozen?

Oh, how funny. Michael would appreciate that. She felt tears sting her nose, her eyes. She stood hunched and miserable, hugging her own elbows in the center of the empty room. She had never felt so alone—or so frightened.

She missed her friends desperately. Dee's courage, Michael's humor, Audrey's practicality. Even Summer would give Jenny someone to protect, and as for Zach—she wanted to find out what was wrong with him. In all the years she'd known him, she'd never seen him act this way.

But most of all she wanted Tom.

Tom, she thought fiercely. *He's* the one in trouble. Not you. He's going through God knows what, getting Julian's *special* attention. And you have no business standing here moaning while that's happening.

The yelling at herself actually helped—it shut up the babbling little voices in the back of her mind telling her that she couldn't deal.

Julian had said it depended on her.

All right. She was calmer now. She knew she had to start moving—but *where*? Jenny tried to gather her scattered thoughts, to remember the configuration of the paper house.

The parlor had been off a long central hallway on the first floor. At the end of that hallway there had been a staircase.

Upstairs, Julian had said.

Jenny found herself moving through the candle-lit hallway, past gold-framed portraits which looked down disapprovingly from the walls.

She looked up at the stairway.

It was wide, carpeted down the middle. There was absolutely nothing strange about it—and Jenny couldn't force herself to put a foot on it.

I could turn around and run, she thought. It was impossible to realize—*emotionally*—that she couldn't just go back into the parlor and find a way home.

But intellectually she knew there was nothing in the parlor to help her. And she didn't want to think what she might see if she opened the front door of this house.

So you can stay here and hide, or you can go up. You have to choose.

She put a foot on the stairway. It was solid. Like any stairway. She started climbing toward the darkness at the top.

The hallway on the second floor seemed to stretch on forever in both directions, so dark that Jenny couldn't see any end to it. There were candles in brass candle holders at intervals on the walls, but they were far apart and didn't give much light. Jenny didn't remember any hall in the paper house looking this way. In fact, what this place *really* looked like was the Haunted

Mansion at Disneyland. Like every other kid in southern California, Jenny had been to Disneyland so often she knew it by heart, and she recognized the creepy wallpaper.

But that was ridiculous. Why should it look like that?

She walked with fingertips brushing the wall. A dozen steps down the hall she saw something far ahead in the dimness, moving under the flickering light of a candle.

Jenny didn't know whether to run toward it or away. Then she noticed something familiar in the long legs and the greyhound build of the figure.

"Dee!"

Dee barely glanced up as Jenny reached her. She was wrestling with a door which bulged just like a door in the Haunted Mansion, the one that had always scared Jenny as a child. A lot of the things in the Haunted Mansion were simply silly, and a lot of others were mind-boggling—but only one thing there had ever really frightened Jenny when she was young . . . and that was a door.

A closed door, which bulged in the middle as if a great weight was leaning on it from the inside, deforming the wood, expanding, relaxing. While all the time guttural snarls, not the sort of sounds a human could make, came from behind it.

The door that Dee was wrestling with was doing exactly the same thing.

Only it was open a little. Dee had her lynxlike body braced against it, head down, knees bent, one long slender leg back so the toe of her sneaker dug into the black carpet of the hallway, but she couldn't quite get the door shut.

Without a word Jenny went and helped her, leaning to press on the door above and below the handle which Dee was grasping. The keyhole had a large key in it.

"Push," Dee gasped.

Jenny leaned harder, throwing her weight behind it, while Dee pushed right above her, body stretched taut beside Jenny's. The door pushed back and bulged. The low, thick snarling rose in tone. Angrily. Jenny felt her muscles begin to tremble. She put her head down and shut her eyes, teeth locking.

"Push!"

The door yielded a crucial fraction of an inch, closing. Dee's hand shot to the key and turned it. There was a click, the sound of a bolt shooting home.

The door wasn't pushing anymore.

Jenny stumbled back, legs weak with the sudden release of strain, and looked at it. No bulging. No snarling now, either. It was just an ordinary six-paneled door, as quiet and innocent as a door could be.

There was utter silence in the hallway.

Jenny backed to the opposite wall, then slowly slid down it until she was resting on her heels. Her forehead was wet around her hair roots.

Dee was leaning one hand against the wall by the door.

"Hi," Jenny said at last.

"Hi."

They continued to look at each other blankly.

"Have you seen the others?"

Dee shook her head.

"Me, either. He said—you know, *him*"—Jenny paused until Dee nodded—"he said you guys were scattered around the house. Waiting for your nightmares." Jenny looked at the door. "Were you in there?"

"No. I was in the parlor watching Tom, and then all of a sudden I got dizzy. I woke up on the floor here. There was only one door, and I wondered what was inside, so I opened it."

"Oh. What *was* inside?"

"Just your average butt-ugly monster."

"Like the ones in the pictures—the Creeper and the Lurker or whatever?"

"No, *really* ugly. Sort of like Coach Rogers."

Dee was taking this rather calmly, Jenny thought. She looked strained and stern, but very beautiful, like a statue carved out of ebony.

"We'd better look around," she said. "See if we can find the others."

"Okay." Jenny didn't move.

Dee, still standing, reached out to her.

"Come on. Up."

"I'm going to faint."

"Don't you *dare*. On your feet, soldier!"

Jenny got up. She looked down the hallway. "I thought you said there was only one door. What's that, then?"

"It wasn't there before."

They both looked at the door. It was just like the other one, six-paneled, innocuous.

"What do you think is behind this one?" Jenny said carefully.

"Let's see." Dee reached for the knob.

"Wait, you lunatic!" Trying not to flinch, Jenny pressed her ear to the wood. She couldn't hear anything but her own breathing. "Okay—but be ready to shut it again fast."

Dee flashed her a barbaric grin and stood ready to kick the door shut. Jenny put her hand on the knob, turned it.

"Now," Dee said, and Jenny flung the door open.

CHAPTER 6

The room behind the door had golden-ocher walls. On one of them an African mask hung in primitive glory. Several clay sculptures rested on built-in teak shelving, including a bust that could have been Nefertiti. Leather cushions were tossed around the floor, one resting beside a complete home gym.

It was Dee's bedroom. The bust was one that Dee's grandmother, Aba, had made of Dee. There was a stack of textbooks by the bed and a pile of half-completed homework on the nightstand.

Jenny loved this room, loved to see what Aba would bring Dee next from her travels. But seeing it now was unnerving.

Once they were inside, the door shut behind them—and

disappeared. When Jenny turned at the sound of slamming, she saw nothing but a blank ocher wall where the door used to be.

"Great—now we're trapped," Jenny said.

Dee was frowning. "There must be a way out."

They tried the window. Instead of the Ice Age outside it was the ordinary view from Dee's upstairs room. Jenny could see the grass below, illuminated by a porch light. But the window wouldn't budge, or—as they discovered when Dee swung a ten-pound barbell against it—break.

"So now what?" Jenny said. "Why are we in your room? I don't understand what's going *on*."

"If this place is like a dream and we know we're dreaming it, we should be able to change things. With our minds. Maybe we're supposed to *make* a way out of here."

They both tried, with no results. No matter how hard Jenny concentrated on making the door reappear, nothing happened.

"I give up." Dee took off her jacket and flopped on the bed—as if this place really were her room.

Jenny sat beside her, trying to think. Her brain wasn't working properly—shock, she supposed. "All right, look. That guy said we're each supposed to face our nightmares. So this must be—" she began, but Dee interrupted.

"What else did he say? Who is he?"

"Oh. Do you . . . do you believe in the devil?"

Dee gave her a scornful look. "The only devil I know is Dakaki, and he only makes you horny. According to Aba."

"I think he wanted me to believe he was the devil," Jenny said softly. "But I don't know."

"And he wants us to play the Game with him? Just like the one in the box, only for real?"

"If we get to the turret by dawn, we can go," Jenny said. "If we don't, he wins." She looked at the other girl. "Dee, aren't you scared?"

"Of the supernatural?" Dee shrugged. "What's to be scared of? I always liked sword-and-sorcery stuff; I'm glad it's true. And I don't see why we can't beat him. I swore to kick the Shadow Man's ass before—and I'm going to. You wait."

"But—this is all so crazy," Jenny said. Now that she had time to sit and think, reaction was setting in. She was shaking again. "It's like you've always thought, sure, maybe there's ESP, maybe there're strange things out there in the dark. But you never think it could happen to *you*."

Dee opened her mouth, but Jenny rushed on.

"And then it does and everything's different and it isn't possible and *it's still happening*." She looked hard into the dark eyes with the slightly amber-tinted whites, desperate for understanding.

"That's right," Dee said briefly, returning Jenny's gaze. "It *is* happening. So all the rules are changed. We have to adapt—fast. Or we're not going to make it."

81

"But—"

"But nothing, Jenny. You know what your problem is? You think too much. There's no point in talking about it anymore. What we have to worry about now is surviving."

Dee's straightforward, razor-sharp mind had gone to the heart of the matter. What was happening was happening, possible or not. They had to deal with it if they wanted to live. Jenny wanted to live.

"Right," she breathed. "So we adapt."

Dee flashed her brilliant smile. "Besides, it's kind of fun," she said. "Don't you think?"

Jenny thought of Tom cowering from something invisible on the floor. She leaned her forehead onto her fingertips.

"Something must scare you, though," she said after a minute, looking up. "You drew a nightmare."

Dee picked up a beaded Ndebele bracelet from the nightstand and examined it. "My mom scares me. Really," she added, at Jenny's disgusted look. "Her stuff at the university—computers and all." Dee glanced toward the window.

Jenny saw only the curtains made of appliqué cloth from Dahomey.

"You're afraid of *technology*?" she said in disbelief.

"I am not afraid of technology. I just like to be able to deal with things—you know, directly." Dee held up a slender clenched fist, and Jenny looked at the corded tendons in the dark forearm. No wonder Dee wasn't afraid of the "sword and sorcery" stuff—she fit right into the heroic mythos.

"It's the same reason I won't go to college," Dee said. "I want to work with my hands. And not at anything arty."

"Aba would smack you," Jenny told her. "And your brain's as good as your hands—" She broke off because Dee was once again looking at the window.

"Dee, what did you draw?" she said, sitting up straight and finally asking the question she should have asked in the first place.

"Nothing's happening."

"What did you draw?"

A red light was blossoming outside the window, like the glow of a distant fire. Jenny whipped her head toward a crackling sound and saw that Dee's stereo had begun to smoke.

"What—?" Jenny breathed. Dee was already moving toward the window.

"What's going to happen?" Jenny yelled, jumping up. She had to yell because of the throbbing sound that suddenly permeated the room. It resonated in Jenny's bones.

Outside, a silhouette appeared against the light.

"Dee!" Jenny grabbed for the other girl, trying to pull her away from the window. She was panicking and she knew it. The thing outside was *huge,* blocking out the stars, dull black and nonreflective itself but haloed in its own red glow. The eucalyptus trees outside were thrashing in a violent wind.

"What is it?" Jenny screamed, dimly aware that Dee was

clutching back at her. But that was a stupid question. What *could* it be, hovering outside a second-story window, shaped like a half-sphere with the flat side down? As Jenny watched, six beams of light, bright as phosphorous flares, shot out from the bottom of the thing.

One of the lights swung around to shine directly through the window. Jenny was blinded, but she heard the shivery tinkle of glass, and a blast of wind blew her hair straight back. The window's gone, she thought.

The wind roaring past her was freezing and felt somehow electric. Behind her a brass tray fell off a wooden stand with a crash.

That was when Jenny found she couldn't move. The light was paralyzing her somehow, her muscles going like jelly. There was the strong pungent odor of an electric storm.

She was losing consciousness.

I'm going to die, she thought. I'll never wake up.

With a great effort she turned her head toward Dee for help. Dee was facing the light stiffly, pupils contracted to pinpoints. Unable to help Jenny or herself.

Fight, Jenny thought weakly.

This time fainting was like oozing into a black puddle of sludge.

The room was round. Jenny was lying on a table that conformed to her body's shape. Her eyes were burning and tearing, and she felt a great disinclination to move. A white light shone down on her from above.

"It's exactly the way I thought it would be," a husky voice said. Jenny fought off the lassitude enough to turn her head. Dee was on another table a few feet away. "It's just like what I've read about the Visitors, just like my dreams."

Jenny had never thought much about UFOs at all, but this wasn't what she would have expected. The only thing she knew about aliens was that they—did things—to people.

"So this was your nightmare," she said.

Dee's perfect profile was tilted up toward the white spotlight above her, looking *exactly* like an Egyptian carving. "Oh, brilliant," she said. "Any other deductions?"

"Yes," said Jenny. "We've got to get out of here."

"Can't move," Dee said. "Can you?"

There were no obvious restraints, but Jenny's arms and legs were too heavy to lift. She could breathe and move her torso a little, but her limbs were dead weights.

I'm scared, Jenny thought. And then she thought about how Dee must feel. As an athlete, physical helplessness was Dee's worst fear. The strong, slim body that she'd cultivated with so much care was no use at all to her now.

"This place—it's so sterile," Dee said, her nostrils flaring. "Smell it? And I bet they're like hive insects, all the same. If we could just get up to fight them . . . but they've got *weapons,* obviously."

Jenny understood. Muscle and ingenuity wouldn't do anything against sterile, hellishly efficient technology. No wonder it was Dee's personal nightmare.

Jenny noticed a movement in her peripheral vision.

They were small—Summer's size. To Jenny they looked like demons: hairless, with slender bodies and large glittering dark eyes. No noses, slits for mouths.

Their skin glowed like bad mushrooms—very pale mushrooms grown in a cellar without ever seeing the light. Jenny noticed an odor of almonds.

They were alive, but they were as alien and *wrong* as the bleached things that crawl around at the bottom of caves. Just the sight of them struck Jenny with sick terror.

They were naked, but Jenny couldn't see anything that would make them male or female. Their bodies were hideous blanks, like dolls' bodies. They're *its,* Jenny thought.

Somehow, Jenny knew they were going to hurt her.

Dee made a faint sound.

Jenny turned toward her. It was easier than it had been the other time, and after an instant she realized that the spotlight above her had dimmed fractionally. Dee's light was brighter, because Dee was trying to get away.

Jenny had never seen Dee frightened before—even in the parlor Dee had looked more alert than anything else. But now Dee looked like a terrified animal. Droplets of sweat stood on her forehead with the effort to move. The more she thrashed, the brighter the light above her got.

"Dee, stop it," Jenny said, agonized. She couldn't stand to watch. "It's just a dream, Dee! Don't let it get to you."

But Julian had said if they got hurt in the dream, they got hurt for real.

The Visitors were clustering around Dee, but they didn't seem alarmed. They seemed absolutely indifferent. One of them pushed a cart over to the far side of Dee's table. Jenny saw a tray of gleaming instruments.

God—no, Jenny thought.

Dee collapsed back on the table, exhausted.

Another being picked up something long and shiny from the tray, examined it with lustrous black eyes. It flexed the thing a few times like a painter making practice runs with a brush. It seemed dissatisfied, although with its masklike face Jenny didn't know how she could tell this. Then it casually flicked the thing up Dee's thigh and Dee screamed.

It was like hearing your father scream. Jenny was so frightened that she tried to get up, and only succeeded in disarranging her legs slightly. One of the beings repositioned them carefully, stretching her feet toward the bottom corners of the table.

She had never felt so open, so utterly vulnerable.

Dee's black spandex legging gaped where the thing had cut it. Jenny could see blood.

The being handed the instrument to one of the others, which took it away. If they were talking or communicating,

Jenny couldn't sense it. Certainly nobody tried to communicate with Dee or Jenny.

They were moving around again. One of them—the same one who had cut Dee?—took up a new instrument and went to Jenny's table. With a swift, deft movement the being touched the instrument to Jenny's hand. Jenny felt a pinch.

Then the probe went in her ear. Outraged, Jenny tried to roll her head away, but small hands—strong as claws inside mushroom flesh—held her forehead. She felt the probe go in deeper, and she squirmed frantically. It touched her eardrum and hurt like a Q-tip stabbed too deep.

She was completely helpless. Whatever they wanted to do to her, they would do.

Tears of pain and fury trickled out of her eyes, down her temples. They put the probe in her other ear. One of them dabbed at her eye, holding the lid open. Jenny felt the touch of cool metal against her eyeball.

"It's just a dream," she called to Dee, almost sobbing, when the probe was withdrawn. "It's not real!"

She couldn't hear any answer from the other table.

What kind of game was this, where you didn't have a chance? Julian had talked about "getting through" the nightmares, but Jenny didn't think that meant just waiting for them to pass. She was supposed to *do* something, but she didn't know what, and she couldn't move. And she didn't think she and Dee were going to survive this if they just lay here.

"What do you want from us?" she shouted. "What are we supposed to do?"

There was a shifting among the Visitors. A new kind of being had arrived. Taller than the others, clearly in command, with skin as white as wax. Its fingers were twice as long as a human's. Although Jenny got only a glimpse of its face, it looked more menacing than the other kind, its features even more exaggerated.

It picked something up from the instrument cart and went over to the far side of Dee's table. It looked up at Jenny, and she saw its eyes were blue.

Not glittering black like the other beings' eyes. Blue lakes endlessly deep, deep as a mountain is high. Eyes that looked *inside* you.

Jenny stared back, her own eyes widening.

Then she saw what it was holding. A needle. Wire-thin, murderously long, longer than the needle for a spinal tap. The tall Visitor was holding it over Dee's stomach.

Dee's stomach was heaving wildly in a fight for breath. Her khaki T-shirt was sticking to her body as she writhed in a futile attempt to escape. Her sweat-soaked hair glistened like mica in the light.

"Don't touch her!" Jenny cried. To watch it happen to Dee was worse than having it happen to herself.

The needle hovered just below Dee's navel. Dee's abdomen went concave trying to avoid it. Dee made rocking, shifting motions as if trying to shimmy up the table, but she only moved in place. The light above her intensified, and abruptly her struggles became weaker.

"You bastard! Leave her alone!"

What can I *do*? Jenny thought. She had to stop this—but how?

The light.

It came to her suddenly. The light above her had dimmed as Dee's had brightened. Maybe she could move now. And if she could move—

She began to rock.

She had some control over her body. Not much. Her arms and legs were still useless, like huge pieces of dead meat attached to her. But she could move her trunk and her head and neck. Using all her strength, she rocked her weight from one side to the other.

Dee saw her. All the other eyes in the room, all those slanted liquidy black eyes, and the one pair of deep blue, were on Dee's stomach, on the needle. But Dee's thrashing head had turned toward Jenny, and just for a moment the two of them were looking at each other, communicating without words. Then Dee began to struggle again.

The harder Dee fought, the brighter the light over Dee. The brighter the light over Dee, the dimmer the light over Jenny.

Fall off this table and you'll have no way to control it,

Jenny's mind told her. A broken arm or leg, at least, and maybe a broken nose. You'll smash into the floor facedown.

She kept on rocking. Maybe Dee thought she was just trying to get away, but what Jenny cared about was distracting them. Stopping that *thing* with its too-long fingers from putting the needle in Dee. If she hurt herself they'd have to come deal with her. They'd leave Dee alone.

She swung her torso harder and harder, like a beetle trying to upend itself. Dee was fighting madly, yelling out insults to keep the aliens' attention. The light above Jenny dimmed further, Jenny surged violently—and felt her momentum take her over the edge. For a moment she teetered there, balanced on her side, then the deadweight of her arms and legs decided the issue, and she felt herself begin to fall.

There was a burst of startled movement from the aliens, and the light flamed into brightness above her. It didn't matter in the least. It wasn't her muscles that were in charge, it was the law of gravity. Something nobody could argue with.

Jenny thought.

Searing illumination was reflecting off the white floor, and Jenny shut her eyes as that floor seemed to come up to meet her. She flinched away from the moment of impact. When the impact didn't come, she opened her eyes.

She was floating, facedown, an inch or so from the floor. Suspended. Paralyzed. The aliens were scuttling around hysterically, as if they weren't programmed to deal with this. As if they were as surprised by her midair arrest as she was.

The painful reflection on the floor softened. Jenny was still floating. It was a very strange sensation.

The small aliens were still moving around in consternation—Jenny could see by their feet. A bunch of them crowded between the tables and lifted Jenny back to hers.

She was positioned too high—she felt her ponytail hanging over the edge of the table. And the light above her was dimmer. Maybe somebody who hadn't been staring up at it for half an hour wouldn't notice, but Jenny did.

The blue-eyed alien with the needle was beside her.

She expected it to touch her, but it didn't. It just looked down, and Jenny looked back.

Why didn't you let me fall? she thought.

Abruptly the tall alien turned away. It motioned to the others, then walked out the octagonal doorway of the round room. Several of the small ones followed it, pushing the cart. Several others came and poured green liquid into Jenny's mouth.

It tasted like sugar and iodine. Jenny spit it out. They restrained her head and poured her mouth full again. This time she shut her lips, holding the liquid inside her mouth, doing her best not to swallow any. She could have struck out at them—she could feel her fingers again—but she pretended she couldn't move.

And then, blessedly, they went away.

Jenny turned her head and spat her mouthful out. Her lips and tongue were numb. She saw Dee doing the same.

They looked at each other, then at the lights.

"Both dimmer," Jenny whispered. Dee nodded.

Then, eyes on the doorway, they squirmed and rocked themselves off the tables. It wasn't easy, but with the lights this dim, it was possible.

Jenny, with no training in how to fall, bruised her arm and knee. But Dee was already pulling her up, out of the influence of the white light. Outside its circle, Jenny could move freely.

"Look," she said, seizing Dee's arm.

It was a door, concave, set in the wall that had been behind Jenny's head. It looked like an airplane door, which Jenny recognized because she'd once spent five hours studying one when her family flew to Florida on vacation.

And which was absurd, Jenny thought fretfully. Why should aliens have airplane doors? Dee wasn't worrying about it—she was moving levers and things. The door swung away outward.

Jenny shrieked.

She'd never liked heights, and this was much higher than she'd ever been in the open air. She could see clouds below.

But we both went for the door instinctively, she thought. It must be right. We went into Dee's room and the door disappeared. This is the first door we've seen since. It's *got* to be the way out.

She still felt faint when she looked down.

"I don't care; I'd rather die than stay here. Besides, I always wanted to skydive," Dee said, grabbed Jenny's hand, and jumped.

Jenny *really* screamed then.

Whistling wind slapped her face. Jenny's eyes screwed shut against it. Everything was icy cold around her. She felt weightless, but she knew she was falling.

If this is flying, I don't think I like it—

She didn't exactly faint then, but things got very confused. She couldn't see or hear anything until she hit an ocher-painted door with a thud, Dee tumbling behind her. From their direction and velocity they might have been thrown through Dee's bedroom window by a giant fist. The door opened as she struck it, and she and Dee both fell into the hallway.

The Haunted Mansion hallway. Dark as a crypt. Jenny stared into the golden glow of Dee's bedroom—

—then the door whisked by her nose and slammed shut.

She and Dee lay panting while their eyes gradually adjusted to the dimness. Dee leaned over and slowly, deliberately punched Jenny in the biceps.

"We did it, killer," she said. "You saved me."

"We're alive," Jenny said wonderingly. "We got through. Dee—do you realize what happened? We *won*."

"Of course," Dee said. She poked her fingers into the hole in her leggings, and Jenny saw that the cut was still there, the blood drying. Then Dee flipped up her shirt. Jenny could count ribs under the velvety night-dark skin, below Dee's dark blue sports bra. But there was no mark above the navel. "I told you, you saved me. That was my worst nightmare—those *things* poking at me, and me not being able to stop them."

"We both did it—by using our brains," Jenny said. "Anyway, now we know what to do in the nightmares. Once we're inside we look for a door—any door. Hey, what's that?"

A scrap of paper showed white against the black carpet. Jenny smoothed it out and saw it was a drawing, done in crayons. A black thing like a bowler hat was hovering above stick trees, with rays of scribbled light around it.

"I never could draw very well," Dee said. "But you get the idea. Now what do we do?"

Fear of the aliens had left its mark on Dee's face, but she also looked exhilarated, triumphant. Ready for anything.

Jenny was suddenly very grateful to have this beautiful, brave girl on her side. "We find the others," she said. "We look for another door."

She dropped the crumpled paper on the floor and stood, offering Dee a hand up.

An unseen clock struck eleven.

Jenny stiffened. "That's it—the clock I heard in the parlor. It's counting off the hours. He said dawn was at six-eleven."

"Seven hours and change," Dee said. "Plenty of time."

Jenny said nothing, but her little fingers tingled. She couldn't explain it, but she had the feeling Dee was going to be proved very wrong.

CHAPTER 7

The hallway seemed to stretch forever in both directions. The stairway had disappeared.

"It's changed," she said. "It keeps changing—why?"

Dee shook her head. "And who knows which way to go? We'd better separate."

Jenny nearly objected to this, but after what they'd been through—well, she should be able to handle a hallway alone. She started down it and immediately lost sight of Dee.

It seemed almost normal to be walking down an impossible black-carpeted hall like something out of a horror movie. I guess you can get used to anything, Jenny thought. After the blinding-white sterility of the alien ship, this dim place looked almost cozy.

There were no doors. Even the monster one, which should have been somewhere back this way, had disappeared. The tiny flames of the candles went on endlessly ahead. As Jenny stopped under one to rest, she thought suddenly of the riddle she'd pushed to the back of her mind earlier. If it would get one of them out of here, she ought to try to solve it.

> *I am just two and two. I am hot. I am cold.*
> *I'm the parent of numbers that cannot be told.*
> *I'm a gift beyond measure, a matter of course,*
> *And I'm yielded with pleasure—when taken by force.*

What could it possibly mean? Two and two, hot and cold—it was probably something childishly simple.

"How do you like the Game so far?" The voice was like silk-wrapped steel.

Jenny turned fast. Julian was leaning against the wall. He'd changed clothes again; he was wearing ordinary black jeans and a black T-shirt with the sleeves rolled up.

Seeing him suddenly was like the first moment in the morning when the shower flicks on, a shock of cold awareness.

"Was it you?" she said. "In the ship up there?"

"That would be telling," he said, but for an instant his eyelids drooped, heavy lashes coming down.

"Why didn't you let me fall?"

"Did you know your eyes are dark as cypress trees? That means you're unhappy. When you're happy they get lighter, they go all goldy-green."

"How would you know? You've never *seen* me happy."

He gave her a laughing glance. "Is that what you think? I'm a Shadow Man, Jenny." While Jenny was trying to figure this out, he went right on. "Cypress eyes and sun-glowing skin . . . and your hair's like liquid amber. Why do you wear it back like that?"

"Because Tom likes it," Jenny said reflexively, her standard response. "Look, what did you mean—"

He shook his head, clicking his tongue. "May I?" he said politely, straightening up. His tone was so normal, so solicitous, that Jenny nodded automatically. She was still intent on her question.

"What did you—no, *don't.*"

He had pulled the elastic band out of her ponytail. Jenny felt her hair fall about her neck, and then his fingers were in it.

An almost imperceptible shudder went through Jenny. *"Don't,"* she said again. She didn't know how to deal with this situation. He wasn't being rough. He still looked solicitous and friendly. It didn't seem appropriate to hit him in the gut as Dee had taught her to do with guys that annoyed her.

"Beautiful," he murmured. His touch was as light as the soft pat of a cat's paw, and his voice was like black velvet. "Don't you like it?"

"No," Jenny said, but she could feel the heat in her face. She was backed against the wall now. She didn't know how to get away from him—and the worst thing was that her body didn't seem sure it wanted to. His cool fingers moved against her warm hair roots, and she felt a trembling thrill.

"Have I told you about your mouth?" he said. "No? It's soft. Short upper lip, full lower. Just about perfect, except that it's usually a little wistful. There's something you want, Jenny, that you're not getting."

"I have to go now," Jenny said in a rush. Her standard stuck-with-a-jerk-at-a-party response. She was so confused she didn't care if it didn't make sense here.

"You don't have to go anywhere." He seemed unable to take his eyes away from her face for a second. Jenny had never held anyone's gaze for this long—and she had never even dreamed of eyes like his.

"I could show you what it is you've been wanting," he said. "Will you let me? Let me show you, Jenny."

His voice seemed to steal the bones from her body. She was aware of shaking her head slightly, as much in response to the new feelings as to his question. She didn't know what was happening to her. Tom's touch made her feel safe, but this—this made her feel weak inside, as if her stomach were falling.

"Let me show you," he said again, so softly she could barely hear him. His fingers were so gentle as they laced in her hair, urging her to tilt her face up toward him. His lips were bare inches from hers. Jenny felt herself flowing toward him.

"Oh, stop," she said. "Stop."

"Do you really want me to?"

"Yes."

"All right." To her astonishment, he stepped back, fingers trailing out of her hair.

Jenny could still feel them. I almost kissed him, she thought. Not the other way around. In another minute I would have.

Tom. Oh, Tom.

"Why are you *doing* this?" she said, her eyes filling again.

He sighed. "I told you. I fell in love with you. I didn't do it on purpose."

"But we're so different," Jenny whispered. She was still feeling weak at the knees. "Why should you—want me? Why?"

He looked at her, head tilted slightly, quizzically. "Don't you know?" His eyes moved to her lips. "Light to darkness, Jenny. Darkness to light. It's always been that way."

"I don't know what you're talking about." And she didn't. She wouldn't let herself understand it.

"Suppose the devil was just quietly minding his own business—when he saw a girl. A girl who made him forget everything. There've been other girls more beautiful, of course—but this girl had *something*. A goodness, a sweetness about her. An innocence. Something simple he wanted."

"To destroy it."

"No, no. To cherish it. To warm his cold heart. Even a poor devil can dream, can't he?"

"You're trying to trick me."

"Am I?" There was something oddly serious in his blue eyes.

"I won't listen to you. You can't make me listen."

"True." For just an instant Julian looked tired. Then he gave his strange half smile. "Then there's no choice but to keep playing, is there? No choice for either of us."

"Julian—"

"What?"

Jenny caught herself up short, shaking her head.

He was crazy. But one thing she believed, he really was in love with her. She knew, somehow, that it was true. She also knew something else about him—she'd known it since that instant when she'd looked into his eyes and seen the ancient shadows there. She'd known it when he'd humiliated Tom and terrorized Dee.

He was evil. Cruel, capricious, and dangerous as a cobra. A prince of darkness.

Completely evil—and completely in love with her.

How was she supposed to reconcile that?

"If you want me so much," she said, "why don't you just *take* me, then? Why go through all this with the Game? You could grab me anytime—why don't you just do it?"

His heavy lashes drooped again. In that instant he looked

exactly like the boy in the More Games store. Almost vulnerable—almost human.

Realization came to Jenny. "Because you can't," she breathed. "You can't, can you? You can't do just *anything* you want to, not even here."

His eyes flashed up, glittering like a snake's. Jenny saw pure violence there. "This is *my* world. I make the rules here—"

"No." Giddy triumph was swelling through Jenny, an effervescent rush. "Not this one. That's why you asked if you could touch my hair. That's why you tried to make *me* kiss *you*. You can't do it without my permission."

"Be careful, Jenny," he said. His face was cold and cruel.

Jenny just laughed excitedly. "If you can kiss me against my will, then prove it," she said. "Show me—do it now." And then she added an Italian phrase she'd picked up from Audrey. *"Come osi!"*

It meant *I dare you.*

He didn't move.

Jenny laughed again.

"I don't think you understand," he said. "I'm going to have you, at any cost. *Any* cost, Jenny, even if you have to suffer on the way. If I can't force you, I'll persuade you—and I can be very persuasive."

Jenny felt some of the triumph fold up inside her.

"Remember where you are, Jenny. Whose territory you're on. Remember what I can do in the Game."

Jenny was completely sober now.

"You challenged me—now I suppose I'll have to show you what I *am* capable of."

"I don't care what you do to me."

"Maybe it won't be to you. See your friend there? She's playing the Game, too."

He was looking down the hallway, in the same direction Jenny had been going. Barely visible under a far candle was the copper glint of someone's hair. Jenny drew in her breath.

"Don't you dare—" Turning back to speak to him, Jenny broke off. Julian was gone. She was alone.

Jenny bit her lip. It was infuriating to talk to somebody who could do that, and she was beginning to think it hadn't been a very good idea to laugh at him. Nothing to be done about it now.

"Audrey!" she called and started down the hall.

Audrey's skin, usually pale as magnolia blossoms, was touched with a golden glow from the candles, and her auburn hair flashed copper. She and Jenny hugged, and Jenny thought only Audrey could stay so calm, so chic, in such awful circumstances.

"You look as if any minute you're going to be demanding to see your ambassador," Jenny said.

"If Daddy were here he'd take care of things," Audrey agreed. "He'd come out of retirement to take this place on. Are you all right? You look a little flushed."

Jenny put a hand to her cheek self-consciously. "It's the light," she said. "Uh, how long have you been here? I mean, did you see me—before I called?"

"No. I'd been looking and looking—for *anybody*, but all I've seen is this *interminable* hallway."

"Good. I mean—it's good that I found you. The only other person I've seen is Dee. She's back there, and she's just been through hell. And you're next, if I'm right about the way this works. I'll explain as we go."

The explanation, about how they were all scattered, about finding doors in the nightmares, about the dawn time limit and about how things in the nightmares could hurt you, took until they found Dee. They did find Dee, to Jenny's relief, standing beside a door.

"I thought I'd better guard it to make sure it didn't go anywhere," she said after a perfunctory nod at Audrey.

Audrey had only one question. "Is he Nordic, that guy? They're supposed to be sexy as all get-out."

Jenny ignored this. "Since the doors move, how do we know this isn't one of the two we opened before?"

"We don't," Dee said and flashed The Smile. Dee's wild, leaping beauty always annoyed Audrey. "Of course, it doesn't have a key like the first one, but I guess we'd better get in monster position again. Anything could be inside."

She and Jenny did, ready to kick the door shut fast. Audrey's eyebrows lifted into her spiky bangs. "No, thank you," she said politely. "Not in a fitted linen skirt. Listen, you two, why are we doing this at all? Why don't we just sit down and refuse to play?"

"Didn't you listen to me before?" Jenny said. "If we're still here by dawn, we stay for good. We lose automatically."

"I've never lost *anything* by default," Dee said. Then she said, *"Now."*

Behind the door there was a forest.

Cool wind blew out, ruffling Jenny's loose hair against her cheek. It smelled like summer camp.

"God," said Jenny.

"Well, come on," Audrey said, flicking her perfectly polished nails in a gesture of readiness. "We might as well get it over with."

"It's too weird," Jenny said as they stepped inside—outside. "Dee's bedroom was a *room,* at least. But this . . ."

They were on the outskirts of a dark forest on a sloping hill. Above them the night sky was strewn with stars much bigger and brighter than the ones Jenny usually saw from her Vista Grande backyard. A moon of pure silver was rising.

The door had slammed and disappeared, of course, as soon as they stepped through. Behind Jenny were meadows and pastures; before her a tangled mass of pitch-black trunks and bushes. The girls were alone on the hill in the moonlight.

"Now what?" Audrey said, shivering fastidiously.

"Don't you know? It's your nightmare—you drew it."

"I drew a picture of me opening the Bloomies catalog and finding it *blank*," Audrey said. "That's my worst nightmare. Don't look at me that way—shopping is cheaper than therapy."

And that was all she would say about it.

There were a few scattered lights in the valley below them. "But it's too far to hike," Jenny said, "and even if we did get down there, I don't think that there would really be any people."

Audrey looked at her strangely, but Dee nodded.

"It feels like one of those model-train landscapes—or like a stage set," she said. "False fronts. You're right, I don't think we'd find little houses with people in them down there. Which means—"

They faced the forest bleakly.

"Why do I have a bad feeling about this?" Jenny asked.

"Come on," Dee said. "Let's make it happen."

The forest looked solid, but with Dee in the lead they found a way into it. It was mostly pine and fir trees, with the occasional beech shining silvery gray against the darkness of the background.

"Oh, my God," Audrey said after they'd been walking some time. "High ground, evergreen trees, rocks—I know where we are now. It's the Black Forest."

"Sounds like something from a story," Jenny muttered, picking her way through the undergrowth.

"It's a real place. I saw it when I was eight, when Daddy was at the German embassy. It—scared me a little, because it was *the* forest, you know."

Dee threw a derisive glance over her shoulder. "*The* forest?"

"The forest where everything happened—where the Grimm brothers got all their fairy tales. You know, Snow White. Hänsel and Gretel. Little Red Riding-Hood and the—"

Audrey stopped in midsentence. In front of her, Dee had stopped, too. Jenny's knees locked.

Just ahead of them in the tangled blackness, yellow eyes glowed. Jenny even imagined she could see moonlight gleaming off sharp teeth.

All three girls stood very still. Seconds passed and the yellow eyes remained motionless. Then they seemed to shift to a different angle so that one went out. Both flashed toward the girls again, then both went out. Jenny heard underbrush crunching. The sound got fainter. It faded into a profound silence in which Jenny could hear her heart beating strong and very fast in her chest.

Jenny let out her breath.

Dee's shoulders heaved slightly. She reached down and picked up a long stick almost as thick as her own slim wrist. She settled it in her hand, waggling it, testing her grip. It made a good weapon.

"—and the Wolf," said Audrey, her voice suspiciously calm. She tucked stray wisps of hair into her French twist, her lips tight. The three of them looked at one another, then started walking again. What else was there to do?

"It was strange, that wolf coming just when you were talking about one," Dee said.

"Unless—" Jenny stopped dead. "Wait," she said. Something had fallen into place with an almost audible click. "Let me think a minute . . . *yes*. It wasn't strange at all that the wolf came when Audrey was talking about it. Don't you see? He's taking it all from our own minds."

"Who?" Audrey said, her well-bred nostrils flared.

"Who do you think? Julian. The Shadow Man. He's creating the Game around us—or *we're* doing it—but either way it's made up of our own thoughts. That hallway back in the house is the hallway from the Haunted Mansion at Disneyland. It always scared me as a kid—so it came from *my* mind. And the door in the UFO was like a plane door I'd seen."

Dee's eyes flashed like a jaguar's. "And the parlor—I saw a lamp like that once in Jamestown. I wondered what it was doing here."

"Everything—every detail—is coming from us," Jenny said. "Not just big things but little things. He's using our minds against us."

"So what's going to happen next?" Dee asked Audrey. "You're the one who should know what scares you most. I mean, should we be on the lookout for walking trees or little hooded men or what? Or was that wolf it?"

"I was only eight when I lived here," Audrey said coldly. "And, no, I don't remember specifically which story . . . disturbed me . . . most. I had a German nurse, and she told me all of them."

She and Dee glared at each other.

"We could run into something from any of our minds," Jenny said, to make peace. "Anything could happen here. You can feel it."

She knew in her heart that it was going to be something worse than the wolf. Something more *un-mundane*. Audrey didn't like anything supernatural, so it followed that whatever happened was going to be *very*.

Remember, it's all a dream, she told herself. But she could hear Julian's voice in her mind: *"I can tell you right off that one of you probably won't make it."*

They walked. Underbrush clutched at Jenny's skirt like little fingers. The fragrance of evergreens surrounded them like a thousand Christmas trees. All Jenny could see was darkness and the endless tangle of forest ahead. Her nerves stretched and stretched.

They literally stumbled on the clearing.

One large tree grew there—a yew, Jenny thought. It stood in front of a great jumble of rocks and boulders that looked as if they might have been left by a glacier. The tree had rough bark, dark green needles, and red berries.

Gathered around it was a group of young men in weird clothes.

They were wearing pants and long over-tunics of leather trimmed with fur, very old-fashioned looking. Their arms were bare and muscular. The ground beside the tree had been cleared and a circle drawn on it. Inside the circle a fire burned, and red light glinted off daggers and what looked like drinking horns. The whole area was decorated with flowers.

"It's some kind of secret ceremony," Dee whispered. "And we're spying on it," she added with considerable relish.

"They're certainly good-looking," Audrey murmured.

They were. Jenny counted seven of them, four with blond hair and three with blondish-brown. They looked as if they were in their late teens or early twenties, and if what they were doing was secret, they weren't bothering to be quiet about it. Jenny could hear laughter and boisterous singing.

Good grief, it's like a fraternity party, she thought. Even this far away she could smell the beer.

"I think," said Audrey, "I'm beginning to like this Game."

She stepped out before Jenny could stop her. The singing fell silent. Seven faces turned toward the girls. Then one of the German boys lifted a drinking horn over his head, and all the rest cheered.

They all seemed surprised but delighted to see the girls. White, even teeth flashed in friendly smiles, and they bundled the visitors over to the warmth of the fire. Audrey's bare legs caused a lot of appreciative comment, as did Dee's spandex leggings.

"No—no, thanks," Jenny said as one of them tried to get her to drink the stuff in his horn. The horn had angular symbols carved on it that made her nervous somehow—they reminded her of something. "Audrey, what are they *saying*?"

"I can't catch it all. It's not like the German I learned," Audrey said. Seated between two admirers, her cool porcelain beauty contrasted with her flirtatious lashes. "I think it must be archaic. But that one is saying that you're like Sif. It's a compliment—Sif was a goddess with shining golden hair."

"Oh, give me a break!" Dee backed up to sit on a rock.

There was an instant stirring among the German boys. Several pulled Dee away from the rock pile, shaking their heads. Dee barely allowed them to move her, not at all placated by the way they marveled over her dark skin. And she only snorted when one offered her a garland of flowers to wear.

"Oh, put it on," Jenny said, flicking a small bug out of her own wreath. She was starting to enjoy this. The young men were nice, even if they did smell a bit like sweat. They were about the most strapping youths she'd ever seen, but several of them had braids in their hair, and they didn't seem to think weaving garlands was sissy.

"It's a ceremony to greet the spring," Audrey said as one of the blonds cried, *"Ostara!"* and poured beer on the ground. "Ostara's the goddess of spring—that's where we get 'Easter.'"

The young men began to chant.

"It's something about life being renewed," Audrey said. "There's something else—something I can't quite make out. They're . . . asking? Petitioning?"

All the German boys were on their feet by now, urging the girls to rise. They were facing the huge pile of boulders.

"Dokkalfar," they chanted.

"That's dark—something. I don't—*oh, my God.*" Audrey's voice changed completely. She tried to pull away from the circle, but two of the German boys grabbed her. "Dark *elves,*" she said wildly. "That's what they're saying. They came here to ask favors from the elves—and *we're* the yielding."

Jenny had never heard Audrey's voice like that before—bordering on hysteria. "The what?" she demanded. Suddenly the white, even smiles around her didn't look so friendly.

"The gift to the Otherworld. The *sacrifice!*" Audrey cried. She was trying to get away again, but it was no good.

We're outnumbered more than two to one, Jenny thought. And they've all got muscles. She looked at Dee—and felt shock ripple over her. Dee was laughing.

Snickering, actually. Chortling. "Elves?" she gasped. "Little pixies in bluebells? Little guys who sit on acorns?"

"No, you idiot," Audrey said through her teeth. "Dark elves—Outdwellers. Oh, you don't understand—"

Jenny heard rock scraping. One of the huge stones in front of her was *moving.* It swung out slowly, pushing a ridge of dirt

113

along in front of it. A black, gaping hole was revealed in the pile. A tunnel leading down.

Dee's laughter was dying—but it was too late. The girls were pushed forward into the hole. Jenny tried to turn, but her Capezio flats slithered on dust and grit, and she felt herself falling.

CHAPTER 8

Rock scraped on rock and the moonlight was cut off above them. Audrey was lying in a ball beside Jenny near the bottom of the slope. Dee had been shoved in backward and was sprawled at the very bottom, legs higher than her head. In those first moments Jenny didn't stop to wonder how she could still see either of them. She said, "Are you all right?" to Dee and then wrapped her arms around Audrey comfortingly.

Audrey was *shaking*. Making little moaning sounds.

"I'm sorry, I'm so sorry . . ." Jenny said, hugging her.

"It's not *your* fault." Dee was picking herself up, her fine-boned face contemptuous. "What's her problem, anyway?"

Jenny twisted her head to snap at Dee, but the words never

got out. She could now see the reason they weren't in pitch darkness. There was a semicircle of lanterns around the bottom of the slope, and holding the lanterns were people.

Dee had fallen silent. The lantern light reflected off faces that were disturbing to say the least.

The elves were very pale, very beautiful . . . but very strange. Their eyes were slanted in a way that reminded Jenny of the Visitors'. Their cheekbones were almost too high and sharp. And they stood oddly.

They didn't look as if they had any sympathy to appeal to.

One of them said something. Jenny thought it was the same language that the young men outside had used, but the elf's voice was more liquid—and more cold. It was obvious that he was ordering the girls up.

Jenny didn't want to obey. She was irrationally frightened by these pale beautiful people. Then she saw that maybe her fear wasn't so irrational.

They were like animals—or parts of them were. They were deformed.

The elf who had spoken had one normal hand and one hand like a cow's split hoof. It was black and shiny like patent leather. Jenny was afraid she was going to be sick.

Another of them had a tail hanging out of his breeches—a long, pink naked tail like a rat's. It swished. A third had two little horn-buds swelling on his forehead. A fourth had glossy dark hair growing on his neck.

Every one of them had some deformity. And they were *real*. Not like the pasted-together monstrosities Jenny had seen in the Ripley's Believe It or Not! exhibit.

"Audrey, you've got to get up," she whispered, swallowing the bile that had risen in her throat. "Audrey, if you don't I think they'll *make* you." Then, with desperate inspiration: "Do you want them to see you lying here like this? I bet your mascara's smeared halfway down your face."

The appeal to Audrey's pride worked where nothing else might have. She slowly sat up, brushing at her cheeks.

"It's waterproof," she said defiantly. Her fingers went automatically to adjust the combs in her French twist, and then she saw the elves.

Her chestnut eyes widened until they showed white all around. She was staring at the cow's-hoof hand. Jenny gripped her arm tightly.

"Are they what you thought they were?"

Audrey pressed her lips together and nodded.

The elf spoke again, sharply, stepping forward. Audrey cringed back. Slowly and carefully Jenny urged her to stand.

"Audrey, we've got to go with them," she whispered. She was afraid that if Audrey balked, the elves were going to *touch* them. The thought of that—of being touched by that shiny hoof or by the flipper she saw one of the others had—was more than Jenny could bear. "Please, Audrey," she whispered.

It was easy for the elves to lead them. All they had to do

was close in from one direction, and the girls would move in the other.

They walked like that, surrounded by a circle of lanterns, down a passage that sloped on and on. Other passages branched away. Clearly the place was big—and they were going deeper and deeper into it.

Walking calmed Jenny a little. The rocks around them took every imaginable shape—some like twisting antlers, others like windblown grass. There were lacy falls of angel hair, and huge columns covered with formations like exquisite flowers or the gills of mushrooms.

The air smelled like rain-damp earth. It was surprisingly warm.

Jenny tightened her supporting grip on Audrey's arm.

"Say something to them," she suggested. "Ask them where we're going."

In her own way Audrey was as brave as Dee. Her spiky eyelashes were starred together from crying, and she didn't look at the elf beside her. But she spoke to him in level tones.

"He says they're taking us to the Erlking," she said after a moment. Now Jenny could hear taut, shaking control in her voice. "That means—elf king, I think. I remember the story about the Erlking now. He's a kind of evil spirit who haunts the Black Forest. He's supposed to—take people. Especially young girls and children."

Dee pounced. "Why girls?"

Audrey spoke between clenched teeth. "You guess. But all the dark elves are that way. Well, *look* at them. They're all men. It's a male race."

With a shock, Jenny realized that it was true. The delicacy of their features had fooled her. Every one of their captors was beautiful—and male.

Dee's grin was bloodthirsty. "Time to fight."

"No," Jenny said tensely. Her heart was pounding, but she tried to quiet it. "There are too many of them; we wouldn't have a chance. And anyway, we're supposed to *face* our nightmares, remember? If the Erlking is what Audrey's most afraid of, he must be what we have to face."

"It's a *stupid* nightmare anyway," Dee hissed, her supple shoulders hunching as if an ice cube were going down her back.

"Believe me," Audrey said bitingly, "I wish you weren't in it with me."

The two girls ignored each other as they walked on through subterranean caverns of cathedral spaciousness. Glittering white gypsum crystals powdered everything, catching the lantern light. Coarse rock dust crunched underneath Jenny's feet.

"I don't understand," Audrey whispered. "This can't have come out of my mind. I've never seen anything like it."

"I have," Dee said, and even her voice was subdued. "Spelunking in New Mexico. But it wasn't so—*much.*"

At last they reached the biggest cavern of all.

They passed giant red pillars like coral reefs which gave Jenny the disconcerting feeling of being underwater.

They were heading straight for an enormous wall of flame-colored rock. It wasn't flat. It went rippling up and up like an inverted Niagara Falls. At floor level there was an irregularly shaped gap in the wall—like an entrance.

"The castle," Audrey translated quietly.

They passed through the gap in the red walls.

Inside, the elves moved to separate the girls into two groups. It happened so fast that Jenny didn't have time to react. All in an instant she was being herded away, and when she twisted her head frantically she saw Dee and Audrey being borne in the opposite direction. She saw Audrey's copper head bobbing and heard Dee's voice raised in fury. Then Dee's voice faded, and Jenny was led through a gap into a large room.

One of her captors said something ending with *"Erlkönig,"* and they all walked out. When Jenny looked through the gap, she found they were standing sentry on either side.

Now what?

She looked around. The rock formations here were like huge sand castles, half melted by water, in white and gold. Jenny realized she was seeing by moonlight and looked up. The ceiling had openings in it like skylights or chimneys in the rock. She studied them for a while.

Finally there was nothing to do but wait—and worry. What was happening to Tom right now? she wondered.

Think about the riddle, she told herself firmly. It'll pass the time, and it might be useful.

> *I am just two and two. I am hot. I am cold.*
> *I'm the parent of numbers that cannot be told.*
> *I'm a gift beyond measure, a matter of course,*
> *And I'm yielded with pleasure—when taken by force.*

Suddenly she had it. Yes! Something that could be hot and passionate or cold and impersonal. Something that could be the "parent" of untold numbers of people—because there was no counting how many babies had gotten started with it. Something that was just two and two—two lips touching two lips.

A kiss.

Jenny smiled in triumph. She'd solved the riddle. She could get one of the others free.

There was no question, of course, about who it would be. Much as she loved her friends, Tom would always come first.

The only problem with having solved the riddle was that she now had nothing to think about—except whatever was going to happen to her. The elf who'd left had said *"Erlkönig."* The Erlking? Was that who she was waiting for?

What kind of deformity would the Erlking have? she wondered. Hooves? Horns?

If he's king, he probably has something worse than all the others, she thought, and her heart chilled.

Someone came through the gap in the stone, and Jenny braced herself. The next minute she realized how dense she'd been.

He was wearing a white tunic and breeches and soft white boots. They showed off how lithe and smoothly muscled he was. In the moonlight his hair was silver as a mirror, and he was smiling.

"Julian."

"Welcome," he said, "to the Erlking's castle."

The last time they had spoken, Jenny had been furious with him. It was hard to keep that in mind now. The white leather was so soft looking, and it clung to him, hip and thigh. And there was something about a guy who looked at you with eyes like a starving tiger's. All at once Jenny felt disconcerted.

Tom always looked so good in ordinary clothes—but he was very conservative, never would dress up even at Halloween. Julian, by contrast, obviously got off on outrageous.

His broad leather belt showed how flat his stomach was, emphasized his narrow hips. It was modestly encrusted with sapphires. Jenny wished she had one like it.

"The Erlking, huh? Enjoying the part?"

"Immensely," Julian assured her gravely.

"At least you're *talking* to me in this nightmare. Not like the UFO one, I mean."

"Jenny. I will happily talk to you all night."

"Thank you, but there's a time limit, and I'd rather have my friends back."

"Say the word."

Jenny looked at him, startled, and then realized what word he meant. "No," she said. "I'll do it the hard way. We're going to get through all the nightmares, you know. We're going to win the Game."

"I admire your confidence."

"You can admire my success—starting now. I've solved your riddle, and you're a male chauvinist pig. It is *not* given with pleasure when taken by force."

"What isn't?"

"A kiss." She turned to face him fully. "That's the answer, isn't it? And you told me if I solved the riddle, you'd let one of my friends go."

"Wrong." He waited for her reaction, eyes glinting in a wicked smile. "I told you if you *gave me* the answer, I'd let one of your friends go. But you haven't *given* it to me yet." His eyes lingered on her lips. "Would you like to now?"

Fury sparked in Jenny. "You—!" She turned away so he wouldn't have the satisfaction of seeing her angry.

"I've upset you. You're offended," he said. He sounded genuinely penitent. Jenny couldn't keep up with these mercurial changes of mood. "Here, I'll give you something to make it up to you."

Reluctantly Jenny turned again. He was holding a rose—a

white rose. Or maybe it was silver—in this light it was hard to tell. It was the most beautiful thing she'd ever seen.

As she took it, Jenny realized it wasn't real but was exquisitely wrought, perfect down to the tiniest detail. Half opened, the blossom shimmered in her hands. The petals were cool but soft.

"Made from silver dug out by black elves in the deepest mines of the earth," Julian said. Jenny shook her head at him.

"That's all *folklore*. Are you saying you're *really* the Erlking? Do you want me to believe in Hänsel and Gretel, too?"

"I've been more things than you can imagine. And what I want you to believe is that children can go into dark places and disappear. After which people might tell stories to explain it—sometimes true stories, sometimes not."

Jenny felt disconcerted again. "Anyway—it's a beautiful rose," she said and stroked it against her cheek.

Julian's eyes gleamed.

"Let's go walking in the courtyard," he said. "You can really see the moonlight there."

The courtyard had a number of natural chimneys, and moonlight flooded down. Jenny felt almost awestruck at the beauty of the landscape. The moonlight threw a sort of magic sheen over everything, and the cavern was weirdly beautiful with its dark shadows and bright patches of silver.

Julian looked the same. Every shadow on his face was dead black, and there were silver points in his eyes.

"Have you ever wondered why you can go into dangerous places without getting hurt?" he said abruptly. "Why the stray animals you pick up never bite you, why you don't get mugged—or worse—when you wander around bad parts of town at night?"

"I . . ." People were always yelling at Jenny for exactly the things he was talking about. She herself had never given it much thought, but now a wild suspicion was rising in her mind. "No," she said. "No, I haven't."

His eyes remained on hers. "I've been looking after you, Jenny. Watching over you. No one can touch you . . . no one but me."

"That's impossible." It came out in a whisper. "You . . . I've done those things all my life. . . ." Her sentences were coming untangled.

"And I couldn't have been watching you that long? But I have. I've always loved you, Jenny."

The power of his gaze was frightening. Jenny was confused by her own emotions. She knew she should feel only hatred, only anger toward him, but by now she had to admit that part of her was fascinated by him. He was a prince of darkness—

—who had chosen *her*.

She turned and walked away from him, trying to gather herself.

"I have never been in love before," Julian said. "You're my first—and you'll be my only."

There was music in his voice, and the words settled like filigreed snowflakes around her, wrapping her in otherworldliness.

Jenny turned around and he touched her.

His touch was as tenuous as gauze on her cheek. Jenny was so surprised she didn't move. Then she looked down stupidly. He had taken her hand.

But I thought you couldn't . . .

His fingertips were as cool as jade against her skin. Tingles followed in their wake. She had an urge to press her cheek to his open hand.

Don't, she thought. Don't, don't, don't . . .

"Don't," she whispered.

He went on stroking her hand, thumb gently circling in her palm. A sensuous and dangerous feeling. Jenny felt herself start to come undone.

His touch was so delicate—he'd disengaged her hand so gently from the rose. . . .

From the rose, Jenny thought.

His gift. She'd held it in her hand. She'd stroked it against her right cheek—the cheek he was touching now.

She stepped back. "You . . . tricked me."

He still held her hand. "Does it matter?"

"Yes, it *matters,*" Jenny said furiously, trying to pull out of his grasp. How could she have been so stupid? It was a game he was playing with her, to get permission to touch more and more of her. "I understand now—I'll never touch you or anything you give me. That trick won't work again."

His lips were smiling, but there was something hot and deadly serious in his eyes. "Maybe not—but another one will. Believe me, Jenny: I'm going to make you mine—entirely—before you finish the Game."

Jenny wished she could think of something more mature to say than, "In your dreams!"

"No—in yours," he said. "And remember, you're not alone here."

Jenny heard a scream.

"That's Audrey," she said. "That's Audrey! Something's happening to her!" When he wouldn't release her hand, she jerked it out of his.

Then she saw his eyes—and what she saw there froze her.

"You know," she whispered. "You're *doing* it—to get back at me."

"I warned you," he said. The screaming was still going on. "Do you want it to stop?"

Evil, she thought. Absolute evil. Cruel, capricious, and dangerous as a cobra. I won't forget that again.

"I'll stop it myself," she said, her voice soft but fierce. "I told you I was going to win this Game. And I am. And I will *never* give in to you."

She threw the silver rose at his feet.

Then she was running for the sound of Audrey's screams.

Elves rushed at her as she plunged out of the sandcastle room, but she veered sharply and got by them. Audrey's screams were getting clearer and clearer. Jenny saw a gap in the nearest red wall and ducked into it, and suddenly the screams echoed all around her.

She saw Audrey sitting and Dee standing in front of her. She stumbled the last few feet to collapse beside them.

"What's wrong?"

Audrey was half sitting, half lying against the gypsum-encrusted wall of a small cavern. Her features were contorted with horror—and when Jenny turned she saw why.

She would have thought that after all she'd been through, she would be inured to weird creatures. But these things— these things were—

"Oh, *God,* Audrey, what are they?" she choked out.

Audrey's fingernails bit into Jenny's arm. "They're *draugar.* Living corpses. They've come for us. I—" She turned away, retching.

They *smelled* like corpses—the sickly-sweet odor of decay. Some of them had bloated bodies. Some had leathery skin, fallen in and wrinkled. Some, to Jenny's horror, had skin that was sloughing off.

One had thick fingernails turned brown by time and grown into long, dangling spirals. The nails clattered together, making a sound that raised gooseflesh all over Jenny's body.

They were completely blocking the exit. Jenny didn't know

how she'd gotten around them to reach Audrey, but there was no getting out again. They were closing in from all sides.

"When I tell you, run for the door!" Dee said.

"*What* door?"

Dee pointed and Jenny turned. Beyond the nearest *draugr* on the right was a wall—and there was a door in it. A Gothic door with an arched top, painted blue.

"Okay?" Dee shouted. "Get ready for it!"

She had been standing with her left leg back, knee bent, all her weight on it. Her right leg was so bent that only the toe touched the floor. It made her look like a ballerina, but it was called the cat stance—Dee was always trying to teach Jenny kung fu stances.

Suddenly she kicked, her right foot snapping up flat to strike the *draugr* under the jaw with her heel.

With a dry crack the *draugr*'s head fell backward—all the way backward. Its neck was snapped.

The terrible thing was that it kept walking. Head resting on its own shoulder blades, blundering the wrong way, *it kept walking.*

Jenny let go and screamed.

"Get up!" Dee shouted to them. "Now, while I've got them distracted. Get out of here!"

Audrey remained frozen. "We can't leave you—"

"Don't worry about me! Just go! Jenny, take her!"

Jenny obeyed the tone of command instinctively. She

hauled Audrey up by her houndstooth jacket and pulled her to the door. She wrenched it open, and they both fell through.

It slammed behind them before Jenny could stop it. She and Audrey looked at each other in dismay.

And then they waited.

They waited until a sick feeling in Jenny's stomach told her Dee wasn't going to come. Audrey was crying. Jenny tried the door handle. It wouldn't budge.

"It's my fault," Audrey whispered.

"One of you probably won't make it. . . ."

The door flew open. Dee charged through, slammed it behind her, leaned on it. She expelled a great gust of air.

"That was *close,*" she said. "But I've been dying for a fight, and it was a good one."

She was glowing with exertion and the joy of battle. She looked at Audrey.

"Well, aren't you a mess," she said.

Audrey's glossy auburn hair was hanging around her face; her spiky bangs were plastered damply to her forehead. Her cheeks were flushed and wet, her hands and legs scratched and scraped. Her cherry lipstick was gone.

Face inscrutable, Audrey held out one hand and slowly unclenched the fingers. On her palm were the combs from her French twist. "At least I still have these," she said calmly.

All three of them burst into hysterical laughter. They laughed and laughed in a violent release of emotion.

"I guess that counts as winning: getting out of your nightmare alive with your combs intact," Dee gasped finally.

Audrey raised her eyebrows, and then her lips curled again in a smile. She and Dee were smiling at each other.

An unseen clock struck twelve.

"Midnight," Jenny said. It came out softly, almost a whisper. Every time they won, that clock chimed to remind them that time was passing—passing fast. Where *was* it, anyway? The sound seemed to pervade the entire house.

"Six hours until dawn," Dee was saying to Audrey. "And only five nightmares to go. We're fine. We'll make it, easy."

"Easy? I don't *think* so," Audrey said.

"Look," Jenny said quietly, bending to pick up a scrap of paper.

CHAPTER 9

It was an abstract rendition of a forest, very heavy on green swirling lines.

"All right, so I did draw a forest," Audrey said. "I've always had nightmares about them, but I never knew why. I didn't even know *what* forest I was scared of."

"He picks up on our subconscious," said Dee.

"So what happened to you two after we got separated?" Jenny asked.

"Not much," Dee said. "They put us in that room, only there wasn't any door at first. Then we saw the door—and at that exact instant those corpses appeared and Audrey started screaming. What about you? Did you see the Erlking?"

Jenny looked away. "Sort of. It was Julian, playing the part."

She hesitated, then blurted, "You *do* know that it's because of me you're suffering, don't you? It's me he wants. He told me that he'd stop hurting you if I—if I let him—"

"Don't you *dare*," Dee said, sloe eyes flashing.

"Don't even think about it," said Audrey with equal heat.

Jenny nodded, feeling warmth in her eyes. To cover it up she watched Audrey. While they were talking, Audrey had efficiently put her hair back up, fished a quilted pouch out of her jacket pocket, and deftly restored her cherry lipstick. Audrey had always seemed so cosmopolitan, so invulnerable—but now Jenny had seen beneath the facade.

"It must have been hard, living in all those different countries," she said slowly and glanced over at Dee.

Audrey paused a moment in the midst of fluffing her bangs. She snapped her compact shut with a click.

"Frankly, it was awful," she said. "You can't imagine the culture shock. The dislocation—the insecurity—and you never know when you're going to move again. Even now that Daddy's retired I still feel—"

"Like it's hard to make real friends?"

Audrey nodded. "I feel as if we might be picking up and going again any minute."

"You're not, though," Jenny said. "You're staying here with us." She glanced at Dee again. "Right?"

"Oh, naturally," Dee said, but there was no rancor in her voice, and she laid a slender dark hand on Audrey's back.

133

"You know, I don't understand," Jenny said suddenly. "Those guys in the forest seemed nice—so why did they do it? Why did they hand us over?"

"Well—elves are supposed to do people favors. Answer questions, do work for you. But they always want something in return, and if you call them up and try to trap them, they sometimes trap *you*. Take you to their world. I guess those guys figured we were more expendable than they were."

Jenny nodded. "One more thing—"

"Always one more thing!" said Dee.

"—which of you did the door? I know *I* didn't put it there because I've never seen a door like that."

"I did, I suppose," said Audrey. "I saw doors like that in Germany—but I didn't *put* it there. It just appeared."

"You can't change things here by using your mind," Dee said. "You have to deal with everything here as if it's real."

"But where *is* here?" Audrey said bleakly.

"Good question," said Jenny, "It's nowhere on Earth; I know that from what I saw out the window."

"The Shadow World," Dee said. "Remember the instructions? A world that's like ours but different, that exists alongside ours, but never touches it."

"'Some people call it the world of dreams, but it is as real as anything else. . . .'" Jenny quoted. "Well, it touched our world tonight, anyway. What's wrong now, Audrey?"

"It just occurred to me. You know, in Norse and German

legends there are supposed to be nine worlds—our world's just the one in the middle."

"Nine?" said Jenny.

"Nine. There's Asgard, which is a sort of heaven, and Hel, which is a sort of hell, and a world of primal fire and a world of primal water and a world of primal wind—but, listen. There's also a world of primal ice. It's sort of connected to Hel—*and it's also a world of shadows.* It's called Niflheim, and *nifl* means 'dark, shadowy.'"

"Just what are you getting at?" Dee asked.

"I don't know. It's just strange, *nicht wahr?* God, I'm starting to think in German. But it *is* strange, isn't it—with him calling himself the Shadow Man? And I just remembered something else. The things that live in Niflheim are supposed to be terribly destructive, so they're under a rune of restraint to keep them from getting out of their world and into other peoples'. I don't remember which rune, though."

"You're *not* saying runes are real," Jenny said. "I mean, like the one Julian talked about—the one that 'pierced the veil between the worlds.' They can't really work."

"I always assumed they didn't, that it was just a silly superstition. But now . . . I don't know. They work in *legends* all right, to let you—oh, what do they call it? Fare forth between the worlds. Or summon up things from the other ones. The way those German boys summoned the elves."

The talk was making Jenny very uncomfortable. She didn't

know why, and that made her even more uncomfortable. Something to do with runes, a long time ago. After all she had seen, why should it upset her that runes might be real? That day in her grandfather's basement . . .

"Look," she said abruptly, "we've been standing here gabbing forever. Don't you think we'd better start looking for the next person? There *is* a time limit, you know."

"Right," Dee said, always ready for action. "Do you want to split up again?"

"No," Jenny said quickly. "Let's stick together." By whatever weird laws operated in this place, she'd already yielded Julian the right to touch her hand, her cheek, her hair. And he'd made it plain that he wouldn't be satisfied until he got all of her, bit by bit. It was just a question of what kind of ruse or threat he planned to try next. Jenny figured her best chance was not to be caught alone.

They found Michael on the third sweep down the hall. He was wandering back and forth in front of a door, running his hands through his rumpled dark hair and muttering. He brightened considerably at the sight of the girls.

"Audrey, at last! It seems like years!"

"Oh, I've been counting the seconds we've been apart," Audrey said, raising an eyebrow and dimpling at the same time.

"Me, too. I only wish I had a calculator to keep track."

And neither of them meant a word of it. Lucky for them,

thought Jenny. Love for Tom was like an aching bruise in her chest. If only she could see him, just for a moment . . .

They explained to Michael everything that had happened to them. He told them that for him the parlor had simply disappeared while Tom was cowering from the invisible creatures. Then he'd found himself in front of this door. He'd tried the knob, but it wouldn't open. He'd been pacing the hallway ever since.

"And you never saw a staircase?" Jenny asked.

"No staircase, no other doors, no nothing. No people, until you came."

"And yet we've been walking this hallway for hours, and we've seen three doors, and I came up a staircase," Jenny said. "It's just one more weird thing about this place."

"Which we don't have time to discuss," Dee said. "Let's move, people. Who wants to try this door?"

"This time let's try to keep it open after we go in," Jenny said. "That is, if we don't need to slam it shut fast."

"We can't go in at all—it's locked," Michael said.

Dee flashed him a grin as she took up a heel stance, ready to do a forward kick. "Bets?"

The door opened easily when Jenny twisted the knob, and no monsters jumped out. Dee caught it as it swung and held it against the wall. Through the opening Jenny could see dimness.

"Uh, you first. I'm a registered coward," Michael said.

Jenny took a deep breath, squared her shoulders, and stepped over the threshold—

—into a hallway identical to the one she had left.

She looked up and down it in bewilderment.

"What's going on? This door wants to close," Dee called.

"It's—" Jenny gave up and beckoned Audrey and Michael in.

"It's the same place," Audrey said, looking around.

This hallway was the mirror image of the other. Same gloomy carpet, same creepy wallpaper, same candles in brass holders.

Michael went back through to Dee's side. "Look—the candles even have the exact same drops of wax running down. It really is the *same* hallway, not just another one like it."

No matter how many times they went back and forth over the threshold, they kept getting the hallway.

"For some reason it's not letting us into your nightmare," Jenny said. "We just keep getting bounced back here."

"Oh, *too bad*," said Michael. "I'm really going to miss facing it."

"All right, let me see this." Dee finally went through, the door swinging shut behind her. "Yep, same place," she said, looking around. "Like a revolving door to hell."

"Wasn't it Sartre who said hell was eternity spent in a room with your friends?" Michael asked grandly.

"Oh, quit showing off your A in world literature," said Jenny. "Unless—was *that* your nightmare, Mike?"

Michael deflated a bit. "Uh, actually, no. Mine was more of a kid thing, really."

"But what was it?"

Michael seemed to be blushing. Scratching under the collar of his gray sweatshirt, he shook his head.

"'Each of you has a secret you would rather die than reveal. . . .'" Dee quoted portentously from the game card. "I'll bet it was something *really* embarrassing, like the potty monster, huh, Mikey?" As she spoke she turned the doorknob. It wouldn't budge. "Oh, great, it's locked again."

"If we're stuck here again, we might as well sit down," Audrey said.

There didn't seem to be anything else to do. They sat, and Michael talked. One thing you could always count on, Jenny thought—that Michael wouldn't run out of things to talk about.

"When I think," said Michael, "that I could have stayed home and watched 'Ren and Stimpy' tonight . . ."

". . . This isn't much of a game. No reset. It's win, lose, or die," Michael said. "You heard the one about the bunny and the hair dryer?"

"Michael," Audrey said scathingly.

While he was talking, Michael had taken off one of his battered tennis shoes. It had a hole in the toe. Audrey stared in genteel horror at his limp sock on the floor.

"I can't help it—I've got an itch. Ah . . . that's better,"

Michael said, scratching vigorously. "So what'd you say to—that guy—after we all got whooshed out of the parlor?" he said to Jenny. "I mean—" He fumbled for words as all three girls looked at him. "I mean—it was pretty obvious what he wanted—and you said he kept you there alone—"

"Whatever he wants," Jenny said shortly, "he's not getting it."

"Of course not," Audrey huffed. "What an idea."

"She wouldn't give him the time of day," Dee said curtly.

"I don't even know what he sees in me," Jenny said.

The others all looked at each other. Then Dee snorted. "No, you wouldn't, would you? But everybody else does. Except Zach, probably, but then he's your cousin."

"It's not just looks," Audrey said. "You're *good.* Too good, sometimes. I've told you—"

"Aba would say your soul is straight," Dee interrupted.

"Just like a Girl Scout," Michael said helpfully. "Sweet and simple and honest."

"But he's *bad,*" Jenny said.

"That's the point," Dee said. "Badness always wants goodness."

"And opposites attract," Audrey said grimly. "Look at Michael and me."

Michael said hastily, "So who do you think he is, anyway?"

"I think he's a Visitor," Dee said, to Jenny's surprise. "You know, an alien that abducts people."

Michael stared, scratching his chin. Audrey frowned.

"Don't be ridiculous," she said. "He's no alien—just look at him. And where's his spaceship?"

"I think he can look like whatever he wants to," Dee said, scratching her arm. "And maybe they don't really need spaceships. He's taken us to another planet, hasn't he?"

"Another *world,* maybe. There's a difference," Audrey shot back. "And according to him he did it with a rune. Which makes him—"

"What? The Erlking? I don't think so, dear. You're just saying that because it's what you're most afraid of."

"And Visitors are what you're most afraid of, *dear,*" Audrey said, working her perfect nails over her palm. It was turning into a vintage Dee-Audrey feud.

"Girls, girls," Michael said. "Personally, I think he's a demon. Jenny's demon lover." He smiled ingenuously, digging under his collar again. Dee and Audrey both glared. Jenny just felt a chill deep inside.

"Look, I believe in demons," Michael said. "Why shouldn't they exist? And if they *do* exist, that guy has gotta be one."

Throughout this conversation Jenny had gradually become aware of a discomfort. The skin on her arm was tingling—no, itching. She scratched at it absently, but the itching got worse. And worse. She looked down.

Even in the dim light she could see the mark on her arm. A dark spot, like a strawberry birthmark. But she didn't have any birthmarks. And this spot wasn't strawberry-colored . . .

. . . it was green.

At the same moment Michael, who'd thrust one hand inside his sleeve to scratch his arm, made a strange sound. His eyes bulged, his expression changed. He shoved the sweatshirt sleeve up.

Jenny gasped.

There was something growing on his arm.

A plant. There were leaves, fresh and green and young, looking like newly sprouted mint, growing from his flesh.

The next instant they were all on their feet, looking at themselves in the candlelight. Each of them was grow-ing patches of green. Jenny's were like moss, Audrey's like mold.

Jenny gulped. Like Dee and Audrey, she was horrified. But Michael went hysterical.

"Get it off me! *Get it off!*" He thrust his arm out blindly at Jenny.

Even gritting her teeth, she couldn't bring herself to touch the sprigs. Dee took hold of one and pulled.

"Ow!" Michael yelled. Dee stopped. "No, go on! I don't care how much it hurts. Pull it out!"

Dee pulled harder. The plant hung on. Jenny could just glimpse a network of thin roots like white threads connecting it to his arm. Blood began to ooze out of several pores as Dee kept pulling.

Michael was screaming.

Finally Dee swallowed, her nostrils flared.

"Mike, I can't keep pulling. I can't. It's taking your skin with it."

"I don't care! I don't care!" Michael still wouldn't open his eyes. He grabbed at the plants himself with his other hand. Jenny pressed a hand to her mouth to stop from gasping.

Sprigs were growing on his other hand, too. Growing even more luxuriantly than on the first.

"Mike, it's . . . it's all over you," she whispered.

Michael's eyes flew open, and he looked at his hands. "Oh, God. Oh, GodGodGod . . ."

In one frenzied motion he yanked his sweatshirt over his head, pulling his arms out. His chest and stomach were thickly covered with new leaves. They stirred with his breath, brushing one another lightly.

Michael's screams rang from the ceiling.

"Chill out!" Dee finally got him in a choke hold, preventing him from running raving down the hall. His eyes were wild and set, and he was breathing like a lathered horse.

"We've got to do something for him," Jenny said. She could hardly bear the moss on her forearm, but she had to forget about that. Michael was so much worse off.

"Yeah—but what?" Dee was trying to keep Michael under control. He seemed about to go into convulsions, clawing at himself.

Audrey stepped forward. Jenny guessed that she was actually more upset by the growths than anyone but Michael—appearance meant a lot to Audrey. But Audrey had herself in iron control.

"Michael Allen Cohen, look at me!" she rapped out.

He turned wild dark eyes on her.

"You calm down *now*. Understand? *Verstehen Sie?*"

A glimmer of sanity showed in Michael's eyes.

"Right *now*," Audrey said severely, and putting her palms on either side of his face, she kissed him.

When she backed up, Michael had cherry lipstick all over his mouth. He looked a lot calmer.

"I live to obey," he said weakly.

"You live to kibitz," said Audrey.

"We've all got to stay calm," Jenny said. "We've got to *think*. How can we get rid of these things? We can't pull them out. So what else can we do?"

"Weed-killer," Dee muttered. There was some exotic red-and-green-leafed plant growing on her, almost harmonizing with her dark skin.

"We don't have *anything* here to work with," Audrey said. "Never mind anything deadly to plants."

Michael spoke up in a whisper—but a whisper with a new note in it.

"We've got fire."

Jenny looked up at the candle in its brass holder.

144

"You can let go of me, now," Michael told Dee. "I won't go anywhere. I want to see if that candle will come out."

Dee released him. He tried to take a step, then stopped. He squatted down to stare, his head almost at floor level. Jenny bent, too.

His bare foot was rooted to the floor by a mat of white tendrils.

They were growing out of his sole and into the black carpet. He could barely raise his foot an inch, and only by turning it sideways could he see the roots.

As Jenny slowly looked up, she expected him to go frantic again. But Audrey reached out and firmly took his hand, her fingers crushing the leaves on the back.

Michael was shaking, but he stayed rational.

"Get the candle," he said thickly.

Dee lifted it out easily. "I'm going to try it on myself first," she said.

"No. Me."

Dee slanted a sloe-eyed look at him, then nodded. She tilted the candle to apply the flame to a leaf on his arm.

The leaf seemed to melt slightly in a crescent where the flame touched it. There was a bad smell as the edge blackened. Nothing else happened.

"Try the roots."

Dee tried lower, very close to Michael's skin. Michael flinched away from the heat, but Audrey held him steady.

The plant started to shrivel.

"That's it!"

"Can you stand it?" Dee asked.

"I can stand anything to get these off. With the right kind of incentive, of course." He looked hopefully at Audrey, who was still holding him and murmuring encouragement.

Jenny smiled to herself. To be inane and lecherous when you're scared to death required a special kind of bravery.

Dee burned more roots. The plants began to drop off more and more quickly, shriveling at the first touch of the flame.

Michael was almost sobbing in relief. His arms and torso were clear.

"Anything—ah, lower?" Dee gestured with the candle at Michael's sweatpants.

"No! And watch where you're waving that thing. I plan to be a family man."

"Look," Jenny said softly.

The patch of moss on her skin was getting smaller and smaller. In a moment it had faded altogether. The same was happening to Dee and Audrey. Michael's feet came free of the floor.

And then they were all laughing, admiring their clear, perfect skin, touching it, holding it up to the others. Just exactly like the scene at the end of *Ben Hur*, Jenny thought, where the two women are miraculously cured of leprosy. Michael put his sweatshirt back on and kissed Audrey once more.

"You had some mold on your lips before," he said. "I didn't like to mention it."

"No, you didn't, Aud," Dee muttered in Audrey's ear. Audrey looked helplessly at Mike, but with some indulgence.

"So this *was* your nightmare, and we got through it," Jenny said. "This hallway is your nightmare room. Which means that if we go back through that door . . ."

The door opened under Dee's hand. They walked through into the hallway, apparently the same hallway they had just left. But with two differences, Jenny noticed. In this hallway there was no candle missing from the bracket. And there was a scrap of white paper on the floor.

A picture of a huge green plant, something on the order of a rubber plant, with arms and legs sticking out. No head.

"Ugh," Jenny said.

"My nightmare," Michael said, still looking embarrassed. "Turning into a plant. It's so stupid—I think it came from this book I read when I was in third grade. It had a story about a kid who was so dirty that things started to grow on her—little radishes and veggies. And it just freaked me out. I mean, it was this harmless story, but for some reason I just flipped. I kept thinking about that kid, all crusted with dirt, with green stuff sprouting from her—it made me sick."

"You're making *me* sick," Audrey said.

"And then the parents pulled them—the veggies—they pulled them off her—"

"Stop it," Dee commanded.

"Like I said, it was stupid, a kid's thing."

"I don't think it was stupid, I think it was *horrible*. And I think you were smart and brave, the way you dealt with it," Jenny said. Michael's soulful eyes widened at the unprecedented compliments, and he gave her a rumpled grin.

The unseen clock struck one. There was something eerie about the way it echoed. Morning is coming, Jenny thought.

"We'd better get moving," Dee said, just as Michael made a stifled sound.

"What's wrong—" Audrey began, but then she saw it, too, in the darkness of the hall where nothing had been before.

A staircase.

CHAPTER 10

Excitement bubbled up in Jenny. "Finally we can *go* somewhere."

"And get out of this freaking hallway," Dee said.

Michael was looking awed. "It's just like going up to the next level of a video game."

But Audrey pursed her lips. When Jenny asked why, Audrey gave her a sideways glance under spiky dark lashes.

"One thing about video games—the farther you go, the harder they get," she said. *"N'est-ce pas?"*

The stairs had rubber padding with the ridges worn almost to nothing. Jenny couldn't see the top from where she stood—the roof of the Haunted Mansion hall was in the way.

"What are we waiting for?" Dee said and vaulted onto the

steps. Then she grabbed for the railing—as soon as her foot touched a step, the whole staircase had started moving with a jerk. It was a wheezing, groaning, shivering escalator.

"Oh, geez," Michael said. "I hate to tell you this, but when I was a kid I was scared of escalators. I was afraid they might catch the end of my muffler or something—"

"You don't wear mufflers," Audrey said and shoved him on.

"Mike, if you're scared of escalators, then this one is probably your fault," Jenny said, stepping on behind him. "Remember, he gets it all from us."

As they neared the top, Jenny found they were riding directly toward a mirror. In fact, she discovered when she looked down the hall—after helping Mike jump off the escalator at the strategic moment—there were mirrors everywhere.

The hallway downstairs had been dark—this one was exactly the opposite. Light bounced and rainbowed off the mirrors lining the zigzagging walls until Jenny saw colored streaks even with her eyes closed. In fact, the mirrored walls zigged and zagged so sharply that it was impossible to get a clear view for more than a few feet. You had to veer alternately right and left to follow the hallway's path, and anything in the bend before you or behind you was invisible.

"All right, who put *these* here?" Dee demanded.

"Are my legs really that short? Or are these trick mirrors?" Audrey asked, pivoting.

Michael made one effort to straighten his wrinkled gray sweats and then gave up.

Jenny's own reflection made her uncomfortable. She seemed to hear Julian's voice in her mind: *"Eyes as green as cypress and hair like liquid amber. . . ."*

That wasn't what she saw. Just now Jenny saw a girl with flushed cheeks, whose hair was clinging to her forehead in little damp curls, whose tissue-linen blouse was beginning to go limp, and whose flowing cotton skirt was dusty and grass-stained.

"Right or left—take your pick," she said, glancing up and down the hallway.

"Left," Dee said firmly, and they went that way, zigging and zagging with the acute turns.

The mirrors were disconcerting. Everywhere Jenny looked her image was thrown back at her, and thrown from mirror to mirror so that she saw herself coming and going, reflected to infinity on all sides. Stay in this place long enough and you might forget which one is really you, she thought.

As in the other hallway, there were no deviations from the pattern, nothing to distinguish any part of it from any other. It was especially nerve-racking not being able to see more than one turn behind you, and not knowing what might be waiting around the next turn ahead. Images of the Creeper and the Lurker went through Jenny's mind.

"Dee, slow *down*," Jenny said as Dee's long, light step took her out of sight for the third time. Dee was navigating the corridor like a skier on a slalom, plunging in and out of the sharp turns, while the rest of them walked with hands outstretched to help them tell reflection from reality.

"No, you guys hurry *up*—" Dee's voice was responding from the next bend, and then there was a flash.

It seemed to reflect from everywhere at once, but Jenny thought it came from ahead. She and Audrey and Michael stood frozen for a moment, then hurried forward.

Dee was standing, hands on her hips, in front of a door. It was mirrored like the walls, but Jenny figured it *had* to be a door because there was a red button like an elevator button beside it. When she looked hard she could distinguish the door's outline from the mirror around it.

Above the red button was a blue lightbulb, round as a clown's nose.

"It just appeared," Dee said and snapped her fingers. "Like *that*. In that flash."

From the turn ahead they heard whimpering.

"*Summer!*" Jenny, Dee, and Audrey exclaimed simultaneously.

It was Summer, huddled in the next bend, her spun-sugar curls resting on her folded arms, her legs drawn beneath her china blue shirtdress. She looked up with a little hysterical cry at their approach.

"Is it really you?"

"Yes," Jenny said, kneeling. She was a little frightened by the expression in Summer's eyes.

"Really, really you?"

"Yes. Oh, Summer." Worriedly, Jenny put her arms around the smaller girl and felt her trembling.

"I've been alone here so long, and I kept seeing myself, and then sometimes I thought I saw other people, but when I ran toward them they weren't there. . . ."

"Who have you seen?" Jenny asked.

"Sometimes Zachary—and sometimes *him*. He *scares* me, Jenny." Summer buried her small face in Jenny's vest.

He scares me, too, Jenny thought. She said, "There's nothing to be frightened of now. We're really here. See?"

Summer managed a watery smile.

"Poor sun bunny," Michael said. "I guess it must be your nightmare next."

"Good job, Mr. Tactful," Dee said under her breath.

They explained about the nightmares to Summer. She wasn't as disturbed as Jenny thought she might be.

"Anything to get out of *here*," she said.

"I know. I've only been here twenty minutes, and I hate the place already," Dee said. "Anybody for claustrophobia?"

In front of the door Jenny hesitated with her finger on the button. "I don't suppose you want to tell us what you drew for your nightmare," she said. She didn't have much hope; none of the others had told.

"Okay," Summer said readily. "It was a messy room."

"A messy *room*?" Michael said. "Oh, horror."

"No, really, Summer," Audrey said with a briskly adult air. "It'll help if you tell us."

Dee flashed an amused ebony glance at her.

"I did tell you. It's a messy room."

"It's all right, Summer," Jenny said gently. "We'll deal with it when we get there." She pushed the red button. The blue light went on. The door slid open.

It was a messy room.

"You see," Summer said.

It was Summer's bedroom, only more so. Ever since Jenny had known Summer, her room had been messy. Summer's parents were refugees from the sixties, and everything in their house was slightly frayed or weathered, but as Michael said, Summer herself had clutter down to a fine art. When you visited her you usually couldn't see the handmade tie-dyed curtains at the window or the bright patchwork quilt on the bed, because of the things hanging from them or piled up in front of them or scattered on top of them.

In the room behind the mirrored door, Jenny couldn't even see the *bed*. There was a small clear space in front of the closet—everything else was obscured by piles of junk.

Dee and Michael were giggling. "Trust you, Sunshine, to have a nightmare like this," Dee said.

Jenny sighed, not nearly as amused. "All right, everybody,

let's go in. I suppose we have to clean it up—there must be a door somewhere along one of the far walls."

"Hey, wait. I don't do the C-word," Michael protested, alarmed. "Besides, dust is bad for my allergies."

"In," said Audrey, taking him by the ear.

They all squeezed in between the closet and the piles. The door slid noiselessly shut behind them—and disappeared.

"Talk about claustrophobia," Michael gasped.

"Cette chambre est une vrai pagaille," Audrey said under her breath.

"What?" Jenny asked.

"I said this is one messy room. Summer, how can you stand it?"

Summer's delft-blue eyes filled with tears. "My real room isn't as bad as *this*. This is my nightmare, dummy!"

"Well, why this kind of nightmare?" Audrey said, not softening.

"Because my mom never yells about my room, but once my nana came to visit, and she almost passed out. I still dream about what she said."

"Don't make her feel bad," Jenny whispered to Audrey. "Try to clear a path around the edges," she said aloud, "and check every wall for the door."

The piles of junk were amazingly varied. There were heaps of rumpled clothes, year-old magazines, disjointed Ray-Bans, spindled cassette tapes, unstrung string bikinis, crushed frozen yogurt cups, bent photographs, mismatched sandals, dry felt-tip pens, chewed pencils, twisted headphones, musty towels, endless mounds of underwear, and a zoo of bedraggled stuffed animals. Also a dog-chewed Frisbee, a mashed Twister mat, and a futon that smelled like somebody's bottom.

"It's spider city here," Dee said, gathering up one of the heaps. "Haven't you ever heard of Raid?"

"I believe in live and let live," Summer said vaguely.

It really *was* a nightmare of sorts, Jenny thought—a nightmare of tedium. But Dee worked with tireless energy and Audrey with fastidious precision, and slowly they forged a path through the debris. Michael was no good at all—he stopped to leaf through every magazine he picked up.

They were getting to a different type of garbage—a type that made Audrey wrinkle up her nose. Blackened avocado husks, mildewed newspapers, and plastic glasses with the dregs of unidentifiable liquids in them.

Then Jenny lifted a box of odds and ends and saw something like a pressed flower on the hardwood floor underneath. But it wasn't a flower, it was the wrong shape. At first she didn't recognize it, then she saw the little muzzle and the tiny curled-up feet. It was a flat and desiccated mouse.

She couldn't help gasping.

I can't touch that, I can't, I *can't.*

Dee scraped it up with a 1991 calendar and threw it in

the closet. Jenny felt a whisper of terror inside her, unease that went beyond disgust at the mouse.

The garbage got worse and worse—like what you'd find at a dump, nothing that would be in anybody's bedroom. Food in all stages of decomposition. Every kind of refuse, trash, and litter.

No one was smiling anymore.

Dee picked up a tattered Easter basket, paused. An *awful* smell wafted from it. She stirred the cellophane grass with one long finger, and then her face convulsed. In the basket was a solid mass of white, writhing maggots.

"God!" In one fluid motion Dee threw the basket at the closet, where it hit the door and scattered a shower of white. Michael bolted up from his magazine with a yell. Audrey and Summer were shrieking.

Jenny felt the quick, cold touch of real fear.

"Summer—just *what* did your grandmother say about your room?" she said.

"Oh—she said things were growing in it," Summer reported, her eyes large and worried. "She said it would attract bugs. She said it looked like an earthquake hit it. She said someday I would get lost in it and never come out."

Dee, who had been staring at Summer, now cut a glance of startled revelation at Jenny. "Uh-*huh*," she said.

The tension in the room was palpable.

"And just what kind of nightmares do you have about it?" Jenny asked, trying to discipline her voice.

"Oh." Summer shivered. "Well—it's like I hear a scratchy noise, and then I look and it's these cockroaches—but they're big, big as . . . as sneakers. And then I see this thing on the floor. It's like fungus, sort of a column of fungus, but it's got a kind of mouth on the top and it's howling. It's howling fungus."

Summer's lips were trembling by now.

"It may not sound scary, but it was. It was the scariest thing I've ever seen in my life."

A primitive warning was going off in Jenny's brain. She, Audrey, Dee, and Michael all looked at one another. "It sounds plenty scary to me," she said. "I think maybe we'd better get moving."

Michael's lips were puckered in a soundless whistle. "I think maybe you're right," he muttered. He bent to work without another word of complaint.

The closet was full by now, and they were just transferring things from before them to behind them, like digging a tunnel. The garbage kept getting grosser and grosser and scarier and scarier. Things Jenny didn't want to touch with her hands. She wore crumpled T-shirts like oven mitts to move them.

Then the bugs came.

It started with a rustle, a pleasant sound like a taffeta prom dress. Jenny stiffened, then turned slowly to look.

A cockroach, flat and brown. But it was huge, far larger than Jenny's foot. It crawled languidly out of the floor vent, squirming through somehow, its barbed back legs catching on the metal louvers. Its feet made soft ticking sounds on the paper debris.

Summer gave a reedy shriek and pointed at it. Then another one came out of the vent, and another. Summer's pointing finger became a shaky blur.

Jenny reached for a water glass to revive her and snatched her hand back. The glass was jam-packed with crickets, antennae twitching delicately.

Summer saw it. She stopped pointing and went still.

Smaller roaches emerged from a discarded candy box, the frilly paper cups crinkling as the bugs crept out.

Summer's face was so white there were blue patches under her eyes.

Iridescent green beetles the size of footballs began to climb the walls. They flexed their chitinous outer wings, their membranous inner wings hanging out like dragging petticoats.

Summer stood like a statue of ice.

Jenny looked up. A dozen brown moths as big as small kites were clinging flat to the ceiling, their dark-spotted wings outstretched.

"Come on, Summer, *help* us!" Audrey said in a fear-clotted voice as she raked at the trash. Disturbed ants swarmed out of it, forming thick trails like black waterfalls over the debris.

Summer didn't move. She was staring at one of the hard-shelled beetles like a witless rabbit caught in a headlight.

The ground rocked beneath Jenny's feet.

At first she thought it was some effect of the garbage shifting. Then she remembered: *She said it looked like an earthquake hit it. . . .*"

"We have to hurry!" she shouted at the same time as Dee yelled, "Go, go!"

They were clawing through the garbage now, tearing just enough away from the wall to reveal cracked and peeling wallpaper, to make sure there was no door. They climbed on the smaller mounds, wading through them.

The ground shook again.

The whisper of terror inside Jenny had become a scream.

"Hurry," she gasped, clearing refuse with sweeps of her arms. "Hurry, hurry . . ."

The towering piles of rubbish quaked.

They were all working frenetically, even Michael. Only Summer stood rooted in horror.

"The door!" Dee shouted, from the top of a pile.

Jenny's head snapped up. Relief flooded through her. Barely visible above a stinking pile she could see the rectangular molding of the door.

"It opens *in,*" Audrey said. "We have to get all this stuff out of the way."

They scrambled over each other, ripping at the pile. A

cockroach climbed onto Jenny's foot; she kicked it off. Time to scream later.

The room shook again. Jenny looked up and her breath hissed in. There were ominous cracks in the ceiling.

At that moment Dee and Michael cleared the last rubble from the door.

With a thankful sob Jenny helped them pull it open.

Then she turned to look back.

What she saw wasn't anybody's *room.* It was Hell. There were huge cracks in the floor with monstrous, mutant bugs crawling out. The ceiling was buckling and plaster was filtering down. The moths, disturbed, were fluttering through the air, their wings making a sound like huge cards shuffling. And sprouting like grotesque anemones among the refuse were objects Jenny didn't recognize. They looked like drooping sea cucumbers and they were green-gray.

Audrey and Michael had stumbled out into the hall of mirrors. Dee was holding the door. The earth rumbled again.

"Summer, come on!" Jenny shouted.

Summer turned toward her voice, her large blue eyes blind. She took a step toward Jenny.

One of the growths directly in her path straightened up. It became a column. At the top of the column there was an aperture that flared open and shut.

The aperture opened wide. A demented, obscene sound came out.

It was howling.

The other growths were straightening. The moaning siren sound doubled, tripled. They were between Summer and the door.

Summer turned and stumbled back toward the closet, shrieking.

"Summer, *no!* Come back!"

The ground heaved. The piles of garbage were toppling, falling into the clear path. The mutant bugs skittered around in a frenzy. They seemed to be heading toward Summer. The fungus howled.

Summer's shrieks gave way to full-throated screaming.

"Summer!" Adrenaline kicked in and Jenny plunged into the garbage, trying to climb it.

"Jenny, come back!" Dee shouted. More rubbish fell. Jenny couldn't see Summer at all. The screams were fading.

"Jenny, I can't hold the door!"

The screams fell silent. Only the howling went on.

"Summer!"

The earth jerked violently.

"It's coming down!" Dee shouted, and Jenny felt a hand grab her, pull her backward.

"No—we have to get Summer!"

"We can't get anybody! Come on!"

"No—*Summer!*" Jenny screamed, turning again.

Dee ducked and caught Jenny around the waist. Jenny

found herself flying over Dee's shoulders, out the door.

Michael and Audrey grabbed her. Through the open door Jenny saw the ceiling come down. Dee staggered out and fell beside them. Jenny didn't have the strength to stand up.

Then the door slammed shut as the toppling piles fell against it.

"Look," Michael said in a thick voice.

The door was disappearing.

It did a slow fade, like a still frame in a movie. It was a door, it was a slightly misty door, it was a transparent door with mirror showing through, it was a mirrored wall.

Jenny was staring wildly at her own image.

She could see the others in the mirror. Audrey was white as china. Dee's face was gray. Michael looked numb. They huddled on the carpet, stunned.

It had happened with such terrible suddenness.

Jenny whispered, "When Dee was late coming out of Audrey's nightmare, the door didn't disappear. It stayed there—and she came out. But this time . . ."

"God," said Dee in a very low voice.

There was a long silence. Audrey, finally, was the one to say the words.

"She's dead."

Jenny put her face in her hands. It was a gesture she would never have thought she'd use. At the moment it just happened. She wanted to hide from the world. She wanted to make everything that had happened unhappen.

"It's not fair," she whispered. "She never hurt anybody." Then she was standing, shouting to the echoing hallway. "It's not fair. It's not *fair,* damn you! She didn't deserve it! It's not *fair*!"

"Jenny. Jenny, calm down—come on, now. Jenny, please— just sit down, okay?"

They were all trying to hold her. Jenny realized she wasn't in control of herself. She was trembling violently, and her throat hurt from screaming.

As suddenly as it had come, the hysterical energy faded. Jenny felt herself falling.

They set her down.

"It's okay," Dee said, and Jenny felt a hand stroking her hair. At any other time it would have surprised her. Now she felt nothing. "It's okay to be upset," Dee said.

They didn't understand. It was Jenny's fault. She was the one who had gotten them into this. If she had kissed Julian in the Erlking's cavern, she could have gotten Summer out.

As if to mock her, an unseen clock struck two. But Jenny could only sit.

CHAPTER 11

"What's taking them so long?" Dee said.

Audrey and Michael had gone off to see if they could find Zach, who they figured must be around here somewhere. Or if they could find water—or a blanket—or *something*—for Jenny.

Jenny was in bad shape. She was slumped against the slanting mirrored wall opposite Summer's door—what had been Summer's door. There wasn't a trace of the exit from Summer's nightmare left, but Jenny wouldn't leave this place.

Jenny ached. All she could think of, in between waves of grayness, was Summer. Summer had joined their group in fourth grade, after she, Tom, Dee, Zach, and Michael were already friends. Tiny, muddled, and very sweet, Summer had needed to be taken care of, and taking care was what Jenny did best.

But not this time. This time Jenny had screwed up. And Summer was gone.

Jenny still didn't believe it had really happened. Summer would come walking out of that mirror any second now, all thistledown hair and dark blue eyes. Any second now.

Summer didn't.

Jenny let her head drop back against the wall.

"I'm going to look for them," Dee said. "They've been too long, they might be in trouble. You stay here, okay? Promise you'll stay right here." Her voice was slow and clear, the voice you'd use to talk to a child.

Eyes shut, Jenny made some slight motion with her head.

"Okay. I'll be back in a minute."

Jenny's mind drifted back into a haze. Summer climbing a tree at camp, Summer at Newport Beach falling off a surfboard, Summer at school chewing on a pencil. Summer laughing, Summer puzzled, Summer's blue eyes filled with tears.

She didn't have a mean bone in her body, Jenny thought. She was a *good* person. Something like this can't happen to a *good* person.

Can it?

She saw the flash even through closed lids.

Summer! she thought, opening her eyes. But the mirror in

front of her showed only her own pale, anxious face and disarrayed hair.

Maybe it had come from the side. Which way? On her feet, Jenny looked to the right and left, dazzled by the multiple reflections. She didn't even know which way Dee had gone.

She went right, veering back and forth around the zigzag mirrors.

Turning a corner, she saw dozens of reflections of a round blue lightbulb.

She caught her breath sharply. The blue light was on, the red button beneath it was depressed. Beside it was a dark rectangle—an open door.

Numb to caution, Jenny poked her head in. She could see only darkness inside. None of the light from the hallway seemed to penetrate.

Had Audrey and Michael gone in here? Had Dee? Could Summer—

With a click the button popped out, the door began to close. Jenny had an instant to choose: jump back or jump forward. She jumped forward.

The door slid noiselessly shut behind her, and she stared around, trying to see in the gloom. She could make out shapes like a row of shelves, something on a tripod, a tall lamp. Then she knew where she was. It was dim simply because the lights were off.

As her eyes adjusted she recognized a giant mural print

on one wall. It showed cafeteria tables stacked in a glorious pyramid, one trash can on each end at each level—a marvel of engineering. Jenny knew that picture well. She, Tom, and Dee had spent an entire night stacking those tables and listening to Zach's imperious demands for "one more shot." It had been one of the more hysterical and terrifying adventures of their sophomore year.

This was her cousin Zach's garage, converted into a studio. It felt almost like home—but there was no one in sight.

The darkroom, Jenny thought, and followed the special L-shaped hallway Zach had built—a light trap, he called it—to the little room nestled within the garage. She pushed aside the curtain at the entrance.

The amber safe light shone on a single figure's back, on a flannel shirt and a casual ponytail.

"Zach!" Jenny ran to him, but he didn't turn around. "Zach, it's me, Jenny. Zach—what are you *doing*?"

He was gently rocking a tray full of chemicals with a print in it. His body was stiff and resistant, but Jenny turned him by force. Even in this light she could see he looked—tranced. The look she'd seen first in the living room when he'd insisted on turning more game cards, and then in the parlor when all the rest of them were freaking out.

"Oh, Zach, what's wrong with you?" she said and threw her arms around him. She'd been worried about him all night; she'd been planning to comfort him, to help. But now she didn't have the strength. She desperately needed help herself.

He scarcely seemed to notice she was there. He pushed her away and turned back to agitating the tray.

"Zachary, did Dee come in here? Have you seen Audrey or Michael?"

His voice was slow, dragging, but matter-of-fact.

"I haven't seen anybody. I was sitting out there. Where the mirrors are. Then I saw a flashgun go off. When I looked for it, I found a door. I pushed the button and went in."

A flashgun—of course, that was how Zach would interpret the bursts of light in the hallway. "But what are you *doing*?" Jenny said.

"It was all set up for me. The print was already in the developer." Somewhere a timer went off, and he pulled away from Jenny's reaching hand. "I have to rinse it now."

Jenny blinked painfully as he turned the white light on. She watched his careful, clever fingers as he rinsed the print and plastered it wetly against the wall, standing back to evaluate it, frowning.

"Zach, *please*. You have to listen." The numbness over Summer was wearing off. Zach was her blood relative, and right here, and in trouble. In this light she could see how pale his narrow face was. She could also see the fixed look in his clear gray eyes. "Don't you realize this is your nightmare? We can't waste time—we have to find a door to get out. *Zach!*"

169

He pushed her away again. "I have to finish this job. I have to . . ."

She was barely in time to catch him as he collapsed. But when she did he didn't push her away again. He clung to her like a frightened child.

"Jenny . . . sorry . . ."

"It's okay." She held him tightly, almost rocking him. "It's okay, I'm here. That's what cousins are for."

After a minute he tried to straighten up, but she still held him, encouraging him to hold her back. She needed comfort as much as he did, and Zach had always been there for her. Before their families had moved out to California, she and Zach had lived next door to each other. They'd played Indians in the cherry orchard behind their houses. That was in the days before Zach decided he liked photographs better than people, when Zach's gray eyes had been warm instead of winter-cool.

Her cousin's mind was obviously following the same track. "Just like when we were kids," he said with what was probably supposed to be a laugh.

"And you'd get all scraped up climbing trees, and we'd wash you with the hose so Aunt Lil wouldn't get mad," Jenny said. She laughed, herself, muffled against Zach's shoulder. It was almost like crying. "Oh, Zach, I'm so glad I found you."

"Me, too." He sighed. "I've been feeling pretty weird."

"Everything's been awful," Jenny said, and once again her

voice was shaking badly. "I've been so scared—and now . . ."

She couldn't bring herself to mention Summer. The words stuck in her throat.

"It's okay," he said. "We're together now. We'll make things okay."

A hose and a Band-Aid aren't going to help this time, Jenny thought, but it was easier just to hold on to Zach. Tighter and tighter. Exchanging comfort without words. He was stroking her hair and it felt good—soothing. She seemed to feel strength flowing from his body to hers.

And something else. A warmth that surprised her. Zach was usually so cool. Now he was holding her and caressing her almost as if she were some toddler that needed pacifying.

Or—as if he weren't her cousin, but her boyfriend.

She pushed the thought away. Zach was just being kind. He wanted to help—and he was helping. She felt better, simply absorbing his sympathy, his affection. His—tenderness.

She leaned against him, letting him support her weight. Feeling secure. Cared for. Safe.

When he kissed the back of her neck, it was so tenderly it didn't disturb the safe feeling. Zach was nice. She loved him; she was happy to know he loved her.

When he kissed her again, an unexpected tremor ran through her.

Now—she wasn't supposed to feel like *that*. Not with Zach. He shouldn't—he really shouldn't. . . .

But she didn't want to pull away from him or spoil the moment.

His lips were warm on the back of her neck. A shock of sweetness passed through Jenny, this time too strong to be ignored. That felt—she *knew* she mustn't feel that way. Her hands went up to his arms, to push at him.

"Zach," she whispered. "I think we're both—a little upset. We're not ourselves."

"I know," Zach said, as if it hurt him. "I'm sorry—I . . ." He straightened, loosening his grip a little, but then he kissed her hair. She felt his lips moving, felt his warm breath there.

"Zachary," she said. "It's *wrong.* We're cousins." The problem was that although her words were strong, her voice wasn't. She could barely breathe. And she didn't move away.

"Half cousins," he said. It was true, although Jenny seldom thought of it—her mother and his were only half sisters. "And besides, I can't help it. I can't help it." His kisses were coming faster.

His urgency caught Jenny in a rush of elemental feeling. She kept thinking, *but there's something else*—without remembering what the something was. Then she whispered, "But, Tom . . ."—and shock swept over her.

She hadn't thought about Tom since—since—

She couldn't remember when.

Zach was saying that he couldn't help Tom, either.

"He doesn't deserve you." The words came on a warm wave of breath in her ear. "He doesn't love you enough. I was always afraid to say it, but you know it's true."

Despite his slimness Zach's muscles were hard against her. Jenny tried to protest, but the words caught in her throat.

"And now I know you don't love him enough, either. You weren't meant to be with him." Zach's voice was soft and reasonable, his words running together in a velvet sound.

Then he was looking down at her. A clear light seemed to shine through his intense face. His winter-gray eyes looked almost pale blue.

"You can't fight something like this, Jenny," he whispered. "You know you can't."

Jenny shut her eyes and turned her face up.

He kissed her and her senses reeled.

They seemed to melt together. Jenny felt herself sinking beneath his embrace. So soft . . . kissing had never been so soft before. She couldn't think anymore. She was flying. She was deep underwater.

Pure sensation overwhelmed her. She was kissing him back as she had never kissed Tom. His hair was loose under her fingers; it must have come out of the ponytail. She wanted to feel all of it. It was so much softer than she'd realized. She'd always thought of Zach as having rather coarse hair, but this was *so* soft . . . like silk or cat's fur under her fingertips. . . .

She heard the wild, whimpering sound she made, and she

knew, she *knew,* even as she was pulling back. Even as she was jerking away, she knew.

Julian's eyes were like liquid sapphires under sooty lashes. Heavy-lidded and dark with passion. He was wearing a plaid flannel shirt like Zach's shirt, stone-washed denims like Zach's denims, and running shoes like Zach's shoes. But he had a languid, careless grace Zach would never have. His hair looked bright as sand in moonlight.

Jenny was scrubbing her mouth with the back of her hand. A purely reflexive and senseless gesture. She was too shocked to be angry.

Did I know? Did I know underneath before he kissed me or while he was kissing me but before I pulled away did I know could I possibly have known . . . ?

She still couldn't make out what reality was.

"How could you know . . . ?" she whispered. "You acted like Zach—you knew things only he would know—"

"I've watched him," Julian said. "I've watched you. I'm the Shadow Man, Jenny—and I love you." His voice was soft, mesmerizing, and something inside Jenny began to melt at the very sound.

Then she thought of Summer.

Anger, hot and bright, surged through her and gave her strength. She looked into Julian's liquid-blue eyes. Any softness she'd ever had toward him had disappeared. She *hated* him now. Without a word she turned and walked out of the darkroom.

He followed her, flicking the garage lights on. He knew, of course, what she was thinking about.

"She agreed," he said. "Just like all the rest of you, she agreed to play the Game."

"She didn't know it was real!"

He quoted from the instructions. "'I acknowledge that the Game is real. . . .'"

"You can talk all you want, Julian—but you killed her."

"*I* didn't do anything to her. Her own fear did that. She couldn't face her nightmare."

Jenny knew there was no point in arguing with him, but she couldn't help it. In a low, savage voice she said, "It wasn't fair."

He shook his head, looking almost amused. "Life isn't fair, Jenny. Haven't you learned that yet?"

Jenny was raging on. "What gives you the *right* to play with us this way? How can you *justify* it?"

"I don't need the right. Listen to me, Jenny. The worlds—all nine of them—are cruel. They don't care anything about you, or about *right*. There is no ultimate goodness. It's the law of the jungle. You don't need right—if you have strength."

"I don't believe you," Jenny said.

"That the world is cruel?" There was a newspaper on the bench; he picked it up. "Take a look at this and tell me that evil loses and good wins. Tell me that it's not the law of the jungle in your world."

Jenny didn't even want to look at the headlines. She'd seen too many in her life.

"Reality," Julian said, flashing a smile, "has teeth and claws. And since that's true, wouldn't you rather be one of the hunters than one of the hunted?"

Jenny shook her head. She had to admit the truth of what he was saying—about the world, at least. But she felt sick to her stomach.

"I'm offering you a choice," Julian said. His face had hardened. "I told you before that if I couldn't persuade you I would force you—somehow. If you won't agree I'll have to show you what I mean. I'm tired of playing, Jenny. I want this settled—one way or another."

"It is settled," Jenny said. "I'll never come to you. I *hate* you."

Anger flared like a twisting blue flame in Julian's eyes. "Don't you understand," he said, "that what happened to Summer can happen to you?"

Jenny felt a wave of coldness. "Yes," she said slowly. "I do."

And she did, at last. She probably wouldn't have believed it before. Wouldn't have believed Julian was capable of it, or that *she,* Jenny, could be vulnerable to it. Dying was for old people, not kids her age. Bad things—*really* bad things—didn't happen to good people.

But they did.

Now she knew that emotionally. In her heart. Sometimes

bad things, the *worst,* happened to people who didn't deserve it at all. Even Summer. Even her.

Jenny felt as if she had learned some secret, been initiated into some worldwide club or community. The community of sorrow.

She was now one of the people who knew. Strangely, it gave her a sense of comfort to know that there were so many others, so many who'd had friends die, or lost parents, or had other terrible things happen that they never asked for.

There are a lot of us, she thought. Without realizing it, she'd begun to cry. We're everywhere. And we don't all turn hunter and take it out on other people. All of us don't.

Aba hadn't. Jenny suddenly remembered that Dee's grandmother had lost her husband in a racial incident. And she remembered something Aba had taped to her bathroom mirror, incongruous among all the glass and marble and gold fixtures. It was a handmade sign that said:

> Do no harm.
> Help when you can.
> Return good for evil.

Jenny had never asked Aba about the sign. It didn't seem to need explaining.

Now she felt the community of sorrow strengthening her from all over. As if they were sympathizing, silently. Bad things—

the worst—might happen to Jenny, right now. Jenny understood that.

She said, "You're right. Maybe things are that bad. But that doesn't mean I have to give in. I won't join you willingly, so you might as well try force."

"I will," he said.

It started so simply. Jenny heard a whining buzz and a bee landed on her sleeve.

It was just an ordinary bee, dusty-gold. It clung with its little feet to her tissue-linen blouse. But then she heard another buzz, and a second bee landed on her other sleeve.

Another buzz, and another.

Jenny hated bees. She was always the one at picnics shrieking, "Is there one in my hair?" She wanted to shoo these bees away, but she was afraid to provoke them.

She looked at Julian. At his wild, exotic sapphire eyes and his beautifully sculpted face. At that moment, wearing Zach's lackluster clothing, his beauty was so unearthly it was frightening.

Another buzz and a bee *was* in her hair, its wings a blur of motion as it tangled and clung. She could see it in her peripheral vision.

Julian smiled.

Jenny heard a deeper sound, a *thrumming,* and she looked automatically for the source. A swarm of bees was clustered on one of the rafters of the garage, hanging down like some giant, pendulous fruit.

Jenny took a step backward and heard a warning *buzzzzz* from her hair. The ball of bees was moving, breaking up. Becoming a dark cloud.

Heading toward her.

Jenny looked once more at Julian, and then bees began to fall on her like hail. They clung to her arms, her shoulders, her breasts. She had to hold her arms away from her body in order to keep from crushing the ones on her sides. She knew that if she did that they would sting.

Then it simply became a nightmare, unreal.

They were heavy, covering her like a blanket. Too heavy. Jenny staggered. She shut her eyes because they were crawling out of her hair onto her face. She was inundated with bees, layer upon layer of them. They were clinging to each other now, because there was almost no part of her body clear of them. Her fingertips, some parts of her face. She felt their feet on her cheeks and wanted to scream, but she couldn't, she couldn't scream because if she did—if she did—

They'd get into her mouth. And then she'd lose her sanity. But she couldn't breathe well enough through her nose. Her chest was heaving and their weight was crushing her. She was going to have to open her mouth.

She was crying silently, trying not to move, to disturb them more than she could help. Julian's voice came to her.

"Just say the word, Jenny."

She could only shake her head slightly. The barest minimum

of motion. But what she could manage, she did. She was still sobbing without a sound, terrified to move, but she would not—she *would not*—give in.

You can do whatever you like to me, she thought. In the dark beneath her bee-covered eyes she tried to hold on to consciousness, but it was like a thin thread slipping through her fingers. She grasped at it, felt it being snatched away from her.

She was fainting. Falling. But she wouldn't give in.

When I hit the ground and crush them, they'll go mad. They'll kill me, she thought.

But she never said the word to stop it.

She felt the darkness come as she began to fall.

CHAPTER 12

Floating in gray dimness, she heard a clock strike three. Wake up, she thought, but she didn't want to. She floated for a while again.

No, *wake up,* she thought. That's the alarm. You have to go to school . . . or something. You have to go see Zach.

Zach.

She was awake.

She was lying on the cold floor of her cousin's garage, chilled and stiff but bee-less. She looked at her hands and bare ankles. Not a mark. Julian hadn't let it happen.

But now she was stuck in a garage without a door. The light trap had only a curtain. All the other doors—the large one for cars and the regular one to the house—were simply missing, their spaces filled in with blank walls.

She had no idea what she was supposed to do next, and it was after three in the morning and she was tired.

Jenny looked at the corner of the studio where Zach took pictures. Zach's camera stood on a tripod. The tungsten flood-lamp was turned on. The backdrop was a sheet of seamless paper from a roll maybe six feet wide. Zach had done a lot of photos by painting paper like that black and throwing hand-fuls of white flour at it. The result had looked a little like the Milky Way—white splashes on infinite space. Very strange and futuristic; Zach loved that kind of stuff.

This backdrop, though, had a door painted on it, too.

A knob protruded from the paper.

The way out, Jenny thought as she went over to it, but something inside her wasn't so sure. For some reason this black-and-white door made her chilled flesh creep.

What choice have you got? her mind asked simply.

She turned the knob. The door swung out. She stepped inside.

It was like being suspended among the stars. The door closed behind her, but Jenny scarcely noticed. The sky seemed very low, more like a ceiling. It was black with glowing white splotches. The ground was a velvety black dropcloth that went on forever in all directions.

It was awful, this sense of infinity all around, pulling at her. It reminded her of a dream she'd once had, where the ground stretched on endlessly, but the sky was close and solid over-head. Did Zach have the same kind of dreams? Was this Zach's real nightmare?

The only landmarks in the limitless, featureless darkness were lamps—tungsten floodlamps like the ones Zach used. They formed little islands of brightness here and there, some white, some colored, fading out into the distance.

Jenny pivoted, trying to get her bearings—and drew in her breath sharply. The door was still behind her. It hadn't disap-peared. She could walk right out again.

But if this was Zach's nightmare, he must be in here some-where. She couldn't leave without looking for him.

After a moment's hesitation she headed for the nearest floodlamp, a neon pink one. It took courage to step away from the security of the door, and once she did she kept her eyes fixed on the island of light ahead. The black velvet ground was perfectly smooth, without the slightest wrinkle. She could practically skate over it in her flats.

When she reached the floodlamp, she saw it had a pink filter just like the ones Zach used. He got them from the drama department when colored spotlights burned out. And the scene it illuminated was exactly like a print Zach had made—a card-board silhouette of a neon-pink coyote in the grass. The print had been weird and high tech, like all Zach's photos, but Jenny had always liked it. Just now the coyote-shape standing alone with pink light blazing on it was unnerving.

Waiting for the photographer, Jenny thought. It gave the disquieting impression that it had been waiting there forever.

She headed toward the next floodlamp, a white one maybe forty feet away. It was hard to judge distance here.

This one was shining on a wall, a single wall standing alone, its windows broken out. Silver dots and swathes decorated the wall. Zach had gone into deserted houses in Zuma Beach and painted and photographed them. Vandalism, the police said, but Zach insisted it was art.

Jenny looked on both sides of the freestanding wall. It was unnerving, too. Everything was so quiet here. . . .

Just as she thought it, she heard a faint clanking noise.

The light from the pink floodlamp dimmed for a moment—as if something had passed in front of it. Standing rigid, Jenny strained her eyes in the darkness. She couldn't see anything moving. She couldn't hear anything, either.

Just your imagination, she told herself—but it was hard to make it sound convincing.

Glancing back frequently, she walked to the next lamp.

This one had a neon orange filter. A few years ago Zach had photographed baking soda thrown in the air under colored lights. The problem was that here the baking soda *stayed* in the air, a glowing orange cloud suspended—by nothing. Jenny could see individual motes in it twinkle and drift slightly.

God, get me out of here.

She backed away from it and set out for the next island.

When she got closer her heart skipped and she began to run. There were two blue floodlamps close together. Zach was under one.

Jenny opened her mouth to shout to him, but stopped at the last minute. What if it *wasn't* Zach? She'd been fooled once.

She approached cautiously and looked down at the figure in silence.

Same flannel shirt over same T-shirt. Same denims. Same hair in same ponytail.

He was holding a fist-size rock over a gray canvas painted with silver streaks. He put the rock down, looked at it, picked it back up. He put it down again in almost exactly the same place.

"I'm going to call it 'Rock on Water,'" he said. He looked up. "Because rocks don't really float."

"Zach," said Jenny. She knelt down and put a hand on his shoulder. His gray eyes were abstracted and a little glazed, just like the other's had been. But something told Jenny this was really her cousin.

A stealthy noise in the endless dark made her look up fast. The white spotlight winked out, went back on.

"Zach, we've got to go," she said and tightened her grip. "I'll explain later—but there's something out there, and we have to get back to the door."

Zach just gave her one of his absent smiles, the kind that didn't reach his eyes. "I know it's out there," he said. "It doesn't matter. It's all part of my hallucination."

"Your *what*? You mean your nightmare?"

"Whatever." He picked up the rock again, shifted it slightly, considered it. "I've known for a long time that this was going to happen."

Jenny was genuinely astonished. "You knew we were going to get kidnapped by the Shadow Man?"

"I knew I was going to go crazy." Then, adjusting the rock fractionally, he said, "Actually 'kidnapped by the Shadow Man' is a really interesting way of putting it. Really imaginative. I mean, what else is going insane?"

Jenny could feel her mouth hanging open. Then she shut it with a snap and took her cousin by both shoulders.

"Zachary, you are not insane," she said. "Is *that* what your problem is—why you were acting so strange before? Because you thought you'd gone *crazy*?"

"Brain kidnapped by the Shadow Man," he told her. "It was bound to happen sooner or later. It runs in the family."

"Oh, for God's sake, Zach!" She had no idea what he was talking about.

The orange floodlamp, the next one out, seemed to flicker.

"Don't worry," Zach told Jenny. "You're just part of my hallucination. It won't really hurt."

"*What won't really hurt?*"

Zach was gazing at the rock on his canvas. "It's about dimensions. See? The canvas is two dimensional and the—"

An arrow shattered one of the blue floodlamps in a shower of sparks and glass.

No, a bolt, Jenny thought, stunned. A bolt from a crossbow. She recognized it because Zach's father had made it to the National Crossbow Championship three years running. Bolts were even more lethal than arrows—and this one was metal and looked almost futuristic.

Zach was brushing bits of glass off his canvas.

"Zach, *get up!*" Jenny was frantic.

Another bolt shattered the second blue floodlight. Jenny jumped away from the sparks. Zach hunched protectively over his rock.

"Zach, listen to me! This is not a hallucination, it's *real,* and you can die for real here, too! You can bring your rock if you want, but we've got to leave this minute—*this minute!*" Her voice rose hysterically at the end.

It got through to him. She could barely see him by the glow of the white-splattered sky, but he got up—still holding the rock—and went where she was pulling him.

Orange floodlight, Jenny was thinking. Orange, and then white, and then pink. The door should be beyond that.

The orange lamp shattered as they got to it.

"Zach, who's after us? No, don't stop, come on!" Panting, Jenny tugged at his elbow. He'd turned around to look thoughtfully behind them. He didn't seem frightened.

"Me," he said.

187

They reached the freestanding wall by the white flood-lamp. Jenny felt somewhat safer behind it. She looked at her cousin. *"You?"*

"It's me. It's my hallucination and I'm chasing myself. Hunting myself."

"Oh, Zach," she said helplessly. Then: "Zach, it's not a hallucination. The same thing is happening to all of us—we're all here. Dee and Mike and Tom and Audrey and me. And Summer was here, but her nightmare *killed* her because she couldn't cope. So you have to cope, because if you don't . . ." Jenny's eyes were wet.

Zach blinked. "We're all here? It's real?"

"It's real. It really happened, the Game and the Shadow Man and everything. It's not in your head. It almost drove me crazy, too, but you can't let it."

Zach blinked again, then looked through the empty window of the wall, out into the darkness. "If it's real . . ." he began slowly, and continued in a voice with more strength, "If it's real, then who's that?"

Jenny inched over to take a cautious peek. A—person—was standing at the very edge of the light that went through the window. His crossbow *was* futuristic-looking—and so was he. Cyberpunk, Jenny thought. He was wearing black body armor that hugged his lean body sleekly, and he had one normal hand and one that was shining steel and cables. There was some kind of high-tech gun strapped to his thigh.

He wore a helmet with a mirrored face mask that completely obscured his features.

Jenny leaned back against the wall.

"Oh, terrific," she whispered.

"I figured he was my dark side. The part of me that wants to destroy me," Zach said reasonably.

A bolt came through the window—Jenny felt the wind of it—and shattered the white floodlamp.

"Come on!"

This time Zach ran without prompting.

The Cyber-Hunter got to the pink floodlight before them.

He couldn't have, but he did anyway. He stood, backlit by the neon pink glow, a dark silhouette as they approached.

"This way! We have to get to the door!"

Jenny veered sharply, circling to get to the other side of the pink lamp. Zach followed her. But when she got to the place where the door should have been, it wasn't.

"It's *gone*!" Jenny turned to look back. The Cyber-Hunter was facing them now, facing the blazing pink glow.

And what on earth are we supposed to do with him? Jenny thought. Kill him? Bash him with the rock? I don't think so.

One thing she'd learned—the nightmares were fair. There was always a chance, a way to get out, even when there didn't seem to be. She supposed Julian considered that only sporting.

So what could they do with the Cyber-Hunter? How could Zach face his fear?

189

"Zach," she said hesitantly, "you haven't seen his face, right? You don't know if he *looks* like you."

"No, I just figured. He's like the high-tech stuff in my photos—come to get me."

And like some cyberpunk stuff I've seen, Jenny thought grimly. She said, "If you *did* look at him . . . If you pulled off his helmet, say—"

She could feel Zach recoil in the dark.

Jenny shut her eyes, feeling suddenly tired. "Then that's what you have to do, I think. It's your nightmare, and you have to face him. I'll go with you."

It was a risk. Whether the Hunter was Julian or just one of Julian's dream-creatures, like the dark elves or the small Visitors, he might very well look like Zach under the helmet.

"Zach, I think you have to—or we won't ever find the way out of here. I think, even if he looks like you, you have to know he's *not* you."

"But—if he is me . . . if you're not really here and this is all my hallucination . . ."

"Then I'll probably disappear or something!" Jenny said. "And then at least you'll *know* you're crazy. All I know is that Summer wouldn't face her nightmare and she *died*."

There was a silence. Zach turned toward her, but it was too dark to be sure of his expression. "Come on," he said and started for the light.

Jenny's heart rate kept accelerating as they got closer to it.

The Cyber-Hunter could easily shoot them at any minute.

He didn't. He stood as still as a figure in the Movieland Wax Museum. He was exactly Zach's height.

Zach stopped when they were a few feet in front of him.

Jenny could hear blood roaring in her ears.

The Cyber-Hunter shifted the crossbow a little. Pink jewels of light slid up and down it, and over his black armor. Zach's face was reflected in the mirrored faceplate.

"Go on, Zach," Jenny whispered. "Take off the helmet. Tell him he's not you, whatever he looks like."

She wasn't nearly as confident as she sounded. Was it Zach's face under the helmet? Julian's? Maybe it was some hideous android—some kind of killer robot. Maybe Zach would get shot before he could find out. Maybe . . .

The Cyber-Hunter stood waiting.

With a sudden gesture Zach reached out and grabbed the front of the helmet, pulling the face mask away.

There was nothing underneath.

No face, no head. Jenny, prepared for anything else, screamed involuntarily. The Cyber-Hunter's black body armor fell down empty, the crossbow clattering on top of it.

A door appeared beside the pink floodlight.

Zach was staring down at the empty shell of armor. He nudged the dismembered robotic hand with his foot.

Jenny gave a little gasp of relief. It had been so easy—but then she looked at her cousin. The real test was in his head.

"I'm still here, Zach," she said. "Right? Right?"

He turned to look at her, pink light haloing his hair.

Then, slowly, he smiled. "Right," he said.

The awful dazed look had disappeared. He looked like Zach again. She could *see* the sanity return to his eyes. Relief flooded Jenny in painful waves.

Zach dropped the mirrored face mask on the pile of black armor.

"The rock I'll keep. I still want to do that photo."

They stepped through the door to the mirrored hallway.

Zach's slip of paper was on the ground. Jenny picked it up and frowned over it. She could vaguely make out what looked like a profile—a profile with a beaky nose—but behind that was just a futuristic mishmash of colors, streaks and dabs.

"The things in my head," Zach said. He took it from her and tore it up. Jenny watched the colored pieces float down like confetti.

"Zach—what made you think insanity runs in the family?"

Zach just shrugged. The others had explained their nightmares, but it didn't surprise Jenny that Zach wouldn't. Zach protected his privacy.

An unseen clock struck four.

"I hate this place," Zach said, looking at his own gray-eyed reflection. "It reminds me of the fun house at that amusement park we used to go to when we were kids."

"Then *you're* the one who put it here," Jenny said. She'd forgotten the fun house herself—but then she'd forgotten a lot about her childhood, especially the years before she came to California. She didn't want to remember.

She felt a little twist of premonition in her stomach.

She also felt the heat in her cheeks. Now that they were out of danger, now that Zach looked like himself again, she found that her attitude toward him had changed. It was Julian's fault. Jenny knew perfectly well that her cousin had never thought of her romantically—but she couldn't forget what had happened in the darkroom. Every time she looked at Zach, she remembered seeing those gray eyes black with passion.

I'll forget eventually, she told herself. It'll wear off. Just as long as he never finds out.

Aloud she said, "We've got to find the others. Dee and Audrey and Mike are all wandering around here somewhere. I guess"—she hesitated—"I guess we should separate. But I'm afraid we might not be able to find our way back to each other. I know it seems as if the hall only goes two ways, but you can't trust anything here."

"Wait a minute." Zach pulled two crayons out of the pocket of his flannel shirt. "I took them because I thought the colors might work in a photo. Take your pick, cadet blue or Indian red. We can mark a trail."

Jenny chose cadet blue and made a pale, waxy streak on the nearest mirror. "Brilliant," she said. "I'll go this way, you go that way. Whoever finds them can bring them back here."

"Where the two crayons meet," Zach said and began a line of his own. Still drawing, he walked away. The first zigzag of the hall took him out of sight.

No thank-you, no goodbye. Well, *that* should help her forget the darkroom scene. Zach was himself again, all right.

She went her own way, leaving a crayon trail behind her.

The mirrored hallway seemed infinite—and completely deserted. It went on and on with no variations.

Until, to her astonishment, she came to the end.

It was a blank wall, gray as concrete. No mirror, no blue light, no red button.

It scared her.

On the ground in front of it was a white slip of paper.

Jenny approached the paper slowly. It scared her, too. Dee, Audrey, Mike, Summer, and Zach had had their nightmares. And Julian had said Tom was at the top of the house.

Nobody's nightmare left on this floor but hers.

She picked the paper up, turned it over. She recognized the formless doodle around the edges. The middle of the paper was exactly as she'd left it—blank.

Jenny looked up at the blank wall.

"Need any help?" Julian asked from behind her.

The paper crumpled in Jenny's clenched fist as she turned.

He was leaning against a mirror, wearing the sleek black

body armor. No helmet, though. Instead, there was a splash of purple in the shock of white hair falling over his forehead and a triangular blue design on his cheekbone. It looked almost like silk-screening. More cyberpunk, Jenny thought. High-tech body art. Zach would love it—or maybe not.

Jenny looked straight into the strange cat-tilted blue eyes. Things had changed since Julian had set the bees on her. She had a new confidence at her core. Whatever he did to her, even if he killed her, he couldn't break her.

"So it was you shooting at us," she said.

"Personally, I think it was Zach's father. I think he has a little complex there. Rugged, old-fashioned dad; artistic, new-fangled son, you know. On the other hand, I *am* a hunter." He pushed the lock of purple hair out of his eyes, smiling.

"Why don't you just go away?" Jenny said. "I'm trying to figure something out."

"I'm glad to help. I know a lot about you. I've watched you for so many years now. Hour after hour, day after day."

Jenny froze. He'd said similar things before, and she hadn't really listened. Or she hadn't taken it literally. But now, looking at him, she knew he meant it.

It was the most terrible thing she'd ever heard.

He'd *watched* her for hours on end? How many times in her life, when she'd thought she was alone, had he been there?

It was an appalling intimacy, and one Jenny didn't want.

"I'm in love with you," he said simply. "I think everything you do is marvelous."

"You—"

"There's no need to be embarrassed. I don't think the same way you do. Whether your hair's brushed—whether your makeup is on—I don't care. Besides"—he smiled at her—"didn't you know that I was there?"

"Of course not." But she had, Jenny realized. Somewhere deep inside herself she'd known she was being watched. She'd just thought everybody had that feeling.

Those times in the night when she woke up, certain that a tall shape was standing over her in the darkness. Usually when it happened she couldn't move, could hardly breathe. Sometimes she would actually *see* the shape, the outline black against lighter blackness, and she stared until her eyes ached.

If she kicked at it or turned on the light, it would disappear. But she'd sit there breathing hard anyway, choking on her own fear.

Her room always looked strange in that unnatural middle-of-the-night brightness. Subtly different than it did in the daytime. It was always a long time before she would be able to turn the light off again.

And underneath, in her heart of hearts, she would feel it had been real. Not just a dream. Her eyes had been open when she'd seen the thing above her, and it didn't matter if that was stupid and nobody could see in such darkness. She'd seen it anyway. It had been there.

Jenny had thought everybody went through things like that.

"I hate you," she whispered.

"I'd have thought you'd want my help right now." He nodded at the blank wall. "*That's* your nightmare, Jenny—but how are you going to get into it? And if you can't get into it, how are you going to get through it?"

He wants you panicked, Jenny told herself. He wants to scare you, to make you think you need his help.

But she didn't need it. She *refused* to need it.

She smiled suddenly. She could feel it was lopsided. She held up the cadet blue crayon.

"I'll get in with this," she said and smoothed out her blank slip of paper.

His eyelids drooped in amusement, and his voice was a caress. "But how will you *remember*? You don't know what to draw. You've spent all these years trying to forget. . . ."

"I know enough," Jenny said. She wondered just how much Julian knew about her own private nightmare, the one she'd spent so long running away from. She had the chilling feeling that she was about to find out.

"I know what it starts with," she said. "It starts with my grandfather's basement, when I was five years old."

She put the paper flat against a mirror and began to draw.

CHAPTER 13

Cadet blue, which had just looked pale on the mirror, turned out to be gray on paper.

Jenny was no artist, but she could draw simple things. Like a square—that was her grandfather's basement. Steps, going out of the top of the picture up to the house. A desk against one wall. A couch. Three or four large bookcases.

That was all she could remember. She hoped it was enough.

Glancing over her shoulder, she saw that Julian was gone again. Good.

She put the slip of paper on the floor in front of the blank wall.

The flash of light was exactly like a flashgun going off in

her eyes, leaving her with dancing afterimages. Score one for Zach, she thought. When she could see again, she found herself looking in a mirror.

It had worked.

She could feel her pulse in her wrists and throat as well as her chest. God, don't let me run away, she thought.

After so many years of fighting *not* to remember this, she was going to throw herself right into it. It was going to be bad. How bad, she'd have to find out when it happened.

She pressed the red button. The blue light went on. The mirrored door slid open.

She didn't give herself a chance to look at anything before she stepped inside.

Golden sunlight slanted in from small windows set high on the walls. To Jenny's utter surprise she felt a thrill of excitement and recognition.

I remember those windows! I remember . . .

The door slid shut behind her, but she was already stepping out to the center of the room, looking around in wonder. Taking in the colors, the profusion of objects.

It's smaller than I thought it would be—and even more crowded. But it's my grandfather's basement.

Her grandfather, though, wasn't there.

That's right. He wasn't here that day. I remember. I let myself in the house and went looking for him, but I couldn't find him anywhere upstairs.

So . . . I looked down here—I think. I must have. I don't remember doing it, but I must have.

Jenny turned toward the stairs, which ended in a blank wall at the top. No door, of course, because this was a nightmare. The wall was as blank as her mind—her sense of delighted recognition had stopped cold. She had no idea what came next.

But as she stared, she seemed to see the ghost of a child looking down from the top step. A little girl wearing shorts, with wind-ruffled hair and a scab on her knee.

Herself. At age five.

It was almost like watching a movie. She could see the little girl's thongs flap as she ran down the stairs. She could see the child's lips open as she called for her grandfather, see the child standing in surprise at the bottom when he turned out not to be down here.

As long as Jenny watched without trying to guide the images, the ghostly movie went on.

The little girl was looking around, green eyes opening wide as she realized that she was *alone* down here, a thing which had never happened before.

That's right. The door to the basement had always been locked when Jenny's grandfather wasn't down there—but not that day. Jenny remembered the feeling of delicious wickedness at being where she wasn't allowed to be. But she couldn't remember what happened next.

Don't try to remember. You're trying too hard. Relax and *see* what happens.

As soon as she did, she seemed to see the little girl again. The ghostly image was standing uncertainly, swaying on her toes, considering whether to stay or go.

It was stay. The child looked around with elaborate casualness, then, sucking on her lower lip and affecting an air of nonchalance, she wandered over to the first bookcase.

All right, Jenny thought. So let's see what's in the bookcase. She followed the child's image. The little girl was idly running a grimy finger along a row of books—which, of course, she couldn't read. Not even the titles. But sixteen-year-old Jenny could.

Some of them looked fairly normal, like Goethe's *Faust* and *UFO's: A New Look.* But others were completely unfamiliar, like *The Qabalah* and *De Occulta Philosophia* and *The Galdrabók.*

The little girl was moving on to the second bookcase, which held all sorts of objects. One whole shelf was crowded with small wooden boxes with glass tops, filled with what looked like spices. No—herbs, Jenny thought. Dried herbs.

The little girl was running fascinated fingers over some balls of colored glass attached to strings. Sixteen-year-old Jenny was more interested in the looped cross next to them—she was sure it was an ankh. Summer's dad had said the ankh was an Egyptian life symbol that kept away bad luck.

And that diamond-shaped thing made of yarn—that was a Mexican Eye of God. A string design that was supposed to protect you from evil. Jenny's mother had one in the kitchen, for decoration.

But what about the bracelet of cobalt and turquoise beads, alternating with little silver charms? And the gold-plated religious pictures? And the wooden flute wrapped in fur?

. . . items of protection? Jenny thought. She wasn't sure what put the idea in her mind, but the longer she looked at the things in this bookcase, the more certain she felt.

But . . . it wasn't just this bookcase. Slowly Jenny turned to look around the basement again. All these things, all these beautiful, exotic things—could they *all* be for protection?

Who would need that much protection? And why?

The little girl was fingering a large silver bell in the bookcase, but Jenny's eyes were drawn to a group of charts on the wall. *The Theban Alphabet,* one was labeled, and underneath were strange symbols. *The Alphabet of the Magi. The Secret Etruscan Alphabet. The Celtic Tree Alphabet. Numerical Values of the Hebrew Alphabet.* There was also a rather frightening engraving of a skeleton holding a raven on one bony hand.

The ghost child was moving again, wandering over to the large writing desk. Going on tiptoe in her thongs, she leaned her elbows on the felt desk pad. Jenny found herself looking down through a transparent blond head at the papers there.

Lots of papers—which held no interest for the five-year-old Jenny except that she wasn't supposed to touch them. Intrinsic naughtiness was the fun.

Sixteen-year-old Jenny could read them. One was a chart like those on the wall. It was titled *The Elder Futhark* but Jenny recognized the slanty, angular symbols.

Runes.

Like the ones she'd seen on the drinking horns of the young men in the forest. Like the one on the inside cover of the white box. Each had its name written beside it in her grandfather's strong black handwriting, with notes.

Uruz, she read. For piercing the veil between the worlds. She recognized the inverted *U* shape, the two uneven horns pointing downward.

Raidho—it was shaped like an *R* drawn without any curved lines—for journeying in space or time.

Dagaz, which looked like an hourglass on its side. For awakening.

One of the runes was circled with a thick pen stroke.

Nauthiz, Jenny read. Shaped like a backward-leaning *X*, with one stroke longer than the other. For containment.

The last word was underlined heavily.

Jenny took another slow look around the room.

Oh, my God.

She couldn't keep the truth away any longer. She'd been holding it at arm's length, refusing to look at it, but now it burst on her with the force of absolute certainty. There was no way to deny it.

Oh, my God, he was a *sorcerer.*

Her mother's father had been a sorcerer.

Don't think about it . . . don't remember, the voice in her mind whispered. Nobody can *make* you remember. Stay safe behind your walls, or else . . .

It was going to be very bad from here on, she realized.

She had to remember—for Tom. But Tom's image eluded her. So much had happened since she'd seen him last night—could it only be last night? She'd changed so much since then. She tried to conjure up his rakish smile in her mind, his green-flecked eyes, but the picture she got was like a distant, faded photograph. Somebody she'd known long ago.

God, I can't get any *feeling* for him.

Her palms were tingling. Her stomach felt sick.

I still have to remember. For Dee. For Zach. For Audrey and Michael—and Summer. *Yes.* For Summer.

All the others had faced their nightmares. Even Summer had tried. Pictures skittered through Jenny's mind: Dee thrashing like an animal; Audrey huddled and moaning; Michael screaming; Summer's blue-white lips; Zach's glazed gray eyes. They'd all been terrified out of their wits. Was Jenny's nightmare any worse than theirs?

Yes, I think so, the little voice in her mind whispered, but Jenny wasn't listening anymore. From *Don't remember, don't remember,* the chant in her head had changed to *Remember, remember* . . .

Maybe this will help, she told herself rather calmly, and with a feeling of meeting her doom she picked up a leather-bound book on the desk.

It was a journal of sorts. Or at least a record of some kind of experiment. Her grandfather's heavy black writing degenerated into a scrawl in places, but certain sentences stood out clearly as she leafed through.

". . . out of all the methods from different cultures this one seems safest . . . the rune Nyd or Nauthiz provides an eternal constraint, preventing travel in any direction. . . . The rune must be carved, then stained with blood, and finally charged with power by pronouncing its name aloud. . . ."

Jenny flipped through more pages to a later entry.

". . . interesting treatise on the traditional methods of dealing with a *djinn,* or, as the Hausa call them, the *aljunnu.* Why anyone should think this could be accomplished with a bottle is beyond me. . . . I believe the space I've prepared to be just barely sufficient for containing the tremendous energies involved. . . ."

Good grief, he sounded just like a scientist. A mad scientist, Jenny thought. She flipped more pages.

". . . I have achieved the containment at last! I'm very satisfied . . . foolproof methods . . . not the slightest danger . . . the tremendous forces I've harnessed . . . all in complete safety. . . ."

Toward the end there was something stuck in between the pages like a bookmark. It was a torn sheet of yellowing, brittle paper. It looked very old. The writing on it was quite different from her grandfather's—thin and shaky—and part of it was obscured by rusty-brown stains.

It was a poem. There was no title, but the author's name, Johannes Eckhart, and the date, 1943, were scrawled at the top.

> I, slipping on the slime-edged stones,
> To that dark place by rusty foxfire lit,
> Where they lie watching, fingering old bones,
> Go with my question. Deep into the pit
> Of the Black Forest, where the Erlking rules
> And truth is told but always at a cost,
> I take my puzzle. Like the other fools
> Who've slipped on these same stones and played and lost
> I come because I must. I have no choice.
> The Game is timeless and . . .

The rest of it was covered with the dark stains, except for the last two lines:

> I leave them waiting there below.
> I hear them laughing as I go.

Jenny leaned back and let out her breath.

Obviously this poem had impressed her grandfather enough for him to keep it for forty years. She knew her grandfather had fought in World War II—he'd been a prisoner in a German POW camp. Maybe he'd met this Johannes Eckhart then. And maybe this Johannes Eckhart had started him thinking. . . .

She had all the pieces of the puzzle now. She just didn't want to put them together. All she could think about was taking the next step in the drama she was playing out here.

The final step, she thought.

The ghostly child in the thongs had vanished; the internal movie had stopped running. But Jenny didn't try to get it back. She could feel the irresistible tug of real memory at last, and she knew what she had to do.

She stepped back to look at the third bookcase.

It was a massive one built of solid mahogany, and it usually stood against the same wall as the desk. Today it had been moved. Pulled out at an angle. The dust pattern on the wall behind it showed clearly where it normally rested.

It had been moved to expose a door behind it.

Jenny hadn't noticed the door before because the case stuck out enough to block it. You had to actually walk beyond the bookcase to get a good look.

That's what Jenny felt compelled to do now.

It was a perfectly ordinary-looking door. Probably leading to a closet. The only strange thing about it was the huge backward-leaning *X* deeply carved into the wood.

Carved and colored a rusty brown like the stains on the poem.

The internal movie had started up again, even though

Jenny didn't need or want it. The ghostly little girl was standing in surprise in front of the door, swaying from one foot to the other. Obviously temptation was fighting with obedience—and winning. The wind-ruffled hair was shaken back, the tanned legs flashed, two small hands grasped the doorknob—and the ghost disappeared.

And then I opened it, Jenny thought. But no image of opening it, or of what had happened after, would come to her mind. She was going to have to find that out for herself.

All the way to the door her heart was thudding wild disapproval. Her body seemed to have more sense than she did. No-don't-no-don't, no-don't-no-don't, her racing pulse said.

Jenny took hold of the knob. The thudding became a screaming.

No, *don't*. Don't—don't—*don't*. . . .

She flung open the door.

Ice and shadows.

That was all she could see. The closet was wide and very deep, and the inside of it was a whirling, seething mixture of white and black. Frost coated the walls, icicles hung like teeth from the ceiling. A blast of freezing wind went straight through Jenny, chilling her as if she'd been plunged into Arctic waters. The tips of her fingers went numb, the skin shriveling.

It was so cold it stopped her breath. It stopped her from moving. The ice was so bright it blinded her.

She got just one glimpse of what was at the center of that whirlpool of light and dark.

Eyes.

Dark eyes, watching eyes, sardonic, cruel, amused eyes. Ancient eyes. Jenny recognized them. They were the eyes she sometimes saw just at the moment of falling asleep or of waking up. The eyes she saw at night in her room.

Eyes in the shadows. Evil, malicious, knowing eyes.

One pair was an indescribably beautiful blue.

She didn't have the air to scream; her lungs were rebelling against the freezing wind she was trying to draw into them. But she had to scream—she had to do something—because they were coming out. *The eyes were coming out.*

It was as if they were coming from very far away, rushing toward her, riding the storm. She had to move—she had to run. The glittery black eyes of the alien Visitors, the slanted eyes of the dark elves—Jenny had thought those were frightening, but they were nothing compared to this. They were feeble, petty imitations. No horror that human beings had invented to scare themselves came anywhere close. Vampires, aliens, werewolves, ghouls, they were all *nothing*. Stories made up to hide the real fear.

The terror that came in the darkness, the one that *everyone* knew about, and everyone forgot. Only sometimes, waking up between dreams, did the full realization hit. And even then it was seldom remembered, and if it was remembered it was dismissed the next morning. The knowledge couldn't survive in daylight. But at night sometimes people glimpsed the truth. That humans weren't alone.

They shared the world with *them*.

The Others.

The Watchers.

The Hunters.

The Shadow Men.

The ones who walked freely through the human world, and who had another world of their own. They'd been called different things in different ages, but their true nature always came through.

They granted favors—sometimes. They always asked for something in return, usually more than you could afford.

They liked games, riddles, any kind of play. But they were unreliable—whimsical. They balanced any good they did with capricious evil.

They preyed on humans. When people lost time, *they* were responsible. When people disappeared, *they* were laughing. People who got into *their* world usually didn't get back.

They had power. Trying to get a good look at them—or trap them—was always a bad idea. Even being too curious about them could kill you.

One more thing. They were heartbreakingly beautiful.

All this passed through Jenny's mind in a matter of seconds. She didn't need to reason it out. She *knew*. It was as if a crust had fallen away from her mind and she saw the truth as a complete, coherent whole. All she could think was, *So that's it. I remember now.*

The eyes were still rushing toward her. Her loose hair whipped around her face in the wind, her own breath coating it with ice. She couldn't move.

"Jenny!"

Her name called in a terrible voice. Before she could turn, she was caught around the waist and lifted—lifted as if she were five years old and weighed thirty-seven pounds.

"Grandpa," she gasped and threw her arms around his neck.

He was smaller than she remembered, too—and just now his tired, kind face was etched in absolute horror. Jenny tried to cling to him, but he slung her around, thrusting her behind the bookcase.

"Nauthiz! Nauthiz!" he shouted.

He was trying to shut the door, tracing over the rune on the front with stabs of his finger. His slashing motions as he traced the *X* became more and more violent, and his voice was the most dreadful thing Jenny had ever heard. *"Nauthiz!"*

The door wouldn't shut. The old man's shouts were becoming screams of despair.

A white light was coming from the closet. A white storm, with tendrils and lashings of mist. Dark strands were interwoven with the white. The tendrils were writhing around Jenny's grandfather.

Jenny tried to scream. She couldn't.

The wind blasted out, blowing her grandfather's sparse hair. All his clothes were rippling. Frost flowed out on the ceiling, down to the desk, to the ground-level windows. It spread like crystals growing along the walls.

Tears froze in Jenny's eyes. She seemed to be locked in the form of a stricken five-year-old. She couldn't make herself go to him.

The voices that spoke from the mist were as cold as the wind. Like bells made of ice.

"We won't be put back. . . ."

"You know the laws. . . ."

"We have a claim, now. . . ."

And her grandfather's voice, full of desperate fear. "Anything else. You can have anything else—"

"She broke the rune. . . ."

". . . set us free . . ."

". . . and we want her."

"Give her to us." This was all the voices together.

"I can't!" her grandfather said. It was almost a groan.

"Then we'll *take* her. . . ."

"We'll embrace her. . . ."

"No, let's keep her," said a voice full of subtle, elemental music. Like water running over rock. "I want her."

"We all want her. . . ."

". . . We're all *hungry*."

"No," said Jenny's grandfather.

A voice like an ice floe cracking said, "There's only one way to change the consequences. Make a new bargain."

Jenny's grandfather's jaw worked, and he backed away from the closet a few steps. "You mean . . ."

"A life for a life."

"Someone must take her place."

"Come now, that's only fair."

The voices were delicate, reasonable. Evil. Only the water-voice seemed to have an objection.

"I *want* her. . . ." it argued.

"Ah, youth," said a voice as slow as a glacier, and all of them laughed like Christmas bells.

"I'm ready," said Jenny's grandfather.

"No!" Jenny screamed.

She could move at last—but it was too late. She remembered everything now. She had been cowering behind the bookcase, her five-year-old mind probably better able to deal with the reality of the Shadow Men than an adult's. They were the monsters that scare every five-year-old. The Bogeymen. The Bad Things. And they were taking her grandfather.

She'd jumped up then and run, as she was running now. Toward the closet. Toward the white tendrils of mist that were coiling around her grandfather, toward the ice storm of eyes. She'd heard her grandfather screaming that day as the storm dragged him into the closet. She'd reached for him, catching his flailing hand. She'd been screaming, too, just as she was screaming now, and the freezing wind had been howling around her, full of angry, evil, *ravenous* voices.

For one instant, then as now, it had been a horrible tug-of-war. She, Jenny, clinging on to her grandfather's hand with all her strength. *They*, in the ice storm, pulling him away. Into the depths of a closet that had become endless, a tunnel reaching to some other world.

She could never hope to stop them, of course. She succeeded only in being dragged along the floor, her clothes torn, her shoes lost, her bare feet raking up ice.

They were both going in.

Then her grandfather slapped her hands away.

Hitting and scratching, he tore out of her grip. Jenny fell on the floor, the ice cold under her bare legs. She was directly in front of the closet, and she had a perfect view of the screaming, whirling pinwheel that had been a man, disappearing into a white cloud which got smaller and smaller as if speeding away and finally disappeared itself, becoming a closet wall.

Then the shrieking wind stopped and the room was empty and Jenny was sobbing alone in the silence.

CHAPTER 14

Jenny?" Dee's voice said hesitantly. "Jenny, are you okay?"

I've had such a strange dream, Jenny thought, but when she lifted her face from her hands, it was real. She was sitting on the floor of her grandfather's basement, in a puddle of icy-cold water. Dee, Audrey, Zach, and Michael were standing in another puddle, looking at her.

"I found these three in the hallway," Zach said.

"We fell down a shaft," Michael said. "This hole just opened up in front of us. It took us all the way back to the first floor."

"It was a chute," said Dee. "I fell down it, too, and then we had to walk back up here."

"We followed your crayon trail, and it ended at a door," Zach finished. "We pressed the button and . . ."

"It let us in," Audrey said crisply, when he stopped. "But it looks like something's already happened."

"My nightmare," Jenny said. She was having a very hard time bringing herself back to the present. The five-year-old in her mind seemed more real than the sixteen-year-old these people were talking to. Dee and Michael and Audrey looked like strangers.

Not Zach, because Zach had been there when she was five.

Zach, maybe, understood this. In any case he knelt on the floor beside her, ignoring the water soaking into his jeans.

"What happened?" he said, his gray eyes steady.

"I lost," Jenny said dully, feeling strangely removed from everything. "I screwed up. I couldn't save him. I lost."

"It's something about Grandpa Evenson, isn't it?"

"What do you know about it?"

Zach hesitated, then, looking her directly in the face, he said, "Only what my parents told me. They say he—went crazy that day. Tried to—well, hurt you."

Jenny was shocked out of her apathy. *"What?"*

"They found you here, in the basement, with your clothes all torn and your arms all scratched. Your legs and feet were bleeding. . . ."

"From the ice," Jenny whispered. "I got dragged through the ice. And he scratched my hands to make me let him go. They were taking him. He let them take him instead of me."

Then, suddenly, she was sobbing again. She felt a movement, then a slender, hard arm around her. Dee. A rustle and a cool hand on her wrist. Audrey, heedless of her fancy clothes. An awkward, warm grip from behind on her shoulder. Michael. They were all around her, all trying to help.

"You went through our nightmares with all of us," Audrey said softly. "It's not fair you had to face yours alone."

Jenny shook her head. "You don't understand. All of you had nightmares about things you were scared *might* happen. Mine *did* happen—because of me. It was real. It was my fault."

"Tell us," Dee said, her face stern and beautiful.

"He was a sorcerer," Jenny said. She looked at Zach. "You mean, all this time everybody thought he tried to hurt me?"

"What were they supposed to think?" Zach said. "You were here, practically in a coma. You screamed if anyone tried to touch you, but you wouldn't talk. And he was gone. They figured he ran away when he realized what he tried to do. And when they looked around at this place"—Zach looked around the basement himself and snorted—"well, they knew he was crazy. Paranoid. Because all this junk turned out to be—"

"Charms for protection," Jenny said.

"Right. I mean, what kind of nut collects thousands of those from all over the world? And he had piles of books on the occult, all kinds of garbage. . . ."

"He was a sorcerer," Jenny said again. "Not a black one.

217

Maybe not a white one, either, but not black. He wasn't trying to do evil. He was just—a little bit naive. He didn't allow for accidents happening . . . like a five-year-old coming down here on a day he didn't expect her, and opening a door she knew she shouldn't touch."

"That door?" Dee looked at the empty closet.

Jenny nodded.

"But what was in the closet? A monster?"

"Julian."

They all stared at her.

Jenny swallowed the bad taste in her mouth. "My grand-father wanted—well, the same thing those German boys in the forest wanted, I guess." She looked at Audrey. "Power. Or maybe he was just curious. He knew there were—things—out in the darkness, and he caught some. Maybe he used runes to summon them up, I don't know. But I know he used a rune to hold them. On that door."

"And just what," Michael said, his voice unusually grim, "would you call the things he caught?"

"Aliens," Jenny said, looking at Dee. "Dark elves," she said, looking at Audrey. "Demons," she said, turning around to face Michael. "The Shadow Men," she said to Zach.

Dee hissed softly in comprehension.

Once started, Jenny couldn't seem to stop. "Dakaki. The Erlking. The old gods. The fairy folk . . ."

"Okay," Michael said huskily. "Enough, already."

"They're *real*," Jenny said. "They've *always* been here—like genies, you know? The old name for a genie was *djinn*, and in his notes my grandfather called them *aljunnu*. Djinn—aljunnu—Julian—get it? It was a joke. They like to *play* with us. . . ."

Her voice was rising. She felt herself gripped from all sides, but she went on.

"He was keeping them trapped—but *I* let them out, and that changed everything. They said they had the right to take me. But he went instead. He did it for me." She stopped.

"If we're going to get through this," Dee said, "we've got to be strong. We've got to stand together. All right?"

"Right," Audrey said, the first to confirm it. Looking down, Jenny saw Audrey's perfectly polished nails entwined with Dee's slender dark fingers. Both holding on to each other, to Jenny.

"Right," Zach said with no hesitation, no distance in his winter-gray eyes. His long-fingered artist's hand came down over Dee's and Audrey's.

"Right," whispered Michael, and he gripped Zach's hand with his own square pudgy fingers, unembarrassed.

"But there's nothing to *do,*" Jenny said, almost crying again. "He won. I lost. I didn't make it through my nightmare. That door"—nodding at the closet one—"was always here. It's not the way out."

"What about that one?" Michael said, standing back and looking up the stairs.

Jenny had to move around the bookcase to see it. Instead of the blank wall she had seen earlier at the top of the staircase, there was a door.

Directly above them—in the room above—a clock struck five.

"You must have done something right," Dee said.

Jenny's skirt was clammy, clinging to her legs. Her hair, she knew, was in complete disarray. She was exhausted and still shaking inside, and it seemed like years since she had slept.

"I'll go first," she said and led them up the stairs, trying to look like Dee, proud as a princess. She found her slip of paper on the top step and stepped on it.

"If that's the turret—the top of the house—we've won," Audrey said. "Right?"

Somehow Jenny didn't think it was going to be that easy.

She twisted the knob and pushed, and the door swung back on oiled hinges. They all stepped into the room above. It was much larger than any turret could possibly be.

It was the More Games store.

Well, more or less, Jenny thought. There were the same shelves and racks and tables with the same uncanny games on them. There was the same small window—quite dark—and the same lamps with shades of purple and red and blue glass.

But there were differences, too. One was the grandfather clock standing near a corner, ticking loudly and steadily.

The other was Tom.

Jenny ran to him. He was huddled against the clock, chained to it somehow. Her mind registered fury at the humiliation of that, then went on to more important things.

"Tommy," she said, reaching with both hands for him.

He turned weakly, and Jenny was shocked. There were no bruises on his face, but he looked—ravaged. His skin was unhealthily pale, and there were black circles under his eyes. He gave her the ghost of his own rakish smile.

"Hey, Thorny," he said painfully.

Jenny put her face against his shoulder and cried.

The faded-photograph memory had disappeared. What Jenny remembered now was the day of their first kiss, in second grade, behind the hibiscus bushes at George Washington Elementary School. They'd both gotten detention, but it had been worth it.

That kiss, she thought. Everything innocent. Everything sweet. Tom hadn't been arrogant, then, hadn't taken anything for granted. Tom had loved her.

"Tommy," she said. "I missed you so much. What did he do to you?"

Tom shook his head. "Hardly anything . . . I don't understand. There were the rats"—his haunted eyes skittered around the floor—"but they're gone now."

Rats. So that was what Tom had seen in the parlor—the invisible things that had tried to climb up his legs. In second grade Tom had owned a turtle, and his older brother

221

Greg had owned a pet rat. One morning they woke up to find that the rat had eaten the turtle—eaten it right out of the shell.

I knew how upset that made him—how much he hated rats after that, Jenny thought. Why didn't I realize what they were in the parlor?

Because it hadn't seemed bad enough. Tom had been *so* afraid. But one thing Jenny had learned: Everybody's nightmare was scariest to them. You had to see it with them, get into their shoes, to understand just how scary.

"I'm sorry," she whispered. "But, oh, Tom, your wrists—" They were torn, bleeding. He was wearing shackles like the kind his brother Bruce used in police work. The rest of him was wrapped up like Marley's ghost.

"I kept trying to get away," he said. "Not because of the rats. Because I saw you. He would come and hold up a mirror, and I could see you and what was happening to you. I saw you go through everything. When Summer died . . ." He stopped to get control of himself, his face twisting.

Saw me? Jenny thought in horror. Pictures of what Tom might have seen when she and Julian were together flashed through her mind. Then she felt a backwash of relief. If Julian had been standing here holding a mirror, he must have been showing Tom the times when he—Julian—wasn't with Jenny. Still, she had to know.

"Did you ever see—him—in the mirror?"

"No. But he told me—he told me he was doing things to you. To all of you. He laughed about it."

Jenny gripped both his hands. "Don't you worry about him, Tom. He can't hurt us anymore. We're free, Tom—we've *won*. Now we just need to find the way out of here."

Tom looked at her, then nodded behind her. Jenny turned.

She'd missed it before, because Tom had so quickly captured her attention. There was a door, just like the door in the More Games store that led out onto Montevideo Avenue. But this door was partly open, showing darkness outside.

Standing before it, completely blocking the way, were a giant coiled snake and a large wolf.

"The Creeper and the Lurker. At last," Dee said.

"Just a slight problem," Michael said nervously.

They weren't real animals exactly—they looked more as if they'd been painted with luminous paint on the darkness. Like some special effect Zach might make for a photo. But the wolf breathed and the snake's fluorescent tongue flicked in and out. Jenny felt sure that they could move—and do harm.

She fingered Tom's chains. "He has to let us go. The rules were that if we got to the top of the house, we could go free."

"Not exactly," the liquid, elemental voice said from the back of the store.

He was dressed the way he had been in the More Games store, in that weird combination of cyberpunk and Byronic poet. The snake tattoo was back on his wrist.

223

He looked as laconic as he had in the store, and as beautiful. His hair was like moonstone, white with a shimmery blue glow inside. In this dim light his eyes were midnight blue.

He looked—charming, sinister, and slightly mad. A demon prince with the face of an angel.

Jenny was suddenly very frightened.

And much more alert. Seeing Julian cleared the cobwebs out of your brain instantly. She straightened her back, still kneeling.

The others were gathering themselves, too. What light there was caught Zach's light hair and the gold clasp of Audrey's Brunetti calfskin belt. Jenny could see by their faces that they knew Julian better now—not because they'd seen him in the Game but because they understood what he was.

Julian smiled his strange, sweet smile.

"You all wanted to know who I am. Well, I'll give you a final riddle," he said. "I'm a Visitor from the stars. I'm the Erlking. I'm Loki. I'm Puck. I'm the Hunter. I'm the Shadow Man. I'm your nightmares come true."

"We figured that out," Jenny said, quietly, steadily. "And we played your game and won. Now we want to go home."

"You didn't let me finish," Julian said, turning the smile on her. "Do you remember, when you first came in the game store, I showed you the ancient Tibetan game of goats and tigers?" He gestured, one of his easy, flowing motions, and Jenny saw the bronze board on a table. Tiny figures, also bronze, sat on it somewhat like chess pieces.

"Well, that's what you've really been playing," Julian said, and at the sound of his voice Jenny felt the walls closing in. He smiled at her particularly.

"You are all the innocent little goats . . . *and I'm the tiger.*"

Tom's hands were gripping Jenny's numbingly. Dee was in the forward stance, left leg forward, right leg back, ready for action. Zach looked bleak, and Audrey and Michael had moved closer together.

"You didn't really think," Julian said to Jenny, "that I would let you go."

Jenny felt dizzy. Smothering.

"You said . . . you were playing the Game fairly," she got out, with barely the breath to say it. "You promised me—"

"I'm not hidebound by tradition. And I *am* playing fairly— I said if you got to the turret before dawn, you'd find the door home standing open. It is open—it's just that I won't let you get to it."

Jenny looked at the animals guarding the door. What could even Dee do to fight them?

"By the way, *Tommy,* here, hasn't even faced his real nightmare yet. But there'll be plenty of time. We've got something like eternity ahead of us, you know," Julian said. His eyes were like liquid cobalt—and ravenous. Hungrier than the wolf's as he looked at Jenny and Tom together there.

225

God help me, Jenny thought. Please, *someone* help. She looked at Tom, but Tom was looking at Julian with such hatred and fury that it made Jenny afraid for him.

"Then this whole 'Game' has been a farce," Tom said, almost spitting the words. His hazel eyes were burning.

Julian spread his hands and inclined his head slightly—almost a bow. As if someone had complimented him on a job well done. But it was Jenny he spoke to.

"I told you I'd do whatever was necessary to get you. At first I was sure you'd lose the Game—most people do. Then, when I saw you had a chance of winning, I figured I could make you turn to me for help. But you wouldn't. She's very strong, you know," he added, flicking a heavy-lidded glance at Tom. "Much too good for you."

"I know," Tom said, and Jenny looked at him, astonished. "But she's a thousand times too good for *you.*"

"I want her for goodness' sake," Julian said and smiled. "Light to my darkness. You'll see—Tommy. You'll have years and years and years to see how well she and I fit together." He turned back to Jenny. "In any case, you've gotten this far, and I'm afraid I have to tell you the truth. Which is that the whole Game has been just—a game. The kind a cat plays with a mouse."

"Before eating it?" Dee said in a voice like a knife.

Julian barely glanced back at her. "I'm only hungry for one thing at the moment, Deirdre. But my friends by the door have strange appetites. I wouldn't go near them if I were you. And of course there are all the other Shadow Men—all my elders, those ancient, bone-sucking, lip-licking wraiths—they'd all like to get hold of you. This house keeps them outside—but you wouldn't get far if you opened a window."

Jenny felt the trembling in Tom's clenched fists and bowed her head. She was thinking of the poem in her grandfather's room.

Like the other fools/Who've slipped on these same stones and played and lost . . .

Did everyone lose to the Shadow Men?

The dice are loaded, she thought. You can't win.

All bets are off.

"They'd love to sink a tooth in *you,*" Julian was saying to Dee. "Do you know you're the image of Ankhesenamun, one of the greatest beauties of Egypt?" Even as he spoke, Dee snapped her right leg up in a high kick, pulling her toes back at the last minute to deliver a devastating blow with the heel. At least, that was how it should have happened. Julian, with the reflexes of a rattlesnake, caught her foot as it came at him and jerked up, flinging Dee on her back.

"Rule One in this Game," Julian said, smiling. "Don't mess with me. I'll beat you every time."

Dee got up, obviously in pain—there was no way to break a fall like that—and Julian turned back to Jenny.

Jenny met his ravenous eyes and felt something inside her change forever.

"Let the others go," she said clearly and softly, "and I'll stay with you."

Julian stared at her. Everyone stared at her.

Then somebody—she thought it was Michael—started to laugh.

Julian smiled, very slightly, just one corner of his lip up. Not an amused smile. His eyes had gone the blue of gas flames.

"I see," he said.

Jenny detached her hands from Tom's. She stood up.

"I'm serious. Let them go . . . and I'll stay . . . of my own free will. And you know what that means." She was thinking of the darkroom, of the boy masquerading as her cousin who'd held her in his arms. The boy she'd *kissed*—of her own free will. She was hoping Julian remembered, too.

She thought he did. He looked intrigued. A strange, sensuous smile curved his lips.

"Willingly?" he repeated, as if testing the word.

"Willingly."

"No . . ." Tom whispered.

"Willingly," Jenny repeated, looking only at Julian.

Julian looked charmed—but wary. "You'd have to make a promise—seal the bond. In a way that couldn't be broken."

"Yes."

She could see she'd startled him. He'd expected her to play for time, to argue. Didn't he understand that she'd changed?

She raised her eyebrows at him, ironically. "The sooner the better," she said.

Julian blinked, then said slowly, "Beautiful Deirdre can leave, and Audrey. So can Zach and Michael. But *Tommy* stays. I'll keep him as a hostage for your good behavior."

Looking up at him, Jenny felt her lip twitch, not quite a smile. "I don't think you'll need that. . . ."

"All the same."

"All right. It doesn't matter to me." Then, stepping close to him, she spoke quietly, for his ears alone. "Julian, don't you know that I've changed? Can't you *see* that? I still care about Tom, but . . . it's not the same. He'd seem tame after you. Anything would seem tame after you."

His eyes widened slightly in fascination.

Jenny took a deep breath. "I probably would have come to you a lot earlier if you'd just straight out asked me. Didn't that ever occur to you? That you could just appear at my front door, no games, no threats, and just *ask* me?"

He looked disconcerted. "Not exactly. . . ."

"You're too cynical. Do you know, I think the way you look at things has made you blind. You've gotten so hardened that you think you have to *fight* the universe to get what you want. To—sort of wrestle it out of people."

"And—don't I?"

"Not always," Jenny said. Meeting his gaze directly, she said, "Sometimes there's a much simpler solution. There are some things you can't force, Julian, and you can't buy them, either. They have to be *given,* for free. That's what I want to give you."

His fascination was complete.

"Then promise yourself to me," he said, and with a motion like a sleight-of-hand trick, he held something between his fingers. A gold circlet.

Jenny reached for it automatically, taking it between forefinger and thumb. It was a simple ring, with a design she couldn't quite make out on the outside. Inside the band something was written in fancy script. She tilted the ring toward one of the small lamps.

All I refuse & Thee I chuse, she read.

"Put this on your finger and you're sworn mine," Julian said. "No way to break the promise, no way to change the bond. It's a short ceremony. Do you want to go through with it?"

CHAPTER 15

"Yes," Jenny said.

Audrey gasped. "Jenny—for God's sake."

Jenny didn't look at her.

Tom made some movement. Jenny didn't look his way, either.

"Jenny . . ." Dee whispered. "It's not worth it. I know your promises—you keep them. You'll be *trapped*. Don't do it for us."

Jenny turned, then. She looked straight into the dark eyes with the slightly amber-tinted whites. "Dee . . . I'm sorry. I know you don't understand—and I can't explain it to you. But please believe me, I'm staying because I *want* to. Audrey, can't *you* understand?"

Audrey slowly shook her copper head, highlights flaring.

"I don't have a lot of real friends," she said. "I don't want to lose you."

"You're going to anyway," Jenny said. "This way is just easier on everyone. And I *want* to stay. I swear I do."

Dee had been staring at Jenny hard. Now, abruptly, her ebony face went blank. Walled off. Utterly without expression.

"That's right," she said. "You have to look out for number one." She nodded at Jenny, face grim, eyes meeting Jenny's directly. "Go ahead, Sunshine. Good luck."

Jenny nodded back. If it hadn't been manifestly impossible, she would have said the glitter in Dee's eyes was tears.

She turned back to Julian, who took the ring from her.

"A short ceremony," he said again. "Give me your hand."

A stained-glass lampshade threw blue and purple light over him. Jenny gave him her hand, felt that his was as cool as hers.

"Oh, don't," Audrey said, as if involuntarily.

Jenny didn't move.

"Seventeenth-century poesy ring, used to be given as tokens between lovers," Julian explained, holding up the gold circlet. "With the inscription on the inside. It means you refuse all the world except the one who gives it to you. The words touch your skin and bind you with their power."

Jenny smiled at him.

Tom stood slowly, his chains scraping up the sides of the clock with a sound like ball bearings rolling on wood.

Julian ignored everything but Jenny. "Now you repeat after me. But remember—the promise is irrevocable." With a slight, grave formality, he said, as if quoting:

"This ring, the symbol of my oath,
Will hold me to the words I speak:
All I refuse and thee I choose."

Jenny repeated the words and felt the cool band slide onto her finger. Then she looked at it. It shone with a rich, warm light, as if it had always been there.

"Now if we seal the bargain with a kiss, it becomes irrevocable," Julian said again, looking down at her. As if giving her a last chance to back out. The circlet burned on Jenny's finger like cold fire.

Jenny turned her face up. She didn't have to go far on tiptoe to kiss him. It was a soft kiss, but not a quick one.

Julian was the one who lifted his head from it.

"Sworn mine," he whispered. "Now and forever."

The violence came from an unexpected quarter.

"No," said Zachary, surging forward as if he was going to attack Julian.

Julian didn't even bother to look at him. Zach slammed into an invisible wall and fell back into Dee.

Jenny did turn, to look at all of them. Audrey and Zach and Dee and Michael. Her friends.

"I knew you wouldn't like this—" she began, but Zach interrupted her. He was on his feet again, gray eyes flashing in a way Jenny had never seen, face more intense than ever.

"How could you?" he burst out. He seemed as angry on Tom's behalf as if he himself were being betrayed. "How *could* you?"

"Leave her alone," Michael said shortly. Jenny could see his opinion in his dark spaniel eyes—Mike thought she was making the best of a very bad situation. He didn't blame her for it. "What do you want her to do?" he said, and Zach shook his head in contempt.

"Not go willingly," he said. "Not give in—to that."

Tom was watching it all with blank eyes. Jenny could barely make herself look at him, but she did.

"I'm sorry, Tommy," she said. She saw his face twist slightly, and for a terrible moment she thought he was going to cry. Then he shrugged.

"I suppose it had to happen. That's the name of the Game, isn't it?" he said, looking at Julian.

Julian gave him an odd smile, and Jenny realized they were talking about something she didn't understand. "I keep my promises, too," he said. "All of them."

Jenny touched his sleeve. His face changed as he turned toward her, as if he were forgetting everyone else in the room.

"The ceremony's done," he said. "We're promised."

"I know." Jenny let out a deep breath. The ring made a little weight on her finger, but she felt very light, very free. She spoke calmly and casually, as if she were organizing a picnic or a redecorating project. Something that had to be done fast, but right.

"Let the others go now, Julian. I wish you'd let Tom go, too—but if not, can't you please make him more comfortable? I think in a few days you'll realize you don't need a hostage to keep me behaving."

He was searching her face, as if stricken by doubt for the first time. "Jenny—you really want to stay here? It's going to be strange for you. . . ."

"*That* is the understatement of the century." She looked up at him and spoke freely. "I only hope to God we can get a different view out the parlor window. But, yes, I want to stay. I never realized how much more there was to life than what I was getting. Now that I've seen it, I can't go back. I'm not the same person I was before."

He smiled. "No. In less than twelve hours you've changed. You've become . . ."

Jenny raised her eyebrows. "What?"

"I'll tell you later. I'll enjoy telling you, taking a long time to do it." He turned.

"You can all go." Jenny heard Tom's chains rattle and clank to the floor. Out of the corner of her eye, she saw him hold his hands up, free.

"Out!" Julian said with a snap of his fingers. For an instant Jenny thought he meant it for Dee and the others, but then the phantom wolf, which had been bristling, lowered its head and slunk off. Straight through the wall, apparently. The luminous snake slithered and poured itself through the floor. Some compartment in Jenny's mind noticed with awe how long that took, how much length there was to pour.

The door home stood open, unguarded. From this angle Jenny could see the rune Uruz on it, the inverted *U* flaring fire-red with power.

Through the door—and through the small window—she could see midnight blue. She glanced at the clock, which was still ticking away. 5:50 A.M.

Dawn was coming fast.

"Go on," Julian said, as if eager to be rid of them.

"Not without Jenny," Dee said.

Michael, Jenny thought, was surprised. He looked at Dee, opened his mouth. Zach's mouth was curled angrily. Audrey was shaking her head in doubt. Tom just stood.

Jenny looked away.

Julian's voice was impatient. "Well, go, stay, do whatever you want," he said. "I'll leave you to argue it out. But, remember, that door closes at dawn. Six-eleven sharp. If you're still inside, you're here for good—and I might not be in the mood for company."

He turned to Jenny. "This place is crowded."

"I know. There's a couch downstairs. We can sit on it and get acquainted."

They went.

The sofa in Jenny's grandfather's basement was shabby and lumpy but wide and very soft. It sank under their weight. Jenny found it odd to be sitting beside Julian like this, with no animosity, no need to pull away. No battles to fight.

It was a very private place. She knew the others wouldn't open the stairway door and come down, or even look in before they left the Shadow House. Julian's warning about not wanting company was sufficient. They all knew what he could do.

She looked up at him, to find him looking at her. So close. His eyes the color of a May morning.

Very deep, but very gentle.

She could feel his hunger.

And could feel herself trembling slightly. Her nerves jangling with excitement—and fear. But he didn't even touch her, at first. He just looked at her, with an expression she'd never seen on his face before. A look of wonder. The tenderness she'd seen when he was impersonating Zach.

"Are you frightened?" he said.

"A little." She was trying not to show it. She said lightly, "So you're the youngest Shadow Man."

"And the nicest."

"I believe that," Jenny said earnestly.

He did touch her, then, fingers light on her hair. Jenny felt the little inner stillness, the change in perception that comes

237

before response. She shut her eyes and told herself not to think, not to feel anything but the featherlike touch. The lighter it was, the more it moved her.

She was surprised when it stopped. She opened her eyes—and was even more surprised at the anger in his face.

For an instant Jenny was *really* frightened, and the reality of what she was doing came home to her. Then she saw that Julian wasn't angry at her but—for her.

"You're so—innocent," he said. "That boyfriend of yours, that—*Tommy,* that spoiled, swaggering—he never thought about you, did he? Only about himself. And he botched it. I'd like to kill him."

This wasn't at all what Jenny wanted to think about. She started to say so, but Julian was going on, his eyes full of wild blue light.

"You want to watch out for that cousin of yours, too. He really does think about you, you know. I took that impression from life."

Knowing it was completely inappropriate, Jenny burst into slightly hysterical, but genuine laughter.

". . . you're jealous," she said, when she could get her breath. "Of *Zach.* Zach doesn't like people, only lenses and things."

The dark look disappeared from his face. "It doesn't matter," he said. "He won't be able to get at you here. No one will, ever. I'll keep you safe. . . ."

Jenny reached for him and lightly pressed her lips to his. He forgot about talking, then, and kissed back—such a soft kiss, his warm lips barely brushing hers.

But the soft kisses developed into slow shivery kisses and then into white-hot ones. She was still afraid of him, even as she clung to him—was it true that fear had to be a part of passion? Everywhere he touched she felt fire and ice.

Upstairs, the clock struck six.

Jenny pulled away from Julian, reluctantly. "I have to breathe," she whispered. She shook herself a little, then stood up. "Things are happening so fast."

He smiled as she walked around, getting her breath back, feeling her flushed cheeks cool. She couldn't look at him right now; she needed to regain her composure. Scarcely seeing it, she fingered the cobalt bracelet on the shelf.

"Why did you let me through my nightmare?" she said abruptly. "Sentimental reasons?"

"Not at all." He laughed. "I *did* play the Game fairly. I don't lie, even if I sometimes—withhold information. Your nightmare was remembering what happened that day. You couldn't see it, but the door appeared as soon as you remembered opening the closet."

"Oh," Jenny said softly. "The closet." Then she added, "What did he want from you? My grandfather?"

"What everybody else wants. Power, knowledge—the easy way. A free ride."

"And runes really work," Jenny said, shaking her head slightly in wonder.

"A lot of things work. A lot of things don't. People can't tell which are which until they try them—and then they're usually surprised."

Jenny went over to the closet, looked inside. He followed, standing beside her.

"I'm sorry," Jenny said quietly, without looking at him. "I'm sorry he did it. He wasn't a bad man." Then she turned. "I can hardly believe he kept you here."

"Believe it," Julian said grimly.

Jenny shook her head. "I'll always love him. But he was wrong to do what he did." She stepped into the closet. "Not as small as it looks."

"Small enough." He stepped in, too, looked around. "This place brings up bad memories."

"See if we can't make a better one." She smiled up at him, backed up against one wall.

He turned and smiled down at her. In the confined space they were very close. Jenny stood shyly, one leg crossed behind the other.

He bent his head again, his mouth warm and demanding. Jenny gave herself up to it, and the kiss opened like a slow-blooming flower. Became so breathless and urgent that Jenny couldn't break it, even though she knew she had to. She kept thinking, Just one more minute, just one more minute . . .

It was Julian who pulled back.

"It's rather uncomfortable in here."

"Do you think so?" She smiled up at him, breath slowing.

"Definitely."

"Well, then, I suppose we could—"

Now, she thought.

In the middle of her sentence she moved. She had been standing in the cross stance, a kung fu stance Dee had taught her. Good for instant lateral movement. Now, in a split second, she used the power of her left leg to throw her to the right, vaulting out of the closet. In the same motion she slammed shut the door.

"Nauthiz!" she shouted. She slashed the *X* in the air.

As she shouted it, the rune flashed brightly on the closet door. Not red like fire, but blue-white like ice.

She didn't know if she was doing it right, but it was what her grandfather had done—or tried to do. Shut the door, trace the rune, say the name. She pronounced it as her grandfather had pronounced it.

And Julian did *not* come leaping out after her.

The closet door stayed closed.

The silence was deafening.

Jenny turned and ran for the staircase.

He lied, Jenny thought, racing up the steps. He changed the rules and he lied. Sometimes you can't return good for evil; sometimes evil simply has to be *stopped*.

She knew all this, of course; it had been in her mind from the very beginning, from the moment when she'd offered to stay with Julian. She didn't need to explain it to herself.

She was saying it to the whispering, plaintive voices in her own head that were begging her to go back.

Dawn tinted the turret window pink as she burst into the room. The door was a rectangle of pure palest rose with some lacy white clouds thrown in. The view was only slightly obscured by the five people standing around it.

Five. All of them. Dee, she'd expected—she knew Dee. Tom, she'd been worried about; she'd wanted him to understand, but she'd wanted him to leave even more. She'd hoped that Zach would be mad enough to go, and that Audrey would be sensible enough. Michael, she'd assumed, would be out like a shot.

"Go!" she shouted as she ran to them. She couldn't help glancing at the grandfather clock, which showed a scrolled minute hand leaning far too far past the ten. *"Go!"*

Tom's face had lighted with—well, with an expression that sent Jenny soaring the last five feet. "Go on!" he said to the others, reaching for Jenny,

It wasn't as easy a proposition as it sounded. There was nothing outside this door. No Ice Age, no living room. Nothing but dawn. Stepping out into that took guts.

"Oh, what the hell," said Michael, and, holding hands with Audrey, he took the step.

Dee flashed a barbaric grin over her shoulder and jumped out like a skydiver.

Zach was the one who balked. Jenny couldn't believe it. "Where is he?" Zach demanded.

"In the closet. Go, go!"

Zach's face was still dark. "I thought you meant it—"

Tom gave him a good straight-arm shove, running-back style. Zach fell out sprawling, spinning, arms and legs extended.

It didn't look like fun. They were trusting to fate. No—to Julian, a much more dangerous proposition. Trusting that when he'd said Jenny's friends could leave, he had meant alive.

And trusting to Grandpa Evenson, Jenny thought, that the rune of containment would contain. Tom reached to take her hand in both of his. The sky was a blaze of rose and gold.

They looked at each other and stepped out that way, together.

They were falling as the sun appeared. In that instant the entire sky around them turned a color Jenny had seen only once before. An unbelievable luminous blue, the color of Julian's eyes.

No matter how often you faint, you never really get used to it. Jenny came to herself slowly. She was lying down, she knew that first. Lying on something cool and very hard.

Mexican paver tiles.

She sat up much too fast and almost fainted again.

The first thing she saw was the Game.

It was sitting in the middle of her mother's solid ponderosa pine coffee table. The white box lid was on the floor beside the table. The rune Uruz was dull as rust.

The Victorian paper house itself was tall and perfect, its printed colors richly glowing in the rosy eastern light. The only difference Jenny could see was that the slips of paper they'd drawn their nightmares on were gone—as were the paper dolls they'd drawn of themselves.

It all looked so innocent, so wholesome, with the Tupperware tub of Joey's crayons sitting beside it.

"Maybe it was all a dream," Michael said hoarsely.

He was on the other side of the table, with Audrey, who was just straightening up. Her glossy auburn hair was windblown into a lion's mane. It made her look quite different, quite—free.

"It wasn't a dream," Dee said with uncharacteristic quietness, uncoiling her long legs and standing. "Summer's gone."

Zach picked himself up and sat on a leather footstool. He said nothing, but rubbed his forehead as if his head hurt.

Jenny looked at Tom.

He was sitting up very slowly, using the table as help. Jenny put a hand under his arm, and he looked a "thank you" at her. He'd changed. Maybe even more than Audrey. He looked battered and sore, and he'd lost his air of always being in control. There was a new expression in his eyes, a sadness that was almost grateful at the same time. Jenny didn't know the word for it.

Maybe something like *humility.*

"Tommy," she said, worried.

The rakish smile was crooked. Battered as his devilish good looks. "I thought maybe you were really staying with him. To save me—and because you wanted to. And the thing was, I wouldn't have blamed you. I sort of realized that when he gave you the ring."

Jenny, who had been about to protest, looked at her hand. Any lingering doubts about last night being real were shattered. It was there, shining on her finger.

"I thought *definitely* you really were staying with him," Audrey said. "You had me convinced you honestly wanted to—and it was all a trick?"

"It was the truth. I *was* doing it of my own free will, and I did want to stay—long enough to make sure Tom and you guys got out."

"*I* knew," Dee said.

"It's those brains of yours again," Jenny said, looking straight at her.

"And I always thought you were such a sweet little thing," Michael was musing. "So simple, so honest . . ."

"I am—when people treat me fairly. When they don't kill my friends. When they don't break their word. I figured he made up the rules of that game, and trickery was a legal move. So I did it."

Audrey persisted. "And you really never felt anything for him? That was all an act?"

"Just call me Sarah Bernhardt," Jenny said.

She hoped that Audrey wouldn't notice she hadn't answered the question.

"Who cares?" Michael said. "We're home. We did it." He looked around at the sunlight flooding in through the sliding glass door, at the ordinary Thornton backyard outside, at the pastel walls of the living room. "I love each and every one of these baskets," he said. "I could kiss the tiles we sit on. I could kiss *you*, Audrey."

"Oh, if you have to," Audrey said, not bothering to fuss with her hair. She leaned forward and so did Michael.

Dee, though, was still looking at Jenny, her night-dark eyes serious. "What about the betrothal?" she said. "The ring? You're supposed to be promised to him now."

"What about it?" Jenny said quietly. "I'm going to throw the ring away. With the rest of this garbage."

In a single motion that brought Zach's head up, she crushed the paper house, smashing it flat and flatter. She put it in the white box, like filling an overstuffed suitcase, pushing it in where it wouldn't fit. She scooped up the game cards and jammed them in, too.

Then she took the ring off. It came quite easily, not sticking to her finger or anything. She didn't look at the inscription.

She dropped the ring on top of it all.

Then she put in the paper dolls of the Creeper and the Lurker. As she picked up the third doll she paused.

It was the boy with the shocking blue eyes.

They seemed to be looking up at her, but she knew they weren't. It was just a tagboard cutout, and the original was locked away under a rune of constraint that would hold, she hoped, forever.

She hadn't let go of the Shadow Man doll yet.

It was your Game. You hunted us. You told me to become a hunter. You just never expected to be trapped yourself.

What would this world be like without a Julian in it? Safer, certainly. Calmer. But poorer, too, in a way.

She'd beaten the Shadow Man, but it was strangely hard to consign him to oblivion. Jenny felt a pang of something oddly like regret, of something lost forever.

She put the doll in the box and crammed the lid on.

There was a roll of masking tape in with Joey's crayons. Jenny wound tape round and round the bulging white box, sealing it shut. The others all watched in silence.

When she finally ran out of tape she put the box on the table and sat back on her heels. A smile began somewhere in the group and traveled from one person to another. Not a partying kind of smile, just one of quiet relief and joy. They had made it. They'd won. They were alive—most of them.

"What are we going to say about Summer?" Tom asked.

"We're going to tell the truth," Jenny said.

Audrey's eyebrows arched. "No one will ever believe us!"

"I know," Jenny said. "We're going to tell them anyway."

"It'll be all right," said Dee. "After all we've been through, we can deal with it. As long as we're all together."

"We are," Jenny said, and Tom nodded. In the old days—last night—it would have been the other way around.

Audrey and Michael, who couldn't seem to separate from each other, both nodded, too. So did Zach, who was for once paying attention to the rest of them, instead of being off in his own little world.

I think it actually helped him, Jenny thought suddenly, to know that his grandfather was only calling up demons and not insane after all.

"We can call the police from the kitchen," she said aloud.

CHAPTER 16

It was Dee who made the phone call, because Audrey and Michael were looking out the kitchen window together, and Zach wasn't the talking type. Jenny and Tom had moved a little away from the others.

"I wanted to show you this," Tom said.

It was a tattered scrap of paper. It had several things drawn and then crossed out—Jenny thought one was a rat. The only thing not crossed out was in the middle, and Jenny couldn't tell what it was.

"I'm a rotten artist. I thought you could tell by the yellow hair and green eyes."

"*I'm* your worst nightmare?" Jenny said, only half joking because she was completely bewildered.

"No. It was hard to draw, but it was what I meant at the

end when I told Julian I guessed it had to happen. The name of the Game was face your worst nightmare, and that was mine. Losing you."

Jenny could only look at him.

"I'm not good at saying it. Maybe I'm not even good at showing it," he said. "But—I love you. As much as he does. More."

All Jenny could think of was hibiscus bushes. Little Tommy in second grade. The boy she had decided she was going to marry—on sight.

Something was tugging at her inside, but she knew she had to put it—even the memory of it—away forever. Never think of it again. And never let Tom know.

Never.

"I love you, too," she whispered. "Oh, Tom, so much."

It was at that moment they heard the glass break.

Dee was hampered by being on the phone. Tom was hampered by Jenny. The others were just plain frozen.

Still, it was only a few seconds before they ran back to the living room, just in time to see two figures ducking out the broken sliding glass door with really astonishing speed.

The white box wasn't on the coffee table anymore.

Tom and Dee, of course, ran into the backyard. But even Jenny, standing by the broken door, could see there was no chance. The two figures were over the wall and gone before their pursuers got close. After climbing the block wall and looking around, Tom and Dee came slowly back.

"They just disappeared," Dee said in disgust.

"They were *flying*," Tom panted.

"You're not in the best of shape, either of you," Jenny said. "It doesn't matter. I didn't really want to give the Game to the police anyway. It probably won't work for anyone else."

"But who *were* they? Shadow Men?" Michael asked.

"Shadow Men in sneakers," Dee said, pointing to a muddy footprint on the tiles.

"But why would they *want* to—"

Jenny tuned him out. She was looking at the broken glass and trying not to think. Even from behind, those two guys had looked familiar.

But surely what she'd said was true. The Game had been meant for her; it shouldn't work for anyone else. Besides, it was squashed now, ruined. And even if it did work for someone else, what were the chances of them making it all the way up to the third floor, into her grandfather's basement? And even if they did make it there, what were the chances of them opening a white closet door?

"Good riddance to it," Tom said. In the early morning light his dark hair shone, and the green flecks in his eyes looked gold. "Everything I care about is right here," he said. He smiled at Jenny. "No more nightmares," he told her, with open love in his face, in front of them all.

Jenny went into the circle of his arms.

*   *   *

251

In a vacant lot, two boys were panting, looking behind them for pursuers.

"I think we lost them," said the one in the black bandanna and T-shirt.

"They weren't even trying," said the one in the black-and-blue flannels.

They looked at each other in a mixture of triumph and fear.

They didn't know what the box was, despite a night of watching the blond girl's house. It hadn't been until dawn that they'd worked up the nerve to break in—and then the white box had been there on the table, waiting for them.

They knew only that ever since seeing it they'd been compelled to follow it, fearing it and wanting it in equal measure. It had dominated their thoughts, sending them after the girl, keeping them up all night.

And now they had it, at last.

One of them flicked out a knife and slit the tape.

THE CHASE

For Joanne Finucan,
a true heroine and lifelong inspiration

CHAPTER 1

It wasn't so much the hunting. It was the killing.

That was what brought Gordie Wilson out to the Santa Ana foothills on a sunny May morning like this. That was why he was cutting school even though he wasn't sure he'd get away with forging his mom's signature on another re-admit. It wasn't the wildflower-splashed hills, the sky blue lupines, or the fragrant purple sage. It was the wet, plopping sound when lead met flesh.

The kill.

Gordie preferred big game, but rabbits were always available—if you knew how to dodge the rangers. He'd never been caught yet.

He'd always liked killing. When he was seven, he'd gotten

robins and starlings with his BB gun. When he was nine, it had been ground squirrels with a shotgun. Twelve, and his dad took him on a real hunting trip, going after white-tailed deer with an old .243 Winchester.

That had been so special. But then, every kill was special. It was like his dad said: *"Good hunts never end."* Every night in bed Gordie thought about the very best ones, remembering the stalking, the shooting, the electric moment of death. He even hunted in his dreams.

For one instant, as he made his way along the dry creek bed, a memory flickered at him, like a little tongue of flame. A nightmare. Just once Gordie had dreamed that he was on the other side of the rifle sights, the one with dogs snapping behind him, the one being hunted. A chase that had only ended when he woke up dripping sweat.

Stupid dream. He wasn't a rabbit, he was a hunter. Top of the food chain. He'd gotten a moose last year.

Big game like that was worth observing, studying, planning for. But not rabbits. Gordie just liked to come up here and kick them out of the bushes.

This was a good place. A sage-covered slope rising toward a stand of oak and sycamore trees, with some good brush piles underneath for cover. Bound to be a bunny under one of those.

Then he saw it. Right out in the open. Little desert cotton-tail sunning itself near a squat of grass. It was aware of him, but still. Frozen. Ter-*rif*-ic, Gordie thought. He knew how to sneak up on a rabbit, get so close he could practically catch it with bare hands.

The trick was to make the rabbit think you didn't see it. If you only looked at it sideways, if you walked kind of zigzag while slowly getting closer and closer . . .

As long as its ears stayed down, instead of up and swiveling, you were safe.

Gordie edged carefully around a lemonade berry bush, looking out of the corner of his eye. He was so close now that he could see the rabbit's whiskers. Pure happiness filled him, warmth pooling in his stomach. It was going to hold still for him.

God, this was the exciting part, the *gooood* part. Breath held, he raised the rifle, centered the crosshairs. Got ready to gently squeeze the trigger.

There was an explosion of motion, a gray-brown blur and the flash of a white tail. It was getting away!

Gordie's rifle barked, but the slug struck the ground just behind the rabbit, kicking up dust. The rabbit bounded on, down into the dry creek bed, losing itself among the cattails.

Damn! He wished he'd brought a dog. Like his dad's beagle, Aggie. Dogs were crazy about the chase. Gordie loved to watch them do it, loved to draw it out, waiting for the dog to bring the rabbit around in a circle. It was a shame to end a good chase too soon. His dad sometimes let a rabbit go if it ran a good enough race, but that was crazy. What good was a hunt without the kill?

There were times when Gordie . . . wondered about himself.

He sensed vaguely that his hunting was somehow different than his dad's. He did things when he was alone that he never told anybody about. When he was five, he used to pour rubbing alcohol on earwigs. They'd writhed a long time before they died. Even now he would swerve to run over a possum or a cat in the road if he could.

Killing felt so good. Any kind of killing.

That was Gordie Wilson's little secret.

The bunny was gone. He'd spooked it. Or . . .

Maybe something else had.

A strange feeling was growing in Gordie. It had developed so slowly he hadn't even noticed when it started, and it was like nothing he'd ever felt before—at least awake. A . . . rabbit-feeling. Like what a rabbit might feel when it freezes, crouched down, with the hunter's eyes on it. Like what a squirrel might feel when it sees something big creeping slowly closer.

A . . . *watched* feeling.

The skin on the back of his neck began to crawl.

There were eyes watching him. He felt it with the part of his brain that hadn't changed in a hundred million years. The reptile part.

Gingerly, flesh still creeping, he turned.

Directly behind him three old sycamores grew close enough together to cast a shade. But the darkness underneath was too dark to be just a shadow. It was more like a black vapor hanging there.

Something was under those trees. Something else had been watching the rabbit.

Now it was watching him.

The black vapor seemed to stir. White teeth glinted out of the darkness, as bright as sunlight on water.

Gordie's eyes bulged in their sockets.

What the—what *was* it?

The vapor moved again and he saw.

Only—it couldn't be. It couldn't be what he thought he saw, because it—*just couldn't be*. Because there wasn't anything like that in the world, so it *just couldn't*—

It was beyond anything he'd ever imagined. When it moved, it moved *fast*. Gordie got off one shot as it surged toward him. Then he turned and ran.

He went the way the rabbit had, slipping and slithering down the slope, tearing his jeans and his hands on prickly pear cactus. The thing he'd seen was right behind him. He could hear it breathing. His foot caught on a stone, and he fell heavily, arms flailing.

He rolled over and saw it in the full sunlight. His mouth sagged open. He tried to scoot away on his backside, but sheer terror paralyzed his muscles.

Deliberately it closed in.

A loose, blubbery wail came from Gordie's lips. His last wild thought was *Not me—not me—I'm not a rabbit—not meeeeee—*

His heart stopped before it even got its teeth in him.

Jenny was brushing her hair, *really* brushing it, feeling it crackle and lift by itself to meet the plastic bristles in the static electricity of this golden May afternoon. She gazed absently at her own reflection, seeing a girl with forest green eyes, dark as pine needles, and eyebrows that were straight, like two decisive brush strokes. The hair that lifted to meet the brush was the color of honey in sunlight.

"They didn't do it."

Jenny stopped abruptly. A girl was reflected behind her in the mirror.

The girl had dark hair and dark eyes reddened with crying. She looked poised for flight out of the bathroom.

"I'm sorry?"

"I said, they didn't *do* it. Slug and P.C. They didn't kill your friend Summer."

Oh. Jenny found herself gripping the brush hard, unable to even turn her head. She could only look at the girl's eyes reflected in the mirror, but she understood now. "I never said they did," she said softly and carefully. "I just told the police that they were around that night. And that they stole something from my living room. A paper house. A game."

"I *hate* you."

Shocked, Jenny turned.

"You and your preppy friends—*you* did it. You killed her yourselves. And someday everybody will know and you'll pay and you'll be sorry." The girl was twisting a Kleenex between slim olive-tan fingers, tearing it into little bits. Her long hair was absolutely straight except for the slight undersweep of the ends, and her dark eyes were pensive. She didn't belong at Vista Grande High; Jenny had never seen her before.

Jenny put the brush down and went to her, facing her directly. The girl looked taken aback.

"Why were you crying?" Jenny said gently.

"Why should you care? You're a soshe. You wear your fancy clothes to school and hang out with your rich friends—"

"Who's rich? What have my clothes got to do with it?" Jenny could feel her eyebrows come together. She looked pointedly at the girl's fashionably tattered designer jeans.

The girl spoke sullenly. "You're a soshe . . ."

Jenny grabbed her.

"I am not a soshe," she said fiercely. "I am a human being. So are you. So what is your problem?"

The girl wouldn't say anything. She twisted under Jenny's hands, and Jenny felt the small bones in her shoulders. Finally, almost spitting it in Jenny's face, she said, "P.C. was my friend. He never did anything to that girl. You and your friends did something, something so bad that you had to hide her body and tell those lies. But you just wait. I can prove P.C. didn't hurt her. I can *prove* it."

Despite the warm day, hairs rose on Jenny's arms. Her little fingers tingled.

"What do you mean?"

Something in her face must have scared the girl. "Never mind."

"No, you tell me. How could you prove it? Did you—"

"Let *go* of me!"

I'm being rough, Jenny realized. I'm never rough. But she couldn't seem to stop. Chills were sweeping over her, and she wanted to shake the information out of the girl.

"Did you see him or something?" she demanded. "Did he come home the next morning alone? Did you see what he did with the paper hou—"

Pain exploded against her shinbone. The girl had kicked her. Jenny lost her grip, and the girl wrenched away, running to the bathroom door.

"*Wait!* You don't understand—"

The girl jerked the door open and darted out. Jenny hopped after her, but by the time she looked up and down the second-story walkway, the girl was gone. There were only a few bits of twisted Kleenex on the concrete floor.

Jenny hobbled over to the nearest locker bay and looked into it. Nothing but students and lockers. Then she limped back and looked over the railing of the open walkway to the main courtyard. Nothing but students with lunches.

Young. The girl had been young, probably a ninth grader. Maybe she'd come from Magnolia Junior High. It was within walking distance.

Whoever she was, Jenny had to find her. Whoever she was, she'd seen something. She might *know* . . .

I left my purse in the bathroom, Jenny realized. She retrieved it and slowly walked back out.

The pay phone beside the bathroom was ringing. Jenny glanced around—two teachers were locking up a classroom, students were streaming down the stairs on each end of the building. Nobody seemed to be waiting for a call, nobody even seemed to notice the ringing.

Jenny lifted the receiver. "Hello," she said, feeling foolish.

She heard an electronic hiss, white noise. Then there was a click, and in the static she seemed to hear a low whispering in a male voice. It was distorted, drawn out, and there was something weird about the way the syllables were stressed. It sounded like one word whispered over and over.

A as in *amble*. Then a dragging, hissing sigh: *ish. A . . . ish . . .*

Gibberish.

"Hello?"

Shhshhshhshhshhshhshhshhshh. Click. In the background she heard something that might have been speech, a sharp, staccato burst.

Again, the rhythm was weird. It sounded like some *very* foreign language.

Bad connection, Jenny thought. She hung up.

Her little fingers were tingling again. But she didn't have time to think about it now. That girl had to be found.

I'd better get the others, Jenny thought.

CHAPTER 2

She looked in on Tom's business law class first, but he wasn't there. She headed downstairs. Then she began to forge her way across campus, weaving around fellow students who were staking out their favorite benches. She could hear paper bags rustling and smell other peoples' lunches.

Jenny's group hadn't been eating together these last two weeks—it caused too much talk. But today they had no choice.

Audrey next, Jenny thought. She passed the amphitheater with its blistered wooden benches and looked into one of the home ec rooms. Audrey was taking interior decorating, and—of course—acing it.

Jenny just stood in the doorway until Audrey, who was

lingering with the teacher, looked up and caught her eye. Audrey shut her folder, dropped it in her backpack, and came.

"What is it?"

"We've got to get everybody," Jenny said. "Do you have your lunch?"

"Yes." Audrey didn't ask why they had to get everybody. She just shook spiky copper bangs out of her eyes with an expert toss of her head and pressed her cherry-glossed lips together.

They cut across the center of campus toward the girls' gym. The sun shone on Jenny's head, sending a little trickle of dampness down the back of her neck. Too hot for May, even in California. So why did she feel so cold inside?

She and Audrey peered into the girls' locker room. Dee wasn't even dressed yet, snapping towels and snickering with a couple of girls on the swim team. She was naked and completely unself-conscious, beautiful and lithe and supple as a jet-black panther. When she saw Jenny and Audrey looking at her significantly, she hiked an eyebrow at them, then nodded. She reached for a garnet-colored T-shirt and joined them a minute later.

They found Zach in the art block, standing alone outside the photography lab. That wasn't surprising—Zach was usually alone. What surprised Jenny was that he wasn't *inside* the lab, working. Zach's thin, intense face had always been pale, but these days it looked almost chalky, and in the last few weeks he'd taken to wearing black cotton twills and shirts. He's changed, Jenny thought. Well, no wonder. What they'd been through would have changed anyone.

He saw Jenny, who tilted her head in the general direction of the staff parking lot. The usual place. He gave a brief jerk of his head that meant agreement. He'd meet them there.

They found Michael near the English block, picking up scattered papers and books from the concrete floor.

"Jerks, porkers, bozos, *Neanderthals,*" he was muttering.

"Who did it?" Jenny asked as Audrey checked Michael for bruises.

"Carl Vortman and Steve Matsushima." Michael's round face was flushed and his dark hair even more rumpled than usual. "It would help if you kissed it *here,*" he said to Audrey, pointing to the corner of his mouth.

Dee did a swift, flowing punch-and-kick to the air that looked like dancing. "I'll take care of them," she said, flashing her most barbaric smile.

"Come on, we've got to talk," Jenny said. "Has anybody seen Tom?"

"I think he cut this morning," Audrey said. "He wasn't in history or English."

Wonderful, Jenny thought as Michael got his lunch. Zachary was wearing Morbid Black, Michael was getting stomped, and Tom, the super-student, was cutting whole mornings—just when she needed him most.

They sat down by the parking lot on what was commonly

known at Vista Grande High as the grassy knoll. Zach arrived and dropped first his lunch sack, then himself to the ground, folding his long, thin legs in one easy motion.

"What's happening?" Dee said.

Jenny took a deep breath.

"There's this girl," she said, and she did her best to describe the Crying Girl. "Probably a ninth grader," she said. "Do any of you guys know her?"

They all shook their heads.

"Because she said *we* killed Summer and hid her body, and that she knew that P.C. didn't do it. She sounded like somebody who really did know, and not just because she has faith in him or something."

Dee's sloe-black eyes were narrowed. "You think—"

"I think maybe she saw him that morning. And that means—"

"Maybe she knows where the paper house is," Michael said, looking more alarmed than excited.

"If she does, we have to find her," Jenny said.

Michael groaned.

Jenny didn't blame him. Everything about their situation was awful. The way people looked at them now, the questions in people's eyes—and the danger. The danger that no one but their group knew about.

A lot of it was Jenny's fault. It had been her own brilliant idea. *Let's tell the police the truth. . . .*

*   *   *

There were two policewomen. One was Hawaiian or Polynesian and model-beautiful. The other was a stocky motherly person. They both examined the pile of fragments around the sliding glass door.

"But that doesn't have anything to *do* with Summer," Jenny said, and then she and Tom and Michael and Audrey explained it all again.

No, it hadn't been a UFO. Well, it had been sort of like a UFO—Julian was *alien,* all right, but he hadn't broken the door. He had come out of a game—or at least he had sucked them *into* a game. Or at least—

All right. From the beginning again.

Jenny had bought the game on Montevideo Avenue, in a store called More Games. Okay? She'd bought it and brought it home and they had all opened it. Yes, they'd all been here, the six of them, plus Summer. It had been a party for Tom's seventeenth birthday.

Inside had been this cardboard house. This model. They had put it together, a Victorian house, three stories and a turret. Blue.

Then they'd put these paper dolls inside that they'd colored to look like themselves. Yeah, right, they *were* a little old to be playing with paper dolls. But it wasn't just a dollhouse. It was a game.

The game was to draw your worst nightmare and put it in

a room of the house, and then, starting at the bottom, work your way up to the top. Going through each different person's nightmare as you went.

It had seemed like a good game. Only then it turned real.

Yes, real. *Real.* How many different ways were there to say real? *Real!*

They had all sort of passed out, and when they woke up, they were in the house. Inside it. It wasn't cardboard anymore. It was solid, like an ordinary house. Then Julian had showed up.

Who was Julian? *What* was Julian, that was the question. If you thought of him as a demon prince, you wouldn't be too far off. He called himself the Shadow Man.

The Shadow Man. Like the Sandman, only he brings nightmares.

Look, the point was that Julian had killed Summer. He made her face her worst nightmare, which was a messy room. Piles of garbage and giant cockroaches. Yes, it did sound funny, but it wasn't. . . .

No, none of them had read Kafka.

Look, it wasn't funny because it had *killed* Summer. She'd been buried in a garbage dump from hell, under piles of filth and rotting stuff. They'd heard her screaming and screaming, and then finally the screaming had stopped.

The body? For God's sake, where else would the body be? It was *there,* buried in rubbish, in the paper house, in the Shadow World.

No! The sliding glass door did not have anything to do with it. That had happened after they escaped from the Shadow World. Jenny had tricked Julian and locked him behind a door with a rune of constraint on it. When they got back to the real world, Jenny had put the paper house back in the game box, and then they'd called the police. Yes, that was the call made at 6:34 this morning. While they were on the phone, they'd heard glass breaking and come out to see two guys taking the box over the back fence.

Why would anybody want to steal the box? Well, these guys had been following Jenny when she bought the Game. And seeing the Game—it did something to you. Once you saw that glossy white box, you wanted it, no matter what. The guys had probably followed Jenny home just to get the box.

NO, SUMMER DIDN'T GO THAT WAY, TOO! SUMMER WASN'T THERE! SUMMER WAS ALREADY DEAD BY THEN!

It was only after telling it that Jenny saw how crazy the story sounded. At first the police wouldn't believe that Summer was *really* missing, no matter how many times Tom demanded a lie detector test.

The police finally began to believe when they called Summer's parents and found that nobody had seen her since last night. By then Jenny and the others were sitting in the detective bureau around a large table with detectives' desks all around them. By then Jenny had picked out pictures of the two guys who'd stolen

273

the game. P.C. Serrani and Scott Martell, better known as Slug, a name he'd chosen himself. They both had records for shoplifting and joyriding. P.C. was the one who'd been wearing the bandanna and black leather vest, Slug the one in the flannels with the bad complexion.

And it turned out that they were both missing, too.

The worst part was when Summer's parents came down to the station to ask Jenny where Summer really was. They didn't understand why Jenny, who had known Summer since fourth grade, wouldn't tell them the truth now. The kids finally were given a drug-screening test because Summer's father insisted their story sounded exactly like things he'd seen in the sixties. Like a very, very bad trip.

Mrs. Parker-Pearson kept saying, "Whatever Summer's done, it doesn't matter. Just tell us where she is."

It was *horrible.*

Aba was the one who finally stopped it.

Just at the point when the fuss got the biggest and noisiest, she appeared. She was wearing a brilliant orange garment that was more like a robe than a dress, and an orange headcloth like a turban. She was Dee's grandmother, but she looked like visiting royalty. She asked the police to leave her alone with the children.

Then Jenny, shaking all over, told the story again. From the beginning.

When it was over, she looked at each of them. At Tom,

the champion athlete, sitting with his normally neat dark hair wildly tousled. At Audrey, the ever-chic, with her mascara rubbed off from sobbing. At Zach, the unshakable photographer, whose gray eyes were glassy with shock. At Michael, with his rumpled head in his arms. At Dee, the only one of them still sitting up straight, proud and tense and *furious,* her hair glistening like mica with sweat.

At Jenny, who had looked back at her with a mute plea for understanding.

Then Aba looked down at her own interlaced fingers, sculptor's fingers, long and beautiful even if they were knotted with age.

"I've told you a lot of stories," she said to Jenny, "but there's a famous one I don't think you've heard. It's a Hausa story. My ancestors were those-who-speak-Hausa, you know, and my mother told me this when I was just a little girl."

Michael slowly lifted his head from the table.

"Once there was a hunter who went out into the bush, and he found a skull lying on the ground. He said, although he was really speaking to himself, 'Why, how did you get here?'"

"To his astonishment, the skull answered, 'I got here through talking, my friend.'"

Tom leaned forward, listening. Audrey stared. She didn't know Aba as well as the rest of them.

Aba went right on. "The hunter was very excited. He ran back to his village and told everyone that he had seen a talking skull. When the chief of the village heard, he asked the hunter to take him to the marvelous skull.

"So the hunter took the chief to the skull. 'Talk,' he said, but the skull just lay there. The chief was so angry at being tricked that he cut off the hunter's head and left it lying on the ground.

"Once the chief was gone, the skull said to the severed head beside it, 'Why, how did you get here?' And the head replied, 'I got here through talking, my friend!'"

In the long silence afterward, Jenny could hear distant telephones ringing and voices outside the room.

"You mean," Michael said finally, "that we've been talking too much?"

"I mean that you don't need to tell *everything* you know to *everyone*. There is a time to be silent. Also, you don't have to insist that your view is the only one, even if you honestly believe it. That hunter might have lived if he'd said, 'I think a skull talked to me, but I may have dreamed it.'"

"But we didn't dream it," Jenny whispered.

What Aba said then made all the difference. It made everything easier somehow.

"I believe you," she said quietly and laid a gentle, knotted hand on Jenny's.

When the police came back, everyone was calm. Jenny's group now admitted that while they thought they were telling the truth, it could have been some sort of dream or hallucination. The police now theorized that something really *had* happened to Summer, something so awful that the kids just couldn't accept what they'd seen, and so had made up a hysterical story to cover the memory. Teenagers were especially prone to mass hallucination, Inspector Somebody explained to Aba. If they could pass a lie detector test, proving they hadn't done anything to Summer . . .

They passed.

Then the police released them into the custody of their parents, and Jenny went home and slept for sixteen hours straight. When she woke up, it was Sunday and Summer was still missing. So were Slug and P.C.

That was how the Center got started.

The new idea was that Slug and P.C. had made off with Summer, or that someone else had made off with all three. The local shopping mall donated space for a search center. Hundreds of volunteers went out looking in stormpipes and ditches and Dumpsters.

There was nothing Jenny could do to stop any of it. Every day the volunteers did more, the search got bigger.

She felt awful. But then she realized something.

Summer's body wasn't in a Dumpster—but the paper house might be. It wouldn't do any good searching for Summer, but it might do some good to search for Slug and P.C.

"Because," she pointed out bleakly to Dee and the others, "they got into the paper house, all right. And that means they might get up to the third floor. And *that* means they might open a certain door and let Julian out. . . ."

After that they went out every day with the other volunteers, looking for a clue to where Slug Martell and P.C. Serrani might have taken the Game. It was a race against time, Jenny thought. To get to the house before Slug and P.C. got to Julian. Because after what she had done to Julian, tricking him and locking him behind that door, and after what she had promised him—telling him she'd stay with him forever—and then running away . . .

If he ever got out, he would find her. He'd hunt her down. And he'd take his revenge.

CHAPTER 3

On the grassy knoll Michael was still groaning at the thought of finding the Crying Girl.

"She probably doesn't know anything," Zach said, his eyes gray as winter clouds. "She probably just wonders if maybe we did it. Deep down, I think everybody wonders."

Jenny looked around at the group: Dee sprawled lazily on the grass, dark limbs gleaming; Audrey perched on a folder to save her white tuxedo pantsuit; Michael with his teddy-bear body and sarcastic spaniel eyes; and Zach sitting like some kind of Tibetan monk with a ponytail. They didn't look like murderers. But what Zach was saying was true, and it was just like him to say it.

"We've got to go postering today anyway," Audrey said.

"We might as well look for this girl while we're at it."

"It's not going to make any difference," Zach said flatly.

The others turned to Jenny. He's your cousin; you deal with him, their looks said.

Jenny took another deep breath. "You know perfectly well it *will* make a difference," she said tightly. "If we don't get the paper house back—you *know* what could happen."

"And what are you going to do if we *do* get it? Burn it? Shred it? With them inside? Isn't *that* murder, or don't P.C. and Slug count?"

Everyone burst into speech. "They wouldn't care about us—" Audrey began.

"Just cool it," Dee said, standing over Zach like a lioness.

"Maybe they're not inside. Maybe they just took it and skipped town or something," Michael offered.

Jenny gathered all her self-control, then she stood, looking at Zach directly. "If you don't have anything useful to say, then you'd better leave," she said.

She saw the looks of surprise from the others. Zach didn't look surprised. He stood, his thin beaky-nosed face even more intense than usual, staring at Jenny. Then, without a word, he turned around and left.

Jenny sat back down, feeling shaken.

"Good grief," Michael said mildly.

"He deserved it," said Dee.

Jenny knew the point was not whether Zach had deserved

it, but that Michael was surprised Jenny would give it to him.

I've changed, Jenny thought. She tried to push the knowledge away with a "So what," but it nagged at her. She had the feeling that, deep down, she might have changed more than anybody knew yet.

"We have to find the paper house," she said.

"Right," Dee said. "Even though I don't think there's a chance in hell of P.C. and Slug making it all the way to the third floor where Julian is. Not with that snake and that wolf around—"

"The Creeper and the Lurker," Audrey said with precision.

"—but we might as well be safe." A bell rang. "See you in physiology," Dee added to Jenny, grabbed her empty Carbo-Force can, and ran for the art block.

Michael brushed cookie crumbs off his lap, got up, and began the trek to the gym.

Jenny knew she should be hurrying, too. She and Audrey had to get changed for tennis. But at the moment she really didn't care if she was late or not.

"Want to cut?" she said to Audrey.

Audrey stopped dead in the middle of reapplying her lipstick. Then she finished, snapped her compact shut, and put the lipstick away. "What's *happened* to you?" she said.

"Nothing—" Jenny was beginning, when she realized that somebody was walking up to them.

It was a guy, a senior from Jenny's world lit class. Brian

Dettlinger. He looked at Audrey uncertainly, but when it was apparent she wasn't going anywhere he said hi to both of them.

Jenny and Audrey said hi back.

"Just wondering," he said, eyeing a bumblebee hovering over a clump of Mexican lilies, "if you had, you know, a date for the prom."

Prom's over, Jenny thought stupidly. Then she realized that of course he meant senior prom.

Audrey's chestnut eyes had widened. "No, she doesn't," she said instantly, with the slight pursing of lips that brought out her beauty mark.

"But I have a *boyfriend*," Jenny said, astonished. Everyone knew that. Just as everyone knew that she and Tom had been together since elementary school, that for years people had talked about them as Tom-and-Jenny, a single unit, as if they were joined at the hip. Everyone *knew* that.

"Oh, yeah," Brian Dettlinger said, looking vaguely embarrassed. "But I just thought—he isn't around much anymore, and . . ."

"Thank you," Jenny said. "I can't go." She knew she sounded scandalized, and that Brian didn't deserve it. He was only trying to be nice. But she was put off balance by the whole situation. Obviously she couldn't have been his first choice, since today was Monday and the prom was this Saturday, but to have been asked at all by him was a compliment. Brian

Dettlinger wasn't just any scabby senior scrambling for a date at the last minute, he was captain of the football team and went with the head cheerleader. He was a star.

"Ma è pazzo?" Audrey said when he'd gone. "Are you nuts? That was *Brian Dettlinger.*"

"What did you expect me to do? Go with him?"

"No—well—" Audrey shook her head, then tilted it backward, to look at Jenny appraisingly through spiky jet-black lashes. "You *have* changed, you know. It's almost scary. It's like you've blossomed, and everybody's noticed. Like a light went on inside you. Ever since—"

"We have to go to P.E.," Jenny said abruptly.

"I thought you wanted to cut."

"Not anymore." Jenny didn't want anything else to change. She wanted to be safe, the way she was before. She wanted to be a regular junior looking forward to summer vacation in a month or so. She wanted Tom.

"Come on," she said. For a moment, just as they left, dropping iced tea bottles in the metal trash can by the English block, she had the feeling that someone was watching her. She turned her head quickly, but she couldn't see anything there.

Tom watched her go.

He felt bad lurking there in the shadow of the English building, behind the scarred metal pillars that held the porch-like roof up. But he couldn't make himself come out.

He was going to lose her, and it was his own fault.

The thing was, he'd blown it already. He'd screwed up. The most important thing in his life—and he hadn't even realized it was the most important thing until seventeen days ago. April 22. The day of the Game. The day Julian came and took Jenny away.

Of course he'd *loved* Jenny. Loving was easy. But he'd never thought about what it might feel like without her, because he'd always known she'd be there. You don't sit around and think to yourself, "I wonder what it would feel like if the sun didn't come up tomorrow."

He'd assumed things, taken things for granted. He'd been lazy. That was what came of having everything handed to you on a platter. Of never having to prove yourself, of having people fawn on you because of your good looks and your hot car and your knuckleball. Of, essentially, being Tom Locke. You get to think you don't *need* anything.

Then you find out how wrong you are.

The problem was that just when he'd started to realize how much he needed Jenny Thornton, she'd discovered she didn't need him.

He'd *seen* her in that Other Place, inside that paper house that had turned real. She'd been so brave and so beautiful it made his throat hurt. She'd functioned absolutely perfectly without him.

It might still have been all right—except for Julian. The

Shadow Man. The guy with eyes the color of glacier pools, the guy that had kidnapped all of them because he wanted Jenny. Which had been an indisputably evil, but in Tom's view, completely understandable thing to do.

Jenny had changed since Julian had gotten to her. Maybe the others hadn't really noticed yet, but Tom had. She was different now, even more beautiful, and just—different. There were times when she sat with a faraway look as if she were listening to things no one else could hear. Listening to Julian's voice in her mind, maybe.

Because Julian had loved her. Julian had said it, had said all the things that Tom had never thought to mention. And Julian had the charm of the devil.

How could Jenny resist that? Especially being as innocent as she was. Jenny might actually think that she could change Julian, or that he wasn't as evil as he seemed. Tom knew differently, but what was the use of telling her? He'd seen them together, seen Julian's eyes when he looked at her. He'd seen the kind of spell Julian could cast. When Julian came for Jenny next time, Tom was going to lose.

So now all he could do was lurk in shadows, watching her. Noticing the way wisps of her hair blew over the rest of it, light as cornsilk and the color of honey in sunlight. Remembering her eyes, a dark green touched with gold. Everything about her was golden, even her skin. Funny he'd never bothered to tell her that. Maybe that was what Dettlinger had been doing just now. Tom wasn't surprised that the football star had come to talk with Jenny; he was just surprised at how fast he'd gone away. He wished he could have heard the conversation.

It didn't matter. It didn't matter how many guys approached Jenny. Tom was only worried about one—and that one had better watch out.

Tom couldn't have her anymore, but he could protect her. When Julian did come back—not *if*; Tom was virtually certain that he would—*when* Julian did come back for Jenny, and tried to play on her innocence again, Tom would be there to stop it. He didn't quite know how, but he *would* stop it.

Even if it killed him.

And if it made Jenny hate him, so be it. She'd thank him someday.

Moving quietly and purposefully, Tom followed the copper head and the golden one, stalking the girls to the gym.

It might have been his imagination, but he had the odd feeling that something else was stalking them, too.

They drove to the Center in two cars; Jenny and Audrey in Audrey's little red Alpha Spider, and Dee and Michael in Michael's VW Bug. Jenny braced herself as they walked inside.

No matter how she braced, the west wall was still a shock. It was covered with pictures of Summer.

Hundreds of them. Not just the flyers and posters. Summer's parents had brought in dozens of photographs, too, to show

Summer from different angles, or maybe just to remind people what all this efficiency and envelope-stuffing was really about. Somebody had gotten one of the pictures blown up into a monstrous billboard-like print, so that Summer's soft blond curls spanned five feet and Summer's wisteria blue eyes stared out at them like God's.

"Where's the Tomcat?" one of the volunteers asked Jenny. She was a college girl, and she always asked about Tom.

"I don't know," Jenny said briefly. The same question had been stabbing at her since lunch.

"If I were you, *I'd* know. What a hunk. I'd be keeping tabs on him. . . ." Jenny stopped listening. As usual, she wanted to get away from the Center as soon as possible. It was a warm, earnest, busy place, full of hope and good cheer—and it was a farce.

There was a sick feeling in Jenny's stomach as she turned to the large map on the wall. The map showed which areas had been postered and which hadn't. Jenny pretended to study it, even though she already knew where she had to go. If the Crying Girl had been P.C.'s friend, she might live near him.

She scarcely noticed as the Center door opened and one of the volunteers whispered, "It's that psychic who called. The one from Beverly Hills."

"Will you look at that Mercedes?" Michael said.

Jenny turned and saw a woman with frosted blond hair, who was decorated with ropes of expensive-looking gold chains. At the same moment the psychic turned and saw *her*—and gasped.

Her eyes got very large. She took several steps toward Jenny, until her Giorgio perfume overpowered Audrey's Chloé Narcisse. She stared into Jenny's face.

"You," she whispered, "have seen them. Those from the Other Side."

Jenny stood frozen. Lightning-struck.

"I have a message for you," the psychic said.

CHAPTER 4

What message?" Dee said, frowning.

The psychic was still staring at Jenny intently. "You've got the look," she said. "You've seen *them*—the faery folk."

Audrey said sharply, "The faery folk?" In the paper house Audrey's worst nightmare had been a fairy tale. A story about the Erlking, a spirit who haunted the Black Forest and stole children. The Elf-king. Julian had played the part to perfection, had even claimed to be the *real* Erlking.

The Shadow Men. The faery folk. Different names for different ages. Oh, God, Jenny thought, she knows the truth. I should be happy, she thought wildly. But there was a knot in her stomach.

The woman was answering Audrey. "The Elder Race. Some people have the gift of seeing them where everyone else only sees a wind in the grass, or a shadow, or a reflection of light."

Something about the woman's tone brought Jenny up short. The psychic sounded too—pleased—about the subject. Not scared enough. "What do they look like?"

The woman gave her a laughing glance. *As if you didn't know.* "They're the most beautiful things imaginable," she said. "Creatures of light and happiness. I frequently see them dancing at Malibu Creek." She held up one of her chains, and Jenny saw the charm, a beautiful young girl with gauzy wings and floating draperies.

"Pixies in bluebells," Dee said, absolutely straight-faced. Jenny's muscles went slack. This woman didn't know anything about the Shadow Men. Just another kook.

The psychic was still smiling. "The message is: *Vanished.* They told me to tell you that."

"Vanished? Oh," Jenny said. "Well, thank you." She supposed it was as good a message as any, considering Summer's situation.

"Vanished," the woman repeated. "At least—I *think* that was it. Sometimes I only get the vowel sounds. It might have been—" She hesitated, then shook her head and went back to her Mercedes.

"For a moment there I thought she had something," Audrey murmured.

Jenny grabbed a handful of flyers and a map. "Let's go."

Outside, they made their plans. "P.C.'s house is at thirteen-twenty-two Ramona Street," Jenny said. She knew this by heart. It was the first place they had checked, along with Slug's house. Of course, they hadn't been able to search directly, but one of the kinder detectives had let them know that there was no paper house in either of the boys' homes.

"Dee, you and Michael can start there and cover everything west over to, say, Anchor Street. Audrey and I can cover everything east over to where Landana turns into Sycamore. Remember, it's the girl we want now."

"In other words we're canvassing the entire south side of town," Michael said with a groan. "Door to door."

"Obviously we won't cover it all today," Jenny said. "But we'll keep at it until we do." She looked at Dee, who nodded slightly. Dee would keep Michael at it.

Audrey didn't look particularly happy, either. "We've been to a lot of those houses before. What are we supposed to say when they tell us they already have flyers?"

Dee grinned. "Tell them you're selling encyclopedias." She hustled Michael into the Bug.

Audrey shook her head as she and Jenny got back into the Spider and drove away. The top was down, and the wind blew stray wisps of copper-colored hair out of her chignon. Jenny shut her eyes, feeling the rushing air on her face.

She didn't want to think about anything, not about the

psychic, not about Zach, not about Tom. Especially not about Tom. Underneath she'd had some faint hope he might show up at the Center after school. He was avoiding her, that was it.

Her nose and eyes stung. She wanted him *with* her. If she thought any more about him, about his hazel eyes with their flecks of green, about his warmth and his strength and his easy devil-may-care smile, she was going to cry.

"Let's go over by Eastman and Montevideo," she heard herself saying. The words just came out of her mouth, from nowhere.

Audrey cast her a spiky-lashed glance but turned south.

Eastman Avenue, the scene of so many recent riots, was almost deserted. Jenny hadn't been there since the day of Tom's birthday, the day she'd walked there to buy a party game. As they approached Montevideo Avenue, everything Jenny had experienced the last time she'd been here—the blue twilight, the footsteps behind her, the fear—came back to her. She almost expected to see P.C. in his black vest and Slug in his flannels walking down the sidewalk.

Audrey turned the corner on Montevideo and stopped.

The mural on the blank wall still showed a street scene. In the middle of the mural was a realistic-looking store with a sign reading: More Games. But it was just paint and concrete. Flat. There was no handle sticking out of the door.

Behind that blank wall she'd met Julian, in a place that wasn't a real place after all.

Scraps of paper lay in the street. One was the bright yellow of Summer's flyer.

Jenny felt suddenly very hollow. She didn't know what she'd expected to find here, or even what had made her come.

Audrey shivered. "I don't like this place."

"No. It was a bad idea."

They drove north, backtracking. They were actually near Summer's house now, in the kind of neighborhood where cars tended to be slightly dented, on blocks, or in pieces in the side yard. The afternoon seemed brighter here, and on the sidewalks the usual kids with sun-bleached hair and freckled limbs or night-black hair and brown limbs were running around.

They parked the car by George Washington Elementary School and put the top up.

At every house the spiel was the same.

"Hi, we're from the Summer Parker-Pearson Citizen's Search Committee. Can we give you a flyer . . . ?"

If the people in the house looked nice, they tried to get invited in. Then came the transition from "We're looking for Summer" to "We're looking for an important clue in her disappearance"—meaning the paper house. And today, "We're looking for somebody who might know something about her"—meaning the Crying Girl with the long dark hair and haunted eyes.

Most of all, though, they tried to talk to kids.

Kids knew things. Kids saw things. Usually the adults in

the houses only listened politely, but the kids were always eager to help. They followed along on their bicycles, suggesting places to look, remembering that they thought they might have seen someone who could possibly have been Summer yesterday, or maybe it was the day before.

"The paper house is really important, but it could be dangerous. Anybody could have picked it up, thinking it was a toy," Jenny told one nine-year-old while Audrey kept his mother occupied. The nine-year-old nodded, his eyes bright and alert. Behind him, on a cracked leather sofa, a girl of four or five was sitting with a dog-eared book on her lap.

"That's Nori. She can't really read yet."

"I can, too." Tilting her face toward the book, although her eyes still remained on her brother, Nori said, "Then Little Red Riding-Hood says, 'Grandma, what big *eyes* you have.' Then the wolf says, 'The better to *see* you with, my dear.'"

Jenny smiled at her, then turned back to the boy. "So if you see it or the white box, don't touch it, but call the number on the flyer and leave a message for me."

". . . Grandma, what big *ears* you have. . . ."

"I'll know what you mean if you say, 'I've found it.'"

The boy nodded again. He understood about things like clues and secret messages.

". . . The better to *hear* you with, my dear. . . ."

"Or if one of your friends knows about a girl with dark hair that was good friends with P.C. Serrani—"

". . . Grandma, what big *teeth* you have. . . ."

Audrey was finished with the mother. Jenny gave the boy a quick touch on the shoulder and turned to the door.

"*. . . The better to EAT you with, my dear!*" Nori shrieked suddenly, bolting up on the couch. Jenny whirled—and dropped her flyers. Nori was standing, eyes wide, mouth pulled into a grimace. For an instant Jenny saw, not a child, but a small, misshapen goblin.

Then the mother cried, "Nori!" and Jenny was jerked back to reality. She felt herself turn red as she gathered the flyers.

Nori began to giggle. Jenny apologized. The mother scolded. Finally they got out of the house.

"I am *never* going to have children," Audrey said, outside.

They kept going. Some people were friendly, others were rude. A shirtless man laughed unkindly when they started the spiel about Summer and rasped, "Did you check the mall?" Almost all of them already had heard about the missing girl.

Dinnertime came and went. They called their parents to say they'd be out for a little longer, while it was still light.

Jenny glanced sideways at Audrey, a little surprised. Audrey wasn't the suffering-in-silence type. Jenny had expected to have to cajole her to stay out this long.

There was a lot more to Audrey than her glamour-magazine exterior let on.

They came to a street where a lot of kids were playing. Jenny recognized the white-blond head of the one covering his eyes against a tree. It was Summer's ten-year-old brother.

"Cam!" she said, startled. He didn't hear her. He went on counting, leaning on his folded arms. Other kids were scattering, hiding in open garages, behind bushes, in ivy. Jenny recognized two more of them. One was Dee's little sister, Kiah, the other was her own younger brother, Joey.

They came to play with Cam after dinner, she realized. It was a long way for Kiah, even on a bike.

"What are they playing?" Audrey asked.

"It looks like cops and robbers." At Audrey's blank expression Jenny remembered. Audrey had grown up in every place but America; her father was with the diplomatic corps. If he hadn't retired early, she wouldn't be in California now.

"It's a chase game. You capture the robbers and take them back to your home base as prisoners. Hey, watch out!" Jenny caught a small figure that had erupted out of the nearby ivy, tripped, and gone flying. It was Kiah, and Cam was close on her heels.

Kiah looked up. She was never going to be tall like Dee, but she had Dee's fine bones and wild, leaping beauty. Cam had hair like dandelion fluff, even lighter than Summer's. It made him look oddly defenseless, although Jenny knew he was a tough kid.

Unlike Summer, who hadn't had a tough sinew in her, Jenny thought. Summer had been as fragile as spun glass.

Ever since the night of the Game, Jenny's emotions had

been like boats bumping at a thick canvas barrier—cut off from her but still nudging. But suddenly, at the sight of Cam, they burst through. Grief for Summer. Guilt. Tears filled her eyes.

What on earth could she say to him? "I'm sorry" was so inadequate it was pathetic.

Other kids were coming out of hiding at the sight of Audrey and Jenny, gathering around curiously. Jenny still couldn't speak. Audrey came to the rescue, improvising.

"So what are you playing?"

"Lambs and monsters," Cam said. "I'm the monster."

"Oh. So how do you play it?"

Kiah spoke up. "If you're a lamb you hide, and then the monster comes looking for you. And if he tags you, then you're captured and you have to go back to the monster lair. And you have to stay there until another lamb comes and lets you out—"

"Or until the monster eats you," Cam put in harshly.

Kiah's eyes flashed. "But he *can't* eat you until he's got all the lambs there. Ev-er-y sin-gle one."

Cops and robbers, Jenny thought. With only one cop and lots of robbers. The new name seemed a little savage, though, and so did the look in Cam-the-monster's eyes. God, I wonder what it must be like for him at home, she thought.

"Cam," she said. His hard blue eyes fixed on her. "Cam, did your parents tell you what we said happened to Summer?"

He nodded tightly.

"Well—" Jenny had a feeling that Aba might not approve of what she was going to do next. But all these kids knew Cam, they cared. Jenny felt more of a connection here than she had anywhere else.

"Well—I know it sounds crazy. I know your mom and dad don't believe it. But, Cam, it was the *truth*. We didn't hurt Summer, and we didn't mean to let anybody else hurt her. You just don't know how sorry—" The tears spilled suddenly, embarrassingly. Cam looked away and Jenny tried to get a grip on herself.

"And what we're doing now is trying to stop the person who hurt her from hurting anybody else," she whispered, feeling stupidly like somebody on TV—"America's Most Wanted."

Joey had joined the group and was flushed to his yellow hair roots with the humiliation of having a teenage sister bawling on the sidewalk. But Cam's tight look eased slightly.

"You mean all that stuff kids are saying about you guys looking for a cardboard house is true?"

"Are they saying that? Good." It's working, Jenny thought. The junior grapevine. There was something heartening in these kids' expressions. They weren't closed off like adults, but open, interested, speculative. "Listen," she said. "We're still looking for that house, and now we're looking for something else. A girl who was friends with P.C. Serrani." For the hundredth time that day she described the Crying Girl.

The kids listened.

"We really, really want to talk to her," Jenny said.

Then she explained why. Why they needed the girl and why they needed the house. She explained, more or less, about Julian. A watered-down version, but the truth.

When she finished, she let out a long breath—and saw something like determination coalescing in the steady young gazes. They'd weighed her claims, and they were willing to give her the benefit of the doubt. Even Joey, who'd been running away from her for the last two weeks, looked halfway convinced.

"We'll look for the girl tomorrow," he said briefly. "We'll talk to kids who've got, like, brothers or sisters in junior high. Because they might know her."

"Exactly!" Jenny said, pleased. She spared him the humiliation of being kissed by his sister in public. "Just be careful. If you see the paper house, *do not* touch it."

The last traces of doubt were wiped from the young faces, and there were grim nods. Her urgency had gotten through. She felt as if she'd recruited a team of small private detectives.

"Thanks," she said, and, feeling it was time for a judicious retreat, she gestured Audrey toward the next house.

"One more game," somebody behind her said, and somebody else said, "But who's going to be It?"

"Cam, unless he can guess who puts the eye in," Kiah's sweet voice fluted. On the doorstep Jenny glanced toward the street.

Cam was turned around, undergoing some elaborate ritual for picking the next It. "I draw a snake upon your back," Kiah chanted, tracing a wiggly shape. "Who will put in the eye?"

Somebody lunged forward and poked Cam between the shoulder blades. "Courtney!" Cam shouted.

"Wrong! You're the monster again!"

The door opened to Audrey's knocking. "Yes?"

Jenny tried to tear her attention from the game. Something about it . . . and about that snake thing . . . were all children's games that gruesome? And their stories? *The better to eat you with, my dear. . . .*

Maybe kids know something adults don't know, Jenny thought, chilled, as a lady asked them into the house.

When they came out, the sky was periwinkle blue and losing its color to the east. The light was fading. The street was empty.

Good, Jenny thought, glad that Joey was on his way home—maybe even home by now.

"Want to finish this block?" Audrey said, surprising her.

"I—sure. Why not?"

They worked their way down one side of the street and up the other. Jenny could feel herself getting more and more perfunctory at each house. The sky was now midnight blue and the light had gone. She didn't know why, but she was starting to feel anxious.

"Let's stop here," she said when there were still three more houses to go. "I think we should be getting back now."

The midnight blue slowly turned to black. The streetlights seemed far apart, and Jenny was reminded suddenly of the little islands of light in Zach's nightmare. A nightmare where a hunter had chased them through endless darkness.

"Hey, wait up!" Audrey protested.

Jenny grabbed her arm. "No, you hurry up. Come on, Audrey, we have to get back to the car."

"What do you mean? What's wrong with you?

"I don't know. We just have to get back!" A primitive warning was going off in Jenny's brain. A warning from the time when girls took skin bags to get water, she thought wildly, remembering something she'd sensed with Julian. A time when panthers walked in the darkness outside mud huts. When darkness was the greatest danger of all.

"Jenny, this is just so totally unlike you! If there was anything to be scared about, *I'd* be scared of it," Audrey said, resisting as Jenny dragged her along. "You're the one who always used to go off into the bad parts of town—"

"Yes, and look where it got me!" Jenny said. Her heart was pounding, her breath coming fast. "Come on!"

"—and I hate to tell you, but I *can't* run in these shoes. They've been killing me for hours now."

The flickering streetlight showed Audrey's tight Italian

pumps. "Oh, Audrey, why didn't you say something?" Jenny said in dismay. Something made her jerk her head around, looking behind her. Something rustled in the oleanders.

Where everyone else only sees a wind in the grass, or a shadow . . .

"Audrey, take your shoes off. Now!"

"I can't run barefoot—"

"Audrey, there is something behind us. We have to get out of here, fast. Now, *come on!*" She was pulling Audrey again almost before Audrey had gotten the pumps off. Walking as fast as she could without running. If you run, they chase you, she thought wildly. But she wanted to run.

Because there *was* something back there. She could hear the tiny sounds. It was tracking them, behind the hedge of overgrown bushes on her right. She could feel it watching them.

Maybe it's Cam or one of the other kids, she thought, but she knew it wasn't. Whatever it was, she knew in her heart that it wanted to hurt them.

It was moving quickly, lightly, keeping pace with them maybe twenty feet back. "Audrey, hurry. . . ."

Instead, Audrey stopped dead. Jenny could just make out her look of fear as she stood, listening.

"Oh, God, there *is* something!"

The rustling was closer.

We should have run for a house, Jenny realized. Her one thought had been to get to the car. But now they had passed the last houses before the school grounds, and Audrey's car was too far ahead. They weren't going to make it.

"Come on!" Don't run don't run don't run, the hammering inside Jenny said. But her feet, clammy in their summery mesh loafers, wanted to pound down the sidewalk.

It was gaining on them.

It can't be a person—a person would show above those hedges, Jenny thought, casting a look behind her. Suddenly Jenny's brain showed her a terrible picture: little Nori scurrying along spiderlike behind the bushes, her face contorted in a grimace.

Don't run don't run don't run . . .

The car was ahead, looking black instead of red in the darkness beyond a streetlight. Jenny seemed to hear eerily rapid breath behind her.

Dontrundontrundontrundontrun . . .

"Get the keys," she gasped. "Get the *keys*, Audrey—"

Here was the car. But the rustling was right beside Jenny now, just on the other side of the hedge. It was going to come *through* the hedge, she thought. Right *through* the hedge and grab her. . . .

Audrey was fumbling in her purse. She'd dropped her shoes. Jenny grabbed the car door handle.

"Audrey!" she cried, rattling it.

Audrey flung the contents of her purse on the sidewalk. She scattered the pile with a desperate hand, seized the keys.

"Audrey! Get it open!" Jenny watched in agony as Audrey ran to the driver's side of the car, leaving the contents of her purse scattered.

But it was too late. There was a crashing in the hedge directly behind Jenny.

At the same moment a dark shape reared up from the shadows on the sidewalk in front of her.

CHAPTER 5

Jenny screamed.

Or got out half a scream anyway. The rest was cut off as something knocked her to the ground. It was the dark figure in front of her, and it was shouting something.

"Jenny, get down!"

Her brain only made sense of the words after she *was* down. There was a dull crashing and a thudding-and-rushing that might have been the blood in her ears. Then the crashing stopped.

"Wait, stay down until I see if it's gone," Tom's voice said. Jenny got up anyway, looking at him in amazement. What are you doing here? she thought. But what she said was "Did you see it?"

"No, I was looking at you. I *heard* it and then I—"

"—knocked me down," Jenny said. "Did you see it, Audrey?"

"Me? I was trying to get my door open, and then I was trying to get *your* door open. I heard it go by, but when I looked it was gone."

"I don't think it went *by*," Tom said. "I think it went *over*—it ran over the hood of your car."

"It couldn't have," said Jenny. "A person wouldn't—" She stopped. Once again a horrible image of Nori, scampering spiderlike, entered her mind.

"I don't think it was a person," Tom began in a low voice. "I think—"

"Look!" Audrey said. "Down there past that streetlight—some kind of animal—" Her voice was high with fear.

"Turn on your headlights," Tom said.

A wedge of white light pierced the darkness. The animal was caught squarely in the beams, eyes reflecting green.

It was a dog.

Some sort of Lab mix, Jenny guessed. Black enough to blend into the night—or the hedges. It stared at them curiously, then its tail gave a quick, uncertain wag.

Rustlings in the bushes, Jenny thought. That tail wagging! And the quick, panting breath.

"Dog breath," she gasped aloud, almost hysterically. After the tension, the relief was acutely painful.

Audrey leaned her auburn head against the steering wheel.

"And for that I lost my shoes?" she demanded, sitting up and glaring at Jenny, who was hiccuping weakly.

"We'll go back and get them. I'm sorry. Honestly. But I'm glad *you're* here, anyway," Jenny said to Tom.

He was looking at the dog. "I don't think—" he began again. Then he shook his head and turned to her. "I didn't mean to hurt you."

"Didn't you?" Jenny said, not meaning the knocking-down. She looked up into his face.

He ducked away to help Audrey pick up her scattered belongings from the sidewalk. They could only find one shoe.

"Oh, leave it," Audrey said in disgust. "I don't care any-more. I only want to get home and soak for about an hour."

"You go on. Tom can take me home," Jenny said. Tom looked at her, seeming startled. "You do have your car, don't you? Or did you walk?"

"My car's down the street. But—"

"Then you can take me," Jenny said flatly. Audrey raised her eyebrows, then got in her car and drove away with a "Ciao" settling the matter.

Tom and Jenny walked slowly to Tom's RX-7. Once inside, though, Tom didn't start the engine. They just sat.

"Well, you've made yourself pretty scarce today," Jenny said. "While the rest of us were working." That hadn't come out right. She was upset, that was the problem.

Tom was fiddling with the radio, getting static. "I'm sorry, Jenny," he said. "I had things to do."

Where was his smile—that rakish, conspiratorial, sideways grin? He was treating her politely, like *anybody*.

Worse, he was calling her Jenny. When he was happy, he called her Thorny or some other silly name.

"Tom, what the *hell* is going on?"

"Nothing."

"What are you talking about, *nothing*? Tom, look at me! You've been avoiding me all day. What am I supposed to think? What's *happening*?"

Tom just shook his head slightly.

"You really have been avoiding me. On purpose." Jenny hadn't quite believed it herself until she put it into words. "Not just today, either. It's been ever since—" She stopped. "Tom. It's not—it hasn't got anything to do with—" She couldn't make herself say it; it was too ridiculous. But what other explanation was there?

"It hasn't got anything to do with what happened in the Game, has it? With—*him*?"

She could tell from the silence that she was right.

"Are you crazy?" Jenny said in a sort of quiet explosion.

"Let's just not talk about it."

"Let's just not talk about it?" Somewhere inside Jenny hysteria was building up, ready to be released.

"Look, I know the score. Maybe better than you do." In

the faint light from the instrument panel, she could see that his mouth was grim.

Jenny got hold of herself and said carefully, "Tom, I am your girlfriend. I love you. We've always been together. And now suddenly you've changed completely, and you're acting like—like—"

"I'm not the one who's changed," he said. Then, turning fully toward her, he said, "Can you look at me and tell me you don't think about him?"

Jenny was speechless.

"Can you honestly tell me that? That you don't think about him, *ever?*"

"Only to be scared of him," Jenny whispered, her throat dry. She had a terrible feeling, as if earthquakes and tidal waves were ahead of her.

"I saw you with him—I saw you looking at each other."

Oh, *God,* Jenny thought. Her mind was filled with panicked images. Julian's fingers in her hair, light as the soft pat of a cat's paw. Julian tilting her face up, Jenny flowing toward him. Julian supporting her weight, kissing the back of her neck. . . .

But Tom hadn't seen all that. He had only seen her and Julian together at the end, when Jenny's thoughts had been on getting her friends out of the paper house.

"I was trying to save us all," she said, safely on high moral ground. "You know that."

"And that means you didn't feel anything at all for him?"

Lie, Jenny thought. There was no reason she should have to lie. She *didn't* feel anything for Julian. But she was so confused—so frightened and confused—she didn't know what was going on anymore. *"No,"* she said.

"I know you, Jenny—I know when something gets to you. I saw you—respond to him. He brings out another side to you, makes you different."

"Tom—"

"And I saw what he can do, everything he can do. He's superhuman. How can I compete with that?"

And there, Jenny thought, clarity returning, was the problem. If Tom Locke the Flawless had a flaw, this was it. He was used to always winning, and winning easily. Tom didn't *do* anything he couldn't do right the first time. He wouldn't try if he thought he was going to fail.

"Besides, you don't need me anymore."

Oh. So that was what he thought.

Jenny shut her eyes.

"You're wrong," she whispered. "I needed you all day today. And you weren't there. . . ."

"Hey—oh, Jenny, don't cry. Hey, Jen." His voice had changed. He put a hand on her shoulder, then an arm around her. He did it awkwardly, as if it were the first time.

Jenny couldn't stop the tears.

"Don't cry. I didn't mean to make you cry." He leaned over to grip her other shoulder with his other hand.

Jenny opened wet eyes.

He was looking into her face, and he was so close. The grim expression was gone, and in its place was concern—and love. Anguished love. In that instant Jenny saw beneath the smooth, polished exterior of Tom Locke's defenses.

"Tommy . . ." she whispered, and her hand found his, their fingers locking together.

Then one or the other of them made a movement—Jenny never could remember which—and she was in his arms. They were holding on to each other desperately.

Relief flooded Jenny, and she gave a little sob. It felt so good to have Tom holding her again. In a moment he would kiss her, and everything would be all right.

But then—something happened. The RX-7's interior was small, like an airplane cockpit, and the center console curved out. Tom pulled back a bit in order to kiss her, and his hand or elbow knocked into the radio buttons. It must have, because suddenly music spilled into the car.

It was a song Jenny's mother sometimes played, an oldie by Dan Fogelberg. She had never really noticed the words before, but now they rang out clearly through the car.

"*. . . Like the songs that the darkness composes to worship the light. . . .*"

Jenny recoiled, heart jolting.

God, who had thought of that? Who had ever thought of that? What did some seventies songwriter know about darkness worshiping light?

She was staring at the radio, transfixed. Out of the corner of her eye she saw Tom staring at *her*.

Jenny reached out and jabbed at the radio, and the car was plunged into silence.

She had to say something—but her mind was blank. All she could hear was the echo of Julian's voice saying, *"I want her for . . . light to my darkness. You'll see—Tommy."*

The silence became terrible.

"I'd better get you home," Tom said in a voice as empty and polite as he had started with. "It's late."

"It was just a song," Jenny burst out, but she knew the song wasn't the problem. The problem was her reaction.

"You've changed, Jenny."

"I'm so tired of hearing that!" Jenny got her breath and added, "If I've changed so much, maybe you don't want me anymore. Maybe we should break up."

She had said it to shock. Stunned, she realized he wasn't going to contradict her.

"Better get you home," he said again.

Jenny desperately wanted to take the words back, but it was too late. It was too late for anything, and her pride wouldn't let her cry or speak. She sat frozen as they drove to her house. Tom walked her in.

Jenny's mother was standing on the threshold of the living room.

"And just where have you been?" she demanded. She had dark golden hair and a quick temper.

"It's my fault, Mrs. Thornton," Tom said.

"It is *not* his fault. I'm responsible for myself," Jenny said.

"As long as you're home," Mrs. Thornton said, with a sigh. Her temper, like Jenny's, flared quickly and died more quickly. "Are you hungry? Have you had dinner, Tom?"

Tom shook his dark head. "I'd better be getting home," he said, avoiding Jenny's eyes.

"Yes, you had," Mr. Thornton said softly but pointedly from his armchair. Jenny's father was a small man, but he had a sardonic eye that could kill from across the room. "I'm sure *your* parents are expecting you. And next time, be back before dark."

As the door closed behind him, Jenny said with reckless energy, "There probably won't be a next time."

Her mother was startled. "Jenny?"

Jenny turned toward the kitchen, but not before she saw her parents exchange glances. Her father shook his head, then went back to *Time* magazine.

Her mother followed her into the kitchen.

"Dear one—you *can't* be upset because we want you home early. We're just trying to keep you and Joey safe."

"It isn't that." Jenny was struggling with tears. "It's just—I think Tom and I are going to break up."

Her mother stared. "Oh, sweetheart!"

"Yes. And I just don't know—oh, Mom, everything's changing!" Abruptly Jenny threw herself into her mother's arms.

"Things do change, sweetheart. You're at the age when everything starts happening. I know how scary it can be, and I'm sorry about Tom—"

Jenny shook her head mutely. She and her mom had talked about growing up before. Jenny had always felt secretly a little smug at how well she was handling it all. She'd had it all planned out: high school with Tom, and then college with Tom, and then, in some comfortably fuzzy future, marriage to Tom, and an interesting career, and a world tour. After the tour, babies. Boy and girl, like that.

She'd already conquered growing up: she knew exactly what it was going to be like.

Not anymore. Her cozy future was crumbling around her.

She drew away from her mother.

"Jenny . . . Jenny, there isn't anything you're not telling us—say, about Zach? Because Aunt Lily is really worried. She says he's been acting so different. . . . He even seems to have lost interest in his photography. . . ."

Jenny could feel herself stiffen. "What kind of anything?" she said.

"Of course, we know Zach didn't—didn't hurt Summer in any way. But he wasn't the one who made up this story, was he? And you all believed it because you care about him."

It was phrased as a theory, and Jenny was horrified.

"*No,*" she said. "First of all, nobody made up the story." Although Mrs. Thornton continued to face her, Jenny noticed that her mother's golden-brown eyes went shades darker at that, and seemed to wall over. It was how all the parents looked when the kids talked about the reality of what had happened that night. They were listening, but they weren't listening. They believed you because you were their kid, but they *couldn't* believe you. So they ended up staring at you like polite zombies and making excuses behind their eyes.

"Nobody made the story up," Jenny repeated tiredly, already defeated. "Look—I'm really not hungry."

She escaped to the family room, where Joey was playing a video game—but it wasn't escape. The phone rang.

She reached for it automatically. "Hello?"

Shhshhshhshhshhshhshhshhshhshh.

Chills swept over Jenny.

The white noise went on, but over it there was a whispering. "*A . . . ishhshhshht . . .*"

"Joey, turn the TV down!"

The breathy whisper came again, and Jenny heard the psychic's voice in her mind. *Vanished . . .*

"*Van-ishhshhshhed,*" the voice whispered.

Jenny clutched the phone, straining to hear. "Who is this?" She was suddenly angry rather than afraid. She had visions of the frosted-blond psychic on the other end. But the voice seemed like a man's, and it had a distorted quality to it that went beyond foreign. The word *sounded* like *vanished,* but . . .

The phone clicked, then there was a dial tone.

"What's wrong?" her mother said, coming in. "Did someone call?"

"Didn't you hear it ring?"

"I can't hear anything over that TV. Jenny, what is it? You're so pale."

"Nothing." She didn't want to talk about it with her mother. She couldn't stand any more questions—or any more weird stuff—or any more *anything.*

"I'm really tired," she said and headed for the back of the house before her mother could stop her.

In the privacy of her own room, she flopped on the bed. It was a pleasant room, and normally its familiarity would have comforted her. Michael always said it looked like a garden because of the Ralph Lauren comforter in rose and poppy and gold and dusty blue, and the baskets on the dresser twined with silk flowers. On the windowsill were pots of petunias and alyssum.

Just now it made Jenny feel—*alien.* As if she didn't belong to its familiarity any longer.

She lay listening to the house. She heard the distant sounds of the family room TV cut short, and presently heard splashing noises in the bathroom. Joey going to bed. Voices in the hall, and a door shutting. Her parents going to bed. After that, everything was quiet.

Jenny lay there a long time. She couldn't relax for sleep; she had to do something to express the strangeness she felt inside. She wanted—she wanted—

She wanted to do something ritual and—well, *purifying*. By herself.

Then she had it. She went to the door and cautiously turned the knob. She stepped into the darkened hallway, listening. Silence. Everyone was asleep; the house had that hushed middle-of-the-night feeling.

Quietly Jenny opened the linen closet and fished out a towel. Still careful not to make the slightest sound, she unlocked the family room sliding glass door and eased it open.

A three-quarter moon was rising over the foothills. Jenny glanced toward her parents' room, but their Venetian blinds were dark, and a row of tall oleander bushes blocked their view of the pool. No one would see her.

She made her way stealthily to a block-wall alcove, where she turned a switch. The pool light went on.

Magic. It transformed a dark ominous void into a fluorescent blue-green jewel.

Jenny sighed.

Keeping well behind the screening row of bushes, she stripped her clothes off. Then she knelt by the lip of the pool, sat on it, easing her legs into the water. She could feel the porous concrete deck on the backs of her thighs and the cool water on her calves. She looked at her feet, pale green and magnified in the glowing water. With a careful twist and a slide, she dropped in.

A slight shock of coolness. Jenny boosted off the side of the pool with her feet and floated on her back, spreading her arms. The smell of chlorine filled her nostrils.

The moon was pure silver in the sky and very far away. Right now Jenny felt as distant from ordinary emotions.

So what do you do, she thought, floating, when you've sold your soul to the devil?

That was about the size of it. She had let Julian put his ring on her finger. A gold ring with an inscription on the inside: *All I refuse and thee I chuse.*

Magical words, inscribed on the *inside* of the ring so they would rest against her skin and bind her to the promise.

When they'd gotten back from the Shadow World, Jenny had put the ring in the white box, the one with the paper house, the one P.C. and Slug had stolen. Now she wished she had it back. She should have had it melted down or hammered flat.

The water slipped pleasantly between her fingertips. It cradled her whole body, touching all her skin. It was a very—sensual—feeling, to be embraced like this, to stroke out in any direction and feel the coolness flow past you.

Jenny—felt things—more these days.

She'd discovered it that first week after getting back. She'd realized, to her bewilderment and somewhat to her horror, that she found things more beautiful than before. The night air was more fragrant than it used to be, her cat's fur was smoother. She noticed little things—tiny, delicate details she had never seen before.

Something about her time with Julian had—opened her to things. To their sensuality, their *immediacy*. Maybe that was what people were noticing when they said she had changed.

Or maybe she'd always been different. Because she'd been chosen. Julian had chosen her, had fallen in love with her, had begun to watch her, when she was five years old.

Because when she was five she had opened a secret closet in her grandfather's basement, a closet carved with the symbol Nauthiz, a rune of restraint.

It had been a natural thing to do. Let a kid alone in a cellar where a bookcase has been moved to expose a secret door, and what would anyone expect? What would be the harm?

It depended. If your grandfather was like any grandfather, a sweet old guy who liked gardening and golf, no harm. But if your grandfather was a dabbler in the black arts, it might be another story. And if your grandfather had actually succeeded in his ambition to call up spirits from another world, to trap them . . . and if the door you opened was the one that held them in . . .

The consequences had been unimaginable.

Jenny had opened that door and seen a whirling, seething mixture of ice and shadows. And in the shadows—eyes.

Dark eyes, watching eyes, sardonic, cruel, amused eyes. Ancient eyes. The eyes of the Others, the Shadow Men.

They were called different names in different ages, but

319

always their essential nature came through. They were the ones who watched from the shadows. Who sometimes took people to—their own place.

The thing Jenny remembered most about the eyes was that they were hungry. Evil, powerful, and *ravenous.*

"They'd love to get a tooth in you," Julian had told Dee. *"All my elders, those ancient, bone-sucking, lip-licking wraiths."*

Suddenly the water seemed more cold than cool. Jenny swam over to the steps and got out, shivering.

In her room she rubbed herself dry until she stopped shivering. Then she put on a T-shirt and crawled into bed. But the vision of glowing eyes haunted her until she fell asleep from sheer exhaustion.

She woke up very suddenly when the phone rang.

The alarm, she thought, confused, and reached for the clock by her bedside. But the ringing went on.

Her window was dark. The clock in her hand showed a glowing red 3:35 A.M.

The ringing went on, frighteningly loud, like a siren.

Her parents would pick it up any minute now. But they didn't. Jenny waited. The ringing went on.

They *had* to pick it up. Not even Joey slept that soundly. Each burst of noise was like white lightning in the dark and silent house.

Chills ran over Jenny's skin.

She found that she had been counting unconsciously. Nine rings. Ten. Eleven. Twelve. Shattering the stillness.

Maybe it was Dee, maybe she and Michael had found out something important and for some reason hadn't been able to call until now.

Heart pounding, Jenny picked up the receiver.

"A isht," a voice whispered.

Jenny froze.

"A . . . isht . . ."

The formless electronic noise blurred the word. Jenny could only make out the vowel sounds and the soft shush at the end. *A* as in *amble,* then *shht.* It didn't sound exactly like *vanished* anymore.

She wanted to speak, but she couldn't. She could only clutch the phone and listen.

"A isht . . ."

Damaged? No, that was even farther off. A-isht. Am-ish. Amished.

Oh my *God.* Oh God oh God oh God . . .

Sheer black terror swept through her, and every hair on her body erected. She felt her eyes go wide and tears spring to them. In that instant she heard, really heard what the voice was saying. She *knew.*

Not *vanished.* It sounded like *vanished,* but it wasn't. It was something much worse. The whispery, distorted voice with the odd cadence was saying *famished.*

Famished.

Jenny threw the phone as hard as she could across the room. She was on her feet, her skin crawling, body washed with adrenaline. *Famished. Famished.* The eyes in the closet. The Shadow Men.

Those evil, *ravenous* eyes . . .

The better to *eat* you with, my dear.

CHAPTER 6

It was that psychic," Dee said promptly. "She looked like a case of peroxide on the brain to me."

"No," said Michael. "You know what it really is?" Jenny thought he was going to make a joke, but for once he was serious. "It's battle fatigue. We've all got it. We're stressed to the max, and we're seeing—and hearing—things that aren't there."

It was the next day. They were all sitting on the grassy knoll—all but Tom, of course. Jenny was surprised that Zach had shown up. After what she'd said to him at lunch yesterday, she'd have thought he'd have withdrawn from them all. But he was in his place, long legs folded under him, ashyblond head bent over his lunch.

Jenny herself had no appetite. "The calls weren't hallucinations," she said. It was all she could do to keep her voice steady. "Okay, the last one might have been a dream—I woke up my parents screaming, and they said *they* didn't hear the phone ring. But the other times—I was walking around, Michael. I was awake."

"No, no, I'm not saying the phone calls aren't real. I'm saying the phone rang, and maybe somebody even whispered something at you—or maybe it was just static—but you imagined what it was saying. You put your own interpretation on the sounds. You didn't hear *vanished* until the psychic said *vanished,* right?"

"Yes," Jenny said slowly. In the bright May sunshine, the terror of last night seemed less real. "But—it wasn't like imagining it. I *heard* the sounds the first time when the phone rang at school, and in the end they came clear. And the word made sense. Not *vanished,* but *famished*—it fit in with those eyes."

"But that's just why you imagined it." Michael was waving a box of Cracker Jack, warming to his subject. "Maybe *imagined* isn't the right word. See, your brain is like a modeling system. It takes the input it gets from your senses and makes the most reasonable model it can from it. But when you're really stressed, it can take that input—like somebody whispering nonsense on the phone—and make the *wrong* model out of it. Your brain hears something that isn't there. It seems real because it *is* real—to your brain."

Dee was frowning, clearly not liking the idea of not relying on her brain. "Yes, but it *isn't* real."

"It's as real as any of the other models your brain makes all day. Like—last night I was doing homework in my living room, and my brain made a model of a coffee table. That's what it thought of the images my eyes were showing it. It took *wood* and *rectangular* and matched that with *coffee table,* and I recognized it. But if I was really stressed, I might see *wood* and *rectangular,* and my brain might make a model of a coffin. Especially if I'd been asleep or if I was already thinking about coffins. See?"

Jenny did, sort of.

"But the coffin still wouldn't be *real,*" Dee argued.

"But how could I tell?

"Easy. You could touch it—"

"Touching's just another sense. It could be fooled, too. No, if a model's good enough, there would be *no way* to tell it wasn't real," Michael said.

It made sense, Jenny thought. It was like the dog yesterday evening. She'd been jumping at shadows because she was so frightened.

She sat back on the grassy knoll and let out a deep breath. The knot in her stomach had eased slightly—and now she could worry about other things.

Like Tom. As long as he wasn't there, things wouldn't be right.

The others were talking around her.

"—we covered about half the streets yesterday," Dee was saying, "but we didn't find anything—"

"I found blisters," Michael put in.

"And if I keep missing my kung fu classes I'm not going to *live* through the next competition," Dee finished.

"You think you've got problems? *I* found scratches all over the hood of the Spider this morning," Audrey said. "Daddy's going to kill me when he sees it." She told the story of the dog that had followed them. Michael spilled his Cracker Jack in triumph.

"You see? More modeling," he said. But Audrey pushed down her designer sunglasses with one finger to stare over them.

"Jenny?" she said. "What's wrong?"

They were all looking at her.

Jenny could feel her lips tremble slightly, but she tried to sound off-hand. "It's just—Tom and I had a fight. And we sort of . . ." She shrugged. "Well, I don't know if we're together anymore or not."

They all stared as if she'd said the world was ending in a few minutes.

Then Michael whistled and ran his hands through his hair, rumpling it even more wildly. Dee, who normally scorned anything to do with romance, put a slender, night-dark hand on Jenny's arm. Audrey's eyebrows were hiked up into her spiky copper bangs. Zach shook his head, a distant flicker of ice in his winter-gray eyes.

Audrey was the first to recover. "Don't worry, *chéri*," she said, taking the sunglasses off and snapping them into a case briskly. "It's not permanent. Tom just needs some stirring up. Guys need to be reminded of their place every so often," she added with a severe glance at Michael, who spluttered.

"No. It wasn't a regular fight. It was about *him*—Julian. He thinks I belong to Julian or something, like one of those horrible old movies. Bride of the Devil. He thinks he's lost me already, so why compete?" She told them about it as best she could.

Audrey listened, her narrowed eyes turned in the direction of the English building. Suddenly her lips curved in a catlike smile. "Clearly, drastic measures are called for. And I have an idea," she said.

"What idea?"

Audrey nodded toward the building. Taped to the brick was a large poster reading: Come to the Midnight Masquerade. *"Voilà."*

"Voilà?" Jenny said blankly.

"The prom. Brian Dettlinger. Yesterday. Remember?"

"Yes, but—"

"You said Tom thinks he can't compete with a demon lover. But maybe if he sees he's got *human* competition, he'll get a little more motivated."

Jenny stared at her. It was crazy—and it just might work. "But I told Brian no. He'll have another date by now."

"I don't *think* so," Audrey hummed. "I got the dirt from Amy Cheng yesterday in algebra. Brian dumped Karen Lalonde to ask you."

Jenny blinked. Karen Lalonde was the head cheerleader. Beautiful. Brilliant. Magnetic. "He dumped her—for me?"

"They've been on the rocks for a while. Karen's been seeing Davoud Changizi on the side. But Brian put up with it until now."

"But—"

"Listen to me, Jenny. After what Tom's done, who can blame you for looking elsewhere? Besides, you'll probably have a great time—it's *Brian Dettlinger,* for heaven's sake. I tell you what; I'll even go with you. I know I can rustle up a date somewhere."

Michael yowled in protest. *"What?"*

"Now, Michael, don't fuss. I'm not going for *fun*; it's like Mother's charities—all for a good cause. Don't you want Jenny and Tom to get back together?"

Michael was spluttering again. But Dee was grinning her wildest grin. "Go on, Sunshine," she said. "Make it happen."

Zach crumpled his lunch sack, looking bored with the whole situation.

"Now, come on," Audrey said. "If we hurry, we should be able to find him before the bell rings. *Allez!* This will be easy."

It was. Brian looked surprised when Jenny walked up—

but a light went on in his eyes. Seeing that light, Jenny suddenly knew that he hadn't found another date.

It was odd having a senior look at her like that. Suddenly Jenny wondered again if it was fair to do this. She thought about Aba's maxims, the ones Dee's grandmother had taped to the mirror in her bathroom. A simple hand-lettered sign saying:

> Do no harm.
> Help when you can.
> Return good for evil.

In the Game Jenny had understood how necessary those maxims were if the world wasn't going to become the kind of place Julian said it was. She'd resolved to live by them. This didn't seem to fit.

But it was too late now. Audrey was talking with Brian, teasing him, letting him know what Jenny was there for. It was all being arranged.

"I'll pick you up at seven," Brian was saying, and there was something like excitement in his face. He was looking at her eyes, at her hair across her shoulders. She could hardly tell him she'd changed her mind now.

"Fine," Jenny said weakly and let Audrey lead her away.

What have I done? I don't even have a dress—

The bell rang.

* * *

Jenny, Michael, and Audrey had algebra together, then Jenny went to computer applications. That was where Michael's theory about brain modeling was put to the test.

It started with the keyboard fouling up. Jenny's partner was absent, so she was alone at her computer, a glacier-slow IBM clone.

She was typing in her name when the *J* key stuck. She'd barely touched it with her right index finger, but the *J*s went on and on across the line. They got to the right margin and went on, got to the edge of the screen and went on.

The screen scanned right and the rest of Jenny's document moved jerkily to the left, disappearing. She stared in horror, her first thought that she'd broken the computer. Jenny loved computers, unlike Dee who hated technology, but she had to admit there was something a little *odd* about them, a little unnerving. As if *things* might happen unexpectedly there on screen. When she was a kid, after a day of playing with her dad's PC, Jenny had sometimes had dreams of bizarre scenes and impossible games appearing on the monitor. As if a computer wasn't just a machine but some kind of connection that could hook into the unknown.

Now her eyes widened as the *J*s went on. On and on and on. That wasn't right—that couldn't be. Where was word wrap? The letters should just fall down onto the next line.

They didn't. They kept going. A line of *J*s hitting the edge of the screen and then ebbing back as the screen scanned right, then surging to the edge again. Like a snake. Or something pulsing.

Jenny's little fingers were tingling; there was a crawling between her shoulder blades. This was *wrong*. She had a dreadful feeling of the physical distance the line of *J*s had traveled. It was as if she were out in space somewhere, far to the right of her original document—and going on farther. She was lost somewhere in virtual space, and she was terrified of what she might see there.

JJJJJJJJJJJJJJJJJJJJJJJJJJJJJJJJJJJJJJJJJJJJJJJJJJJJJJJJJJJJJJJJJJJJJJJJJJJJJJJ

Jenny had been pressing Escape continuously since the key had stuck. Now she hit Enter to put in a hard return, to break the line. Nothing happened.

JJJJJJJJJJJJJJJJJJJJJJJJJJJJJJJJJJJJJJJJJJJJJJJJJJJJJJJJJJJJJJJJJJJJJJJJJJJJJJJ

Oh, God, what was out here? What were the *J*s heading for? Something miles to the side of her original document, something that just couldn't be there because there wasn't room for it. She was beyond any possible margins. It was like sailing over the edge of the world.

She scrambled in her mind for the screen rewrite code, hit that. Nothing. She stabbed at the Break key. Nothing. Then, teeth sunk in her lip, she pressed Control/Alt/Delete.

The combination should have rebooted the computer. It didn't. The *J*s sailed on.

The screen glowed a deep and beautiful blue. Jenny had never noticed before just how blue that screen really was. A color vivid beyond imagining.

The white *J*s surged on and on. Jenny had a physical sense of falling. She was out *too far. . . .*

She reached out and did something the computer teacher had threatened them with death for doing; she flipped the main switch of the computer off. Depriving it of electricity, killing it in the middle of a program. Crashing it deliberately.

Only it didn't crash.

The switch was off, the CPU light was off—but the *J*s kept on going, pulsing and surging.

Jenny's breath stopped. She stared in disbelief. Her hand went to the monitor and fumbled frantically with the monitor switch. It clicked under he fingers; the monitor light went off.

"What are you *doing*?" the girl to the left of her gasped.

The monitor still glowed blue. The *J*s sailed on.

Jenny yanked the keyboard out of the socket.

She had to stop this. Something was going terribly, unimaginably wrong, and she had to stop those *J*s before . . .

"Ms. Godfrey!" the girl to the left of her cried. "Ms. Godfrey, Jenny's—"

Jenny had just an instant to see what happened next. Even with the keyboard detached, the *J*s kept going—or at least she thought they did. It was hard to tell because everything happened so fast. There was a bright flash—the screen going blindingly white—and a blue afterimage printed on her retinas. Then the monitor went dark.

So did the lights in the room—and all the other computers.

"Now see what you did," the girl beside her hissed.

Jenny sat, scarcely breathing. Pulling out the keyboard cord couldn't have caused a blackout. Even crashing her computer shouldn't have done that. The room wasn't totally dark, but it was very dim; the windows were tinted to protect the equipment. Impressed on the dimness Jenny saw pinwheels and filaments of glowing blue.

Oh, please, she thought, holding herself as still as possible. She could feel her heart beating in her throat.

Then she heard—something—from underneath the computer tables.

Soft as a match strike, but audible. A moving sound, like a rope being dragged. Like something sliding across the floor.

Toward her.

Jenny twisted her head, trying to locate it. The teacher's voice seemed distant. The sliding sound was getting closer, she could hear it clearly now. Like a dry leaf blowing across pavement. Starting and stopping. Surging. Like the *J*s. Coming straight for her legs.

It was almost here. Almost was under her table. And she couldn't move; she was frozen.

She heard a hiss like static. Like white noise. Or—

Something brushed her leg.

Jenny screamed. Released from her paralysis all at once, she jumped to her feet, beating at her leg. The thing brushed her again, and she grabbed at it, throttling it, trying to kill it—

—and found herself holding the keyboard cord.

It must have fallen over the edge of the table when she yanked it out, and dangled there. Jenny was holding on to its spiraling length so tightly that she could feel dents in her palms. This close she could see it clearly. Just a cord.

The lights went on. People were gathering around her, putting their hands on her, asking questions.

It's just your brain making models, she told herself desperately, ignoring everyone else. The computer malfunctioned and you freaked. You heard static when the power went off, and you freaked more and made it into a hiss. But it wasn't real. It was just models in your brain.

"I think you'd better go home for the day," Ms. Godfrey said. "You look as if you could use some rest."

"I've got it figured out now," she said to Michael that night. "It must have been something to do with the UPS—the uninterruptible power supply. That's a kind of battery that keeps the computers going when the power goes out."

"Oh, right," said Michael, who knew very little about computers but would never admit it.

"That's what kept the computer going, but then somehow I managed to blow the whole system," Jenny said. "That knocked the power out, and all the rest of it was in my mind."

"You must have looked pretty funny holding that cord," Michael said.

They talked about what had happened to him and the others that afternoon. He and Dee and Audrey had gone postering together and had covered most of the area between Ramona and Anchor streets. They hadn't found anything.

Jenny told him what she'd told Dee and Audrey earlier. She was okay now. She'd slept all afternoon. Her mother had wanted to take her to the doctor, but Jenny had said no.

She was very proud of herself for realizing it had all been in her mind. She planned to stay calmer in the future.

"Well, that's good," Michael said. His voice sounded surprisingly weak for somebody whose theory had been confirmed, "Uh, Jenny—"

"What?"

"Oh, nothing. See you tomorrow. Take care of yourself."

"You, too," Jenny said, a little startled. "Bye."

Michael stared at the cordless phone he'd just clicked off. Then he glanced uneasily at his bedroom window. He wondered if he should have told Jenny—but Jenny had enough to worry about.

Besides, there was no reason to do anything to tarnish his

own brilliant theory. It *was* just battle fatigue, and he was as subject to it as anyone else.

Stress. Tension. In his own case combined with a rather nervous temperament. Michael had always claimed to be an unashamed coward.

That would account for the feeling he'd had all day of being watched. And there was nothing really moving outside that window. It was a second-floor apartment, after all.

Audrey stretched in her Christian Dior nightgown and deposited herself more haphazardly across the peach satin sheets. Even after forty-five minutes in the Jacuzzi her feet hurt. She was sure she was getting calluses.

Worse, she couldn't shake the strange sensation she'd had ever since this afternoon. It was the feeling Audrey usually had when entering a room—of eyes on her. Only these eyes today hadn't been admiring. They had been watchful—and malicious. She'd felt as if something were following her.

Stalking her.

Probably just the remnants of yesterday's fright. There was nothing to worry about—she was safe at home. In bed.

Audrey stretched again and her mind wandered. Eyes . . . hmm. No eyes now. *C'est* okay. *Va bène.*

She slept.

And dreamed, pleasantly. She was a cat. Not a repulsive

scroungy cat like Jenny's, but an elegant Abyssinian. She was curled up with another cat, getting a cat-bath.

Audrey smiled responsively, ducking her head, exposing the nape of her neck to the seductive feeling. The other cat's tongue was rough but nice. It must be a *big* cat, though, she thought, half-waking. Maybe a tiger. Maybe—

With a shriek Audrey bolted straight up in bed. She was awake—but she could swear the sensation had followed her out of the dream. She *had* felt a rough tongue licking her neck.

She clapped a hand to the back of her neck and felt the dampness there.

A strange, musky smell filled the room.

Audrey almost knocked the bedside lamp over getting it turned on. Then she stared around wildly, looking for the thing that had been in her bed.

CHAPTER 7

Dee woke with a start. At least she thought she woke—but she couldn't move.

Someone was leaning over her.

The room was very dark. It shouldn't have been, because Dee liked to sleep with the window open, the curtains drawn back. Breathing fresh air, not the stale refrigerated stuff that came out of the air conditioner.

Tonight she must have forgotten to open the curtains. Dee couldn't tell because she couldn't move her head. She could only see what was directly above her—the figure.

It was a thick darkness against the thinner darkness of the room. It was a human shape, upside-down because it was leaning over from the headboard side.

Dee's heart was pounding like a trip-hammer. She could feel her lips draw back from her teeth savagely.

Then she realized something horrifying.

The headboard side—the figure was leaning over her from the headboard side. *But there was a wall there.* It was leaning out of the *wall.*

"Get away from me!"

Shouting broke the spell. She vaulted off the bed, landing in a tangle of sheets in the middle of her room. She kicked the sheets free and was at the light switch by the door in one movement.

Light filled the room, glowing off the ocher walls. There was no dark figure anywhere.

Tacked over the bed between an African mask and a length of embroidered cloth from Syria was a poster. A poster of Bruce Lee. It was just where the figure had been.

Dee approached it slowly, warily, ready for anything. She got close and looked at it. Just an ordinary poster. Bruce Lee's image stared out blandly over her head. There was something almost smug about his expression. . . .

Abruptly Dee reached out and ripped the poster off the wall, scattering pushpins. She crumpled it with both hands and threw it in the general direction of the wastebasket.

Then she sat back against the headboard, breathing hard.

Zach had been lying for hours, unable to get to sleep. Too many thoughts crowding his brain. Thoughts—and images.

Him and Jenny as kids. Playing Indians in the cherry orchard. Playing pirates in the creek. Always playing something, lost in some imaginary world. Because imaginary worlds were better than the real thing. Safer, Zach had always thought.

Zach breathed out hard. His eyes fluttered open—and he shouted.

Suspended in the air above him was the head of a twelve-point buck.

It was hanging inches from his nose, so close his dark-adjusted eyes could see it clearly. But he was paralyzed. He wanted to twist to the side, to get away from it, but his arms and legs wouldn't obey.

It was falling on him!

His whole body gave a terrible jerk and adrenaline burst through him. His arm flung up to ward the thing off. His eyes shut, anticipating the blow.

It never came. He dropped his arm, opened his eyes.

Empty air above him.

Zach struck out at it anyway. Only believing it was gone when his hand encountered no resistance.

He got up and turned on the lights. He didn't stay to look around the room, though. He went downstairs, to the den, flipping on the lights there.

On the wood-paneled wall where his father's trophies hung, the twelve-pointer rested in its usual place.

Zach looked into its liquid-dark glass eyes. His gaze

traveled over the splendid antlers, the shockingly delicate muzzle, the glossy brown neck.

It was all real and solid. Too heavy to move, bolted to the wall.

Which means maybe I'm losing my mind. Imagination gone completely wild. That would be a laugh, wouldn't it, to get through the Game and then come home and lose my mind over nothing?

Ha ha.

The den was as still as a photograph around him.

He wasn't going to get any sleep tonight. Normally, he would have gone out to his darkroom in the garage and done some work. That was what he'd always done before when he couldn't sleep.

But that had been—before. Tonight he'd rather just stare at the ceiling. Nothing else was any use.

"Hypnopompic hallucination," Michael said to Dee the next morning. "That's when you think you've woken up, but your mind is still dreaming. The dark figure in your room is a classic example. They even have a name for it—the Old Hag Syndrome. Because some people think it's an old lady sitting on their chest, paralyzing them."

"Right," Dee said. "Well, that's what it must have been, then. Of course."

"Same with you, Zach," Michael said, turning to look

at him. "Only yours was *hypnagogic* hallucination—you thought you weren't asleep yet, but your brain was in la-la land already."

Zach said nothing.

"What about me?" Audrey said. "I *was* asleep—but when I woke up, my dream was true." She touched polished fingernails to the back of her neck, just beneath the burnished copper French twist. "I was *wet*."

"Sweat," Michael said succinctly.

"I don't sweat."

"Well, ladylike perspiration, then. It's been hot."

Jenny looked around at the group on the knoll. They all sounded so calm and rational. But Michael's grin was strained, and Zach was paler than ever. Dee's nervous energy was like an electrical field. Audrey's lips were pressed together.

In spite of the brave words, they were all on edge.

And where's Tom? Jenny thought. He should *be* here. No matter what he thinks of me, he should be here for the sake of the others. What's he doing?

"I heard there was a body found up in the Santa Ana foothills," Dee said. "A guy from this school."

"Gordon Wilson," Audrey said, wrinkling her nose. "You know—that senior with the cowboy boots. People say he runs over cats."

"Well, he's not going to run over any more. They think a mountain lion got him."

* * *

Tom had heard about the body yesterday afternoon, and his first irrational thought had been: *Zach? Michael?*

But they had both been safe. And Jenny was safe at school today—although maybe school wasn't so safe, either. Yesterday, she'd gotten herself sent home from computer applications after something—it was hard to figure out exactly what from the conflicting stories—had happened.

A brief thought crossed his mind that he might call her and ask—but Tom had already chosen his course. He couldn't change it now, and she probably wouldn't want him to. He'd *seen* her in the car, that look when the song came on. Scared, yes, but with something underneath the scaredness. She'd never looked like that at him.

It didn't matter. He'd protect her anyway. But yesterday, knowing she was home for good, he'd taken the afternoon off and gone to the police station. He'd used charm on a female detective and learned exactly where the body had been found.

Today he was skipping school completely. Teachers were going to start asking questions about that soon.

So what?

Tom found the dry creek bed. It wasn't too far from the famous Bell Canyon Trail, where a six-year-old had been attacked by a mountain lion. The air was scented with sage.

There was a crinkled yellow "crime scene" ribbon straggling along the creek bed and little flags of various colors planted in the ground. Tom scrambled down the slope and stood where tiny traces of a dark stain on the rocks still showed.

He looked around. One place on the opposite bank had seen a lot of activity. Cactus had been broken, pineapple weed uprooted. There were footprints in the dirt.

Tom followed the trail up to a slope covered with purple sage. Coastal live oak and spreading sycamores cast an inviting shade nearby.

Tom studied the ground.

After a moment he began to walk, slowly, toward the trees. He skirted brush. He came to three old sycamores growing so closely that their branches were entwined.

The air was heavier here. It had a strange smell. Very faint, but disturbing. Feral.

Like a predator.

Sometimes there were huge patches of poison ivy under these old trees. Tom looked carefully, then stirred the brush underneath with his foot. The smell came stronger. Something heavy had lain here for quite some time.

He turned and retraced his steps slowly.

Then he saw it. On a dusty rock directly between the trees and the place where the creek bank was disturbed. A splatter of black like tar. A thick, viscous substance that looked as if it had bubbled at the edges.

Tom's breath hissed in, and he knelt, eyes narrowed.

There was no sign that any of it had been scraped off.

Either the police hadn't seen it or they hadn't cared. It clearly wasn't the blood of anything on earth. It didn't look like anything important.

It was. It was very important. Tom took out a Swiss army knife and scraped some of the gunk up to examine it. It had an odd, musky smell, and spread very thin it was not black but red.

Then he sat back on his heels and shut his eyes, trying to maintain the control he was famous for.

By Thursday Jenny noticed that Zach had dark circles under his eyes and Dee was jumpier than ever. Michael's face was blotchy, and one of Audrey's nails actually looked bitten.

They were all falling apart.

Because of dreams. That was all they were. Nothing really happened at night, nothing hurt them. But the dreams were enough.

Friday they were scheduled to go postering, but Jenny had to stop by the YMCA first, a few blocks from the Center. And it was there that something really did happen at last.

Jenny had been waiting so long, searching for so long, that she ought to have been prepared. But when the time came, she found she wasn't prepared at all.

She was inside the Y, talking to Mrs. Birkenkamp, the swim coach. Jenny volunteered every Friday with the swim class for disabled kids. She loved it and hated to miss.

"But I have to," she said miserably. "And maybe next Friday, too. I should have told you before, but I forgot—"

"Jenny, it's okay. Are *you* okay?"

Jenny lifted her eyes to the clear blue ones which looked at her steadily. There was something so wise about them—Jenny had the sudden impulse to throw herself into the woman's arms and tell her everything.

Mrs. Birkenkamp had been Jenny's hero for years. She never gave up or lost faith. She'd taught a child without arms to swim. Maybe she would have an answer.

But what could Jenny say? Nothing that an adult would believe. Besides, it was up to Jenny to do things for herself now. She couldn't rely on Tom anymore; she had to stand on her own feet.

"I'll be fine," she said unsteadily. "Tell all the kids hello—"

That was when Cam came in.

Dee was behind him. She had been waiting outside in her jeep. "He came over from the Center. He won't talk to anybody but you," she said.

Cam said simply, "I found her."

Jenny gasped. She actually felt dizzy for an instant. Then she said, *"Where?"*

"I got her address." Cam thrust a hand into the pocket of his skin-tight jeans and pulled out a grimy slip of paper.

"Right," Jenny said. "Let's go."

"Wait," Mrs. Birkenkamp said. "Jenny, what's all this about—"

"It's all right, Mrs. Birkenkamp," Jenny said, whirling around and hugging the willowy coach. "Everything's going to be all right now." She really did feel that way.

Cam directed them to the house. "Her name's Angela Seecombe. Kimberly Hall's big sister Jolie knows a guy who knows her. This is the street."

Filbert Street. East of Ramona Street, where P.C. lived, just south of Landana. Audrey and Jenny had been there, distributing flyers.

But not inside this yellow two-story house with the paint-chipped black iron fence. Jenny couldn't remember why they hadn't been let in here, but they hadn't.

"You stay here," she said. "I've got to do this myself. But, Cam—thank you." She turned to look at him, this tough kid with dandelion-fluff hair whose life had changed because his sister had gone to a party.

He shrugged, but his eyes met hers, grateful for the acknowledgment. "I wanted to."

No one answered the door of the yellow house. Jenny leaned on the bell.

Still no answer. But faintly, from inside, came the sound of a TV set.

Jenny glanced at the driveway. No car there. Maybe no adults home. She waved to Dee and Cam to stay in the car, then went around the side of the house. She unlatched the creaking iron gate and waded through thigh-deep foxtails to the back porch.

347

She grasped the knob of the back door firmly. Then she cast a look heavenward, took a deep breath, and tried it.

It was unlocked. Jenny stepped inside and followed the sound of the TV into a small family room.

Sitting on a rust-colored couch was the Crying Girl.

She jumped up in astonishment at the sight of Jenny, spilling popcorn from a microwave bag onto the carpet. Her long dark hair swung over her shoulders. Her haunted eyes were wide, and her mouth was open.

"Don't be afraid," Jenny said. "I'm not going to hurt you. I told you before, I need to talk to you."

Hatred flashed through the girl's face.

"I don't want to talk to *you*!" She darted to the telephone. "I'm calling the police—you're trespassing."

"Go ahead and call them," Jenny said with a calm she didn't feel. "And I'll tell them that you know things you haven't told them about the morning P.C. disappeared. You saw P.C., didn't you? You know where he went." She was gambling. Angela had threatened to tell in the beginning; in the bathroom she'd said she could prove P.C. didn't kill Summer. But she *hadn't* told— which must mean she didn't want to. Jenny was gambling that Angela would rather tell her than the police.

The girl said nothing, her slim olive-tan hand resting on the phone limply.

"Angela." Jenny went to her as she had four days ago in the

high school bathroom. She put her hands on the girl's shoulders, gently this time.

"You *did* see P.C., didn't you? And you saw what he had with him. Angela, you've got to tell me. You don't understand how important it is. If you don't tell me, the thing that happened to P.C. could happen to other people."

The small bones under Jenny's hands lifted as Angela heaved in a shaky breath.

"I hate you. . . ."

"No, you don't. You want something to hate because you hurt so much. I understand that. But I'm not your enemy, and I'm not a soshe or a prep or any of those things. I'm just another girl like you, trying to cope, trying to stop something bad from happening. And I hurt, too."

Dark, pensive eyes studied her face. "Oh, yeah?"

"*Yeah.* Like hell. And if you don't believe it, you're not as smart as you look." Jenny's nose and eyes were stinging. "Listen, Summer Parker-Pearson was one of my best friends. I lost her. Now I've lost my boyfriend over this, too. I just don't want anything worse to happen—which it will, if you don't help me.

Angela's eyes dropped, but not before Jenny saw the shimmer of tears.

Jenny spoke softly. "If you know where P.C. went that morning, then you have to tell me now."

Angela shrugged off Jenny's hands and turned away. Her entire body was tense for a moment, then it slumped. "I won't tell you—but I'll show you," she said.

"Jenny? Are you in there?"

Dee's voice, from the back door. As Dee appeared, narrow-eyed and moving like a jaguar, Jenny reached out quickly to Angela. "It's okay. She's my friend. You can show us both."

The girl hesitated, then nodded, giving in.

To Jenny's surprise, she didn't head for the front door, but led them out back. Cam followed them through the foxtails. The backyard sloped down to dense brush; there was far more land here than Jenny had realized. Beside an overhanging clump of trees was a warped and leaning toolshed.

"There," Angela said. "That's where P.C. went."

"Oh, no you don't." Jenny caught Dee in mid-lunge and held her back. "This isn't the time to be yanking doors open. Remember the Game?" She herself was trembling with anxiety, triumph, and anticipation.

Angela was fumbling with a large old-fashioned locket she had tucked into her tank top. "You need this to open it, anyway. I locked it again—afterward. It was our secret place, P.C.'s and mine. Nobody else wanted it."

Jenny took the key. "So you saw him go in that morning. And then . . . ?"

"Slug went in, too. P.C. climbed the porch and woke me up to get the key. That's my bedroom." She pointed to a second-story window above the porch roof. "Then he and Slug went down and unlocked the shed and went in. I could see everything from my room. I waited for them to come out—usually they just stashed stuff there and came out."

"But this time they didn't."

"No . . . so I waited and waited, then I got dressed. When I came down here, the door was still shut. So I opened it—but they weren't inside." She turned on Jenny suddenly, her dark eyes huge and brilliant with unshed tears. "They weren't inside! And there aren't any windows, and they didn't go out the door. And the key was on the ground. P.C. would never leave the key on the ground; he always locked up and gave it back to me. Where did they *go*?"

Jenny answered with a question. "There was something else on the ground, wasn't there? Besides the key?"

Angela nodded slowly.

"A . . ." Jenny took a breath. "A paper house."

"Yeah. A baby thing. It wasn't even new, it was kind of crumpled, and it was taped up with electrician's tape from the shed. I don't know why they took it. They usually took stuff like—" She broke off.

Dee cut a glance at Jenny, amused at the admission.

"It doesn't matter," Jenny said. "At least we know everything now. And it should still be inside if this place has been locked ever since that morning."

Angela nodded. "I didn't touch anything, even though—

well, I sort of wanted to look at the house. But I didn't; I left it there on the floor. And nobody else has a key."

"Then let's go get it," Jenny said. Deep inside she was shaking. The paper house was here. They'd found it—and no wonder it had eluded them so long, sitting in a locked toolshed used by juvenile delinquents for hiding stolen goods.

"Monster positions?" Dee suggested with a flash of white teeth. She was clearly enjoying this.

"Right." Jenny took up a position beside the door. Dee stood in front of it in a kung fu stance, ready to kick it shut. It was the way they'd learned to open doors in the paper house. "Stand back, Angela. You, too, Cam."

"Now." Jenny turned the key, pulled the door open.

Nothing frightening happened. A rectangle of sunlight fell into the dusty shed. Jenny blocked it off with her own shadow as she stepped into the doorway. Then she moved inside, and Dee blocked the light.

"Come on in—I can't see—"

Then she did see—and her mind reeled.

The blank white box was on the floor, open. Beside it was the paper house Jenny had described to the police. A Victorian house, three stories and a turret. Blue.

Dee made a guttural sound.

When Jenny had last seen the paper house, it had been crushed flat to fit in the box. It was different now. It had been straightened and reinforced with black tape. But that wasn't what made Jenny's head spin and her breath catch. That wasn't what made her knees start to give way.

The paper house was exploded.

In shreds. Roof gone. Outer walls in tatters. Floors gutted.

As if something very large had burst out from the inside.

On the floor nearby, scratched impossibly deep into the concrete, was a mark. The rune Uruz. A letter from a magical alphabet, a spell to pierce the veil between the worlds. Jenny had seen it before on the inside of the box that had led them into the Shadow World. It was shaped like an angular and inverted *U,* with one stroke shorter than the other.

Right now she was looking at it upside-down, so that it should have looked like a regular *U.* But this particular rune was *very* uneven, the short stroke *very* short. From where she was standing it looked almost like a squared-off *J.*

Like a signature.

Even as Jenny turned toward Dee, she felt herself falling.

"We're too late," she whispered. "He's out."

"Okay," Dee said, some minutes later, still holding her. "Okay, okay . . ."

"It's *not* okay." She saw Cam and Angela peering in the doorway, and her head cleared a bit. "You two get back."

They came forward. "Is that it? What you've been looking for?" Cam squatted by the ruined house, his eyes as large and blue as Summer's. Light from the doorway made his dandelion hair glow at the edges. "What happened to it?"

Angela's dark eyes were huge—and despairing. "What happened to P.C.?"

Jenny looked at the house. It was gutted, every floor shredded. Her eyes filled again and she swallowed.

"I think he's probably dead," she said softly. "I'm sorry." The sight of Angela's misery cleared her head a little, brought her out of herself.

"Are you going to tell the police? About P.C. and me and this place?"

"The police," Jenny said bleakly, "are useless. We've learned that. There's nothing they can do. Maybe nothing *anybody* can do—" She stopped as an idea came to her. A desperate hope. "Angela, you said you didn't touch anything here—but are you sure? You didn't see anything on the floor, did you—like any jewelry?"

Angela shook her head. Jenny searched for it anyway. It had been inside the box; maybe it had just rolled away. It wouldn't make the police believe them, but it might just save her—if they could find it and destroy it—

She looked in the opened box and all around on the concrete floor. She shook out the ruins of the paper house.

But it wasn't anywhere. The gold ring that Julian had put on her finger, the one she tried to throw away, was gone.

CHAPTER 8

What can we do?"

They were at Audrey's house, in the second-best family room where no adults would disturb them. Michael was looking at Jenny, his spaniel eyes glazed.

"Well, that's the question, isn't it?" Zachary said crisply. "What *can* we do?"

"I don't know," Jenny whispered.

The paper house—or rather its remains—sat on the coffee table. Jenny had brought it with them, to keep it safe. Although what they were going to do with it, she had no idea.

She'd taken both Angela and Cam by the hand before they left Angela's house. Scared as she was, she wanted to thank them—and to give them what comfort she could.

"I know it wasn't easy to help us," she said. "Now you need to forget all about this, if you can. We're the ones who have to take care of it. But I'll always remember what you've done—both of you."

Then she and Angela, the soshe and the Crying Girl, had hugged.

Outside, on Filbert Street, she and Dee had found Tom. His RX-7 was parked behind Dee's jeep. Clearly, he'd been following them, although Jenny still didn't understand why.

Now he sat beside Jenny, his hazel eyes thoughtful. "You know, I don't think they'll hurt *you*," he said to her. The emphasis on the last word was slight but noticeable.

"What do you mean, *they*?"

"The wolf and the snake. What did Julian call them? The Lurker and the Creeper."

Everyone stared.

"Tom, what are you talking about?"

"They're out, too. It was the wolf that followed you and Audrey on Monday. The Shadow Wolf. I only got a glimpse of it that night, but it wasn't a dog."

Audrey choked. "I've got *wolf* scratches on my car?"

"And that snake—I think maybe it's been around, too."

Jenny shut her eyes, remembering the dry sliding on the computer room floor. The brush against her leg. The hiss.

"Oh, God—then it's all been *real*," she said. "And the

phone calls—oh, my God, oh, my *God*. They were *real*. They really were saying—" She couldn't finish.

"Models in your brain, my ass," Dee said to Michael.

Michael looked wretched. He bent his head, clutching his rumpled hair with his hands.

"And the dreams?" Audrey said thinly. "You think they were real, too? There was some—thing—in my bed with me?"

"Sounds like," Zach said, with morbid satisfaction. "Or maybe Julian can just make us dream what he wants."

"We have to do *something*," Dee said.

"Like what?" Zach's gray eyes shone with devastating logic. "What can we do against Julian? Plus that snake and that wolf. Don't you remember what they looked like?"

"I think they're the ones who got Gordie Wilson, incidentally," Tom said quietly. "I went up to the place where they found him."

"Oh, great. We don't have a chance," Michael said.

"Look, we're all in shock now," Dee said. "Let's get together this weekend at somebody's house and make plans. We can spend all Saturday thinking."

"At Tom's, maybe," Michael said. "I'm going to be there anyway; my dad's going to New York for a week."

Audrey looked at Jenny, then at Tom. Her camellia skin was pink, and she rubbed at her spiky lashes with one hand.

"I hate to say this, but we can't," she said. "At least Jenny and I can't. You're forgetting about the senior prom."

Tom looked up. *". . . What?"*

"Jenny and I," Audrey said helplessly, "are going to the senior prom."

"With Brian Dettlinger and Eric Rankin," Michael said, in a misery-loves-company voice.

Tom was staring at Jenny. His face was perfectly white, and the green flecks in his eyes seemed to flare. Something seemed to have gone wrong with his mouth—it was trembling. Jenny looked back at him in absolute horror, her mind a thundering blank.

Then Tom said, slowly, "I see."

"No," Jenny whispered, stricken. She had never seen Tom look like this. Not when his grandmother died, not even when his father had had a heart attack. Tom Locke the invulnerable didn't have a face like that.

"It's okay. I should have expected it." He got up.

"Tom—"

"You ought to be safe enough. Like I said, I don't think they'll hurt *you.*"

"Tom—oh, God, *Tom*—"

He was walking out the door.

Jenny whirled on Audrey and Michael, lashing out in her misery. "Are you happy now? You made him leave!"

"Do you think that means he doesn't want me for the weekend?" Michael asked, but Dee spoke seriously.

"He wasn't really here, Jenny. He's not with us anymore, Sunshine, and you can't make him be."

Jenny waited a moment while Dee's words slowly sank in. It was true. There was no way to deny it. Jenny hadn't lost anything just now, because she had nothing left to lose.

She sat down and said dully, "Obviously not. And somehow I don't think going to the prom with Brian is going to help, either." She looked at Audrey.

Audrey, however, refused to be fazed. "Who knows? He might feel differently when he sees you actually doing it."

"I'm not *going* to be doing it."

"So you're going to call Brian and dump him at the last minute?"

"Yes." Jenny fumbled in her purse for her address book. She went to Audrey's gold-and-white antique phone and dialed.

"Hello, Brian? It's Jenny—"

"Jenny! I'm so glad you called."

Jenny faltered. "You are?"

"Yeah, I was going to call you—look, I'm so stupid. I forgot to ask you what color your dress is."

"My dress?"

"I know I should have asked before." His voice was full of eagerness and—oh, God—boyish enthusiasm. "It's not that I haven't been thinking about you. The limo's all lined up, and I made reservations at L'Avenue—do you like French food?"

"Oh . . ." Jenny felt limp as seaweed. "Oh . . . sure."

"Great. And your dress is what color?"

Audrey had come over and was leaning her copper head close to the earpiece. "Tell him gold," she whispered.

"Gold," Jenny repeated automatically, then looked at Audrey. "Oh, no, not that one," she whispered fiercely.

"What? Gold's great. I'll see you tomorrow."

Jenny hung up dazedly. She hadn't been able to do it.

"You see?" Audrey said grimly. "I'm stuck, too. Stop looking like that, Michael. I don't care about Eric—much."

Dee stretched. "When you get down to it, what difference does it make where you are? They can get into our houses if they want."

It was true. It wasn't much comfort. Jenny still didn't see how she could go—or how she could get out of it now.

"I can't wear *that* dress," she said to Audrey. "Tom wouldn't even let me wear it with *him*. If he hears I wore it with Brian, he'll have a fit. . . ." Her voice trailed off as new hope ignited suddenly in her chest.

Audrey smiled knowingly. "Then maybe," she said archly, "the prom will do some good after all."

Jenny picked up the handful of liquid gold, put it down again. She couldn't believe she was doing this.

On the other hand, Dee was right. What difference did it make where Jenny was? There was nowhere safe. At least the Monarch Hotel was a large public place. She and Audrey would be surrounded by people.

Last night and today had been very quiet. No dreams, no disturbances. The calm before the storm? Or maybe . . . maybe some miracle had happened and all the bad things had gone away. Spontaneously popped back into the Shadow World. Maybe Julian was going to leave her alone from now on.

Don't be ridiculous, Jenny.

She sighed and shook her head. Too much worrying had sapped her energy and put her in a fatalistic mood.

She picked up the liquid gold again. It was the Dress.

The material was gold foil, which showed a subtle pattern of flowers and leaves when the light hit it the right way—almost like tapestry. The colors were rich and shimmering, and the thin fabric was silky-soft. Audrey had been crazy over it, but Audrey only wore black and white.

"You *have* to get it," she'd told Jenny, tilting the shining fabric back and forth under the lights and ignoring the bevy of trailing saleswomen—saleswomen always trailed when Audrey shopped.

"But Tom—"

"Forget Tom. When are you going to stop letting him tell you what to wear? *You must buy this dress.* With your gold-y skin and hair it will be *exquisite.*"

So Jenny had bought it. But she'd been right; Tom wouldn't let her wear it to the junior prom. It was too short, too cling-ing, molding itself to her like a shining skin. Her legs looked as long as Dee's underneath.

Now she put it on and reached for a brush. She bent over,

brushing, then stood, flipping her hair back. She ran her fingers through her hair to fluff it.

Then she stepped to the full-length maple mirror. She had to admit it; the dress was a masterpiece. A glittering, shameless work of art. Her hair was a mass of dark gold around her face, different from her usual soft look. Her entire image seemed touched with gold.

She looked like a crown princess. She felt like a virgin sacrifice.

"Jenny." Her mother was tapping at her bedroom door. "He's here."

Jenny stared at herself for another moment hopelessly. "Right," she said and came out.

Brian's jaw dropped when he saw her. So, unfortunately, did Mr. Thornton's.

"Jim, now, Jim," her mother said. She led Jenny's father off into the kitchen, talking to him about how responsible Jenny was and how Brian's mother was a member of the Assistance League.

"Are those my flowers?" Jenny said, since Brian was still gaping at her. He held out the corsage box dumbly.

The plastic was clouded with mist, but when Jenny opened it, she saw an ethereal bunch of palest lemon miniature roses. "But they're beautiful!"

"Uh. Um." Brian blinked at the flowers, then shook his head slightly. He took them out, looked at her low neckline.

He reached toward her doubtfully, pulled back. "Uh . . ."

"I'll do it," Jenny said and fastened them on her shoulder. Then she put on his boutonniere and they left.

The limo was champagne-colored, and they weren't sharing it with anybody. Brian looked nice, blond and handsome, with a royal blue cummerbund and tie. All the way to the restaurant Jenny concentrated on the tiny shiny buttons on his tux in order to keep from crying.

She'd never been out with any boy besides Tom.

Dinner was uneventful. Brian was awed by everything she said and did, which made him easy to get along with. He wasn't smart like Tom, but he was a nice guy. A really nice guy.

Palm trees lined the private drive of the hotel. It was a beautiful and dreamlike setting, a cliff above the sea. Mercedes and Cadillacs were parked everywhere and bellhops in red uniforms were running around.

As Jenny got out of the limo, she began to realize something. The senior prom was like a junior prom some fairy godmother had waved a wand over. Everything grander, bigger, more glittery. More grown-up. It was scary, but kind of wonderful.

They walked between marble columns into an enchanted world. Acres of Italian marble. Huge urns of flowers—all arranged in exquisitely simple good taste. Persian carpets, silk wallcoverings, Bohemian crystal chandeliers.

Audrey must be loving this, Jenny thought, stopping somewhere along the miles of hallway to look at an oil painting.

When they finally reached the ballroom, Jenny drew in her breath.

It was . . . fabulous. In the old sense, meaning like something out of a fable. Like a castle. The ceilings were incredibly high, with huge chandeliers in deep recesses. Potted trees—full-size trees entwined with tiny lights—stood here and there among the tables. At one end of the room poufy curtains were drawn back to reveal a balcony, which Jenny guessed looked down on the ocean.

"It's beautiful," Jenny breathed, forgetting everything for a moment.

"It sure is." When she looked, Brian was looking at her.

The tables were as incredible as everything else. There were fresh flowers in blown-glass stands that reached above Jenny's head when she was sitting down. At each place was a little metallic mask as a favor.

"The Midnight Masquerade," Brian said, holding a silver one up to his eyes. "Don't put yours on, though; you're too pretty without it."

Jenny looked away.

"These flowers are beautiful," she said hastily. They were. The roses had a pale gold shimmer unlike anything she'd ever seen, and they smelled so sweet it almost made her giddy.

"Yeah, well, I have to confess—I can't take the credit for them. I ordered white ones for Ka—I mean, I ordered plain white ones. The florist must have screwed up, but it turned out great."

Jenny stirred. For some reason prickles of unease were touching her delicately.

Just then some of Brian's friends came by. One of them stared at Jenny, blinked, then whispered something to Brian that ended with "I bet *you're* planning to stay out late!"

Brian blushed. Jenny leaned across him and said directly to the other guy, *"Vada via, cretino."* Audrey had taught her that. It meant "Get lost, jerk," and it sounded like it.

The guy left, muttering, "And I heard she was sweet!"

Brian, still blushing, was embarrassed and apologetic. A nice guy, Jenny thought, feeling sorry for him. A really, really nice guy. . . .

They talked. Jenny looked at the snowy-white tablecloth and the shining crystal glasses, she played with her prom program and her raffle ticket. She stared at the Oriental border of the carpet. Finally, though, there was no way to avoid the subject that was looming over both of them.

"You want to dance?" Brian said.

What could she say?

Okay, she thought as they walked onto the floor. It's not as if you've never danced with another guy before. But she hadn't, often. Tom didn't like it. Besides, she'd always been *with* Tom, and the guy had always known it.

Naturally, the next dance turned out to be a slow one. The room was just dim enough to be romantic. Brian's arms settled around Jenny's shoulders, and Jenny clasped his waist as lightly as possible. She rested her head on his chest and looked intently at the refreshment table.

It was a marble-topped buffet with huge urns of flowers on either side. Jenny concentrated on identifying the flowers, one by one. Then she saw a glimmer of burnished copper.

"Look, there's *Audrey*!" she said. "Let's go see her!"

Audrey was wearing a saucy little black dress with a pink satin sash at the back. Diamonds glittered in her ears. Her chestnut eyes widened at the sight of Jenny.

"Will you look at you! Jenny, you're sensational. *Wunderschön!*"

Jenny clung to Audrey and made wild small talk. Other people went by. She saw dresses in every color of the rainbow; she saw lime green cummerbunds and pink cummerbunds and plaid ones. But at last Eric and Audrey went out to dance, and Jenny had no choice but to follow with Brian.

When the next slow dance came, she rested stiffly in Brian's arms, staring at the dark wood of the dance floor.

He was too interested. Jenny had seen it all night: the look in his eyes, the way he held her, the way he talked to her. He was such a nice guy, so handsome, and she felt *nothing*.

"Later we can go down to the beach," he was saying.

"Mmm," Jenny said, thinking that she had to get away from the smell of his lime aftershave, and hating herself for it. She wished desperately that someone would rescue her.

Someone did.

It was another guy, and he wanted to cut in. Jenny tried to hide her gratitude as she transferred herself to the new guy's shoulder. He looked like a senior, although she didn't recognize him because he was actually wearing one of those thematic little masks. A black one.

Jenny didn't care who he was. He'd saved her from Brian, and from her guilt at coming with Brian under false pretenses. She saw now that she was going to have to apologize to Brian before tonight was over, apologize and explain everything. He'd probably hate her. He'd probably leave her stranded at the hotel. Jenny kind of hoped he would; it would make her feel better.

The new guy held her very lightly. Jenny floated in his arms and let her mind drift back to junior prom. She had worn ivory lace, soft and romantic and old-fashioned, the kind Tom liked. Audrey had worn a different classic black dress. Summer had been in pale aquamarine, with fringe all over, like a flapper. Tom had looked wonderful in severe black and white. Afterward they'd all gone to McDonald's in their fancy clothes, laughing and fooling around. It had been a wonderful night because they'd been together.

Now here she was in fairyland, surrounded by strangers.

That thought was a little disturbing.

She and the new guy had swayed a little away from the other dancers. He actually seemed to know something about dancing, or at least he was semimobile. It was darker here near the balcony. Jenny felt strangely isolated.

367

And—it was curious, but everything seemed to have slowed. The music had changed. The band seemed to have segued into another slow dance, a haunting melody by some female vocalist Jenny knew but couldn't put her finger on at the moment. Otherworldly. Weird of them to do that without giving people a chance to change partners.

Weird melody, too, but beautiful. It was music that got into your blood, that made you feel strange.

Jenny was feeling very strange.

Time seemed to be stretching.

She didn't want to look up, because that was bad manners unless you wanted to be kissed. And Jenny didn't, whatever kind of music it was. Safer just to keep her head down.

They were on the threshold of the balcony now, and Jenny could look out over it onto the ocean. It was even darker here, so you could see the ocean below. Spotlights reflected off the water, looking like a handful of moons.

Oddly, there was no one on the balcony. Jenny would have thought it would have been crammed body-to-body, but there was nobody here—or at least nobody she could see in the dark. Her partner was leading her toward the darkest corner.

I shouldn't go. . . . *Oh, God, I'm going to have to say Vada via, cretino again.* . . .

But she couldn't seem to resist.

Here on the balcony she could feel the night air, just faintly cool on her arms and the back of her neck. The music seemed distant. She could no longer make out words, only single notes, pure and clear as drops of water falling into a still pool. Falling slowly. Jenny had the queer feeling that she herself was falling.

As loud as the music was the roar of the ocean. They were near the edge of the balcony now. The waves were hissing and crashing on the beach below. An eerie sound, Jenny thought, her mind strangely muddled. A formless, featureless, endless sound. Like white noise . . .

Shhshhshhshhshhshhshh.

All at once she was awake. Awake, with chills sweeping over her and icy terror in her stomach. Not only her little fingers but the sides of her hands were tingling.

Get out of here!

Then, at last, she tried to pull away. But her partner wouldn't let her. She was held in a grip of steel. One of his arms was trapping her arms, the other was holding the back of her head.

She couldn't move. There was no question of screaming. She was alone with him on the balcony, separated by what seemed like miles from the rest of the dance. She could no longer hear any music, only wind in the palm trees and the ocean crashing below. They were very close to a very long drop.

She could see a strand of her partner's hair now, above a

shirt collar as black as his tux. She hadn't realized that before—
he was all in black and his hair was blond. Blonder than Brian's,
blonder even than Cam's. Almost white—

—as white as frost or icicles or mist, as white as winter—

—as white as death—

A voice whispered in her ear, *"Famished."*

Not like that. Longer. *"Faaamishhshhed . . ."*

CHAPTER 9

Everything went gray.

Blood roared in Jenny's ears like the ocean. She was thrown back, in one instant, to the moment when she and Tom and the others had been sucked into the Game, dragged into the Shadow World. She felt the same riptide dragging at her now, the same dark fog overcoming her senses. The same mindless, helpless terror. She was falling into the emptiness.

She didn't faint. She wished she could, but she didn't. She hung in his arms, barely supporting her own weight, feeling darkness all around her, and remained conscious.

He was going to kill her. He was the voice on the phone. He'd sent the Shadow Wolf after her and Audrey, he'd sent the snake after her in computer class. He'd killed Gordie Wilson.

She could still hear the distorted, malign whisper in her head: *"Famished. . ."*

Jenny sobbed.

Sheer terror gave her the strength to take her own weight again, to try and get free again. To her astonishment, he let her. She reeled backward two steps and came up against the balcony railing. Then she just stared at him.

Her first thought was that she should have been more prepared—but there was no way to prepare for Julian. He was always a shock to the senses.

His eyes behind the black mask were like liquid cobalt. His entire face was shadowed. His hair shone in the dimness, as white as moonlight on water.

He wasn't like a human. He was sharper, fiercer, brighter than any human could be. More *real*—which was strange, since *this* was supposed to be the real world.

He was in her world now, not even in some halfway place like the More Games store which seemed to exist between the worlds. He was here, walking around, capable of *anything*.

And just now he radiated menace. Danger.

Jenny's heart was beating so hard and erratically that she thought she might shatter.

"Yellow roses mean infidelity, you know," he said casually.

She remembered his voice now. Once away from it, she'd forgotten. She'd only remembered what she'd *thought* about it, which was that it was musical and elemental, like water running over rock, but that didn't really give any sense of its beauty—or its coldness.

She put a hand to the cluster of miniature roses at her shoulder. The lovely pale flowers with their golden sheen. In her mind she saw Brian blinking at the sight of them, heard him saying, *"The florist must have screwed up. . . ."*

"You sent them," she said. Her voice came out oddly—choked and so openly frightened that she was ashamed. She wanted to tear the roses off, but her hands were shaking.

"Of course. Didn't you know?"

She should have known, but she'd been too stupid. All night she'd been too stupid. She had gone off with a boy in a mask because he didn't look like Julian, forgetting that Julian could look like anyone he wanted. Or *had* she forgotten? Maybe some part of her had known, and had wanted to get it over with. She'd been so frightened for so long.

With good reason. The last time she'd been with Julian, she'd betrayed him. She'd lied to him, made him believe her—maybe even trust her. And then she'd slammed a door on him, meaning to trap him behind it forever. She'd left him imprisoned like a genie in a bottle. She could only imagine what he must have felt when he realized what she'd done. Now he'd come for his revenge.

"Why don't you just do it?" she said. She was more pleased with her voice this time; it was clear, if not quite steady. She'd die with dignity. "Go ahead and kill me."

He tilted his silvery-blond head slightly. "Is that what I want to do?" he said.

"It's what you did to Gordie Wilson."

He smiled—oh, God, she'd forgotten that smile. Wolf-hungry. The sort of smile to send you running and screaming—or to make you collapse in a heap on the floor.

"Not personally," he said.

"But it's what you brought me here for, isn't it?" Jenny glanced back at the drop behind her. Her fragile composure was splintering. Hysteria was bubbling up inside her, and she couldn't stop it. If he wasn't going to throw her over, then maybe she ought to jump, because dying fast would be better than whatever he *was* going to do with her. . . . "Just go ahead and *do* it. Just get it over with."

"All right," he said, and kissed her.

Oh.

She'd thought she remembered how it was with Julian, how it felt to be kissed by him. Her memories had lied. Or maybe this kind of thing was too strong for memory to be anything but a shadow of it. In one instant she was transported back to the paper house, back to the shock she'd felt at his first touch. When Tom held her—back in the old days, when Tom still loved her—his arms had made her feel safe. Comforted.

Julian didn't make her feel safe at all. She was trembling instantly. Falling. Soaring. The electricity he carried around with him flooding into her, tingling in every nerve ending. Sweet shocks that sent her mind reeling.

Oh, God, I *can't*—it's wrong. It's wrong, he's *evil*. I can't feel anything for him. I told Tom I didn't feel anything. . . .

Her body didn't listen to her.

He wants to *kill* me. . . .

But he was kissing her as softly as twilight, tiny sweet kisses and long ones that turned wild. As if they were lovers reunited, instead of hunter and prey.

And Jenny was kissing him back. Her arms were around his neck. He changed the pressure of his lips on hers and light flashed through her. She opened her eyes in shock.

"Jenny," Julian said, not moving away, speaking with his lips brushing hers. He sounded glad—exalted. Full of discovery. "You see how it is with us? You can't fight it any more than I can. You've tried; you've done everything you can to kill it. But you can't kill my love for you."

"No," Jenny whispered. His face was so close, the mask making him look more dangerous than ever. He was terrifying—and beautiful. She couldn't look away from him.

"We were meant to be together. It's our destiny. You've put up a good fight, but it's over now. Give in, Jenny. Let me love you."

"*No!*" With sudden strength she pushed him—hard. Shoving him away. The force sent her backward against the railing.

Fury swept over his face. Then it ebbed and he sighed

deeply. "You're going to fight to the end, aren't you? All right. You're exciting when you're angry, and personally I'm starved for the sight of you. In fact, you might say I'm famished—"

"Don't."

"I like the dress," he continued, as if she hadn't spoken. "In a purely aesthetic sense, of course. And I like your hair like that. It makes you look wild and beautiful."

Terrifyingly, Jenny felt wild and beautiful. Felt desirable. It wasn't right, but his eyes on her made her feel as if no one had ever been as beautiful as she was, since the beginning of time.

But she never stopped feeling frightened, either.

He took her hand. She felt—not saw, because she couldn't take her eyes from his—something slip onto her finger. A cold circlet. A ring. She felt the chill of it all around her as if she'd been banded with ice.

The gold ring she'd thrown away.

Julian said, as if quoting:

"This ring, the symbol of my oath,
Will hold me to the words I speak:
All I refuse and thee I choose."

Jenny shut her eyes.

"Don't you remember? I told you the promise was irrevocable. You are sworn mine, Jenny. Now and forever."

If Darkness had taken on a face and a voice, if the powers

of night had gathered themselves together and formed themselves into a human being, they would have made something
like Julian.

And she was his.

Like some horrible old movie, yes. Bride of the Devil. She'd
promised herself to him, and now she had no choice.

Or at least some part of her believed that. A part of her
she hadn't even known existed before she'd met Julian. A part
that had changed her recently, so that people noticed. The wild
part, a part that craved risks. Like the thing in Dee that loved
danger.

It was this part that responded to him, that found the rest
of the world tame by comparison. The part that made her
heart pound and her stomach melt. Her knees literally felt
weak—the way they had after the last big earthquake in L.A.,
when the ground did things solid ground wasn't supposed to
do, when she'd thought she was going to die. Afterward, her
legs had actually felt like wax. The way they did now.

"I've only come to claim what's mine. You cast your own
fate, Jenny, you doomed yourself. That's the way it works with
runes and oaths. You spoke the words, you let them be written, and that's it. Didn't you ever think you'd have to make
good?"

Jenny didn't know what she'd thought. She'd done it to
save Tom and the others—she would have done anything to
save them at that point.

"It was—I couldn't—it wasn't *fair*," she said, fumbling. She was at a disadvantage; she couldn't think properly.

"Fair—let's not get on that again. Life isn't fair. That's not the point. You promised yourself to me."

Jenny opened her mouth to explain, but she couldn't seem to summon up any words.

Because the terrible thing was that he was right. There was no real way to justify what she'd done. She'd given him her word. She'd sworn the oath, knowing it would bind her forever. And she supposed the shameful truth was that she'd hoped to get rid of Julian so that he couldn't collect.

With one finger Julian sketched some lines in the air, a shape like a vase turned on its side. "That's Perthro, the rune of gambling and divination. It's the cup that holds the runes or dice when they're cast."

"Oh, really?" Jenny said weakly, not having the first idea what he was talking about.

"I'll tell you something interesting about the people who discovered those runes. They loved gambling. Crazy about it. They would bet everything—including their freedom—on one throw of the dice. And if they lost, they'd go into slavery cheerfully, because they had made a promise and they always played by the rules. Honor meant more than anything to them."

Jenny looked away, hugging her own arms. She felt very cold. She wished there were somewhere to hide.

"Are you going to keep your promise?"

What could she say? That it was a promise she never should have had to make? Julian had forced her to play the Game in the beginning—but Jenny had come to him looking for a game. Looking for something scary and sexy, something to provide excitement at a party. Julian had just given her what she'd asked for. It was her own fault for meddling with forbidden things.

But she couldn't—she *couldn't.*

Teeth sunk into her lower lip, she looked at Julian. She could hardly meet his eyes, but she did. She shook her head.

There. Now it was out. She didn't have any excuses, but she wasn't going to keep her word.

"You know I could just make you."

She nodded. It was what she expected. But at least she wouldn't have gone to him willingly.

He turned to look down at the ocean, and Jenny waited.

"What do you say we play another game?"

"Oh, *no,*" Jenny whispered, but he was going on.

"I could just force you—but I'll give you a sporting chance. One throw of the dice, Jenny. One more game. If you win, you're free of the promise. If you lose, you keep it." He turned back to look at her, and in the eyeholes of the mask she could see midnight blue. "Do you want to play, or do we just resolve this here and now?"

Don't panic—*think.* It's your only chance. It's better than no chance.

And the wild part in her was responding to his challenge, surging to meet it. Danger. Risk. Excitement.

"One throw of the dice," she said softly. "I'll play."

He flashed her the wolfish smile. "No holds barred, then. No quarter asked or given—for any of the players."

Jenny froze. "Wait a minute—" she began.

"Did you think I was going to fool around? This game is deadly serious—like the last one."

"But it's between *us*," Jenny said desperately. "Just you and me—"

"No." The eyes behind the mask were narrow. "This is a game for the original players, for everyone who was in the paper house. No more and no less. On my side, myself and the Creeper and the Lurker. On your side—everyone who helped trick me and betray me. I'm going to catch them one by one, starting with Little Red Riding-Hood."

"No," Jenny said, in terror. Oh, God, what had she done? Summer had *died* in the last Game. . . .

"Yes. And it starts now. Ready or not, here I come. Find my base and you can stop me from taking them to the Shadow World."

"Taking *who*—?"

"Your friends. Find them after I take them and you all go free. If not"—he smiled—"I keep them all."

Jenny didn't understand. Panic was rioting inside her. She

wasn't ready—she didn't know the rules. She didn't even know what game they were playing.

"Julian—"

Quick as a cat, quick as a striking snake, he kissed her. A hard kiss, and Jenny was responding before she knew it.

When it was over, he held her tightly to his chest a moment. She could hear his heart beating—just like a human heart, she thought dizzily. Then he whispered in her ear, "The new game is lambs and monsters." And he was gone.

Gone from the balcony, just like that. The warmth dissolved from Jenny's arms, and she was standing alone.

She could hear the music again. It might all have been a dream, but she could still feel Julian's hard kiss on her mouth.

The shadows on the balcony had lightened in his absence. Jenny looked around fearfully. Julian had said that the Game would start now. Julian didn't say things he didn't mean.

But she couldn't see anything unusual. The dance was going on inside the ballroom. Jenny turned and gripped the railing of the balcony, looking over.

Spotlights softly lit the beach below. One of them caught the glint of copper.

Audrey! That was Audrey down there, and the dark-haired figure beside her must be Eric. They were yards away from the other people on the sand, walking hand in hand down the beach. Into the darkness.

The Game starts now. . . . I'm going to catch them one by one, starting with Little Red Riding-Hood.

Red—like Audrey's hair.

"Audrey! *Audrey!*" Jenny screamed. Her voice disappeared into the background of music without even a ripple. She could feel how small and faint it was compared to the roaring of the ocean. Jenny looked around wildly; there was no way from the balcony down to the beach.

Audrey and Eric were walking out of the range of the lights now, heading into the shadows.

"Audrey!"

Audrey didn't hear her.

Something about dances always went to Audrey's head.

For instance, she didn't really like Eric, the boy she was presently kissing. She just couldn't help it—something about dances got to her. All the lights—and the dark corners. The sparkly dresses and the compliments and the music. It was better than shopping.

And Eric was a pretty good kisser, for an American boy.

Not as good as Michael, though. Michael Cohen was a world-class kisser, although you'd never think it to look at him. It was one of the best-kept secrets at Vista Grande High, and Audrey meant it to remain that way.

She felt a slight twinge of guilt, thinking of Michael. Well, but she'd told him she didn't care about Eric. She was doing it to help Jenny.

Who was up in the hotel trying to deal with Brian and his unwanted attentions. Maybe it was time Audrey did something about that.

"Eric," she said, detaching herself and neatening her hair. "We'd better get back."

He started to protest, but Audrey was already turning. She hadn't realized how far they'd walked away from the lights of the hotel.

"Come on," she said uneasily.

She had only taken a few steps when she caught movement out of the corner of her eye. It was on her left, on the land side. Something in the shadows, a quick bright flicker.

Maybe just some small animal or bird. "Eric, come on."

He was sulking. "You go, if you want to."

Oh, fine. She began walking as quickly as she could. Her bare feet sank with each step into the soft, crumbly, faintly damp sand.

The hotel spotlights seemed miles away. The ocean stretched out to her right, unimaginably vast. To her left darkness blanketed a slope covered with ice plant. Between the darkness and the sea, Audrey felt small and vulnerable in comparison. It was a bad feeling.

She turned suddenly and looked into the darkness. She couldn't see anything now. Maybe nothing was there.

Then she heard a cry behind her. Audrey whirled, straining to see in the darkness. Something was going on back there— some kind of activity.

"Eric? Eric!"

Another cry. And, louder, a terrible sound that Audrey could hear over the ocean. A guttural, vibrating snarl. A bestial noise.

Sand was spraying. Audrey could see some kind of thrashing. "*Eric!* Eric, what's happening?"

The thrashing had stopped. Audrey took an uncertain step forward. "Eric?"

Something glimmered, coming toward her.

Not Eric. Something blue and shining. Like an optical illusion, there and then gone. Audrey tried to make her eyes focus—and the lost time was fatal. By the time she saw it clearly it was almost on her.

Oh, God—it was unbelievable. In the Shadow World the wolf had looked like a wolf. Huge, massive, but just a wolf. This thing . . . was a phantom.

Like something painted with luminous paint on the air. Nothing in between the brush strokes. Not exactly a skeleton—something worse. A specter. A wraith-wolf.

The growling was real.

Audrey turned and ran.

It was right behind her. She could hear its growling over the roar of the ocean, over her own sobbing breath. Her legs were beginning to ache already. The thick sand sucked at her, dragging her down. It was like running in slow motion.

She was closer to the lights. If she could just get there—but it was too far. She would never make it.

The ground opened up in front of her.

That was what it looked like. A hole, black against the gray sand. Black with flickering electric-blue edges.

The sand that had been her enemy helped her now, allowed her to catch herself and fall to her knees. She fell right on the brink of the hole, staring down in disbelief.

God—God. It was like nothing she had ever seen. Endless blackness forever. Down at the very bottom there might have been the shimmer of a blue flame.

Audrey didn't want to see any more. She staggered to her feet and ran toward the slope on her left. If she could climb up through the ice plant—maybe she could lose herself there.

But it was fast. It came up on her left side, cutting her off, forcing her to swerve. It turned with her, forcing her to swerve again. To circle back toward the hole.

Audrey stumbled again and heard a snarl right behind her. Hot breath on her neck.

She didn't have the breath to scream, although there was a screaming in her brain. She clawed her way up and was running again.

The way it wanted her to go. She realized that too late. The hole was in front of her, almost beneath her feet. She couldn't stop herself this time.

CHAPTER 10

In midair she was knocked to the side with stunning force. A brutal blocking tackle. She landed with her face crushed into the sand. Not in the hole, on the beach.

Chaos was going on above her. On top of her. A whole football team scrimmaging there. Thick snarls, gasping breath, then suddenly a yelp. Sand fountained around her.

Then it all stopped.

Audrey lay still for a moment longer, then rolled over to look.

Tom was half sitting, half crouching in the sand, his dark hair wildly mussed, his face scratched. He was breathing in gasps. In his hand was a Swiss Army knife, the blade not shining but dark. The wolf was gone. So was the hole.

"Is it dead?" Audrey panted. She could hear the hysteria in her own voice.

"No. It went into that crater thing. Then the crater disappeared."

"Oh," Audrey said. She looked at him, blinked. "You know, we've got to stop meeting like this." Then she collapsed back on the sand.

"*Audrey!* Audrey, where are you? *Audrey!*"

Audrey had seldom heard a voice filled with so much terror, but she was drifting in an endorphin cloud of overexertion. She could barely rouse herself to wave a hand without looking.

"We're here!" Tom shouted. "Here!"

The next moment Jenny was on her knees beside them. "Oh, God, what happened? Are you all right?"

"The wolf happened," Tom said. "She's all right, it's just reaction."

"Are *you* all right? Oh, Tom, you're bleeding!"

Sounds of hugging. Normally, Audrey would have let them have their reunion in peace, but now she said, "Eric's back there. I don't know if he's all right."

"I'll go see." Tom detached himself from Jenny's arms and went. Jenny turned to Audrey, golden dress shining in the gloom. "*What happened?*"

"It tried to chase me into a hole. A hole," she repeated, before Jenny could ask, and described the thing she'd seen. "I don't know why, but it wanted me to fall in."

"Oh, my God," Jenny whispered. "Oh, God, Audrey, it's all my fault. And if Eric is dead—"

"He's not dead," Tom said, coming back up. "He's breathing, and I can't even find any bleeding or anything. The wolf didn't want him; it wanted Audrey."

It was only then that Jenny asked, "What are you doing here?"

Tom looked at the ocean. "I didn't think anything would happen here—but I wasn't sure. I hung around in the hotel just in case. When I saw Audrey going down to the beach, I kept an eye on her from the deck up there."

"Oh, Tom," Jenny said again.

"Thank God you did," Audrey said, picking herself up. She was bruised, but everything seemed to be in working order. Her brand new Oscar de la Renta, though, was another matter. "It's a pity you couldn't have saved the dress, too."

As they climbed the sandy ocean ramp up to the hotel grounds, she said thoughtfully, "Actually, I suppose you saved my life. It doesn't really matter about the dress."

"We can't be the ones to tell the police about Eric," Jenny said. "Because we can't afford to lose the time, and because they might separate us. But we can't just leave him there, either."

There was a fine trembling in all her muscles, her reaction nearly as severe as Audrey's. Deep inside her, though, was a steel core of determination. She knew what had to be done.

"Why can't we lose the time?" Tom asked.

"Because we've got to get the others," Jenny said. "We all need to go somewhere and talk." She saw Audrey, who was slowly making repairs to her hair and dress, give her a sharp glance. "I'll explain later; for now just *trust me*, Tom."

Tom's hazel eyes were dark, puzzled, but after a moment he nodded. "Let me get cleaned up a little; then I'll go tell them at the front desk that there's somebody unconscious on the beach. Then we can go."

When he went, he took a note to send up to the ballroom, too. It was from Jenny to Brian, explaining that she had to leave the prom without him, and that she was sorry.

Jenny shut her eyes and leaned against the wall. Think, she told herself. Don't collapse yet, think.

"Audrey, we both need to call our parents. We've got to tell them—something—some reason why we're not coming home tonight. And then we need to think of somewhere we can go. I wonder how much a hotel room costs?"

Audrey, with two bobby pins in her mouth, just looked at Jenny. She couldn't speak, but the look was enough.

"We're not doing anything dangerous," Jenny assured her. "But we've *got* to talk. And I think we'll only be safe when we're all together."

Audrey removed the pins and licked her lips. "What about Michael's apartment?" she said. "His dad's gone for the week."

"Audrey, you're brilliant. Now think of what we say to our parents, and we'll be fine."

In the end they settled for the old double-bluff. Jenny called her house and told her mother she would be staying at Audrey's; Audrey called her house and told Gabrielle the housekeeper that she would be staying at Jenny's. Then they called Dee, who had her own phone, and had her come out to the hotel in her jeep, while Tom took the RX-7 to his house to pick up Michael. Finally Tom went back out for Zach, while a cross and sleep-wrinkled Michael let the others into his apartment.

It was nearly one-thirty in the morning when they were all together.

"Caffeine," Michael mumbled. "For God's sake."

"Stunts your growth," said Dee. "Makes you blind."

"Why isn't there anything in this refrigerator except mayonnaise and Diet Coke?" Audrey called.

"There should be some cream cheese in there somewhere," Michael said. "And there's Cracker Jack in the cupboard; Dad bought a case at the Price Club. If you love me at all, bring me a Coke and tell me what's going on. I was asleep."

"And I nearly got killed," Audrey said, coming around the corner in time to see his eyes widen. "Here." She distributed Diet Cokes and Cracker Jack to everyone except Dee, who just snorted.

What a mismatched group we are, Jenny thought, looking

around at them. Michael and Audrey were on the couch, Michael in the faded gray sweats he wore as pajamas, and Audrey in the ruins of her saucy little black dress. Dee was on the other side of Audrey, dressed for action in biking shorts and a khaki tank top, long legs sprawled in front of her.

Tom, on the love seat, was windblown and handsome in jeans and a dark blue jersey. Zach sat on the floor by the table wearing a vaguely Oriental black outfit—maybe pajamas, maybe a jogging suit, Jenny thought. Jenny herself was perched on the arm of the love seat in her shimmering and totally inappropriate gold dress. She hadn't thought about changing.

She could see Dee's eyes on the dress, but she couldn't return the amused glance. She was too wrought-up.

"Isn't *somebody* going to explain what's going on?" Michael said, tearing into the Cracker Jack.

"Audrey can start," Jenny said, clasping her hands together and trying to keep them still.

Audrey quickly described what had happened.

"But what's with this hole?" Michael said when she finished. "Pardon me for asking, but how come the wolf didn't just kill you? If it's the same one that attacked Gordie Wilson."

"Because it's a Game," Jenny said. "A new Game."

Dee's piercing night-dark gaze was on her. "You've seen Julian," she said without hesitation.

Jenny nodded, clenching her hands even more tightly together. Tom turned to look at her sharply, then turned away, his shoulders tense. Zach stared at her with an inscrutable expression, the black outfit accentuating his pallor. Michael whistled.

Audrey, her back very straight, said, "Tell us."

Jenny told them. Not everything, but the essence of what had happened, leaving out the bits that nobody needed to know. Like the kissing.

"He said that he'd give me a chance to get free of my promise," she finished. "That he was going to play a new Game with us, and that we were all players. And at the end he said that the new Game was lambs and monsters."

Audrey drew in her breath, frowning. "Like that thing we saw those kids playing?"

"*What* lambs and monsters?" Michael demanded. "I never heard of it."

"It's like cops and robbers," Jenny said. "It starts like hide-and-seek—if you're the monster, you count while all the lambs hide. Then when you find a lamb, you chase it—and if you tag it, it's caught. Then you bring it back to your base and keep it as a prisoner until somebody else sneaks up to let it free."

"Or until all the lambs are caught and they get eaten," Audrey said darkly.

"Cute game," said Zach, then relapsed into silence.

"If we're playing, we'd better figure out the rules," Dee said.

"We may not have to play," Jenny said.

They all looked at her. She knew she was flushed. She had

been thinking ever since she'd looked over the balcony railing to see Audrey's tiny figure disappear into darkness, and by now she'd worked herself into a rather odd state.

"What do you mean?" Dee said, lynx-eyed.

Jenny heard herself give a strange little overstrained laugh. "Well, maybe I should just stop it right now."

She was surprised by the volume of the protest.

"*No!*" Audrey cried. "Give in to a guy—any guy? Absolutely not. Never."

"We have to fight him," Dee said, smacking a slender fist into her palm. "You know that, Jenny."

"We're *going* to fight him," Tom said grimly.

"Uh, look," Michael said, and then got Audrey's elbow in his ribs. "I mean—you'd better not."

"That's right, you'd *better* not," Audrey said. "And I'm the one who got chased tonight, so I'm the one who's got the right to say it."

"We won't *let* you," Dee said, both long legs on the floor now, leaning forward in the intensity of her emotion. "It's our problem, too."

Jenny could feel herself flushing more deeply as a wave of guilt swept her. They didn't understand—they didn't know that she'd almost surrendered of her own free will.

"He's evil," Tom was saying. "You can't just give up and let evil win because of us. You *can't*, Jenny."

Zach's dry voice cut through the impassioned atmosphere.

"I don't think," he said, "that there's much point in arguing about it. Because from what Jenny said before, it sounded like she agreed to the new Game."

"I did," Jenny said. "I didn't know—when I agreed I thought he'd leave the rest of you alone. I didn't think you'd be involved."

"And he said the Game had started. Which means—"

"There's nothing she can do to change it now, even if she wanted to." Audrey finished Zach's sentence crisply.

"Like I said"—Dee gave her most bloodthirsty smile—"I think we'd better figure out the rules."

They all looked at one another. Jenny saw the consensus in all their faces. They were all together now, even Tom. Like the old days. All for one and one for all.

She sat down on the love seat beside Tom.

"So what do we need to do to win?" Audrey asked.

"Avoid getting caught," Zach said tersely.

Michael, rummaging glumly in his Cracker Jack, said, "*How?* We can't stay here forever."

"It's not as simple as that," Dee said. "Look—there are different kinds of games, right? The first Game, the one in the paper house, was like a race game. In a race game the point is to get from the start to the goal in a certain amount of time— or before everybody else does."

"Like Parcheesi," Jenny said.

"No, like Chutes and Ladders!" Michael said, looking up

excitedly. "Remember that? You throw the dice and go across the board—and sometimes you can go up a ladder, the way we went up the stairs in the paper house. And sometimes you fall down a chute—"

"—which we did, on the third floor," Dee said.

"We had that game as kids," Zach said with a half glance at Jenny. "Only ours was called *Snakes* and Ladders."

"Okay, the point is that lots of games are race games," Dee went on. She jumped up and began to pace the room. "But then there are hunting games, too—those are actually the oldest games of all. Like hide-and-seek. That started out as practice for stalking wild animals."

"How do you know?" Michael said suspiciously.

"Aba told me. And tag is like capturing domestic animals. This new game Julian is playing is a hunting and capturing game."

Tom shrugged bleakly. "So he's planning to hunt down and capture each of us animals."

"Trophies," Zach said in a low voice. "Like my father's."

"Not like your father's," Dee said, stopping to look at him. "Your father's are dead. This is more like a game where you catch each of the animals and put them in a big pen to wait for the slaughter."

Michael choked on his Coke.

"Well, it's true," Dee said. "He didn't say he was going to kill us one by one. He said he was going to capture us—until the free ones find his base."

Wiping his mouth, Michael said hoarsely, "Let's find it now and avoid the whole thing."

"But that's the *point*," Dee said, sitting on the windowsill. "How do we find it?"

"How *can* we?" Zach said. "It's hopeless."

Tom was still looking into the distance. "There might be another way," he began, and then stopped and shook his head. Jenny didn't like the expression on his face. She didn't like the way the green flecks in his eyes showed.

"Tom . . ." she said, but Audrey was talking to her.

"Didn't he tell you anything about it, Jenny? His base?"

"No," Jenny said. "Only that it was somewhere to keep us before he takes us to the Shadow World."

"Which means it's not in the Shadow World itself," Dee said, and Michael muttered, "Thank God."

"But wherever it is, you get there through the holes?" Audrey said. "Oh, wonderful. I'll pass, thank you."

"These holes, now," Michael said thoughtfully. "I think they're very interesting."

"Maybe because you have one for a brain," Audrey said with a snappishness she hadn't shown to Michael in weeks.

Michael gave her a startled glance quite different from his standard wounded look. "No, really," he said. "You know, they make me think of something. There's a story by Ambrose Bierce—the book's probably around here somewhere." He twisted his head toward the wall-to-wall bookcases that were the main feature of the living room. Michael's father wrote science fiction, and the apartment was filled with strange things. Models of spaceships, posters of obscure SF movies, weird masks—but mainly books. Books overflowing the shelves and lying in piles on the floor. As usual, Michael couldn't find the one he was looking for.

"Well, anyway," he said, "Ambrose Bierce wrote this trilogy about weird disappearances, and there was this one story about a sixteen-year-old boy. His name was Charles Ashmore, and one night after it snowed he went out to the spring to get water. Well, the thing was, he went out the door and he never came back. Afterward, his family went outside to see what was the matter, and they saw his tracks in the snow—and the tracks went halfway to the spring and just stopped dead." Michael lowered his voice dramatically. "Nobody ever saw him again."

"Great," Jenny said. "But what has that got to do with things?"

"Well, the story was *supposed* to be fiction, right? But there was another part in the book, where this German doctor—Dr. Hern, or something—had a theory about how people disappeared. He said that 'in the visible world there are void places'—sort of like the holes in Swiss cheese."

"And that guy fell into one?" Dee said, looking intrigued.

"Fell—or was dragged. Like I said, the stories were *supposed* to be fiction. But what if there really are voids like that? And what if Julian can—well, control them?"

"That's a nasty idea," Dee said. "I like it."

"Are you saying all people who disappear fall into the Shadow World?" Audrey asked.

"Maybe not all of them, but maybe some of them. And maybe not all the way in, maybe just partway. In the story, when Charles Ashmore's mother went by the place where he disappeared the next day, she could hear his voice. She heard it fainter and fainter every day, until it finally just faded completely."

"A halfway place," Jenny whispered. "Like the More Games store—some place halfway between the Shadow World and here."

Dee was looking at her shrewdly. "Like Julian's base, huh? Somewhere to keep us until he takes us to the Shadow World."

"And you hear about vortex things in Stonehenge and Sedona, Arizona," Michael said. "Was it like a vortex, Audrey?"

"It was big and black," Audrey said shortly. "I don't know how much more vortexy you can get." But she gave Michael the prize from her Cracker Jack, a blue plastic magnifying glass. He put it beside his prize, a mini baseball card.

Jenny was playing absently at her own prize package, not really seeing it. "But it doesn't help us find the base," she said. "Unless we jump into one of those voids, and then I don't think we're coming back."

"It closed up completely," Tom said. "After the wolf jumped

into it, it just disappeared. I don't even think I could find the place again."

"Anyway, I'll bet he can move them around," Michael was beginning, when Jenny gasped.

She had torn open her prize package. She'd been fiddling with the prize, completely preoccupied with the question of voids—until something caught her eye.

"What is it?" Dee said, jumping up from the windowsill.

"It's a book of poetry—or something." It was a very small book, on cheap paper with large print. One sentence per page. But it was a very strange poem for a Cracker Jack prize.

Jenny read:

"In the midst of the word she was trying to say,
In the midst of her laughter and glee,
She had softly and suddenly vanished away—
For the Snark *was* a Boojum, you see."

There was dead silence in the room.

"It could be a coincidence," Zach said slowly.

Michael was shaking his rumpled head. "But those lines are wrong. That's not the way they go—look, *that* book I know I've got." He went into his bedroom and came out with *Alice in Wonderland and Other Favorites*. "They're from a poem about these guys who go out hunting imaginary animals—Snarks.

399

Only some of the Snarks are Boojums, and those hunt *you*. And in the end one of them finds a Snark, and it turns out to be a Boojum. But it's *he* in the poem—'In the midst of the word *he* was trying to say, / In the midst of *his* laughter and glee . . .' You see?"

"Cracker Jack wouldn't make a mistake like that," Tom said, with a wry smile.

"No," Jenny whispered. "It's from Julian. But is it about what almost happened tonight—or about something that's *going* to happen?"

The silence stretched. Tom's brows were drawn together. Dee had her jaguar look on and was pacing again. Zachary's gray eyes were narrow, his lean body tense and still.

Michael had put down the book. "You think he's giving us clues in advance?"

"It would be—sporting, I guess," Jenny said. "And he gave me a kind of clue on the balcony, remember. He said he'd go after 'Little Red Riding-Hood' first."

Everyone looked at everyone else speculatively. Suddenly Dee whirled and did a swift, flowing punch-and-kick. "Then we might just have a chance!"

Excitement was passing from one of them to another like sparks traveling down a fuse.

"If we can figure the clues out beforehand—and then just *surround* the person they're about . . ." Dee said.

"I know we can! I always wanted to be Sherlock Holmes," said Michael.

"I think it might actually work," Tom said. A new light had kindled in his hazel eyes.

Dee laughed exultantly. "Of course it will work! We're going to beat him."

Jenny was caught up in the fervor herself. Maybe they *could* outthink Julian. "It's not going to be easy—"

"But we'll do it," Audrey said. "Because we have to." She gave Jenny a spiky-lashed glance and picked up several empty Coke cans to take to the kitchen.

"We'd better start with the one we have, then," Zach said, turning a cool, analytical gaze on Jenny's riddle book.

"Unless that one's already finished," Michael said. "I mean, if it was about Audrey—or should I call you Little Red Riding-Hood?" he shouted to the kitchen.

"Call me madam," Audrey said from around the corner, her good humor clearly restored. "Call me Al." She began to sing a Paul Simon song. "'I can call you Betty, and Betty, when you call me, you can call me—'"

"Well?" Michael yelled when she didn't finish. "What can I call you?"

Audrey didn't answer, and Michael snorted, "Women!"

Zach was saying, "Yeah, but what if it's a new clue? It says *she,* so it's got to be either—"

Jenny heard him as if from a distance. She was listening, listening, and all at once she couldn't breathe.

"Audrey?" she said. The sound of rattling cans in the kitchen had stopped. "Audrey? *Audrey?*"

Everyone was looking at her, frightened by something in her voice. The sound of raw panic, Jenny guessed. Jenny stared back at them, and their images seemed to waver. Utter silence came from the kitchen.

Then she was on her feet and moving. She reached the corner before any of them, even Dee. She looked into the kitchen.

Her screams rang off the light fixture in the ceiling.

"No! No! Oh, God, no!"

CHAPTER 11

The kitchen was empty. A trickle of water ran out of the faucet, and there was an odd, sharp smell. Sitting grotesquely in the middle of the green linoleum floor was a paper doll.

It was folded to allow it to sit, and one arm was twisted up to give it a mockingly casual air. As if Audrey were saying: "Here I am. Where have *you* been?" It was obscene.

Tom's hands were on Jenny's shoulders, trying to calm her. She wrenched away from him and picked the macabre little figure up. It was the doll Audrey had used in the Game, her playing piece in the paper house. Audrey herself had drawn the face, had colored in the hair and clothes with Joey's crayons. Jenny hadn't seen it since she'd packed it up with the rest of the

Game in the white box. She realized suddenly that it hadn't been in Angela's toolshed. None of the dolls had.

The waxy face looked up at Jenny with a terrible cunning smile. A *U* of bright pink. As if this doll knew what had happened to the real Audrey, and was glad about it.

"Oh, God—God," Jenny was gasping, almost sobbing. The doll crumpled in her hand. Everything in the kitchen was wavering.

"I don't believe it," Michael said, pushing past the others. "Where is she?" He stared at Jenny, grabbed her arm. "Where is she?"

Tom grabbed Michael. "Let go of her."

"Where's Audrey?"

"I said, let go of her!"

Dee's voice rang out dangerously. "Cool off, both of you!"

"But how did she get out of the kitchen?" Michael said wildly. "We were right around the corner—we didn't hear anything. Nothing could have happened to her. We were right there."

Dee was kneeling on the floor, running her fingers across the linoleum.

"It's darker here—see? This whole area is darker. And it smells burned."

Jenny could see it now, a circle of darker green several feet in diameter.

Tom was still gripping Michael, but his voice was quiet.

"You didn't see that thing on the beach—that void, Mike. It didn't make any noise at all. That's how she got out of the kitchen."

"'In the midst of the word she was trying to say, / In the midst of her laughter and glee,'" Zachary quoted, behind them.

Jenny turned sharply to see him standing there. With his thin, intense face and his dark-circled eyes, he looked like a prophet of doom. But when his gray eyes met Jenny's, she knew he cared. He was still holding the poem.

The last of the cloudiness in Jenny's head vanished. Tears and hysterics weren't going to help Audrey. They weren't going to help anyone. She looked down at the crumpled paper doll in her hand.

It was her fault. Audrey had fallen into a black hole, and it was Jenny's fault, just as Summer's death had been. But Audrey wasn't dead yet.

"I'll find her," Jenny said softly to the paper thing she held. "I'll find her, and then I'll rip you to pieces. I'm going to win this Game."

It went on smiling its cunning waxy smile, bland and malevolent.

Michael was sniffling and rubbing his nose. Dee was investigating the floor like an ebony huntress.

"It's like the marks a UFO might leave," she said. "When it lands, I mean. A perfect circle."

"Or a fairy ring," Michael said thickly. "She was so scared of that kind of stuff—legend stuff, you know?" Tom patted him on the back.

"The Erlking," Jenny said grimly. She reached across Tom to grip the sleeve of Michael's sweatshirt. "But we got her back from him last time, Michael. We'll get here back now."

Dee stood in one fluid, graceful motion. "I think we'd all better stay together from now on," she said.

Zach had moved up behind Jenny. The five of them *were* together, standing in one connected knot in the center of the kitchen. Jenny felt herself draw strength from all the others.

"We can sleep in the living room," Michael said. "On the floor. We can push the furniture back."

They raided the bedrooms for blankets and mattresses and found sleeping bags in the closet. In the bathroom Jenny stripped off her golden dress and put on an old sweatsuit of Michael's. She jammed the shimmering material in the laundry hamper, never wanting to see it again.

It scared her to be alone even for a minute.

But we haven't had another clue, she thought. He can't do anything else without another clue. It wouldn't be fair.

"It wouldn't be *sporting*," she said through her teeth to the wall. It had suddenly occurred to her that Julian might be able to hear her. To see her, even—he'd watched her from the shadows for years. It was a disturbing thought, to know that no place was private, but right now Jenny hoped he was listening.

"It's no Game at all if we don't have a chance," she told the wall softly but fiercely.

In the living room she sat down on a mattress next to Tom. He put an arm around her, and she rested against him, glad of his warmth and solidity.

If there was one tiny comfort in all of this, it was that Tom was with her again. She snuggled into his arm and shut her eyes. This was where she could forget about Julian—forget about everything dark and terrible. Tom's strong warm hand clasped hers, held tightly.

Then she felt the pressure released and sensed the change in Tom's body. Tension flooding in. He was holding her hand up, looking at it.

No, not at her hand. At the ring.

The golden band which had felt like ice on her finger earlier that night had warmed to her body temperature. She hadn't even noticed it for hours.

Now, horrified, she snatched her hand back from Tom's. She tried to pull the ring off. It wouldn't come.

Soap, she thought. She pulled frantically, twisting the circlet, reddening her finger. Soap or butter or—

It was no good.

She knew without even trying. The ring was on to stay. She could do anything she liked, but it wouldn't come off until Julian wanted it to. If she could have gotten it off, she might have been able to change the words inside—and Julian would never risk that. He'd said that speaking and writing words made them true. He would never take the chance that Jenny might change the words and change her fate.

"We're going to win the Game," she said to the shuttered darkness in Tom's eyes. "When we win, I'm free of my promise." She said it almost pleadingly—but Tom's face remained closed. He'd gone away again, leaving a polite stranger in his place.

"We'd better get to sleep," he said and turned to his own pile of blankets.

Jenny was left sitting there, feeling the inscription on the inside of the ring as if the letters were burning their way into her skin.

Nothing is as frightening as waking up and not knowing who you are, not knowing it's *you* waking. It happened to Jenny Sunday morning. She opened her eyes and didn't know which direction was which. She didn't know her place in the world, where she was in time and space.

Then she remembered. Michael's living room. They were there because of Julian.

She sat up so suddenly that it made her dizzy, and she frantically looked for the others.

They were all there. Michael was curled almost in a ball under his blanket; Dee was sprawled lazily on the couch like a sleeping lioness. Zach was on his back on the floor, his blond ponytail streaming on his pillow. Tom was beside him, face turned toward Jenny, one hand stretched toward her. As if he'd reached out in his sleep, unaware of it.

Jenny took a moment to look at him. He looked different asleep, very young and vulnerable. At times she loved him so much it was like a physical ache, a pain in her chest.

Dee yawned and stretched, sitting up. "Everybody here?" she said, instantly alert and oriented. "Then let's kick Michael and make him get us some breakfast. We're guests."

Tom pulled his hand away when he woke up, and avoided Jenny's eyes.

"Do you really think we can get away with it?" Michael asked doubtfully.

"We've got to," Jenny said. "What else are we going to say to them? 'I'm sorry; your daughter's been kidnapped, but don't worry because we're going to get her back'?"

"It'll be all right as long as we get the housekeeper," Dee said. "I'll talk to her while you go upstairs."

"Then we'll go by your place," Jenny said, "and you can tell your parents you're staying with me. And Zach can tell his parents he's staying with Tom, and Tom—"

"But the question is: will they buy it?" Michael said. "I mean, we're not talking about just one night, here. It could be days before we find that base."

"We'll tell them we've got a school project," Jenny said,

"and it may take a few nights of working on it. We'll *make* them buy it. We have to."

She and Dee and Zach went in Dee's jeep, while Tom and Michael followed in the RX-7. Tom hadn't said a word to her all morning, and Jenny tried to hide her left hand whenever she could. She felt as if the ring were a badge of shame.

They'd decided to go everywhere together from now on. Nobody was ever to be alone, and whenever possible all five of them were to be in the same place. They pulled up in tandem to Audrey's house, and Dee and Jenny knocked on the door while the boys watched from the sidewalk.

"Hi, Gabrielle," Dee said to the housekeeper who answered. "Are Mr. and Mrs. Myers here? Oh, too bad. Well, could you tell them that Audrey's going to spend a couple nights with Jenny and me at Jenny's?"

Meanwhile, Jenny speedily headed up the stairs of the stately house and came back a few minutes later with an armful of clothes. "Audrey just asked me to pick up a few things for her," she said brightly to Gabrielle, and then she and Dee made a fast retreat.

"Whew!" Dee said when they were back in the jeep. Jenny blinked away tears. Handling Audrey's clothes had brought the sense of guilt back. But it had to be done. Audrey would never go anywhere overnight without a few different outfits.

"We probably should have taken her car," Dee said. "She takes *that* everywhere, too."

"Maybe later," said Jenny. "I picked up her keys while I was in her bedroom."

"Next victim," Zachary said from the back seat.

Tom disposed of his parents quickly; he and Michael came out of his Spanish-style house with a bundle of clothes each.

"And a few textbooks," Michael said. "For authenticity."

Jenny's mother was at church. Jenny shouted her message to her father, who was bent over the pool, wrestling with the floating cleaner. "Gonna stay with Dee for a few days, Dad! We're working on a big physiology project!"

"Call us occasionally to let us know you're alive," her father said, pushing his glasses up by hunching his shoulder and not releasing his grip on the pool cleaner.

Jenny gave him one quick frightened glance before she realized it was a joke. Mr. Thornton complained a lot about being the father of a teenager with an active social schedule. She surprised him by running up and kissing his sweaty cheek.

"I will, Daddy. I love you." Then she ran away again.

It was at Zach's house that they ran into trouble.

They were giddy with their previous successes, and not prepared when they pulled up to the mock Tudor house on Quail Run. Jenny went into the garage with Zach while the others talked to Jenny's aunt Lily.

"You keep your textbooks out here?"

"The art ones. And I figure we might as well bring a flashlight." He took one off a hook on the wall.

Jenny looked around the studio Zach had made in the garage. Being here made her think about Julian, about the time in the paper house when he had impersonated Zach. Flustered, she stared at a print on the wall. It was a giant mural print showing school cafeteria tables stacked in a glorious pyramid, four high and four deep, almost blocking the exit. Zach had taken it last year after she and Tom and Dee and he had stacked the tables one night. They'd left the tables that way for the VGHS staff to find the next morning.

Jenny tried to concentrate on the fun of that night, her mind adding color to the gray tones of the picture, but a soft assault on all her senses had begun. She kept seeing Zach's face in her mind, watching it turn to Julian's. Feeling the softness of Julian's hair under her fingers.

"You okay, Jenny? You look kind of red."

"Oh, no, no, I'm fine." More flustered than ever, she added hastily, "So what have you done lately? You haven't shown me any new prints for a while."

Zach's shoulders hunched slightly, and he looked away. "I've been busy with other things," he said.

Jenny blinked. That was a new one. Zach too busy for his photos? But she had to make conversation; she was afraid to let the silence go on.

"What's this?" she said, touching a textbook that lay open on the desk.

"Magritte," Zach said succinctly.

"Magritte? He was a painter, right?"

"A Belgian surrealist." Suddenly focused, Zach picked up the textbook. He looked at it almost fiercely, his features sharp. "Look at this," he said, opening it to a new page. "I was thinking about doing something that would catch the same mood. I just wish . . ." His voice trailed off.

Jenny looked and saw an extremely weird picture. It showed a brown pipe, the kind Audrey's father smoked, with the words *This is not a pipe* under it.

Jenny stared at it, feeling stupid. Beside her, Zach was tense, waiting for her response.

"But—it is a pipe," she said timidly, tapping her finger on the brown bowl.

Zach's gray eyes were still on the book. "No, it isn't."

"Yes, it is."

"No, it isn't. A picture of a pipe is not a pipe."

For a moment she got it—then it slipped away. It made her head hurt, but it also gave her a vaguely excited feeling. Mystical.

"The image isn't reality," Zach said quietly but with force. "Even though we're used to thinking that way a lot of the time. We show a kid a picture of a dog and say 'This is a doggie'— but it's *not*. It's just an image." He glanced at her sideways and added, "A paper house is not a house."

"Unless you have somebody who can *make* an image into reality," Jenny said, giving him a meaningful glance back.

413

"Maybe he's an artist, in a way," Zach said. He flipped to another page. "See this? It's a famous painting."

It was another extremely weird picture, but it took you a moment to see the weirdness. It showed a window in a room, and through the window a pretty landscape. Hills and trees and clouds. Only—it was odd, but under the window were three metal things like the legs of a stand. The legs of an easel, Jenny realized suddenly. There was actually an easel with a canvas on it in front of the window, but the painting on the canvas blended in so exactly with the landscape behind it that it was almost invisible.

It left you wondering: Where was the artist who had left the easel? And who could have painted a picture that blended in so exactly with reality, anyway?

"It's bizarre," Jenny said. "I like it." She smiled at Zach, feeling as if they had a secret. She saw his expression change, and then he looked away, his gray eyes distant.

"It's important to know the difference between image and reality," he said softly. He glanced at her sideways again, as if considering whether to tell her another secret. Considering whether she could be trusted. Then he said almost casually, "You know, I used to think that imaginary worlds were safer than the real one. Then I saw a *real* imaginary world. And it was—" He stopped.

Jenny was startled at his expression. She put her hand on his arm. "I know."

He looked at her. "Remember how we used to play in the

orchard when we were kids? It didn't seem important then to know the difference between what's real and what isn't. But it's important now. It's important to me."

Oh. All at once, Jenny understood. No wonder Zach had been so moody lately. His photography, his art—it wasn't safe anymore. It had been contaminated by their experience in the Shadow World. For the first time in his life Zach was having to face squarely up to reality.

"That's why you haven't done any new prints," she said. "Isn't it, Zach? It's—it's artist's block."

He hunched one shoulder again. "I just haven't seen anything I wanted to photograph. I used to see things all the time and want to shoot them—but lately I just don't care."

"I'm sorry, Zach." But I'm glad you told me, Jenny thought. She felt very close to her cousin just then. She went on in a low voice, "Maybe when this is all over—"

She was cut off by the bang of a door. The quiet moment was shattered. Zach's father stood in the doorway.

He said hello briefly to Jenny, then turned to Zach.

"So here you are," he said. "What's this about you taking off without telling anyone last night?"

Jenny had never been sure she liked her uncle Bill. He was a big man, and he had large hairy hands. His face always seemed rather flushed.

Zach's voice was cool and bloodless. "I just went to spend the night somewhere. Is that a crime?"

"It is when you don't tell your mother or me."

"I left a note."

Mr. Taylor's face got more flushed. "I'm not talking about a note. I don't know what's going on with you anymore. You used to spend most of your time holed up out here"—he gestured around the garage—"and now you're gone all the time. Your mother says you think you're going to spend another night away from home."

"I've got a project to do—"

"Then you can do it right here. You're not staying out overnight on a school night. If you think that, you've got another think coming."

Jenny's stomach had a falling-elevator feeling. She opened her mouth, trying to think of something, anything to say. But she could see by her uncle's face that it wouldn't do any good. He was as stubborn as Zach; stubborner.

The door banged again as he left.

Jenny whirled in dismay. "What are we going to do?"

"Nothing." Face turned from her, Zach slapped the art book shut and put it back on the pressed-wood shelf.

"But, Zach, we have to—"

"Look, if you argue with him, he'll just get madder—and he might start calling around. Do you want him to talk to *your* parents?" He turned back, and his thin face was calm, although Jenny thought his eyes looked a little sore. "Don't rock the boat, Jenny. Maybe he'll let me come tomorrow."

416

"But for tonight—"

"I'll be okay. You just—just watch out for yourself, all right?" He moved when Jenny tried to put a hand on his arm and added, "Tell everybody else what happened, will you? I think I'll just stay here a while. Do some work."

Jenny's hand dropped. "Okay, Zach," she said softly. She blinked. "Goodbye. I mean—see you later." She turned and went quickly out of the garage.

"Now what?" Dee said when they were back at the apartment. They were all quiet, their triumph deflated.

"Now we order some pizza and wait," Michael said.

"And *think,*" Jenny said. "We have to figure out where that base is."

Jenny woke up with a start and thought, hypnopompic hallucination? I think I'm awake, but I'm still dreaming.

Julian was leaning over her.

"Tom!" she cried, turning to see him lying on the floor beside her, his breathing deep and even. Her cry didn't wake him.

"Don't bother. It's only a dream. Come in the other room, where we can have a little privacy."

Jenny, who was wearing her own sweatsuit tonight instead of Michael's, pulled her blanket up higher. Like some Victorian girl in a lacy nightgown. "You're crazy," she told him with dream-calmness. "If I go in there, you'll kidnap me."

"I won't. I promise." His teeth gleamed at her briefly, wolf-like. "Remember Perthro?"

The rune of gambling, Jenny thought, seeing in her mind's eye the lines he'd sketched in the air on the night of the prom. The rune of fair play, of sticking to the rules. Meaning he kept his promises, she supposed. Or that he would keep this one. Or that he *said* he would.

But he might give me a clue about the base, Jenny thought. She and the others hadn't had much luck figuring it out for themselves. And it was a dream, anyway. She got up and followed him to Michael's bedroom, where the clock radio said 4:33 A.M.

"Where's Audrey?" she demanded as he turned to face her. If this had been reality, she would have been frightened of him, maybe too frightened to speak. But it was a dream, and everything she did was governed by dream-logic.

"Safe."

"But where *is* she?"

"That would be telling." His eyes swept over her and he smiled. "I have to say it; you look equally good in grunge and high fashion."

It wasn't a dream. The way he disturbed and excited Jenny was too real. By Michael's bedside lamp she could see his eyes, which at the prom had been shadowed by his mask. She had finally figured out what color they were. It was the blue you see when you're washing your face in the shower and your fingers press on your closed lids. You see filaments of brightness etched against the black, more vibrant than electric blue. A color that isn't really in the wavelengths of light that the human eye can perceive. The color Jenny had seen in afterimage when the computer flashed.

Jenny looked away, simultaneously holding out her hand to him. "I want this off, please. Just until the Game is over, take the ring off."

He took her hand instead, stroking her palm with his thumb. "Is it making Tommy nervous?"

"No—I don't know. I don't like it." She looked at him again, trying to pull her hand away. His fingers were cooler than Tom's, but just as strong. "I *hate* you, you know," she said earnestly. She couldn't see why he never seemed to understand this. "You make me hate you."

"Is that what you're feeling? Hate?"

Jenny was trembling. Stubbornly she nodded.

Very gently he reeled her in by the captive hand, drawing her to him. She'd been wrong. He wasn't as strong as Tom; he was stronger. Fight or scream? Jenny thought. But he was so close now. She could feel the movement of his breathing. Her heart was beating in the base of her throat.

She could feel her eyes widen as she looked up at him. His expression made her stomach flutter. "What are you going to do?"

"I'm going to kiss you . . ."

Oh, was that all?

". . . until you faint."

419

Then shadows seemed to fill all the corners of the room and close in about her.

But some part of her mind still had strength. She didn't faint, although her legs went weak again. She pushed him away.

"You're *evil*," she whispered. "How do you think I could ever love something evil? Unless I'm evil, too. . . ."

She was beginning to wonder about this. But he laughed. "There is no good and evil, only black and white. But either black or white on its own is boring, Jenny. If you mix them you get so many colors—so many colors. . . ."

She turned away. She heard him pick something up, one of Michael's books.

"Here," he said. "Have you read this one?"

It was a poem, "The Human Condition" by Howard Nemerov. Jenny's eyes skimmed over it, not really understanding any of it. It muddled her.

"It's about world and thought," Julian explained. "World being the world, you see, and thought being—everything else. Image. As opposed to reality. He smiled at her. "That's a hint, incidentally."

Jenny was still muddled. She couldn't seem to focus on the poem, and she was strangely tired. Like the old hypnotist's saying, her eyes were heavy. Her whole body felt warm and heavy.

Julian put his arms around her, supporting her. "You'd better wake up now."

"You mean I'd better go to sleep."

420

"I mean wake up. If you don't want to be late." She felt his lips on her forehead and realized her eyes were shut.

She had to open them . . . she had to open her eyes . . . But she was drifting, somewhere dark and silent and warm. Just drifting . . . floating . . .

Some time later Jenny forced her eyes open. Blinked. She was lying on Michael's living room floor.

It had been a dream after all.

But beside her was an open book, facedown. *Contemporary Poetry.* Jenny picked it up and saw the poem Julian had shown her.

Now that she was awake and thinking clearly, the poem made more sense; it was even vaguely exciting. But she didn't have time to appreciate it; her eye fixed on certain words and her heart began to pound.

> Once I saw world and thought exactly meet,
> But only in a picture by Magritte. . . .

The poem went on about the picture of a picture by Magritte—the one Zach had shown Jenny. The one of a painting that stood in front of an open window, matching the landscape outside exactly. Fitting in like a puzzle piece, standing alone in an empty room.

Magritte, Jenny thought. Oh, God! *An empty room.*

Dropping the book, she seized Tom's shoulder. "Tom! Tom, get up! Dee! Michael! It's Zach!"

CHAPTER 12

Zach was asleep when he first felt the creeping around his legs. Or half asleep, anyway—he hadn't really slept for days now. He hadn't dreamed. His daytime thoughts went on going even when he lay there with his eyes shut for hours.

He'd wondered what happened to you when you didn't dream for days. Hallucinations while you were walking around?

Tonight, though, he was definitely drifting when he felt the touch on his ankle. A smooth, rubbery feeling. For a moment he was paralyzed, and a moment was all it took. The rubbery feeling wound its way up his leg, his stomach, his chest. It tightened like a living rope, cutting off his breathing.

Zach's eyes flew open, and he saw clearly the head of the

snake staring into his face. Its eyes were two dots of shining light; its mouth was open so wide it looked as if its jaw were dislocated. As if it were going to *eat* him. Out of that gaping mouth came an endless menacing *hissssssss*. . . .

Unable to move, Zach stared up at the swaying shape. Then, somehow, his perspective changed. His eyes ached from staring, but he couldn't see the snake's head anymore. The two dots of light looked more like two of the glow-in-the-dark stars he'd stuck on his ceiling when he was eight—he'd scraped most of them off when his father yelled, but a few remained.

He couldn't hear the hiss now, either. Only the *shhshhshhshh* of the air-conditioning.

His arms and legs were tangled up in the bedclothes.

God, he thought, and kicked the sheet and blanket off. He got up and turned on the light. Now he knew what happened when you went for days without dreaming. Of course there was no snake in his bed.

The last thing he wanted to do was lie down again, though. Might as well go out to the garage. Even if he couldn't work, it might take his mind off things.

When he got to the garage, the snake was waiting for him.

It wasn't like a real snake. It was a surrealist painter's idea of a snake—swirls of darkness that bunched and surged in a snakelike motion. Blue-white light connecting murky segments of body. A sort of combination between a snake and a lightning bolt in a storm.

It came toward him with the blind hunching of a tomato worm. It was at least ten feet long.

If I could get it over into the corner, Zach thought, his mind cold and clear . . . He glanced at the corner of the garage where his 6x6 SLR stood on a tripod. If he could get it over there, he was almost sure he could get a picture of it.

He wasn't stupid. He saw the danger he was in. But the idea of photographing this thing—seeing what it would look like on film—drove every other thought out of his mind.

It was the first time he'd cared about getting a picture since the day of the Game. All at once his artist's block disappeared, his creativity came rushing back. This was *real* unreality. It might be unsafe, but it was strangely beautiful, too. It was Art.

He was desperate to capture it.

Try the 35 millimeter first, his mind told him. It's closer. Eyes fixed on the wonderfully artistic monster, he reached for the camera on the desk.

The clock in Dee's jeep said 5:45. More than an hour later than it had been in Jenny's dream of Michael's room.

"Oh, God, we're going to be too late," she whispered.

And it was her fault. She hadn't woken up in time. Even with Julian's warning, she hadn't woken up in time.

"Hurry up, Dee! Hurry!"

Trees were silhouetted against a flamingo dawn when they reached Zach's house.

"Let's go through the garage," Tom said as they all jumped out of the jeep. "Last time I was here, the door was unlocked."

Zach wouldn't be so stupid tonight, Jenny thought, but there was no time to argue. She was following the others at a run to the side door of the garage. The door opened under Tom's hand, and they all burst inside.

The garage light was on. There was a sharp, strange smell to the air. A dark circle of soot on the floor.

In its center was a paper doll with gray eyes.

"I was too late," Jenny said stupidly, looking down at the paper-doll Zach she was holding. It stared back at her, the fine lines of its face shaded by Zach's artist's hand. The penciled eyes seemed vaguely surprised.

Dee was rubbing the soot between her fingers. Tom was standing in front of the corner where Zach's camera and a tungsten floodlamp lay knocked over.

"There was a fight," he said.

Michael just licked his lips and shivered.

"His parents must not have heard anything," Jenny said slowly, after a moment. "Or they'd be down here. So we'd better write them a note—from Zach, saying that he's gone to school already."

Michael's voice was subdued. "You're crazy. We can't keep this up. Eventually some of your parents are going to *talk* to each other—"

"What good is it going to do my aunt and uncle to know Zach's gone? What can they do?"

"Put us in orange coveralls," Dee said from the floor. "Too many disappearances," she added succinctly. "If we lose any more friends, we're going to jail. Now, come on, stop talking, and let's get out of here."

Jenny crept into the house and wrote the note before they left.

Back in the car Tom said, "I don't see how *we* can go to school ourselves. Not and stick together."

"Then we'll have to take the day off," Dee said. "Gosh, too bad."

Michael looked at her balefully from the front passenger seat. "You're enjoying this, aren't you?"

She gave him a distinctly uncivilized smile.

"We've *got* to figure out where the base is," Jenny was saying in the back seat. She'd controlled herself very well this time, she thought: no screaming or crying even when she saw the paper doll of Zach. But the rasping feeling of guilt was still with her. "I haven't been very good at figuring out the clues so far," she said, keeping her voice level so the others wouldn't think she was drowning in self-pity.

"Because Julian *wants* it that way," Dee said. Jenny had told them about the dream—leaving out the kiss—on the drive to Zach's house. "He's not playing this Game straight. We got the first clue in plenty of time, but it was too hard. The second clue

426

was dead easy, but there wasn't time to do anything about it."

"I should have woken up sooner," Jenny said in a low voice.

Beside her, Tom started to reach for her, and Jenny saw his face, all planes and shadows in the early morning light. Tom Locke even looked good at the crack of dawn; he woke up looking that way.

Tom's hand dropped back to his side. Jenny knew what it was without asking. She was sitting on his right in the car, and her left hand, with the ring, was in between them.

She looked out the window fiercely and pretended she didn't mind.

"You know, there's one reason I did want to go to school today," she said. "To try and find out about Eric—the guy Audrey was with. See if he's okay."

"I could probably call his house and ask. I know him a little," Tom said, to show he was still talking to her, even if he wouldn't touch her. Oh, we're terribly courteous, Jenny thought. For all the good that does.

"We can call from the apartment," Michael said. "We should probably get some food first."

"No, I tell you what let's do," Dee said, her voice excited. "Let's go see Aba."

"*This* early?"

"Not everybody sleeps like you, Mikey. Besides, she'll give us breakfast."

In the back seat Jenny leaned forward. A heavy weight seemed to have lifted from her chest, at least for the moment. "You're right," she said to Dee. "Let's go see Aba. Maybe she knows what we should do."

Aba lived in a house beside Dee's mother's house. The two buildings were on the same property, but Aba's house had a distinctly different character. Dee and her friends always called it the Art Pavilion.

One entire wing was devoted to Aba's craft, centering around the studio where she did her sculpting. The large, airy room was all soaring asymmetrical walls and skylights.

Aba was at work when the children came in, taking moist gray clay from a bowl and slapping it on a wire armature.

"What's it going to be?" Dee asked, coming up behind her.

"Good morning," Aba said firmly, and when they'd all said good morning, she said, "A bust of Neetu Badhu, your mother's manicurist. She has a very interesting face, and she's due here at seven."

"Then we'd better hurry," Dee said. "Is it okay if we use your phone? And get some breakfast?"

"There are caramel rolls in the kitchen," Aba said. "Get them—and then come back and tell me why you're here."

While the others went to the kitchen, Tom got on the phone.

"Eric's okay," he said when he hung up. "He was home

from school today, but there's nothing really wrong with him. The police are interested in talking with anybody who saw the attack, though—which means Audrey."

Michael stopped eating his roll. "Which means they might be trying to track her down," he said. "Great."

"Don't worry about it, Mikey," Dee said comfortingly. "You'll probably be next, so you won't be here when our Great Deception comes crashing down."

"Dee," Aba said, "have you been telling lies?"

"Yup. Our whole life these last few days has been a tissue of fibs."

Aba shook her head and wiped her clay-smeared hands on her denim smock. "Now," she said to the group, "tell me."

And they did. They told her the truth about what had been happening since they'd been released from the police station; how they'd been looking for the paper house, how they'd found it, what Julian had said to Jenny about the new Game. And what had happened to Zach and Audrey.

Aba listened to it all, her beautiful old face grave and attentive. When seven o'clock came, she sent the manicurist away, covered the bust with a wet cloth, and kept listening.

When they finished, she sat quietly for a moment. Jenny half expected her to say something about how wrong it was to deceive their parents—Aba was an adult, after all. She half expected Aba to say that Dee couldn't stay with the rest of them because it was too dangerous. And, although she didn't expect it, she wished passionately that Aba would say, "Here's the answer," and solve all their problems for them.

Aba did none of these things. Instead, after several minutes of quiet sitting, she said, "You know, last night I dreamed a Hausa story my mother used to tell me. It's been a long, long time since I thought of that story. I wonder if I didn't dream it for you."

"For us?"

"Yes. Maybe I was meant to tell it to you." She sat back and thought for a moment, then began, "The story is about a boy and a girl who were in love. But one day, as they were sitting on their mat together, Iblis came along and cut off the boy's head and killed him."

"Iblis?" The name sounded vaguely familiar to Jenny. "Who's that?"

"Iblis," Aba said gravely, "is the prince of darkness, the prince of the *aljunnu*—"

"The genies," Dee said, her eyes flashing at Jenny.

"Yes," Aba said. "But in our folklore the *aljunnu* were not kind genies. They were powerful and evil spirits, and Iblis was their leader. My mother never told me why he cut the boy's head off—but then Iblis always liked to do evil and mischief; maybe he had no particular reason. In any case, Iblis killed the boy, and the girl could do nothing but sit on the mat and cry. After a while the boy's parents came along, and when they saw what had happened, they began to cry, too.

"Then Iblis came back. He waved his hand, and the ground rocked. In front of the boy there appeared a river of fire, a river of water, and a river of cobras. And Iblis turned to the boy's mother and said, "If you would like to bring your son back to life, all you have to do is swim through the three rivers to get him.""

"Yeah, right," Michael muttered almost inaudibly. Aba smiled at him and went on.

"But," she said, "the boy's mother was afraid. She turned to her husband, but he was just as frightened.

"Then the girl jumped up. 'I'll do it,' she said. Naturally, she was terribly afraid, but her love for the boy was stronger than her fear. Without another word the girl dived into the river of fire. The fire burned her, of course—my mother always said the fire burned her like fire'—but she swam through it and leaped into the river of water. And the water choked her—like water—but the girl struggled through it and fell into the river of snakes. And the snakes struck at her—"

"—like snakes—" Dee put in, grinning.

"—but the girl managed to stumble through them, and the next thing she knew she had reached the boy.

"As soon as she touched him, the boy's head flew to his shoulders and he jumped up, alive and well. Iblis left, cursing, to do his mischief in some other part of the world. And I suppose the boy and the girl got married, although I don't really remember what my mother said about that.

"Well," Aba said, looking around at them. "That's the story as my mother told it to me. I don't know what meaning it has for you—maybe none. But you've heard it now."

"Maybe it just means that love can be stronger than fear," Jenny said softly.

"Maybe it means you can't trust your parents," Michael said, absolutely deadpan, and Aba laughed.

"I like Jenny's interpretation better. But as I said, there may be no meaning. Or possibly it's just a story about the relative powers of good and evil."

Jenny looked up quickly. "Do you believe in good and evil?"

"Oh, yes. Very strongly. And I believe that evil sometimes has to be fought—personally. Hand to hand. If you care enough to do it."

Michael stirred. "You know what they say about kids our age. That we don't care about right or wrong or anything. That we don't even care about the future."

"Yeah, like the Baby Busters," Dee said, grinning.

"Naw, we're too young even to be Baby Busters. We're the Busted Babies."

Jenny spoke seriously. "It's not *true*. We do care. You care, Michael, more than just about anybody I've ever known. You pretend you don't, but you do. And that's why Audrey loves—" She stopped because Michael was looking away, his sarcastic spaniel eyes filmed over. "We're going to *find* Audrey," she said, her own throat tight.

"I know," Michael said and rubbed at the bridge of his nose with his fingers.

"I wish I could help," Aba said. "But I'm an old woman. My fighting days are over."

"Well, mine aren't," Dee said, raising a slim arm to examine the hard muscle under velvet skin. "Mine are just starting." Aba looked at her and smiled slightly. For years she and Dee had fought about Dee preferring kung fu to college and insisting that she didn't want to do anything brainy like her mother or arty like her grandmother. But just then Jenny knew Aba was proud of her warrior granddaughter.

"It's our fight anyway," Jenny said. "He won't let anyone else into the Game. The original players, he said."

"I think," Aba said, looking directly at her, "that if anyone can find your friends, it will be you, Jenny." Her eyes were very gentle and very sad; they reminded Jenny of pictures of Albert Einstein. At that moment Jenny thought that Aba really was *more* beautiful than Dee.

"I'll try," Jenny said. As the old woman turned away, Jenny just caught the murmured words, "But I wonder what the cost will be."

Before they left, Aba let them raid the kitchen. They took cottage cheese and cold chicken breasts; cereal and microwave brownies and grapes and pippin apples.

On the way back they stopped by Audrey's house and picked up Audrey's car.

Michael's living room was beginning to look like the aftermath of a very long party, Jenny thought as they walked into the apartment. The furniture had been pushed to the extreme edges of the room to make room for the mattresses and sleeping bags on the floor. The plaid couch was a nest of rumpled blankets. Empty Coke cans were scattered everywhere, and most flat surfaces were crowded with books or clothes or stacks of dirty dishes.

"Okay," Dee said, coming in from the kitchen with Michael. "Now what about that base?" She sat down on a footstool with a bowl of cottage cheese and chopped apple.

"We don't have enough information," Jenny said. "He hasn't told me enough." Every time she said *he,* Tom walled up. There was no help for it, just as there was no help for the shining thing on her finger. It caught every glint of the spring sunlight coming in Michael's front window, and she swore she could feel the words on the inside of the band.

"I've been trying to think," she said, "about abandoned buildings or things—places around here he might hold them. But that doesn't seem right."

"In mysteries," Michael said thoughtfully, "things are always hidden in the least likely place. Or the most obvious place—because you always think that's the least likely. I guess it couldn't be the paper house."

"It was trashed," Jenny said. "I don't think it would hold anything. Besides, how could we get in on our own? It was

434

Julian who brought us in last time." She knew, somehow, that Julian's base wasn't in the paper house. And she knew something else: Julian wouldn't find the Game amusing unless there was a *chance* of them finding the base. He would put it somewhere they could get to—if they were smart enough to figure out where to look.

"I guess the More Games store is *too* obvious," Michael murmured.

"Too obvious and gone," said Jenny. "It's just a mural now. No, Julian would put it somewhere *clever*."

"What is it, Tom?" Dee said. "You have an idea?"

Tom was wearing the look he wore mostly these days—one of abstraction. Just now he also seemed disturbed. He got up and walked toward the kitchen, fingers in his back pockets.

"If you think you know something . . ." Dee said.

"No. Nothing." Tom shook his head and sat back down.

"Okay, let's go back to the beginning," Michael said.

But it didn't help. They talked uselessly through the morning and most of the afternoon, until an elderly woman came and rang the doorbell, demanding that Michael move Audrey's car because it was in her parking space.

Dee went down with him. Tom paced the hallway slowly while Jenny sat on the couch staring aimlessly out the window. They were stuck, no closer to figuring out where the base was than they had been two days ago.

And she was tired. She let her eyelids shut, seeing the

golden afternoon sunlight on her closed lids. Then suddenly the light went dark.

Jenny's eyes flew open. Although it had been a bright, cloudless day, there was some sort of mist coating the window. Preventing her from seeing out. Jenny stared at it, pulse quickening, then she drew in her breath and leaned closer.

It wasn't mist—that would have been strange enough. But it was something stranger than that. It was ice.

Touched by the Frost King, Jenny's mother used to say back in Pennsylvania when the windows iced up like that. Jenny hadn't seen it since she was five years old. In those days she'd loved to trace things in the frost with the warmth of her finger. . . .

Something was appearing on the window as if traced by an unseen finger. A letter.

L.

Jenny couldn't breathe. Her mouth opened to call for Tom, but no sound came out.

I. T. T .L. E. . . .

Little. The letters appeared slowly as if a fingertip were tracing them on the icy window.

M. I. S. S. M. U. F. F. E. T. S. A. T. . . .

Jenny watched, scalp crawling. She couldn't seem to make herself move. It was too *strange,* to be sitting here in daylight and seeing something that simply couldn't happen.

O. N. A. T. U. F. F. E. T. E. A. T. I. N. G. H. E. R. . . .

It's me, Jenny thought, gripped by an irrational certainty. This time it's me he's after. I'm Miss Muffet.

C. U. R. D. S. A. N. D. W. H. E. Y. A. L. O. N. G. . . .

Still unable to move, Jenny's eyes shifted upward. A spider. She was afraid of spiders, and crickets, and all crawly, jumpy things. She expected to see a thread descending from the ceiling, but there was nothing.

C. A. M. E. A. S. P. I. D. E. R. A. N. D. S. A. T. D. O. W. N. B. E. S. I. D. E. H. E. R. . . .

The Spider. *The Spider,* Jenny thought. *Audrey's car.*

"Tom," she whispered. And then suddenly she was moving, tearing her eyes from the letters that were still appearing. "Tom, come here. *Tom!*"

As she ran she almost fell over the footstool where Dee had been sitting earlier. Eating cottage cheese, small curd. Curds and whey.

CHAPTER 13

Stupid old lady," Michael said as Dee pulled the Spider out of the carport. "She doesn't even use this space, but will she let anybody else park here? God forbid. Now we have to go all the way down to the garage—take a left up there and go around the trash cans."

"I didn't even know this place had a garage," Dee said.

"Dad and I never use it," Michael said as Dee pulled into a dark entrance and headed down a ramp. "The carports are a lot more convenient."

"Yeah, but right now it's probably a good idea to have Audrey's car down here. In fact, we might want to put *all* the cars here—if somebody notices them outside your apartment, it's a dead give-away that we're all here. We should have thought of that before."

"I guess," Michael said without enthusiasm. "I dunno—when I was a kid I always hated this place. I had the idea there ought to be a dragon at the bottom of it."

Dee grinned. "It's just a garage, Mikey." But he was right, she thought. There was something unpleasant about the garage. It was dingy and badly lit, and she could see how a kid with an active imagination might think of dragons.

Don't be ridiculous, she told herself. It's broad daylight—but it wasn't. They had turned the corner to the lower level of the garage, and it was as dark as twilight down here with the flickering bluish fluorescents on the ceiling. A strange and unnatural twilight.

Even as she thought it, the lights around them flickered wildly and went out.

It was like being plunged into the tunnel on a roller coaster. Dee suddenly felt that everything was happening too fast—while at the same time it was all happening in slow motion, frame by frame.

Her eyes weren't dark-adapted yet—in that first instant she could see nothing. But she heard the growl from the back of the car clearly.

It was a thick, clotted, animal sound. A *large* sound—the timbre alone let you know that only something big could have produced it. So low and dragging that it sounded like a sound-track in slow motion. It sounded like a hallucination.

"*What*—" Michael was tearing at his seat belt, turning to

look. Dee saw the whites of his eyes. Then, as she twisted her head over her shoulder, she got a glimpse of what was in the back of the car.

Pale eyes and white teeth in gaping jaws. Dee's vision was adapting. She saw a hulking shape materializing in that incredibly small space—as if it were coming through a door in the area between the cabin and the trunk. Coming and coming like a genie emerging from a bottle.

It isn't all the way out yet, Dee realized.

There was no time to think about anything. "Get out!" she shouted. Michael was frozen, clutching the seat and gasping. Dee reached across him, fingers clenching on the Spider's door handle. She flung the door open and shoved him, braking automatically at the same instant.

Michael went tumbling and thudding out. Dee felt a rush of air on her cheek—warm as the blast from under a microwave, and wet. A feral, musky odor made her nostrils flare.

The snarl was directly in her ear.

Move, girl!

She hit the accelerator. The snarl fell back, and she heard the scrabbling of claws just behind her. In one motion Dee opened her own door and vaulted out.

To-jin-ho was the art of falling on hard surfaces. Dee took this fall rolling and was on her feet in time to see the Spider cruise into the block wall of the garage.

Some distant part of her mind watched the impact with

a sort of joyful awe. Now *there* was a crash, she thought, and flashed a barbaric smile at nothing.

Then she saw movement. Something was emerging from the Spider. She heard a rising snarl.

Dee spun on her heel and ran.

She could see the light of the stairwell in front of her. If she could make it there—

She felt her Nikes rebound from the concrete, felt her arms swinging, her lungs pumping. Her teeth drew back again in a grin. In that moment Dee Eliade was filled with a joy in living so intense she felt she could fly.

"C'mon, you freakin' fleabag!" she shouted over her shoulder and heard herself laugh wildly. "Come and get me!"

She'd never fought a four-legged opponent before, but she was sure going to give it a try. She'd see how a wolf reacted to a roundhouse kick.

She reached the stairwell and spun, still laughing. The blood was singing in her veins, every breath she took was sweet. Her muscles were electric with vibrant energy. She felt balanced and dynamic and ready for anything.

Then she heard the creak of a door behind her—and an endless, savage hiss.

Michael was picking himself up as Jenny and Tom turned the corner, staring into the depths of the dim garage. He was clutching at one ankle.

441

"*Dee—?*" Jenny gasped. Echoes of a metallic crash were still reverberating in her mind.

Michael waved toward the back of the garage. Jenny saw it then—a large, dim shape against the wall. The Spider.

The lights flickered and went on, and she saw color.

The Spider's front end was crumpled. There was no sign of Dee.

"Come on!" Tom was already running toward the car. Then he looked left and shouted, "The stairway!"

The door there was swinging shut. Jenny heard it clang, felt her chest heave as they ran. Tom reached it and seized the handle with both hands, wrenching at it.

The door swung open, slamming against the wall. A single fluorescent panel flickered high above in the stairwell, and Jenny could hear echoes of her own panting breath in the little room. But nothing moved except shadows.

Dee's paper doll was on the floor, in a lightly scorched circle on the concrete.

"He's going to get us all."

Jenny tightened the Ace bandage around Michael's ankle.

"If Dee couldn't get away from them, what kind of chance do we have?"

Jenny fixed the little metal clips in the bandage and sat back.

"The clues aren't *fair*," Michael said. He was still breathing hard, and his eyes were too wide, showing white around the dark irises. "You said you and Tom ran straight down there once you got this one—which means you didn't have *time*. He's not going to give any of us enough time. And we're never going to find the base."

Jenny closed the plastic first aid kit. The paper doll was lying on the coffee table beside it. On its back, which wasn't characteristic of Dee at all. The black crayon eyes stared up at the ceiling with a crafty look.

They had pushed Audrey's car to the very back of the garage, where they hoped no one would find it. Jenny supposed they were lucky no one had come to investigate the crash—but did it really matter anymore? Did anything really matter?

"Am I just talking to myself here? Isn't anybody going to say something?"

Jenny looked at Michael, then at Tom, who was pacing the hall, not looking at them. She turned back to Michael, and her eyes met his. Their gazes locked a moment, then he sank back on the couch, his anger fading.

"What is there to say?" Jenny said.

They spent the evening in silence; Tom pacing and Michael and Jenny sitting. Staring at a blank TV screen.

It was all going to come crashing down soon—their carefully built structure of deception. Jenny had called her aunt Lily to say that Zach was upset and was spending the night with Tom. She'd called Dee's mother and told her Dee was staying with her. Neither mother had been happy. It was only a matter of time before one of them called Tom's house or Jenny's house and everything came out.

And Michael was right. They weren't going to find the base—not on the information they had now. They needed more.

She was actually glad that night when Julian showed up in her dreams.

It had taken her a long time to get to sleep—she'd lain for hours staring at the empty couch where Dee should have been. The last clear thing she remembered was deciding she was never going to sleep at all that night—and then she must have shut her eyes. When she opened them, she knew she hadn't really opened them at all. She was dreaming again.

She was standing in a white room. Julian was standing in front of a table, with the oddest thing stretched out in front of him. It was a sort of model, with houses and trees and roads and street lights. Like a railway model, only without the train, Jenny thought. But it was the most elaborate model she'd ever seen; the miniature trees and bushes were exquisitely made, and the little houses had various windows alight.

Not just a model, Jenny realized. It's Vista Grande—it's my neighborhood. There's my house.

Julian was holding a small figure of a wolf above one of the streets. He set it down carefully, looked up at Jenny, and smiled.

444

Jenny didn't smile back. Although she was dreaming, her head was clear—and she had a purpose in mind. She was going to get all the information she could from him.

"Is that how you tell them what to do? The wolf and the snake?"

"Possibly." He added, just as seriously as she had asked her question, "What's black inside, white outside, and hot?"

Jenny, mouth opened to speak again, shut it and gave him the kind of look Audrey frequently gave Michael. "What?" she said tightly.

"A wolf in sheep's clothing."

"Is that what you are?"

"Me? No, I'm a wolf in wolf's clothing." He looked up at her, and light flashed in his wild, exotic sapphire eyes.

I don't know how I ever mistook him for a human, Jenny thought. Julian was from an older and wilder race. One that had fascinated and terrified humans from the beginning.

I will not be distracted, she told herself. Not this time. I will remember what I want from him.

"What do you think of the new Game?"

"It isn't fair," Jenny said promptly. "Isn't *sporting*," she added, remembering what Julian thought of the idea of fairness. "It's not a game at all if we don't have a chance to find your base."

"And you think you don't have a chance?"

"Not without some kind of information."

445

Julian threw back his head and laughed, his hair shining like white jade. "You want a hint?" He looked at her with those veiled, liquid-blue eyes.

"Yes," Jenny said flatly. "And you'd give it to me if you wanted it to be any kind of real contest. But you probably don't."

He clicked his tongue at her. "You really think I'm an ogre, don't you? But I'm not so bad. You know, if I wanted, I could manipulate the Game so I couldn't lose. For instance . . ." He lifted the wolf and held it judiciously over another street. Jenny recognized the pale gray wood-frame house and the tiny towheaded figure in front of it.

"Cam!" She looked at Julian. "You wouldn't! You said—"

His long lashes drooped. "I said I'd keep this Game to the original players—and I will. I'm just telling you what I *could* do. So you see I'm not so bad after all."

"Gordie Wilson wasn't a player."

"He put his nose in where he wasn't wanted."

"And what about P.C. and Slug?"

Julian's smile was chilling. "Oh, they were players, all right. They played their own game—and they lost."

So now I know, Jenny thought. I suppose I'll have to tell Angela—if I live to do it.

She was staring down at the tiny towheaded figure of Cam when something else occurred to her. She looked up.

"Was it you who made those kids play lambs and monsters?"

she asked. "All that violence—were you influencing them?"

"Me?" He gave his black velvet laugh again. "Oh, Jenny—they don't need me. Children are that way naturally. Children's games are that way. Haven't you noticed?"

Jenny had, but she said nothing. She turned away.

"War and hunting and chasing—that's all there is. That's life, Jenny—no one can escape it."

He was standing behind her now.

"And why should we? There's excitement in the chase, Jenny. It gets the blood going. It sends chills through the body. . . ."

Jenny stepped away. *Her* blood was going. His voice, strange and haunting as the melody she'd heard on the hotel balcony at the prom, sent a shiver of awareness through her.

Cat-quiet, he followed her. I will not turn around, she thought. I will not.

"Love and death are everything, Jenny. Danger is the best part of the game. I thought you knew that."

Part of her did. The wild part that he had changed. The part of her, Jenny thought suddenly, that would always belong to him.

"And *I* thought you were going to give me a hint," she said.

"Of course, if you want—but nothing is free."

Jenny nodded without turning. She'd expected this. "Give the hint first," she said flatly.

"You can find your friends behind a door."

Jenny frowned. "What kind of a door? Have I seen it?"

"Yes."

"Have I been through it?"

"Yes—and no."

"What kind of an answer is that?" she said, angry enough to turn. She could face him when she was furious.

"It's as clear as black and white—if you know the right way to look at it. Now," he said, "the price." He stepped to her and bent his head.

It took all her self-control to remain rigid and unresponsive in his arms. At last she gasped and pulled away.

"Oh, Jenny. Let's stop playing—we don't need to play this Game anymore. You can have your friends back—you want Dee back, don't you?"

"I'll get her back," Jenny said shakily. She still felt tingles of electricity in every place Julian had touched her. "I'll get them all back—my way."

"As usual, I admire your confidence," he said. "But you can't win. Not against me, Jenny. I'm the master player."

"A door I've been through but haven't been through," she said. "A door that needs to be looked at in the right way."

He smiled. "A door in the shadows. But you won't find it until I take you through it."

We'll see, Jenny thought. Things were getting blurry around her—the shadows were growing. The dream fading.

"Here," Julian said. "To remember me by."

He put a silver rose in her hand.

Jenny recognized it. It was the rose he had given her in the Erlking's cavern, a shimmering half-open blossom, perfect down to the tiniest detail. The petals cool but soft in her palm.

There was something like a slip of white paper wrapped around the stem.

This time I'm going to wake up right away, she thought.

She did. The silver rose was lying on her pillow. She almost knocked it off, sitting up quickly to look at the bundles of blankets on the living room floor.

Tom and Michael were both there. Two dark heads on white pillows. Jenny leaned over and shook the nearest shoulder.

"Michael, Tom, wake up. I've got the next clue."

But when she unraveled the slip of paper from the stem, she wasn't sure.

"It's French," Michael said. "And none of us speaks French. It isn't fair."

"Life isn't fair," Jenny muttered, staring at the words on the paper in frustration. There were only six of them.

Pas de lieu Rhône que nous.

"If we only had Audrey," she said. "*Nous* means 'we,' I think—or is it 'you'?"

"Maybe Dad's got a French-English dictionary some-where," Michael said.

Tom didn't even try to join in the conversation. He had looked at the silver rose, and then at Jenny, and then he had settled back. Now he was staring down at his own hands.

Jenny started to speak to him, then stopped. As she'd told Michael before, what was there to say?

The ring felt as cold as ice and as heavy as lead on her finger.

Michael found the French dictionary the next morning, but Jenny still couldn't make much sense of the clue. The words were French, but they didn't seem to make any sense when you put them together.

"It's about me, I know it is," Michael said. "Because it's French, and Audrey's connected with French, and I'm connected with Audrey. I'm next."

"You're ridiculous," Jenny said. "We don't know which of us it is—but if we all stay together—"

"Staying together didn't do Michael and Dee much good," Tom said from what had become his habitual position, pacing the hallway.

"He's going to get us all. One by one," Michael said softly. "And I'm next."

Jenny stared down at the dictionary and rubbed her eyes.

It was dark and stuffy in the apartment. Outside the sky was cloudy, gray as concrete. Jenny felt like a rat in a trap.

She tried thinking about the base instead of the French clue. She'd told Michael and Tom what Julian had said about the door, but none of them could make anything of it. Now

Tom was pacing endlessly, and Michael was staring at nothing, and Jenny was very tired.

Her head felt stuffy and her eyes hurt. She'd had almost no sleep last night. Maybe if she shut her eyes she could think better. If she shut them just for a few minutes . . .

The crash woke her up with a jerk.

"Sorry," Michael whispered guiltily, picking up a TV tray. He looked even more nervous than usual—almost wild. His hair was sticking up all over his head, and his eyes reminded Jenny of a hamster she'd once had—a frantic hamster that had always tried to run away from her.

"What time is it?" Jenny whispered back, trying to clear her head. It was almost as dark as night.

"About four. You slept for a while."

Jenny wondered vaguely why they were whispering, then saw the bundle of blankets on the floor in Tom's place. He was wrapped like a mummy, even his head covered.

Good—he needs rest, too, Jenny thought, shifting. The slip of paper rustled on her lap. Jenny's blurred eyes focused on the writing on it, her foggy brain seeing the words not as words but merely as letters—sounds. *Pas de lieu* . . .

She straightened suddenly, her breath hissing. Michael nearly jumped out of his skin.

"What is it?" He limped hastily over to her. "What—did you figure it out? Is it me?"

"Yes—oh, we've been so stupid, Michael. We didn't need the dictionary. It's not French at all."

"Even I can recognize that much French."

Jenny clutched at his arm. "The *words* are French, but it isn't a French sentence. I figured that out with the dictionary— the words don't make any sense when you put them together. It only makes sense in *English*."

"What are you talking about, English?" Michael forgot to whisper.

"Just say the words to yourself, Michael. Pronounce them the French way, but kind of run them together."

"*Pas . . . de . . . lieu . . . Rhône . . . que . . . nous*—it doesn't say anything!"

"Yes, it does. It says 'Paddle your own canoe.'"

Michael's lips formed the words silently as he stared at the paper, then he hit himself in the forehead. "Oh, my God. You're right. But, Jenny"—he dropped his hand and looked at her— "what does it *mean*?"

"I don't know." Jenny glanced out the window, where large drops were hanging from the eaves of the walkway and small drops pattered on the concrete. "But it's got something to do with water, I bet—so none of us can go outside. But don't you realize, Michael"—she turned to him excitedly—"we've done it! We've finally done it! We have a clue, and we have all of *us* here and safe. We can win this one!"

Something about Michael's expression made her heart jolt.

And then she realized—she and Michael hadn't been whispering for some time. They'd almost been shouting—but Tom's blankets hadn't stirred.

"Michael—" He was staring at her in terror. The hamster look again. In a single motion Jenny darted to seize Tom's blankets, to yank them away.

She just stared at the bunched-up pillows underneath. She could feel herself folding inside. Collapsing.

"Michael." She spoke without moving, still holding the blankets. Then she lifted her head and looked at him. He flinched and raised a hand defensively.

"Where is he, Michael?"—deceptively softly.

"He made me, Jenny—I told him not to, but he wouldn't listen—"

"Michael, where is he?" Somehow Jenny had gotten two fistfuls of Michael's gray sweatshirt, and she was shaking him. Where did he go?"

Speechlessly Michael looked toward the gray and dripping window. There were tears in his dark spaniel eyes.

"He went to the mountains," he gasped after a moment. "You know the place he told us about—where they found Gordie Wilson. He thought he could find the base there—or maybe just kill the wolf or the snake. He said that killing them might help you and me, even if he—" He stopped and began again. "I told him not to, Jenny—I told him not to go—"

Jenny heard her own voice, sounding strangely quiet and

detached. Almost musical. "To the mountains. Where they found Gordie Wilson—in a creek bed. Isn't that right, Michael?"

Michael blinked at the lines of slanting gray outside. "In a creek . . ." he whispered.

Then they just looked at each other.

"Come on," Jenny said at last. "We've got to find him."

"He told me to keep you here—"

"Nothing will keep me here. I'm going, Michael. The only question is whether you're going with me."

Michael gulped, then said, "I'm going."

"Then let's get out of here. We may already be too late."

CHAPTER 14

Tom had never shot a gun before. He'd taken this rifle from a case in Zach's father's den. Zach's father wasn't going to be happy when he found it missing, or when he found the back door jimmied open, either.

But Tom wasn't going to be around to hear about it.

He had no illusions on that. If he was right, this was strictly a one-way trip.

Of course, Julian's base might not be up here after all. There weren't any doors on this mountain slope, and Julian had told Jenny the others were behind a door. But this was definitely a place where the wolf and the snake hung out—and Tom didn't expect them to pass up the chance to attack him.

If he even got one of them, Jenny's chances would be better. If he got both, maybe she could actually make it.

The idea had first come to him the night Audrey had disappeared, when they'd all been talking in Michael's living room. Michael and Dee had been saying that the only way to win Julian's game was to find the base, and Tom had said, *"There might be another way"*—and then stopped. The other way that he'd thought of was too dangerous. Too dangerous for Jenny, anyway. It wasn't a trip he wanted her making.

He'd thought about his idea during the next two days, going over it, debating about whether to tell Dee. She'd want to be in on it, he knew. But that would mean leaving Jenny practically unprotected. That was the basic problem with the idea—if Tom left Jenny, he left her vulnerable.

Then Dee had disappeared—and suddenly the choice had become critical. Soon Jenny wouldn't have *anyone* to protect her . . . and Julian could creep in through her dreams.

That was what had decided Tom in the end. He couldn't keep Julian out of the apartment—which meant he was no good to Jenny there. What he could do—maybe—was to give her one less enemy to fight.

I'll bet it took both of them—the wolf and the snake—to get Dee, he thought, trudging through the damp and puddling creek bed. Dee could've stood up to either one of them alone—but not both.

Maybe Jenny would have a chance against one or the other

of them alone. Or maybe—if Tom's luck *really* held—he could get both before Julian killed him.

No one else had even suggested going after the animals. It simply hadn't occurred to them. They all thought of the creatures as phantoms—and, God, no wonder. The Shadow Wolf Tom had seen on the beach had looked like a moving nightmare, a luminous specter. But it had been flesh and blood.

That was what Tom's first trip out here had shown. The black and tarry stuff he'd scraped off that rock was blood. Gordie must have wounded one of the animals before it got him. The creatures could bleed—as Tom had proved for himself on the beach. He'd cut the wolf, and his knife had come away dark.

They could bleed, and they left physical marks behind, like the scratches on Audrey's car. They had some sort of material existence. Maybe they could die.

Tom was going to find out.

Rain was splattering his face. Cold rain, stinging drops—not like a spring shower. The cattails in the creek bed were swaying and dripping. Everything was gray.

He was getting near the place. Not far now. Tom was coming from the south, downwind of the three sycamores. Maybe he could surprise them.

In the gray cold he comforted himself with a picture of Jenny. Jenny—all warmth and sunlight. Golden-glowing, her hair streaming back in the wind. Jenny in the summertime, safe and happy and laughing. That was what Tom wanted—for Jenny to see another summer. In this world instead of the world of ice and shadows.

Even if he wasn't there to see it with her.

Movement ahead. Tom squinted into the rain, then smiled grimly. Yes, it was there. Black against the gray background, impossibly big, glowing with its own blue light like a rotten log full of foxfire. A creature that looked like a wolf painted with luminous paint on darkness. The sight of it alone was enough to send a human running and screaming, mind broken.

Because it wasn't real—it was *super*-real. It was the archetypical Wolf—the one kids dreamed about. The one that had inspired stories like Little Red Riding-Hood. The one that lurked at the back of the human brain, eternally crouched and ready. Reminding people of what the world had once been like, a savage place where humans were the prey. When teeth and claws came at you in the night, and you got *eaten*.

Funny, Tom thought, how most people these days took it for granted that they weren't going to get eaten. Not so long ago—a few thousand years, maybe—it had been a pretty serious problem. A constant danger, the way it still was for birds and kittens and mice and gazelles.

The sight of the Lurker, the Shadow Wolf, brought it all back clearly. One look at it and your brain stem remembered everything. How it felt to be chased by something that wanted to tear into your entrails. By something you couldn't bargain with, couldn't reason with, something without mercy to appeal to. Something only interested in tearing your flesh off in chunks.

Tom couldn't let a thing like that near Jenny.

He was almost close enough now. It was moving toward him, slowly, crouched. He could hear the thick snarls over the patter of rain.

Tom raised the gun to his shoulder.

Careful—steady. He was pretty good at this at carnivals, an excellent shot. The wolf was almost in range. Tom centered the crosshairs—

—and heard a noise behind him.

A slithering, dragging noise. The Creeper. The Snake.

He didn't turn. He knew that it was almost on him, that if he didn't run now—this instant—it would get him. He didn't turn. With every ounce of his will, he kept his eyes on the wolf.

In range. *Now! Now!*

A horrifying hiss right behind him—

Ignoring it, Tom squeezed the trigger.

The recoil staggered him. Carnival guns didn't buck like that. But the wolf was more than staggered. The force of the bullet dropped it in its tracks.

Got it! I got it! I did it—

The snake struck.

Tom felt the blow in the middle of his back. Already off

balance, he fell. But he twisted even as he went down. One more shot—if he could get off one more shot—

He was lying in the mud. The snake was towering over him, a column of swaying darkness. Huge, and hugely powerful. Eyes shining with an unearthly light, mouth wide in a hiss. Giant dark head rearing back to strike—

Now! For Jenny—

Tom fired straight into the gaping mouth.

The snake's head exploded.

It was terrible. Dark blood spurted everywhere, stinging Tom's face, blinding him. Heavy coils, whipping in their death throes, fell on top of him, flogging him. He couldn't get them off. Everything was blood and darkness and struggling terror.

But I did it, Tom thought, clawing wildly at the flailing, spurting length of the snake. Oh, God, if I can just get out of here . . . *I did it.* They're dead.

That was when he heard the noise.

A roaring like a waterfall in the distance—or a river. Getting closer fast. And he couldn't see, couldn't get up.

Jenny, Tom thought—and then the water reached him.

"Jenny, you're scaring me," Michael said. It was almost a whimper.

Jenny herself wasn't scared. She was cold and clear and furiously angry.

The idea that Julian's base might be at the creek had passed through her mind once or twice. But she'd dismissed it last night because it didn't fit in with the door.

Tom had obviously felt differently.

"Keep walking," she said. It seemed as if they'd been walking forever. She knew they were in the right area because they'd found Tom's car—but where was the creek bed? Michael was limping badly.

"What's that?"

It was a rushing, liquid sound, louder than the rain. Jenny knew what she would see even before they crested the next rise of ground and looked down.

An unusual sight for southern California, where most creek beds were cracked and dusty. This one was full of dark, swiftly moving water—much too full for the little rain that had fallen. There was no natural explanation for it. It was a freak event, a flash flood that should have been impossible.

But it was there. A swollen river by a sage-covered slope leading to three large sycamore trees.

And in a little eddy directly below Jenny, swirling round and round between some rocks, was a neatly folded paper boat manned by a dark-haired paper doll.

She didn't realize the boat was the next clue until they were back at the apartment.

She had been playing with it all the way. She'd set Tom's doll on the coffee table with the others, arranging them with mad precision beside the car keys Michael had thrown there. A little line of paper dolls that sat and looked at her as she sat on the couch. She'd been turning the boat over and over in her hands while Michael huddled in a blanket on the love seat.

Then she saw the writing on the waxy paper.

It was very simple, a kid's riddle. The simplest clue of all.

What gets bigger the more you take away from it?

She'd heard that one in kindergarten, and both she and Michael knew the answer.

A hole.

"It doesn't say who's next—but I guess it doesn't need to," Michael said, pulling the blanket closer around him. "He'll save you for last—the best for last, you know. So it's me. And it doesn't say how it's going to happen, but that doesn't really matter, does it? As long as you know it's going to happen, and it is. We know that, huh, Jenny? It's going to happen, and there's nothing we can do to stop it. That Julian, he's like the Mounties, he always gets his man. . . ." He began to giggle.

"Michael, calm down. . . ."

"So there's a hole somewhere, and I'm going to fall into it. That's all we need to know. That's all, folks."

"Maybe not. You said Tom went to get the snake or the wolf—maybe he did. And the base wasn't there, but maybe we can still find it."

"May be, may be—it's still May, isn't it?" He looked at the

curtained window. It was fully dark outside. He turned back to Jenny. "You know we're never going to find it."

"I *don't* know that." Jenny's hands were icy cold, but her voice was fierce. "I have an idea—something else Julian said. Something about the hint being as clear as black and white. And before, in my first dream, he said something about image and reality."

"What is this reality thing, anyway?" Michael said. "I mean, how do we know we ever got out of the paper house? Maybe this is all an illusion, like when you think you've woken up but you're still dreaming. Maybe we're still in the old Game. Maybe nothing is solid." He leaned over and hit the coffee table and giggled again.

"Michael, why don't you lie down? Look, I'll get you some water—"

"No! Don't leave me!" He clutched at her as she went by. "If you leave me, he'll get me! The Shadow Man will get me!"

"Okay, Michael. Okay." Jenny looked down into the terrified dark eyes and stroked Michael's hair as if he were younger than Joey. "Okay."

"It's not okay. I have to go to the bathroom—but he can get me there, too."

"No, look, I'll go with you. I'll stand right outside the door."

"He'll get me. Didn't you ever hear about snakes coming out of the toilet? He'll get me, but I have to go. . . . What a dilemma, huh? Let him get me or bust." Michael was almost crying, even while he continued to giggle.

"Michael, stop it. Stop it!" For the second time that day Jenny shook him. "Just calm down! The potty monster is not going to get you, I promise. We'll look for snakes before you go. Let's do it now and get it over with, and then we can think about the base."

Michael shut his eyes and gulped in a deep breath. When he let it out, he seemed calmer. "Okay." But he still staggered like somebody half-asleep when Jenny led him to the bathroom.

"You see? No snakes in there. And I'll stand right outside."

"Leave the door open a crack."

"Okay, Michael." Jenny stood patiently.

"Jenny?" Michael's voice behind the door sounded very small. "A toilet's a lot like a hole. . . ."

"Just do it, Michael!"

"Okay." After a minute the toilet flushed.

"You see? You're all right."

Michael didn't answer. The toilet went on flushing.

"Michael?"

The sound of rushing water. "Michael, it's not funny! Come out of there, or I'm coming in."

The water rushed on.

"*Damn* it, Michael! All right, I warned you—" She jerked the door open.

The bathroom was empty. The toilet was flushing madly, water swirling round and round. Perched on the edge of the porcelain seat was a paper doll.

Five little dollies all in a row. Audrey sitting with her arm twisted up as if to say, "Can we talk?" Zach with his pencil-shaded face looking sharp and malicious. Dee, who kept falling on her back no matter how Jenny folded her. Tom, with a drop or two of rain still beaded on his wax. And Michael, whose crayon eyes seemed to stare at Jenny in accusation.

She'd promised it wouldn't get him, and it had.

Jenny was guilty, just as she was guilty of Summer's death. Not in the sense the police had meant, not the hacking-off-Summer's-head-and-burying-her-body-in-the-backyard sense, but because she was the one who'd gotten Summer into it. Jenny had invited Summer to play a game that had turned out to be deadly. Jenny had come out alive and Summer hadn't. Jenny's Game had killed Summer.

Now it might have killed the rest of her friends.

And she was alone. The apartment practically echoed with aloneness. There was no sound since she had jammed a book under the toilet ball to keep it from flushing anymore.

The rest of them had been picked off one by one. Like ten little Indians. Now she was the only one left, and she was next.

The base. I have to find the base. I have to get them out before Julian gets me.

But how?

The hints. She had to remember them. But her mind was so confused. She was all alone—she could feel the air around her. She could *feel* how each room in the apartment was empty. The emptiness was crushing her.

The hints. Think of them, nothing else. Get them in mind.

But I'm alone—

Image as opposed to reality.

A door she'd seen. A door she'd been through, but hadn't been through.

Not in the Shadow World. Maybe somewhere halfway.

What else was halfway? Like the More Games store—

Black and white.

A tiny light went on in Jenny's mind. Yes. It would fit. A door she'd seen and gone through—but that she couldn't possibly have gone through, depending on how you looked at it. A black and white door.

It was just then that the piece of paper came fluttering down.

From nowhere. It came out of thin air as if someone had dropped it from the ceiling. It skimmed and side-slipped and landed almost in her lap.

Jenny picked it up and looked at the writing.

I'm something. I'm nothing.
I am short. I am tall.

When you fall at your sport, then I stumble and fall.

I have never been seen yet beneath a new moon.

I thrive in the evening but vanish at noon.

I am lighter than air, I weigh less than a breath;

Darkness destroys me, and light is my death.

A little over three weeks ago Jenny might have had trouble with that one. What could be destroyed by both light and darkness? What could be both short and tall? What was something and nothing at once?

But ever since April 22, the day of the Game, the subject of this particular riddle had been on Jenny's mind. She'd been haunted by it, she'd thought about almost nothing else.

She saw shadows everywhere these days.

She had no doubt about what the riddle meant, either. A shadow was coming to get her—*the* shadow. The Shadow Man. Julian was going to take care of this personally.

She had barely thought this when all the lights in the apartment went out.

Chills swept over Jenny. Icy fingers stirred the hairs at the back of her neck. Her palms were tingling wildly.

I'm in trouble. Bad trouble. But I think I know the answer now. I know where the base is. If I can just get there . . . if I can get to it before he gets to me. . . .

First, find the way out of the apartment.

There was some light coming in through the curtains from

the walkway. All right—the front door was over there. Jenny picked up Michael's keys and made her way to it, arms outstretched.

As she reached the walkway, the lights there went out.

Cat and mouse. He's playing games with me. All right, play! This mouse is running.

Her hand slid on the wet iron railing as she hurried down the stairs. In the carport Michael's VW Bug was swathed in shadows. Jenny pulled the door open and slipped in, turning the key in the ignition almost before the door was shut. She pulled out just as the parking lot lights went off.

Right behind me . . .

She wrenched the wheel and sped out of the apartment complex.

The rain had started again, droplets splattering the windshield. Hard to drive safely. Jenny sped on, hoping no one was in her way.

A stoplight—the brakes screeched. Please, God, don't let me hit anyone. Please—

The red light winked out, but the green didn't come on. The stoplight stayed dark, swaying in the rain.

Jenny hit the accelerator.

Canyonwood Avenue—Sequoia Street—Tassajara . . .

The Bug's engine coughed.

No—let me make it. I've got to make it. I'm so close—

Jacqueline Drive . . .

The engine coughed again.

Quail Run! Jenny took the turn dangerously fast, tires skidding. The Bug lurched and a horrible grinding sound came from the engine. Still skidding, it hit the curb—and stopped.

Frantically Jenny turned the key. She got a squeal of metal that set her teeth on edge. Then silence.

Get out! Quick!

Abandoning the key, she fumbled with the door, jumped into the rain. She left the door open and ran.

Up there, just a few more houses. Go, go! She made her legs pump, flying over the wet sidewalk. Don't look back! Don't think! Just go!

There it is! You can see it! A few more yards—

Lungs burning, she reached the driveway of the mock Tudor house. Zach's house. The driveway was empty. She staggered to the garage, seized the handle in the middle of the big door. She pulled as hard as she could.

It was stuck fast. Locked.

Oh, God! Don't panic. The side door, quick!

As she started for it, she could see down Quail Run, could see the deserted Bug nosed against the curb under a streetlight.

The streetlight went out.

Then the next closest one did. Then the next.

A wave of darkness coming toward her. Bearing down on her. The side door was that way.

Jenny turned and ran toward the front door of the house.

She grabbed at the doorknob while knocking, and to her surprise it turned. It was unlocked. Were they crazy?

"Uncle Bill! Aunt Lily! It's me!"

She yelled because she didn't want them to shoot her for a burglar, and because she didn't care about keeping her secret any longer. She desperately wanted people, any people.

The house echoed emptily in answer.

"Uncle Bill! Aunt Lily!"

The silence was ponderous, a tangible presence. There was no one here. For some unfathomable reason they had gone away, leaving their front door unlocked. Jenny was alone.

I won't cry. I won't scream. I just have to get to the garage, that's all. Nothing's changed. I can get there easily. It's just the length of the house away.

Her heart was frozen in panic.

Just go! One foot in front of the other. It's just an empty house!

The hallway light went off.

Oh, my God—he's here! Oh, God, he's *here,* he's in the house, he's got me—

Go!

She stumbled into the darkness, heading for the lighted living room. Her legs were shaking so badly she could hardly walk. Her outstretched hands were numb.

She got one glimpse of the living room, then the brass

lamp beside the leather couch went out. She banged into a wastebasket made of an elephant's foot—a thing that had always filled her with horror. She could hardly keep from screaming.

Every inch of her skin was tingling. Shrinking—as if expecting an attack from any side.

It was pitch dark. He could be anywhere around her. Anywhere in the darkness, moving quietly as a shadow himself. If she took a step, she might run right up against him.

She had to do it. She had to find the garage. For Tom—for Dee. They were waiting for her to rescue them. She'd promised Michael . . .

Sobbing without making a noise, she took a step.

Now another one, she ordered herself. Feel your way. But it was almost more than she could do to reach out into that darkness. Anything might grab her hand. She might reach out and feel *anything.* . . .

Do it!

She took another step, groping blindly. Shuffling across the floor. Her hand struck a wall, with emptiness beside it.

The entrance to the dining room. That's it. And the garage is just on the other side, through the kitchen. You can make it.

She shuffled into the dining room, one hand on the cool smoothness of wallpaper. She could feel the immensity of the darkness on her exposed side. Something could come at her from that side—

471

—or from the wall. Oh, God, he makes things come out of walls. Jenny snatched her hand away from the wallpaper. Nothing was safe. He could grab her from any direction.

Just go!

She staggered forward in the dark and found another empty space—the doorway to the kitchen. Thank God. Now just a few more steps. Turn left around the refrigerator. Good. Now the way was clear until the garage—

She stepped against something warm and hard in the darkness. She screamed.

"You didn't think," the voice like water over rock said gently, "that I would actually let you get there, did you?"

He was holding her by the upper arms, not roughly but inescapably. Jenny's eyes were filled with darkness, and the rushing of her own blood filled her ears.

"Actually, I'm surprised you got this far. I didn't think you would—but I got your aunt and uncle out of the way just in case. An urgent message from their missing son."

I'm going to faint. I really am, this time.

Jenny couldn't keep her knees steady. He was half supporting her now.

"Shh. You don't need to cry. You've lost the Game, that's all. It's over now."

Dark. She was in complete darkness. She looked around wildly, turning as far as he would let her. If she could only see a tiny light—but there was nothing. The wolf and the snake weren't here; she would have seen their sickly, phosphorescent glow. She was alone with the Shadow Man.

And he was going to take her.

"Oh, God, where are we? Are we there already—at the base?" she said hysterically. It was impossible to tell in this complete darkness.

"No. Shh, shh, Jenny. We're going in a moment. You see, here's the way."

Then Jenny did see a light—just a glimmer. A weird, eldritch light like blue electricity. Defining a space opening in the floor behind Julian. A gap, a vortex. A hole.

CHAPTER 15

No . . . Jenny couldn't stand to look at the hole. She turned from it and buried her face in Julian's chest.

"It's all right. Just a little step. Then we'll be together, Jenny." He tipped her face up in the darkness, touching it with fingertips cool as marble.

His touch—so light, so certain. Commanding. As if he could see easily in this utter blackness. So cool. His fingertips traced her wet cheekbone, thumb wiping away the tears. Jenny shut her eyes involuntarily.

"Together, forever."

The cool fingertips brushed over her eyelashes, stroked the hair back from her temple. She felt one trace her eyebrow.

"It was meant to be, Jenny. You know that. You can't fight it any longer."

The finger ran down her cheek like a cool tear. It traced the outline of her lips, the join between upper and lower. A touch so light she could barely feel it. It took the bones out of her legs.

Melting, falling . . .

"Come with me, now, Jenny." His fingertips brushed the line of her jaw, sending delightful shivers through her. She realized her head had fallen back. Her face was turned up as if for a kiss. "I'll go with you. It's time to concede the Game. To surrender . . ."

A tiny light went on in Jenny's mind.

No wolf and no snake. And they were still in Zach's kitchen, which she knew very well. And the hole was behind Julian—and just beyond that the garage door . . .

"All right," she whispered. "All right, but let go of me. I can walk."

Dee always said surprise was the most important element of any attack. Don't give your opponent a second to consider.

The instant Julian's grip loosened, Jenny shoved him.

She didn't think about it, she just pushed as hard as she could. And he was taken by surprise. Even his snake-quick reflexes couldn't save him. With a shout the Shadow Man fell backward into his own black vortex.

Jenny leaped over the hole at the same moment.

A jump straight into darkness. If she'd miscalculated, she'd knock herself out against the wall. As it was her hands struck the door, almost upsetting her backward—but she kept her balance. Her fingers closed on the doorknob, she wrenched it—then she was in the garage.

Zach's flashlight would be on the wall. At least, she prayed it still would be. She flew across the length of the garage recklessly, groping for it. Julian wouldn't take long to recover—he could be here any second—

Flashlight! Jenny thumbed the switch. She had never been so glad to see anything as she was to see the white circular beam that shot out. Light, at last, light.

She swung the beam to the wall, aiming with dead certainty at what she'd come for. The mural photograph Zach had taken of the high school cafeteria.

Julian had told her that black and white mixed make so many colors—but not in a photograph. A photograph—an image of reality—an image that included a door. The exit door that the pyramid of tables had almost blocked, a door in the shadows behind the tables. A door Jenny had been through in real life many times. But she'd never been through it—because you can't open a picture of a door.

Unless, like the mural on Montevideo Avenue, it was a door into unreality. Into a place halfway to the Shadow World, like the More Games store. Julian could make images into reality. He could make posters and murals come alive. If Jenny looked at this picture in the right way . . .

As Jenny stared at the door, the handle seemed to bulge out at her. Three-dimensional. Like the doorknob to the More Games store which had stuck out of the mural.

"Jenny!"

Julian's voice behind her, sharp and dangerous. The flashlight went out.

But Jenny had seen where the handle was. She reached for it in the darkness. Her fingers brushed it—it was cold. Real metal in her hand. She had it!

She pulled.

Rushing wind surrounded her. The cold metal seemed to melt from under her fingers, and she was falling. Her scream was snatched away by the thunder of the air.

She had never seen anyone look as surprised as Audrey and Zach and Dee and Tom and Michael did. Their five faces were turned toward her, staring, mouths and eyes open, as she staggered forward and landed on her knees.

Now, what just happened—? Jenny thought, but before she could look behind her, they were all around her.

"You came through the *door*," Audrey said, greatly excited. She was still wearing the black Oscar de la Renta dress Jenny had last seen her in, and it was more bedraggled than ever. Her copper hair was down.

"Are you all right?" Tom asked. There were muddy streaks on his cheekbones. He reached out to take her hand, her left hand, without seeming to care about the ring on it.

"Of course she's all right. She came through the door," Dee said gleefully. She patted Jenny's head in a frenzy of affection. "Eat that, monster!" she shouted to the ceiling.

"You lied to me," Michael said. He still had the hamster look, only now his lower lip was pushed out pathetically, too. "You said it wouldn't get me, and it did."

Jenny leaned against Tom's warmth and solidity and shut her eyes—which made tears trickle out. She had never been so glad to hear Michael's complaining in her life.

"It's you—it's all of you," she said, opening her eyes with a little sob that sounded strange even to herself. "You're really here."

"Of course we're here," Audrey said. She sounded cross, which meant she was feeling affectionate. "Where else would we be?"

Dee grinned. "We've been waiting for you to come get us, Tiger. Didn't I say she would? Didn't I?"

Jenny looked at Zach. He had black circles under his eyes and his skin had a waxy tint, but there was something oddly peaceful in his expression. "Are you okay?" she said. "Are you all okay?"

Zach shrugged. "We're alive. It seems like a week we've been here, but Tom says it's only a couple of days. I just wish

I could get back and develop these." He jangled the camera around his neck, and Jenny looked at him in surprise. "Got some great shots of that snake." His eyes met Jenny's, and he smiled.

Jenny smiled back.

"I was here alone first," Audrey was saying. "For more than a whole day. *That* was fun." She pressed her lips together.

"It's not so bad," Dee said. "It's sort of like the army. We sleep on the tables—see, there're blankets over there. And there's a bathroom, and food comes out *there*. A cafeteria's actually a pretty good place to keep people. But we never could get that door open, and none of us came in through it."

Jenny looked around. It was a cafeteria, all right. The Vista Grande High School cafeteria. Exactly like the photograph, except that the tables had been unstacked and the six of them were standing around.

The only really peculiar thing was that there was only one door in all the four walls, the only door that had been visible in the picture.

"How did you guys get here, then?" she asked.

"Through the ceiling," Michael said grimly. "I kid you not."

Jenny blinked up at the ceiling. There was a large black hole in the center. Blue electricity crackled through the darkness.

Tom spoke quietly beside her. "We can't get up there. We

tried. There aren't enough tables—and something really strange happens when you get anywhere near that high. Time seems to slow down and you start to pass out."

Jenny looked down from the hole. "But you're all okay. The snake and the wolf didn't hurt anybody?"

"No," Dee said. "They just wanted us to fall in the vortexes. And they're dead now, you know. Tom got 'em."

"I *think* I got them," Tom said cautiously. "Michael was just telling us that you hadn't seen them tonight. . . ."

"You did get them," Jenny said. "You must have, because they're gone. It was a stupid, *stupid* thing to do, going off alone like that"—she squeezed his hand hard—"but I'm glad you did, because if you hadn't I wouldn't be here. I had to jump over a hole—a vortex or whatever you call it—and if they'd been around, I'm sure they'd have chased me back in."

Dee looked interested. "So just where was Julian when you were jumping?"

"In the vortex. I pushed him."

Dee stared at her, then snorted with laughter. In a minute they were all laughing hysterically. Even Zach was chuckling. Dee punched Jenny in the arm.

"He's gonna be mad," Michael hiccuped weakly as the hysteria subsided.

"He is. What difference does it make?" Jenny said coolly. "I found the base. I won." She waved a hand at them. "All you little lambs are free." Then she looked around and waited.

Nothing happened.

Everyone settled back. The joyful frenzy showed the first cracks as they stared around them, waiting for some change. Tom's eyebrows were drawing together darkly. Dee's beautifully sculpted lips lifted to show teeth.

"Oh, you would, would you?" she said softly and dangerously to nothing. "You cheat."

"Maybe we have to yell," Michael said. "Oly-oly-oxen free!"

"Don't be stupid," said Zach. "We *are* in. We want to get out."

"And he's got to let us out," Jenny said. She stood up, looking at the hole in the ceiling. "It's the rules of the Game. Unless he *is* planning to cheat," she added loudly, feeling reckless and bold with Tom's hand in hers.

"I never cheat," Julian said, from behind them. "I practice Gamesmanship—the art of winning games without *actually* cheating."

Jenny turned. Julian was standing just in front of the door—which was now open. The red Exit sign blinked and glowed madly above it, looking as if it would blow a fuse at any moment. That should have been a good omen, but the look on Julian's face wasn't encouraging at all. His eyes were glittering like blue glass, and there was something cruel and predatory about his mouth.

"Then you'll let us go," Jenny said, not quite so boldly as before. She steadied her voice and made herself meet his eyes, lifting her chin proudly. "I got in myself, Julian," she said. "I found the base."

"Yes, you did." Even here, in the well-lit cafeteria, it seemed like twilight around him. A strange, enchanted twilight that was somehow brighter and more real than any daytime Jenny had ever seen. "You found the base. You won the Game. Now all you have to do is walk out."

"While you block the door," Dee said scornfully. "Looks like you'll have to do it yourself this time, since your animal friends aren't here to do it for you."

"Block the door?" Julian widened his cat-tilted eyes innocently, somehow looking more disturbingly beautiful than ever. And more triumphant. "I wouldn't *dream* of it." He stepped away from the exit, gesturing with languid, careless grace, as if to usher them in. "Go on. All you have to do is walk through there, and you'll be outside the photograph. In Zach's garage. Safe and sound."

"I wouldn't trust him as far as I could throw him," Michael whispered in Jenny's ear. But Dee, always eager for a challenge, was already moving toward the door. She flashed an ebony glance toward Julian as she passed him, and he bowed gracefully. Then he lifted his head and smiled at Jenny, who was standing in the protective circle of Tom's arm.

"I told you once not to mess with me," he said. Under his heavy lashes his eyes were blue as flame.

Alarm spurted through Jenny. *"Dee—"* she began. But it was already happening.

Just as Dee reached the door, there was a tremendous

sound—a sound that was both loud and soft at the same time. It was almost like the sound a gas burner makes when you turn it on and the gas ignites. A muffled *whompf.*

Only this was a hundred times louder, and it came from all around them. Jenny's ears popped. Heat struck her from every direction at once, and a blast of burning air sent her hair streaming straight upward.

Dee was thrown backward by the force of the explosion, breaking her fall by striking the ground first with her forearms and palms. The next instant Jenny was holding her, her voice hard with anxiety.

"Are you okay? Are you okay?"

Dee's sooty lashes fluttered. Her slim chest was heaving, and her neck, long and graceful as a black swan's, lay arched back on Jenny's arm.

"Dee!"

"I'll give him gamesmanship," Dee gasped at last. Her eyes opened into narrow onyx slits, her breath still hitching. "I'll give him gamesmanship right up the—"

"He's gone," Zach interrupted flatly. "And we're all in trouble, so I wouldn't waste your breath."

For a moment Jenny was so glad to see Dee unhurt that she didn't care. Then she looked up and understood what Zach meant.

They were inside a ring of fire.

It was just slightly smaller than the dimensions of the

cafeteria—and for all Jenny knew the cafeteria walls were still outside of it. You couldn't see through it to tell. It was as high as the cafeteria ceiling, and it was hot.

And *loud*.

Incredibly loud. Jenny realized that she and the others had been shouting over it to be heard. It made an unbelievable, unremitting roaring. Like the thundering of Niagara Falls, or the blast of a hurricane.

How weird, Jenny thought, part of her mind examining this fact with a curious calm. I guess when you get to a certain extreme, the elements all sound like one another—fire sounds like water sounds like wind. I'll have to remember that.

There was something else about the sound. It was deadly.

You knew, somehow, listening to it, that it was absolutely lethal. If destruction had a voice, this was it.

"I suppose that's why people jump out of windows, even from the twentieth floor, or whatever," she said to Tom, almost dreamily. "You know, from a burning building, I mean."

He gave her a sharp look, then lifted her, practically carrying her to one of the cafeteria tables. "Lie down."

"I'm all right—"

"Jenny, lie down before you pass out."

Jenny suddenly realized that she'd better. She was shaking violently all over, tiny tremors that seemed to come from deep inside her. Her fingers and lips were numb.

"She's in shock," Audrey said as Jenny lay back on the

bench. "And no wonder, after everything that's happened. Jenny, shut your eyes for a while. Try to relax."

Jenny shut her eyes obediently. She could see the fire just as well that way as with them open. A wave of dizziness rolled over her. She could hear the others speaking, but their shouts seemed thin and far away.

"—not going to last long with this heat," Tom was saying.

"No—but what can we *do*?" That was Zach.

"We're going to get *roasted*." And that was Michael. "Better find some *mint* sauce."

"Shut up or I'll croak you myself, Mikey," Dee said.

I can't let them get roasted, Jenny thought. Her thoughts were vague and dreamlike, held together by the thinnest of floating strings. It was a state almost like the moments before sleep, when nonsense seems perfectly sensible, and words and pictures come from nowhere.

Right now she was experiencing something like drowning. Her life flashing before her—or at least the last three weeks— or at least bits of them. Disconnected, jumbled images, each sharp as a clip from a high-grade home video.

Julian appeared, beautiful as a December morning, his eyes like liquid cobalt, his hair moon-wet. *"I never cheat. I practice Gamesmanship. . . ."*

And Aba, her old face with its fine bones under velvety night-black skin. *"Last night I dreamed a Hausa story. . . ."*

And Michael, dear Michael, his hair wildly mussed, dark

485

eyes shining with enthusiasm: *"See, your brain is like a modeling system. It takes the input from your senses and makes the most reasonable model it can. . . ."*

And Zach, thin and beaky-nosed, gray eyes alight with a fierce gleam. *"A picture of a pipe is not a pipe."*

As Jenny drifted, ears filled with the noise of the fire, all the images seemed to float together, merging and intertwining. As if Aba and Michael and Zach were speaking at once.

"Without another word the girl dived into the river of fire. . . ."

"Touching's just another sense. It could be fooled, too. . . ."

"The image isn't reality. Even though we're used to thinking that way. . . ."

"The fire burned her, of course—my mother always said 'The fire burned her like fire. . . .'"

"If a model's good enough, there would be no way *to tell it wasn't real. . . ."*

"We show a kid a picture of a dog and say 'This is a doggie'— but it's not. . . ."

Jenny sat up. The fire was burning as fiercely as ever, like all the beach bonfires in the world fused into one. Tom and Dee and the others were standing in a sort of football huddle a few feet away. Jenny felt light-headed but good. She felt light all over, in fact, as if carbonated bubbles were lifting her toward the ceiling, bursting inside her. She felt glorious.

"That's it," she whispered. "That's it."

She had to shout to make them hear her. "Tom. Tom, come

here—everybody come here. I've got it. I know how to get out."

They crowded around her. "What?" "You're kidding!" *"Tell us."*

Jenny laughed for the sheer pleasure of laughing, feeling crystal clear and brilliant. Like a sphere filled with moonlight. She lifted her arms joyfully, shook back her hair, and laughed again.

The others exchanged glances, their expressions changing from excitement to consternation.

"No, it's okay," Jenny assured them. "I know how we get out—we just *walk*. Don't you see? The fire isn't real! It's a model our brains are making."

They didn't look nearly as happy as she would have thought. They blinked at her, then at one another. Michael opened his mouth and then shut it again, looking nervously at Audrey. Audrey sighed.

"Ah." Dee glanced at the others, then patted Jenny's shoulder. "Okay, Sunshine. You go back to sleep, and later we'll talk about it."

"What, you think I'm joking? I'm not. I'm telling you—we can walk right out of here."

"Uh, Tiger—" Dee looked over her shoulder at the fire, then back at Jenny. "I hate to tell you, but that fire is not a model in my brain. It's *hot*. I've got blisters." She showed Jenny several fluid-filled bumps on her hand.

Jenny looked at them, briefly shaken. Then she recovered.

"That's because you let it happen. You believed in the heat, and it gave you blisters," she said. "No, Dee, don't humor me, damn it!" she added. "I'm serious. You know how hypnotized people can get a blister if you tell them that you're touching them with something hot—even if it isn't hot. It's like that."

Michael ran his hands through his hair. "No, but Jenny, it's *really* hot. You can't even get near it."

"That's because you *believe* it's hot. You were the one who said it, Michael: If a model is good enough, you can't tell the difference between it and reality." She looked from one face to another. The glorious lightness had disappeared; now she felt crushing disappointment. "You think I'm crazy, don't you? All of you."

"Jenny, you've been through so much—"

"I don't want sympathy, Audrey! I want you to listen. Will *you* listen, Zach?" She turned to him desperately. "Remember Magritte? You told me that the image is not the reality, and I said, 'Unless you have somebody who can *make* an image into reality.' But what if that's not what Julian does? What if he doesn't make an image into reality, but he makes us *think* it's reality? If he shows our senses something so convincing that our brains make a model of it and believe it—even though it's just an illusion? Like a dream."

"'What if?'" Zach quoted back to her. "That's a pretty big *if,* Jenny. What if you're wrong?"

"Then we're toast," Michael muttered.

"But it's the only thing that makes *sense,*" Jenny said. "Remember, Julian said he wouldn't actually cheat. If the fire's real and there's no way to get through it, then that's cheating. Right? Don't you think?"

"I think your faith in him is charming," Audrey said acidly, her copper-colored eyebrows raised. She looked at Tom, but Tom looked away. Refusing to side against Jenny—but not looking at Jenny, either.

"It's not just faith in him. It's *sense,*" Jenny said. "Don't you see: Aba had a dream almost exactly like this. And the girl in that story came through all right. Her will was strong enough."

"But the fire burned her," Michael pointed out.

"But it didn't kill her. I'm not saying it won't hurt—I'm sure it will, from the look of Dee's blisters. But I don't think it will kill unless we let it. If our will is strong enough, we can get through." But she could see by their faces that they were still unconvinced.

Despair clutched at Jenny's chest. "Dee?" she said, almost pleading.

Dee shifted uncomfortably. "Sunshine—if it were anything else . . . but I've *been* there. It sure felt like a real fire to me. And even if I could convince myself to walk in—what happens if I get into the middle of it and my will suddenly isn't strong enough?"

". . . toast," Michael said.

Audrey spoke decisively. "It's too big a risk."

"When an illusion is that good," Zach said, "it might as well be real. It can still kill us."

Jenny stood.

"Okay," she said. "I understand—if it wasn't my own idea, I'd probably think it was crazy, too. And I'm the one who got you all into this, so it's only fair I get you out. I'm going in alone."

Tom's head jerked around. "Now, *wait* a minute—" he said at the same moment Zach said, "Now, look—"

"No, it's decided," Jenny said. "I have the best chance, since I'm the one who believes I can get through it."

"That's only if your theory is *right,*" Dee said, standing in front of Jenny to block her. "If you're wrong, you're *dead* wrong. No, Sunshine, you're not going anywhere."

"Yes, I am." Jenny leaned forward, eye to eye with Dee, matching the other girl's volume and ferocity. "This is my decision. I'm going and no one is going to stop me. Get it?"

Dee let out her breath sharply. She glared—but she fell back to let Jenny pass. Michael, eyes wide, moved hastily out of the way, tugging Audrey with him. Even Zach, although his face was white and furious, recoiled a step, unable to hold Jenny's gaze.

It was Tom who caught Jenny's arm. "Just hang on a minute," he said, his voice reasonable. Jenny turned on him, holding her head up like a queen because she was frightened to death, because he was the only one here who might be able to undermine her determination. In her mind's eye she could see herself standing there, drawn up to her full height, with her hair loose on her shoulders in the firelight. She hoped she looked commanding. She felt tall and proud—and beautiful.

"I said nobody is going to stop me, Tom. Not even you."

"I'm not trying to stop you," Tom said, still quiet and reasonable. His hazel eyes were steady, almost luminous in the light of the fire, and his face was clear. Tranquil, with a look of utter conviction. "I'm going with you."

Jenny felt a rush of warmth and dizzy gratification. She grabbed his hand and squeezed hard. "You believe me!"

"Let's go." He squeezed her hand back, then looked at it and took the other one, the one with the ring. His fingers interlocked with hers, and Jenny felt strong enough to *jump* over the fire. "Come on."

They turned to face the fire together.

It was good that Jenny was feeling invulnerable just then, because the fire was terrible. Hotter than putting your hand in an oven. Jenny could feel sweat trickle down her sides as they approached it; the skin on her face felt tight and hot and tingling.

"We'd better do it fast!" Tom shouted over the roar.

Jenny pointed with her free hand. "I think the door is *there*."

"You guys, now, wait, you guys—" Michael was yelling.

Jenny looked at the firelight reflected in Tom's eyes. "One, two, *three*—" They nodded at each other and started for the flames, ignoring the panicked shouts behind them.

"Cool, wet grass! Cool, wet grass!" Tom shouted, and then the fire was all around them.

CHAPTER 16

Jenny's skin burnt off.

That was what it felt like. As if it were flaying off in strips. Searing crisp and black until it cracked open. Charring. Frying like bacon. Her hair igniting, burning like a torch on her head.

It had been easy to say *"Just walk through the fire, it's a model, it isn't real."* But the moment she stepped into it, she understood what Dee meant about it *feeling* real. If she'd gotten close enough before to feel anything of this heat, she would never have dared to suggest it.

That first second was the most horrible thing that had ever happened to Jenny. It was agonizing—and she panicked. She lost her head completely. She'd been wrong, it wasn't an illusion after all, and she was in the middle of a *fire*. She was on fire. She had to run—to run—to get away from this. But she didn't know which way to go. The roaring, crackling, *killing* flames were all around her, burning her like a wax doll thrown in a furnace, roasting her alive.

I'm dying, she thought wildly. *I'm dying—*

Then she heard the faint shout from beside her: "Cool-wet-grass! Cool-wet-grass!"

And she felt Tom's hand in hers. Tom was pulling her, dragging her along.

I've got to make it—for Tom, she thought. If I collapse, he won't leave me. He'll die, too. We've got to keep going. . . .

Somehow she made her legs move, lunging desperately through the flames in the direction Tom was leading her. She just prayed it was the right direction.

"She was terribly afraid, but her love for the boy was stronger than her fear. . . ."

"Cool, wet grass!" Tom shouted.

Then a great, rushing coolness burst over Jenny. She fell headlong into darkness and then into light. She hit something hard and unyielding, and she and Tom were rolling.

They were through.

She was on the floor of Zach's garage. The concrete felt as cold as ice, and she pressed her cheek against it. She stretched her whole body out on it, soaking up the blessed chill. She wanted to kiss it.

Instead, she scrambled to one elbow and looked at Tom. The garage light was on; she could see him. He was all right, his eyes just opening, his chest heaving. She kissed him.

"We did it," he whispered, staring at the ceiling, then at her. His voice was awed. "We did it. We're actually alive."

"I know! I know!" She hugged and kissed him again, in an agony of joyous affection. "We're alive! We're alive!" She was wildly exhilarated. She'd never known how good it was to be alive until she thought she was dying.

Tom was shaking his head. "But I mean—it was impossible. Nobody could have lived through that fire."

"Tom—" She stopped and stared at him. "But, Tom—it was an illusion. You knew that—didn't you?"

"Uh." He gazed around, then puffed his cheeks sheepishly, for a moment looking like Michael. "Actually, no."

"You didn't *believe* me?"

"Well—"

"Then why did you go *with* me?"

He looked at her, then, with eyes that were green and gold and brown like autumn leaves swirling on a pool. "I wanted to," he said simply. "Whatever happened, I wanted to be with you."

Jenny just stared at him a moment. Thunderstruck. Then she whispered. "Oh, Tom!"

And then she was in his arms, sobbing breathlessly. Just his name, over and over. She thought her heart would burst.

I could have lost him. I could have lost him forever. All his brave goodness—all his love for me. I could have lost him . . . I could have lost myself in Julian's darkness.

Never again, she thought fiercely to herself, clinging to Tom as if something were trying to rip her away. The shadows have no power over me anymore. It was as if the fire, the great cleansing fire, had scorched all the dark thoughts out of her. Burning away the part of her that had responded to Julian, that had craved his danger and wildness. Taking that part like a sacrifice. Now that Jenny had come through the fire, she felt purified—renewed. A phoenix reborn.

But the strength that she'd gained from fighting Julian was still with her—that hadn't changed. She was stronger than ever since she'd come through the fire. And she could love Tom more because of her strength. They were equals. They could stand side by side, neither eclipsing the other.

And she knew now that she could trust him to the end. She only hoped he knew the same thing about her—or that she could prove it to him. She was happy to spend the next few decades trying.

Tom's grip on her hand changed. He'd been holding it bruisingly hard; now he turned it over and pulled back to look.

Jenny lifted her head from his shoulder.

"It's gone," Tom said wonderingly. "The ring."

"Of course," Jenny said and nipped his chin. Nothing could

surprise her now. Everything was going to be all right. "It's gone—because we won. I'm free. Know anybody who wants one girlfriend, low maintenance, good sense of humor?"

"God, Jenny." His arms tightened rushingly. "Nope, guess you'll have to put an ad in the classifieds," he said into her hair. "Oh, Thorny, I love you."

"You must, you called me Thorny," Jenny said, blinking away tears. "I love you, too, Tommy. For always and always."

Then, in the midst of her euphoria, she thought of something.

"We've got to get the others, you know—oh, my God!" She had just looked at the mural photograph on the wall.

It was on fire.

"You stay here!" Tom was on his feet, whipping off his jacket. He reached for the metal handle of the door in the picture unerringly.

"I'm coming with you!" Jenny shouted back. She grabbed his hand as he pulled on the handle. "You never go anywhere without me again—"

The darkness snatched them up, sucked them in. Deposited them in fire.

It wasn't as bad this time. Jenny put her head down, clung to Tom's hand, and made her legs run. It'll be over in a minute, she told herself as the agony surrounded her. Over in a minute, over in a minute—

Then it *was* over. Cool air was around them. Dee, Zach,

Audrey, and Michael were in a row, staring at them, reaching out to catch them as they tumbled in.

"You see?" Jenny gasped to Dee, who was nearest. "All in your mind."

"Oh, God, you're alive!" Dee's hug bruised like Tom's.

"Not a very original observation," Tom said. "Now, look, here's the deal. It's hot and it hurts, but it doesn't kill you. You count about to ten and you're through. Okay?"

Only ten? Jenny thought, sagging a little in Dee's arms. "It feels like a hundred," she confided to Dee's shoulder.

"Think 'cool, wet grass,'" Tom said. "Like firewalkers do. Keep thinking and keep going and you'll be okay."

Dee nodded. "Let's do it!"

But Michael's eyes were wide and uneasy, and Audrey recoiled a step. Zach remained very still, looking at Jenny. Then he let out his breath.

"Okay," he said. "It's just an illusion. Unreality, here we come."

"Hurry up, *move*," Tom said to the others. "We have to get out before this damn photograph burns up. Who knows *what* happens then." He grabbed Michael by the sweatshirt, then took firm hold of his hand. He held out his other hand to Dee.

Jenny grabbed Audrey.

"No!" Audrey screamed. "I don't want to—"

"That way!" Tom shouted to Michael. "Go on! Straight

ahead!" He gave Michael a push that sent him stumbling forward. Dee reached behind her to grab Audrey's hand and pull her along. Jenny shoved Audrey on from behind and held out her free hand to Zach. She felt his thin strong fingers close over it. She felt heat billow up around her.

Then it was like a wild game of crack-the-whip, with everyone surging and running and pulling—and Audrey, at least, trying to pull in the wrong direction. Fire filled Jenny's eyes and ears. She tried to count to ten, but it was impossible—her whole mind was occupied with the struggle of keeping Audrey going forward.

Fire and pain and heat and yanking on her arms—

Then Zach stumbled.

Jenny didn't know how it happened. Her hand was suddenly empty. She groped wildly with it and found nothing. She turned her head, looking frantically behind her. For an instant she thought she saw a black silhouette in the orange inferno, then the flames blotted it out.

Zach . . .

She opened her mouth to scream, and burning air filled her lungs. She choked. She was being pulled forward. There was nothing she could do—unless she let go of Audrey. She was being dragged along. Zach was far behind now.

Then she burst out into coolness and fell.

She landed on top of Audrey. Audrey was whimpering. Jenny was still choking, unable to get her breath.

She was so hot and exhausted and sore. Everything hurt. Her ears were ringing. Her eyes and nose stung, and when she tried to get up, her legs collapsed under her.

But she was alive. And Audrey was alive, because she was making noise. Michael was alive, coughing and gagging and beating at his smoking clothes. Dee was alive, pounding the concrete and shouting joyously.

Tom was alive, and on his feet. Tall and handsome and stern.

"Where's Zach?"

Jenny's throat was raw. "He let go," she said, almost in a whisper. "He tripped and he let go of my hand—"

Dee's grin collapsed. She stared up at the photo on the wall. Flames were licking out of it.

"I couldn't hold on to him," Jenny said, ashamed. "I couldn't help it. . . ."

"I'll get him," Tom said.

"Are you crazy?" Michael shouted. He broke off, bending over in a fit of coughing. Then he spat and lifted his head again. "Are you nuts? It'll kill you!"

Audrey had rolled over to look up at the photograph with terrified eyes, her spiky lashes matted together.

"We should get a fire extinguisher—" Dee began.

"No! Not till we get back. It might do something—close the door or something. Just wait for us—we'll be back in a minute."

Jenny swallowed dryly. The fire had been worse this time; it must be getting worse every second.

But Zach. Her gray-eyed cousin. He was lost somewhere in that fire. She couldn't just leave him. . . .

"Oh, God," she sobbed. "Tom, I'm going with you." She tried to get up again, but her legs simply wouldn't obey. She looked down at them in astonishment.

"No!" Tom said. "Dee, take care of her!"

"Tom—" Jenny screamed.

"I'll be back. I promise."

He was reaching into the picture—pulling the handle. Then he simply disappeared. The flames shot out and seemed to grab him like hungry hands, snatching him inside. He was gone—and the photograph was ablaze.

Every inch of it was burning now, flames bursting up and fanning out. Leaping so high that at any other time Jenny would have been terrified at the mere sight, afraid for Zach's house. She'd never seen an uncontrolled fire this high.

At this moment all she cared about was the photograph. The entire picture was on fire, blackening and peeling. The image was fading under the flames.

"No!" she screamed. "Tom! *Tom!*"

"We've got to get water!" Dee shouted.

"No! He said not to . . . oh, Tom!"

It was burning. Burning up. Burning out of all recognition. Turning into a black curling mess. The pyramid of tables

501

disappearing as flames licked over them. The door was gone now. The Exit sign was gone.

"Tommeeeeeee!"

Dee's strong hands held her back, keeping her from trying to jump into the photograph. It was no use anyway. There was no handle sticking out of the picture any longer. There was nothing left at all.

The flames began to die as the last of the photo was consumed. Bits of it fell off. Other bits floated in the air, drifting down slowly. Sparks danced upward.

Then it was just a charred and smoldering rectangle on the wall.

Jenny fell to her knees, hands over her face. She hadn't known she could make sounds like that.

"Jenny, don't. Don't. Oh, God, Jenny, please stop." Dee was crying, too, dripping tears down her neck. Dee, who never cried. Audrey crawled up on the other side, wrapping her arms around both of them. They were all sobbing.

"Look, you guys—you guys, don't," Michael gasped. Jenny felt a new pair of arms around her, trying to shake all of them. "Jenny—Jenny, it might not be so bad. He might have made it through. If he made it through to the cafeteria, he's okay."

Jenny couldn't stop sobbing, but she raised her head a little. Michael's face was grimy and anxious and deadly earnest.

"Let's just think about this. It took more than ten seconds for that picture to burn up. And he could go faster without all of us to hold him back. So he probably *did* make it through—and that means at least he's alive."

There was a shaking in Jenny's middle. "But—but Zach—"

"He may have made it back, too," Michael said desperately. "He may be okay."

Jenny looked up at him. The shaking didn't stop, but it lessened. She felt more connected to the world. "Really?" she whispered. "Do you think?"

Just then Dee made an odd sound, as if something had bitten her.

"Look!" she said.

Jenny twisted her neck and followed Dee's gaze to the photograph. Then she hissed and turned around all the way to stare at it.

Letters were appearing on the blackened surface, just as letters had appeared on Michael's window in the unnatural frost. Only these were graceful, looping letters, flowing script that ran along the length of the picture. As if a giant calligraphy brush were painting them on the blackness. They glowed red as coals, and wisps of smoke rose from them as they appeared.

Your friends are with me—in the Shadow World. If you want them, come on a treasure hunt. But remember: If you lose, there's the devil to pay.

"Oh, no," Michael whispered.

"But they're not dead," Audrey said, a little tremulously.

The red letters were fading already. "You see, they're not dead. Julian's keeping them to bargain with."

Dee just said, "God."

Jenny, though, sat back on her heels, her hands opening and closing. Working, getting ready for action. She thought of the Shadow World, of the swirling ice and darkness in the closet, and the cruel, ancient, hungry eyes there. Tom was somewhere among those eyes, and so was her cousin.

She knew this—but she wasn't shaking anymore. All her weakness and confusion had evaporated. She had heard the challenge and understood.

She wasn't afraid of Julian now. She was stronger than she had ever been before—stronger than she had known she could be. And she knew what she had to do.

"Right," she said and heard her own voice, clear and cold, like a trumpet. "He wants a new game? He'll get it. I know I can beat him now."

"Jenny—" Michael began, looking at her fearfully.

Jenny shook her head, straightened her shoulders. "I can beat him," she said again with complete confidence. To the smoking photograph, black and empty again, she said, "*En garde,* Julian. It's not over till it's over."

THE KILL

For the real Sue Carson, the inspiration for her namesake.

And for John G. Check III, with love and thanks.

CHAPTER 1

The flight attendant started toward them, and the back of Jenny's neck began to prickle. Her little fingers tingled.

Be casual, she told herself. Be calm.

But her heart began to pound as the flight attendant reached their row. She was dressed in navy blue with cream accents and looked rather military. Her face was pleasant but authoritative, like an alert teacher.

Don't look at her. Look out the window.

Jenny wedged her fingernails into the bottom of the plastic trim around the oval window and stared at the darkness outside. She could feel Michael beside her, his teddy-bear-shaped body rigid with tension. Out of the corner of her eye she could see Audrey in the aisle seat, her burnished copper head bent over the in-flight magazine. The flight attendant was blocking the view of Dee across the aisle.

Please let her go away, Jenny thought. Please, anything, why is she *standing* there so long?

Any minute now Michael was going to break into hysterical giggles—or, worse, a hysterical confession. Without moving a muscle, Jenny silently willed him to stay quiet. The flight attendant *had* to go away. She couldn't just keep standing there.

She did. It became clear that she wasn't just stopping casually, a little rest on the route from the galley. She was *looking* at them, looking at each of them in turn. A grave, searching look.

We're debate club students, flying to the finals. Our chaperon got sick, but we're meeting a new one in Pittsburgh. We're debate club students, flying to the finals. Our chaperon got sick, but . . .

The flight attendant leaned toward Jenny.

Oh, my God, I'm going to be sick.

Audrey stayed frozen over her magazine, spiky lashes motionless on her camellia-pale cheek. Michael stopped breathing.

Calm, calm, calm, calm . . .

"Is it you," the flight attendant said, "who ordered the fruit plate?"

Jenny's mind swooped into a nosedive and stalled. For a terrible second she thought she was going to go ahead and babble out the excuse she'd been practicing. Then she licked the dry roof of her mouth and whispered, "No. It's her—across the aisle there."

The flight attendant backed up and turned. Dee, with one long leg folded so she could tuck her toe into the little pouch on the back of the seat in front of her, lifted her eyes from her Gameboy and smiled. Except for the Gameboy and the army fatigue jacket she was wearing, she looked exactly like Nefertiti. Even her smile was regal.

"Fruit plate," the flight attendant said. "Seat eighteen-D. Lovely, got it." The next moment she was gone.

"You and your damned, damned fruit plates," Jenny hissed across the aisle. And to Michael: "For God's sake, Michael, breathe!"

Michael let out his breath with a *whoosh.*

"What could they do to us, anyway?" Audrey said. She was still looking at her magazine, and she spoke without moving her lips, her voice barely audible above the deep roar of the 757's engines. "Throw us off? We're six miles up."

"Don't remind me," Jenny said to the window as Michael began to describe to Audrey, in hushed detail, exactly what he imagined they could do with four runaways in Pittsburgh.

Runaways. I'm a runaway, Jenny thought wonderingly. It was such an unlikely thing for her, Jenny Thornton, to be.

In the darkened window she could see her own face—or part of it. A girl with forest-green eyes, dark as pine needles, and eyebrows that were straight, like two decisive brush strokes. Hair the color of honey in sunlight.

Jenny looked past the ghostly reflection to the black clouds outside the plane. Now that the stewardess danger had passed, all she had to worry about was dying.

She *really* hated heights.

What was strange was that even though she was scared, she was also excited. The way people get excited when an emergency, a natural disaster, happens. When all normal rules are suspended, and ordinary things that used to be important suddenly become meaningless.

Like school. Like her parents' approval. Like being a good girl.

All blown when she ran away. And her parents wouldn't even understand why, because the note Jenny had left them had said almost nothing. *I'm going somewhere and I hope I'll come back. I love you. This is something I have to do.*

I'm sorry. IOU $600.00.

Not very informative. But what was she supposed to say? *Dear Mom and Dad, A terrible thing happened at Tom's birthday party last month. You see, we built this paper house and it became real. And suddenly we were all inside it, and this guy called Julian made us play a game there with him. We had to face our worst nightmares and win, or he would have kept us with him in the Shadow World forever. And we all made it out except Summer—poor Summer, you know she was never the brightest— and that's why Summer's been missing for weeks. She died in her nightmare.*

But the thing is, Mom and Dad, that Julian followed *us out of the Shadow World. He came into our world and he was after one thing—me.* Me. *He made us play another game, and this one turned out bad. It ended with him taking Tom and Zach back to the Shadow World. That's where they are now—they didn't run away like everybody thinks. And the last thing Julian said to me after taking them was: If you want them, come on a treasure hunt.*

So that's what I'm doing. Only there's just a slight problem about getting into the Shadow World—I don't have any idea how to do it. So I'm flying to Pennsylvania, to Grandpa Evenson's house. He opened a door to the Shadow World a long time ago, and maybe he left some clues behind.

Say that? God, no, Jenny thought. The first part her parents had already heard, and didn't believe. The second part would just let them know where Jenny was going—and give them a chance to stop her. *Excuse me, Doctor, but my daughter has flipped. She thinks some demon prince has taken her boyfriend and her cousin. We've got to lock her up and keep her safe. Oh, yes, get that* biiiiig *hypodermic over there.*

No, Jenny couldn't tell anyone. She and Audrey and Dee and Michael had spent three days planning this trip. It had taken them that long to get enough money for plane tickets, each collecting two hundred dollars a day using their parents' ATM cards. Now they were on the red-eye from LAX to Pittsburgh, alone and vulnerable, six miles off the ground. Their parents thought they were asleep in their beds.

And Jenny was excited. Do or die. It was do or die, now, literally. There wasn't such a thing as safety anymore. She was going to a place where nightmares came true—and killed you. She would never forget Summer's blond head disappearing in that pile of garbage.

When she got there, all she'd have to rely on were her own wits—and her friends.

She glanced at them. Michael Cohen, with his rumpled dark hair and soulful eyes, wearing clothes that were clean, wrinkled, and bore no resemblance to any fashion trend that had ever existed. Audrey Myers, cool and elegant in a black-and-white Italian pantsuit, keeping any turmoil she might be feeling hidden under a perfectly polished exterior. And Dee Eliade, a night princess with a skewed sense of humor and a black belt in kung fu. They were all sixteen, juniors in high school, and they were on their way to fight the devil.

The flight attendants served dinner. Dee ate her fruit plate brazenly. Once the trays were cleared, lights began to go out all over the plane. One by one they winked off.

Funeral parlor lighting, Jenny thought, looking at the dim, diffused ceiling-glow that was left. It reminded her of the visitation room where she'd last seen her great-aunt Sheila. She felt too keyed-up to sleep, but she had to try.

Think of anything but *him,* she ordered herself, leaning her head against the cool, vibrating wall of the plane. Oh, who cares, think of him if you want to. He's lost his power over you. The part of you that rushed up to meet his darkness is gone. This time you can beat him—because you don't feel anything for him.

To prove it, she let images drift through her mind. Julian laughing at her, his face beautiful in the most exotic, uncanny way imaginable—more beautiful than any human's could ever be. Julian's hair, as white as frost, as tendrils of mist. No, whiter than that, an impossible icy color. His eyes just as impossible. A blue that she couldn't describe because there was nothing to compare it to.

As long as she was proving a point, she could remember other things, too. His body, slim but powerfully built, hard-muscled when he held her close. His touch all the more shockingly soft. His long, slow kisses—so slow, so confident, because he was absolutely certain of what he was doing. He might look like a boy Jenny's age, he might be the youngest of his kind, but he was older than Jenny could imagine. He was expert far beyond her experience. He'd had girls through the centuries, any he wanted, all helpless to resist his touch in the darkness.

Jenny's lips parted, her tongue against her teeth. Maybe

this wasn't such a good idea after all. Julian had no power over her, but it was stupid to tempt fate by thinking about him.

She would think of Tom instead, of little Tommy kissing her behind the ficus bushes in second grade, of Tom Locke, star of the athletic field. Of his hazel eyes with their flecks of green, his neat dark hair, his devil-may-care smile. Of the way he looked at her when he whispered, "Oh, Thorny, I love you"—as if the words themselves hurt him.

He was only human—not some eerily beautiful prince of shadows. He was real, and human, and her equal . . . and he needed her. Especially now.

Jenny wasn't going to betray his trust. She was going to find him and bring him back from the hellish place Julian had taken him. And once she got him safe, she wasn't going to let him go again.

She relaxed. Just the thought of Tom brought her comfort. In a few minutes her thoughts unwound, and then . . .

She was in an elevator. A silver mask covered the little man's entire face. He was so small she wondered if he was a dwarf.

"Will you go with us? Can we take you?" Jenny realized he'd been asking the same question for quite some time.

"We can carry you," he said. Jenny was frightened.

"No," she said. "Who are you?"

He kept asking it. "Can we take you?" On the elevator wall behind him was a large poster of Joyland Park, an amusement park that Jenny had loved as a kid. "Can we take you?"

Finally she said, "Yes . . ." and he leaned forward eagerly, his eyes flashing in the mask's eyeholes.

"We can?"

"Yes . . . if you tell me who you really are," she said.

The little man fell back, disappointed.

"Tell me who you really are," Jenny demanded. She was holding a bottle over his head, ready to brain him. She knew somehow that he wasn't actually there; it was only his image. But she thought he might materialize briefly to show her what he really was.

He didn't. Jenny kept hitting the image, but the bottle just swung through it. Then the image disappeared.

Jenny was pleased. She'd proved he wasn't real and that she was in control.

The elevator stopped. Jenny walked through the open doors—into another elevator.

"Can we take you? We can carry you."

The little man in the silver mask was laughing.

Jenny's head jerked up and she sat staring. A plane. She was in a plane, not an elevator. A plane which, at the moment, seemed crammed to its dim corners with menace. She was alone, because everyone else was asleep. The other passengers could all have been wax museum figures. Beside her Michael was completely motionless, his head on Audrey's shoulder.

As she watched, his eyes flew open and he made a terrible

sound. He sat bolt upright, hands at his throat. He looked like someone who couldn't get air.

"What is it?" Audrey had jerked awake. There were times when Audrey acted as if she didn't care about Michael at all, but this wasn't one of them.

Michael went on staring, looking absolutely terrified. Jenny's skin was rippling with fear.

"Michael, can you breathe? Are you all right?" Audrey said.

He did breathe, then, a long shaky intake of air. He let it out and slumped back against the seat. His dark brown eyes, normally heavy-lidded, were still wide.

"I had a dream."

"You, too?" Jenny said. Dee was leaning over the armrest of her seat across the aisle. Other people were looking at them, disturbed from sleep. Jenny avoided their eyes.

"What about?" she said, keeping her voice low. "Was it—it wasn't about an elevator, was it?" She had no idea what her own dream meant, but she felt sure it was bad.

"What? No. It was about Summer," he said, licking his lips as if to get rid of a bad taste.

"Oh . . ."

"But it wasn't all of Summer. It was her head. It was on a table, and it was talking to me."

A sensation of unspeakable horror washed over Jenny.

That was when the plane plummeted.

CHAPTER 2

Jenny screamed. It didn't matter, everyone was screaming. Dee, who had unbuckled her seat belt to lean toward Michael, was bounced upward so hard her head almost hit the ceiling.

They were falling, and the sensation was worse than a thousand elevators. There was nothing beneath Jenny because the seat was falling away.

What do people think about when they're going to die? What should I be thinking?

Tom. She should think about Tom and how she loved him. But it was impossible, there was no room inside her for anything but astonishment and fear.

Then the plane lurched up. Instead of falling, her seat was

pressing against her. The whole thing had taken only a second or so.

The pilot's voice came on over the intercom, smooth and rich as cream soda. "Ah, sorry about that, folks—we hit a little turbulence. We're going to try to get above this weather; in the meantime please keep your seat belts fastened."

Just turbulence. Ordinary stuff. They weren't going to die.

Jenny looked out the window again. She couldn't see much; they were in the middle of clouds. Mist and darkness—

Just like the mist and darkness the Shadow Men bring, her mind raced on irresistibly. Any minute now you'll see the eyes, the hungry, hungry eyes . . .

But she didn't see anything.

"Hey, listen," Michael was saying huskily. "About my dream—"

"It was just a dream," Audrey said, ever practical. Jenny was grateful for the little edge in Audrey's voice, the sharp edge of reason. Like a wake-up slap.

"Just a dream. Didn't mean anything," Jenny echoed— unfairly, because she didn't for a moment believe that. But she had no idea what it *did* mean, and ganging up on Michael was the only comfort available. Was Julian behind it? Torturing them with images of Summer? Nightmares were the Shadow Man's specialty.

The Shadow Man. Like the Sandman, only he brings nightmares. And by now he knows us all, knows our weak points.

He can bring our worst fears to life, and they may not be real, but we won't be able to tell the difference.

What are we getting into?

She spent the rest of the flight staring out the oval window, her hands clutching the cold metal ends of her armrests.

Pittsburgh at 6:56 A.M. was cool. Breezy. The sky a blue that early morning skies in southern California seldom aspired to. In Vista Grande, where Jenny lived, May skies were usually the color of wet concrete until it got hot enough to break the clouds up.

They had to take a taxi from the airport because Hertz wouldn't rent a car to anyone under twenty-five. Dee thought this was outrageous and wanted to argue, but Jenny dragged her away.

"We're trying to be inconspicuous," she said.

On the way to Monessen they saw a river with large, flat, ugly ships on it. "The Monongahela and coal barges," Jenny said, remembering. They saw delicate trees with slender trunks and airy little pink buds. "Redbud trees," Jenny said. "And those over there with the white flowers are dogwoods." They saw one steel mill with white smoke turning to gray as it rose. "There used to be blast furnaces all over here," Jenny said. "When they were going, it looked like hell. Really. All these chimneys with fire and black smoke coming out of them. When I was a kid, I thought that was what hell must look like."

By the time they got to the little town of Monessen, Michael was eyeing the taxi meter with deep concern. Everyone else, though, was staring out the windows.

"Cobblestone streets," Dee said. "D'you believe that?"

"*C'est drôle ca.*" Audrey said. "How quaint."

"They're not *all* cobblestone," Jenny said.

"They're all steep," Dee said.

Because the town was built on hills—seven hills, Jenny remembered. When she and Zach had been kids here, that had seemed a magical fact, like a seventh son of a seventh son being psychic.

Don't think about Zach now. And especially don't think about Tom. But, as always, Tom's name alone started an aching in her chest. Like a bruise just slightly to the left of her breastbone.

"We're here," she said aloud, forcibly distracting herself.

"Three Center Drive," the taxi driver said and got out to unload their duffel bags from the trunk.

Audrey, whose father was with the diplomatic corps and who had grown up all over the world, paid the man. She knew how to do things like that, and carried it off with cosmopolitan flair, adding an extravagant tip.

"Money—" Michael began in an anguished whisper. Audrey ignored him. The taxi drove off.

Jenny held her breath as she looked around. All the way from Pittsburgh she'd had flashes of familiarity. But here, in front of her grandfather's house, the familiarity came in a great, sweeping rush, engulfing her.

I know this! I know this place! I remember!

Of course she remembered. She'd grown up here. The broad green lawn that grew all the way to the street with no sidewalk in between—she and Zach had played there. This low brick house with the little white porch—she couldn't tell how many times she'd gone running up to it.

It was a strange sort of remembering, though. The house seemed smaller, and not exactly the way she'd pictured it. Old and new at the same time.

Maybe because it's been empty for ten years, Jenny thought. *Or maybe it's changed—*

No. It hadn't changed—*she* had. The last time she'd stood here she'd been five years old.

And the memory of *that* was like a light splash of icy water. It reminded her of what she'd come here to do.

Am I brave enough? Am I really brave enough to go back down to that room and face everything that happened there?

A slender arm, hard as a boy's, went around her shoulders. Jenny blinked back wetness and saw that everyone was looking at her. Audrey was standing silently, her glossy auburn hair shining like copper in the early morning light. Her chestnut eyes were quietly sympathetic. Michael's round face was solemn.

Dee, with her arm still around Jenny, gave a barbaric grin.

"C'mon, Tiger. Let's do it," she said.

Jenny let out her breath and tried to grin the same way herself. "Around back. There should be, um, stone steps down to the basement and a back door. If memory serves."

Memory did. On the back porch Dee pulled a crowbar out of her duffel bag.

They'd come prepared. In the duffel bags there were also towels to lay over the frames of any windows they might have to break, and a hammer, and a screwdriver.

"It's a good thing the house is empty. If it weren't, we couldn't do this," Dee said, placing the crowbar judiciously.

"If it weren't, there wouldn't be any point in doing it," Jenny said. "Whoever moved in would have cleared out the basement. For that matter, we can't be sure somebody *hasn't*—"

"Wait!" Audrey yelled.

Everyone froze.

"Look at that." Audrey pointed to something beside the door. A black-and-silver sticker with curling edges. When Michael wiped the dirt off with his fingers, Jenny could make out lettering.

THIS PROPERTY PROTECTED BY MONONGAHELA VALLEY SECURITY. ARMED RESPONSE.

"A security alarm," Michael said. "Oh, terrific."

Audrey looked at Jenny. "Do you think it's still working?"

Dee was still holding the crowbar at the door. "We can try and see," she said, grinning.

"No, we can't," Jenny said. "That's just exactly what we

can't do. If it *is* working, we won't be able to come back today, because *they'll* be all over the place."

"I think we're in fairly serious trouble here," Michael said.

Jenny shut her eyes.

Why hadn't she thought of this? Her grandfather had probably always had that alarm system—but it wasn't the kind of thing a kid would notice.

But I'm not a kid anymore. I should have thought *now*.

"There's got to be a way to get in," Dee was saying.

"Why?" Audrey's voice was snappish—because she felt bad, Jenny knew. Because she was scared. "There doesn't always have to be a way just because you want one, Dee."

Think, Jenny. Think, think, think. You forgot the alarm—is there anything else you've forgotten?

"If we're going to get philosophical—" Michael began.

"Mrs. Durash," said Jenny.

They all looked at her.

"She was my grandfather's housekeeper. Maybe she still takes care of the place. Maybe she has a key."

"Brilliant!" Dee said and finally removed the crowbar.

"We've got to find her telephone number—oh, God, if she still even *lives* here. There should be a phone at—at—oh, I guess the dairy bar. It's that way, I think. It's a long walk."

Michael looked cagey. "I'll stay here and guard the bags."

"You'll come with us, and like it," Audrey said. "We can hide the bags in the bushes."

"Yes, dear," Michael muttered. "Yes, dear, yes, dear . . ."

Petro's Dairy Bar, like everything they had passed on the way, had an air of gently going to seed. Jenny stepped into the blue-and-white metal booth outside and was relieved to find a phone book dangling from a chain. She balanced it on her knee and thumbed pages.

"Yes! B. Durash—there *can't* be another Durash in Monessen. It's got to be her."

She stuck in a quarter and dialed before she realized she hadn't planned out what to say.

"*Hel*-lo." The voice on the other end made the word sound almost like *yellow*. There was a faint accent, earthy, not as slow as a drawl.

"Hi. Hi. Uh, this is Jenny Thornton and—" Debate team, Jenny thought. Vacation, hometown, late spring break—parents. Where are my parents supposed to be?

"Is this Mrs. Durash?" she blurted.

There was a pause that seemed very long. Then: "Mrs. Durash isn't here right now. This is her daughter-in-law."

"Oh . . . but she does live there? Mrs. Durash? And—look, okay, do you happen to know if she's the same Mrs. Durash that worked for Mr. Eric Evenson?" I am making a total fool of myself, Jenny realized, staring at the graffiti on the glass door.

Another pause. "Ye-e-es, she's the caretaker for the Evenson house."

Wonderful! Caretakers *had* to have keys. Jenny was so

buoyed up that she forgot about making a fool of herself.

"Thank you—that's great. I mean—it'll be really great to talk to her. Do you know when she'll be back?"

"She always goes over to her son's in Charleroi on Saturday. She'll be back around seven. Call then."

"Seven P.M.?" Michael said bitterly when Jenny repeated the conversation. He flopped onto the splintered green bench against the dairy bar wall. "And we have to wait outside until then. I'm not walking back until I get some ice cream."

"Money," Audrey said with a toss of her copper head.

A bus roared up to the corner. Jenny stared at it absently as she thought. Nine hours to kill. They'd be conspicuous in this little town. They'd have to hide in her grandfather's backyard or—

Something on the side of the bus came into focus.

JOYLAND PARK, ROLLER COASTER CAPITAL OF THE WORLD. The poster was illustrated with roller coasters and merry-go-rounds.

The wooden bench seemed to drop away beneath Jenny.

When she could breathe again, the bus was revving its engine to drive away. Jenny made her decision in an instant.

"Let's go!"

Dee bounded up, ready at once. Michael leaned his head against the wall and shut his eyes. Audrey said, "Where?"

"On that bus. Come on, quick!" Jenny ran up and grabbed the dusty glass door before it could straighten shut. "Do you go to Joyland Park?" she shouted.

527

"Clairton, Duquesne, West Mifflin—West Mifflin's Joyland," he said laconically.

"Right. Four, please."

The others straggled up the steps. The bus was almost empty and smelled like old tires. They sat on the torn leather seats in the very back, and Audrey looked at Jenny.

"Now will you please explain where we're going?"

"Joyland Park," Jenny said a little breathlessly.

"Why?"

"'Cause they've got corn dogs," Michael said, very quietly.

Jenny looked Audrey straight in the eye. "Did you see that poster on the side of the bus? It was in my dream. I had a dream on the plane, while Michael was dreaming about Summer, and that poster was in it."

Audrey considered, teeth set in her cherry-glossed lower lip. "It might be perfectly natural. You might have had the park on your mind, since you were coming back here and all."

"Or it might be something else," Jenny said. "Like—I don't know, some kind of a message." She shifted. "Look, do any of you ever wonder if—well, if Summer is really dead?"

Audrey looked shocked. Dee said dryly, "We've been telling the police so for a month."

But Michael, eyes round and thoroughly awake now, said, "She was alive in my dream. She talked just like her."

Jenny felt uneasy. "What did she say?"

"She was mad at us for leaving her. She was scared."

Jenny felt even more uneasy. Audrey said, "So you think maybe both dreams were connected or something? And that it was some kind of a message?"

"I don't know. It's so complicated. And I don't even know why anyone could possibly want to send us to an amusement park. . . ." She could feel herself deflating.

"Never mind." Dee grinned wickedly and thumped her on the back. "You went with your instinct; that can't be wrong. And even if it wasn't a message—so what? It's an amusement park. Good, clean fun. Right, guys?"

"I'd rather go shopping," Audrey said. "But it's a way to kill the time."

Michael slumped and jammed his knees against the battered metal seat in front of him. "And kill our money. Did I ever tell you about this amusement park nightmare I had when I was a kid—?"

"Shut up, Michael," three female voices chorused, and he shut up.

It was a long, rather lonely drive to West Mifflin. Joyland Park seemed to be one of the few places still in business in a rundown and isolated area. It was almost a surprise to find it out here, in the middle of nowhere.

Michael made an inarticulate noise of awe as they filed off the bus. "Good grief," he said mildly. "It's Noah's Ark."

"That's the fun house," Jenny said. "You go in the whale by the side there."

Even in the bright sunshine she felt strange as they walked through the gates. Maybe because it's changed, she told herself. This place really *had* changed. The fun house was the same, but a lot of other things were different.

The old train ride roller coaster was gone, and there was a mine ride called the Pit in its place. There was a new metal coaster called the Steel Demon and a new water ride—the kind where you slosh around in giant inner tubes.

The biggest shock was the new arcade. It was full of shining video games, holograms, virtual reality. Jenny missed the old penny arcade, which had been dark and somewhat spooky, filled with machines from the turn of the century. Ancient, beautifully carved wood and genuine brass—not this steel and neon stuff.

But as time passed, she felt less anxious. She couldn't help it—the park was irresistible. She breathed in the smell of popcorn and ride-grease—and something else, something that was *like* a smell, but wasn't. A cotton-candy feeling of excitement.

"I don't see why Summer would want us to come *here,*" Audrey said when they stopped to buy corn dogs.

"No. I don't think it was a message after all." Jenny was glad to say it. Whatever horrible things they might have to face that night, they could enjoy themselves now.

Michael's blissful corn-dog smile broke up for a moment. "Maybe it's better that way," he said indistinctly. "I'd rather be dead than be what Summer was in that dream."

They went on the roller coasters, screaming, Jenny's loose hair blowing like a banner. The Steel Demon was good, but everyone agreed they liked the creaking, clattering old wooden coasters best. "Scarier," Dee said with relish. "Could break any minute—it *feels* like."

The mine ride was supposed to be scary. "This is a gold mine?" Audrey asked skeptically while lights strobed wildly to simulate dynamite exploding.

"Use your imagination," Michael said, slipping an arm around her.

Jenny looked away. It made her so homesick for Tom that she had to hold her eyes wide open and blinking, willing the tears back where they belonged.

The fun house really *was* scary. A barrel-shaped brick "wall" revolved around them until nobody but Dee could walk straight. The floor shifted and swayed until Michael threatened to sue—or throw up.

"C'mere," Dee said gleefully, beckoning Jenny closer. Behind a glass wall a red figure was vaguely visible. As Jenny stepped up to look, the scene went dark. She leaned forward, her nose almost against the glass—and with a terrible yelling sound the figure swooped straight toward her. It rode down a wire, actually striking the glass. Jenny leaped back with a shriek.

"Good, clean fun," Dee said, chuckling as Jenny leaned against a wall weakly.

Jenny made a fist, but just then something about the red figure caught her eye.

It was a red devil, with horns and split hooves and a tail. But its eyes—its eyes were blue. A blue that shone eerily under the black lights. And just before it was drawn back up the wire—it winked at her.

Jenny's little fingers started to tingle.

After that, things in the park seemed wrong. The barker for the ring-toss game seemed to have an odd gleam in his eye. Even Leo the Paper-Eating Lion seemed vaguely sinister.

"What in the name of God is it?" Michael asked as he sat down heavily on a bench. He was staring at what looked like a car from a circus train, with a red roof and silver bars. Thrust between the bars was a lion's head, muzzle gaping open in a big friendly smile.

"I'm Leo the Paper-Eating Lion!" The voice was bright and peppy and it came from the muzzle. The timing bothered Jenny; she felt something like the quick cold touch of an ice cube at her neck.

"I eat all kinds of paper," the voice continued joyfully. "I eat cardboard, too. Old gum wrappers, orange peel, popcorn containers. So feed me."

"It's a trash can," Dee explained, squatting to look up the lion's muzzle. "It sucks stuff up like a vacuum cleaner."

A mother wheeled a double stroller up to the car. Both kids stared at the lion with hard expressions.

"Want to feed him?" the mom said.

The kid in front nodded, still unsmiling. She wadded up a paper napkin and threw it at the lion's mouth.

"No, you have to *give* it to him. Here." The mom retrieved the napkin for the kid. The kid, still unsmiling, leaned forward, hand outstretched.

"I bet I'll have a tummyache tomorrow!" Leo caroled.

Forward, forward—the little hand reaching—

"Leo's *always* hungry. . . ."

Jenny jumped up and clapped her hand over the hole in the lion's muzzle just before the kid's fingers got there.

The kid stared at her, never changing expression. The mom squeaked.

"Sorry," Jenny said. *Everyone* was staring at her, even Dee and Audrey and Michael. She didn't move her hand. The kid sat back. The mother, after a flummoxed moment, turned the stroller sharply and wheeled it away.

The back of Jenny's neck was still prickling as she slowly withdrew her hand. She'd been afraid that—what?

"All right," she said defiantly to the others. "So it was a stupid thing to do. So sue me."

"We're all kind of jumpy—" Michael began soothingly, and then proved it, by ducking as two small figures charged him with a blood-freezing battle yell.

Jenny crouched defensively by the lion before she realized that the two figures were children.

They dived under the wrought-iron bench and came up screaming triumph. "We got it! We got another one!"

"Got what?" Dee said, blocking them with her hightop.

"A doubloon, dummy," the boy said in friendly tones, holding up something round and shining between dirty-nailed fingers. To Jenny, it looked like one of those chocolate candies covered with cheap gold foil. Then he pointed. "Cancha read?"

Jenny twisted her neck. There was a large billboard behind them. Swashbuckling crimson letters announced:

ALL-NEW ATTRACTION! COLLECT THREE GOLD DOUBLOONS AND BE THE FIRST TO SET FOOT ON . . . TREASURE ISLAND.

"You get three tokens and they letcha in free the day it opens. You get to go over the bridge first. They've got 'em hidden all over the park."

Spotting something else interesting, the kids ran away. On the billboard a pirate's treasure chest slowly opened and shut, like a clam's shell. Behind it Jenny could see the central island of Joyland Park, a manmade island in an artificial lagoon. The last time Jenny had been here, it had been a sort of stage, with acrobatic shows and bands. Now it was clearly under construction, with a tall lighthouse in the middle. She couldn't see any bridge to it.

Why should that make her feel uneasy?

"Just pop those discards in my mouth! Leo's waiting . . ."

"Let's go," Jenny said. Her stomach was churning and she

felt she *had* to distract herself. "Let's do something stupid—something *kiddie*. Let's go fishing."

Dark water swirled around and around a channel at the Fish Pond booth. "Like a sushi bar," Michael said, watching the water come in one side and go out the other. "You know, those kinds where the plates float around."

For a quarter you could dip a line into the water. A claw at the end picked up a number and you got a prize.

"When I was a kid all these prizes seemed like treasure," Jenny said. She lowered the claw into the opaque swirl.

"A bite," Dee said. She raised her rod. At the end, dripping, was a wooden bar with a number on it. The attendant glanced at it, then tossed it back into the water. He handed Dee a plastic change purse. Pink.

"Just what I always wanted."

Jenny felt a pull on her line, a sharp tug, almost as if it were a live fish on the hook. She lifted it—

—and gasped.

Oh, God! Oh, *God* . . .

Beside her, Michael's breath hissed in. He was staring, his chocolate-colored eyes wide and frightened.

There was no wooden bar on the end of Jenny's line. Instead, hanging neatly over one claw of the hook, was a slender, dripping circlet of gold. Jenny didn't need to look at it twice.

It was the ring.

The ring Julian had given her. The one with seven words inscribed on the *inside* of the band, where they would rest against her skin and bind her with their magical power.

All I refuse & thee I chuse. Meaning that Jenny refused all the world and chose—him. A promise that Julian had tried to hold her to. She was free of it, now—but the reminder was chilling.

She'd been wrong about them being able to enjoy themselves until tonight. Julian was watching her this minute, the way he'd watched her for years. There was no getting away from him, not here, not anywhere.

Nothing to do except go and face him.

"Let's go home," Jenny said, surprised at the steadiness of her own voice. She took the ring off the claw and dropped it into the dark, swirling water.

CHAPTER 3

"You-uns want the *key?*"

"Well, my parents do. They were kind of jet-lagged so they stayed back at the hotel, you know. They just thought they'd look the place over, you know. Gosh, Mrs. Durash, do you remember that old washing machine that belonged to my great-grandma? And the wringer? That was hysterical, huh, a *wringer.*" I'm being winsome, Jenny realized with a jolt. I'm a con artist.

A smile softened Mrs. Durash's thin features. She was a small woman, slight, wearing what Jenny always remembered her wearing: a print dress and a sweater. "I used to use that washing machine," she said warningly. She pronounced it *warsh*-ing machine.

"I know. That's what's so hysterical!" If I get any cuter, I'm going to throw up, Jenny thought. Oh, Lord—I think I just wrinkled my nose.

But it worked. Mrs. Durash was rummaging in a shiny black purse. "Let me tell you how to turn off the alarm system."

Jenny let out a silent breath of thanksgiving, and listened as intently as she had to the opening instructions of the PSAT. She went down the porch stairs muttering, "Three-six-five-five on the pad, then press Enter, Off, Enter. Three-six-five-five, then Enter . . ."

"We've got a time limit," she added to the others who were waiting around the corner. "The last thing she said was to have my parents call her tomorrow, because she didn't even know we were visiting. When they don't call, she's going to know something's wrong."

"But we didn't get any *sleep*," Michael pointed out. "And it's a mile back to your grandfather's house. At *least*."

"Let's take a taxi, then," Audrey said impatiently.

"We can't." Dee jingled the fanny pack which contained their pooled funds. "We paid thirteen ninety-five apiece to get into that park, not to mention all the corn dogs Michael ate. We've spent all the money that was supposed to last us for days. We're broke, princess."

"It's my fault," Jenny said after the first horrible moment. "I should have thought. We'll just have to try to get everything done tonight—once we *go,* we won't need to worry about money. Some of us can sleep while the others look through my grandfather's things—we'll take turns, okay? And we can eat some of the Power Bars from the camping stuff we brought."

"But if we don't find it tonight—?"

"We have to," Jenny said. "We'll do it because we *have* to, Michael."

The old brick house still had electricity, presumably to fuel the alarm system. It was spooky inside anyway; furniture draped with white sheets, clocks stopped on the walls. Jenny kept having the same lurching feeling: familiarity—unfamiliarity. Back and forth, or sometimes both at once.

By far the worst was the basement. Jenny's legs didn't want to take her down the stairs. She'd seen this place last month in a sort of dream, a hallucination created by Julian—but she hadn't *really* been here in over ten years. Not since the day neighbors had heard terrible screaming next door and the police had clattered down the stairs to find five-year-old Jenny on the floor, arms scratched, clothes torn, hair a wild yellow tangle. And screaming. Screaming and staring at an open closet door with a strange symbol carved on the front. Screaming in a way that made the biggest policeman *run* back upstairs to call the paramedics.

The police thought her grandfather had done it to her. The scratches, the torn clothes. The blood. They paid no attention at all to the five-year-old's story about ice and shadows in the closet, about hungry eyes that had seen her and tried to take her. About how her grandfather had been taken in her place.

Instead, the police had thought her grandfather had been a lunatic—and just now, looking at the basement, sixteen-year-old Jenny could see why. Every wall, every bookcase, every available surface was jammed with charms of protection.

Not such a bad idea for somebody trying to summon up and trap demons. But, undeniably, it looked weird.

"Will you look at this stuff?" Audrey breathed, enthralled. "Some of it's junk, but I'll bet some of it's priceless. Like this." She stepped forward and lightly touched a silver bell on a shelf. "This is Chinese—I saw these when Daddy was stationed in Hong Kong. You ring them to clear away evil spirits. And that—that's a genuine Tibetan prayer wheel. And this—" She lifted a bracelet of agate and gold beads.

"That's Egyptian," Dee interrupted. "Seven strands, see? Aba says the number seven was sacred to the Egyptians." Dee's grandmother traveled a lot.

"And those are Russian icons," Audrey said, nodding at some gold-plated pictures. "Very rare, very expensive."

"And *that's* from the *Qabalah*," Michael said, joining the conversation triumphantly and pointing to a chart on the wall labeled *Numerical Values of the Hebrew Alphabet.* "Magical Hebrew divination system."

"A lot of this stuff belongs in a museum," Audrey said.

Jenny was busy trying to breathe. The room was *heavy*

somehow—overloaded, oppressive. Stale air mixed with thick, quivering energy.

Magic, I guess, she thought, trying to feel as if she dealt with magical rooms every day. Well, that's what we came for. It's time to start the search.

She made herself go to her grandfather's desk. In her dream of this room—the dream created by Julian—her grandfather's journal had been lying open on the desk. In real life it wasn't so convenient. There was nothing on the desk but a faded green desk pad.

"Maybe on the shelves," she said.

She went to one of the bookcases and tilted her head sideways to read. It had been a brown leather-bound book, and she was sure she would recognize it when she—

"Found it!" she said, darting forward. She opened it to see her grandfather's heavy black handwriting, then looked back at the shelf. "Oh, God, but there isn't just *one* journal. There're three. We'll have to read through them all."

"We'll take turns, like you said." Dee nodded toward the stairway. "You and Michael go up and get some sleep—you're the most tired. Audrey and I can start reading."

Jenny slept for three hours on the living room couch—she couldn't face going into one of the bedrooms—and then went downstairs to take her place beside Michael. She chewed one of Dee's malt-nut Power Bars as she read. She wasn't hungry and she hated the texture of the protein bar, but she knew she needed the energy.

The journals were strange. Her grandfather had written everything up with the precision of a scientist, but what he was writing about was bizarre—and sometimes frightening. Almost all of it dealt with ways to call up the Shadow Men.

The Shadow Men, Jenny thought. Known by different names in different ages: the aliens, the faery folk, the Visitors, the Others. The ones who watched from the shadows and who sometimes took people to—their own place.

Jenny looked up involuntarily at the closet door which stood open, and something like a fist clenched in her gut. That was where they'd taken him. Through that portal into—the other place, the place that existed alongside the human world, always there, never touching. The Shadow World.

Her grandfather had called them up because he wanted their power. But in the end they'd been too powerful for him.

A phrase from the journal caught Jenny's eye. *Walker between the worlds.* Her heart began to pound as she deciphered the dense black writing around it. Something illegible and then *becoming a Walker between the Worlds myself, if the danger wasn't so great. There are several methods to*—something else illegible—*but the one I consider most likely to succeed would be the circle of runes. . . .*

"Runes," Jenny whispered. The magical alphabet that Julian and her grandfather had used to pierce the veil between the worlds. She looked at the drawing below the writing. "Michael, I've got it."

"Really?"

Jenny read a little further and her fingers tightened on the leather cover of the book. "Really. Get Dee and Audrey. And get a knife."

They'd brought Tom's Swiss Army knife, and Dee had a wicked-looking river knife with a five-inch blade. It was meant for rescuing kayakers who needed their ropes cut—quick.

"We have to carve these runes on a door," Jenny said. "Then we stain them and say their names to charge them with power, and then we open the door."

"Stain them with *what*?" Michael said suspiciously.

"Blood. What else? Don't worry, Michael, I'll take care of it. Let's use the door to the basement—not from the downstairs side, from the other side. It's smooth, good for drawing."

It was funny how simple and everyday it seemed, doing what her grandfather had said he wouldn't try because it was too dangerous. Nobody said, "Are we really going through with this?" Nobody kibitzed—not even Michael. They went about it the same way they'd built the pressed-wood stereo cabinet in Tom's bedroom. Michael read the instructions from the journal aloud; the others followed them.

"Two circles, one inside the other. It doesn't say how big they're supposed to be," Michael said. "But leave room for the runes to go in between them."

Jenny sketched the circles freehand on the smooth oak door with a felt pen.

"Okay, now the runes. First, Dagaz. It goes right at the top and it's shaped like this, like an hourglass on its side," he said. Jenny sketched the angular shape at the top of the inner circle. "It says here that Dagaz is like a catalyst. It represents times like twilight and dawn, when things are just changing. It 'operates between light and darkness.'"

Dawn. Jenny thought about the brilliant blue of the Pennsylvania dawn—and about eyes that were just that color. Julian was like Dagaz, she thought. A catalyst, operating between light and darkness. One foot in either world.

"The next one is Thurisaz, the thorn. It goes to the right— no, a little farther down. It's shaped like—look at this. A straight line with a triangle attached to the side. Like a thorn sticking out of a stem."

"There are a lot of fairy tales about thorns," Audrey said grimly. "You get pricked with a thorn or a spindle or a needle and then you die, or go blind, or you sleep forever."

Silently Jenny drew the rune.

"The next one's Gebo. It stands for a lot of things: a gift, sacrifice, death. The yielding up of the spirit. It's shaped like an *X*, see?"

Sacrifice. Death. A queer shudder went up Jenny's backbone. She stared at the book. It was a straight *X*, not like the slanted *X* of the rune Nauthiz, the one that her grandfather had carved on the closet to restrain the Shadow Men.

"See, Jenny?"

544

She nodded and drew. But the strange feeling didn't go away. A *bad* feeling—and it was connected with Gebo, somehow. Gebo the rune of sacrifice. Something was going to happen. . . .

Not now. Not right now. In the future.

Michael's voice startled her. "Next is Isa. It's a rune for the power of primal ice. It's just one straight line, up and down."

Jenny tore her mind away from the thought of sacrifice and made herself draw.

"Kenaz, the torch. It's for the power of primal fire, and it's shaped like an angle, see. . . ."

"Raidho, for movement, traveling. Like riding a horse. For protection walking between the worlds. It's shaped like an *R*. . . ."

"Uruz, the ox . . . it's shaped like an upside-down *U*—"

"I know, Michael." Uruz was the rune on the game box that Julian had sold her. "It's supposed to look like ox horns pointing downward, ready to pierce the veil between the worlds," Jenny said. "Is that the last one?"

"Yeah. Now we carve it."

Carving the runes wasn't as hard as Jenny had expected The door was good thick wood, but the runes were all straight lines and angles, which was much easier to carve than any rounded shape. Still, there were times when Tom's Swiss Army knife stuck or slipped. Jenny was a little frightened of how sharp it was.

And she was worried about the blood. How was she going

to do it? She was scared of razor blades, and a pin was out of the question. If they were going to stain all these runes, they'd need a lot more blood than you could squeeze out of a pinprick.

Don't think about it now. When the time comes, you'll just have to use the knife—and hope you don't cut your finger off.

Just then the problem solved itself. The knife slipped.

"God!"

Jenny felt a flash of something, gone almost too quickly to identify as pain. She dropped the knife, and she could feel her eyes widen as she stared at her hand—wondering in that first second how bad it was.

Not bad. A half-inch gash across the meat of her thumb. The lips of the wound showed white before bright red welled up to obscure them. Blood began to slide down her thumb.

Jenny felt just slightly sick. Seeing *inside* your skin—even a little way inside—was disconcerting.

"Quick, use it," Michael said. "Don't waste it—that stuff's precious."

The cut was beginning to sting. Jenny looked around for something to use as a pen, then collected the blood on top of one fingernail and began to trace the runes that were already carved. It stained the pale grooves in the wood a clear light red, the color of a teacher's red ballpoint pen.

Audrey and Dee did the rest of the carving, and Jenny

stuck to her gory task. She had to squeeze the cut in the end, but there was enough blood to go around.

The final product of their labors was slightly wobbly but impressive. Two concentric circles, with the runes running between them. Looking at the carving, Jenny wondered for the first time what somebody—a neighbor, say—would think if they caught the kids doing this. Destroying property. Vandalism. As bad as gangs spraypainting graffiti.

Jenny didn't care. She was still operating in crisis mode, in which all normal rules were suspended. She and the others had stepped out of the mainstream, into a place where anything could happen and the only rules were their own. It was scary— and tremendously liberating. Jenny felt as if she were flying toward Tom on wings of fire.

Take him from *me,* will you? she thought to Julian. I don't *think* so. By the time I'm done with you, you'll wish you'd never started this Game.

Dee was regarding the circle critically. "So what now? How does it work?"

"Apparently the idea is that writing runes makes whatever you've written happen," Michael said. "It's like when we drew our nightmares for the first Game, remember? We drew a picture of what we were afraid of, and then our pictures came true. Runes are the same. You make a—a *representation* of something, and it becomes real. You change reality by making the representation."

"That's what Julian told me," Jenny said quietly. "When I put on his ring and said the words, I made my own fate. The words came true when I said them."

"And that's what we have to do with this," Michael said. "We already did the first two steps, carving the runes and staining them. Now all we have to do is charge the runes with power by saying their names out loud. That activates them, and then—"

"And then, look out," Dee said, and her sloe-black eyes flashed. "Let's do it, people."

"We need to get our stuff first," Jenny said. She was trembling-calm now, wrought up to a fine pitch, but determined to do this right, not to jump in without thinking. "We don't know what happens once those runes are activated—we might not have time to do anything then."

They scattered to change their clothes and get things out of their duffel bags. When Jenny came back to the door, she was wearing Levi's and a denim shirt, with a sweater over the shirt and a nylon windbreaker over the sweater. On her feet were thick socks and hiking boots, and at her belt was a bota bag full of water and a pair of leather gloves. A miniature survival kit was in her fanny pack.

Everything in the kit had been chosen for lightness and efficiency. A small waterproof matchbox, a yard of toilet paper, a space rescue blanket folded into a four-inch square. Two heavy-duty plastic bags. Two aspirins. A Hershey's Bar. Three tea bags, three bouillon cubes. A string of safety pins. All that was packed in an old tin cup. Tucked in beside the cup were fifty feet of nylon cord, two Power Bars, and a flashlight.

The last thing she put in was Tom's red-handled Swiss Army knife with the six attachments.

They had no idea what they'd be facing in the Shadow World. What kind of terrain, what kind of weather. The glimpse Jenny had gotten through the window of the paper house had shown twisted pinnacles of rock scoured by an endless blizzard and lit by blue and green flashes like lightning. But was the entire world like that?

I'm about to find out, Jenny thought. Very soon. At least this time we're going prepared.

The others arrived, dressed the same way she was. Even Audrey was wearing light hiking boots and a nylon jacket. Dee had tucked the river knife into a black plastic sheath at her belt, but her most deadly weapons were her slender hands and hightop-encased feet.

They all looked at one another, and then, silently, turned to face the door.

Michael gave the book to Jenny. "You should be the one to do it."

Jenny took a deep breath. Holding the journal lightly, she began to read the names.

"Dagaz." *Rune of change.* "Thurisaz." *The thorn.* "Gebo." *For sacrifice.* Jenny's voice was beginning to shake and she couldn't breathe easily. Unconsciously she raised her voice. "Isa." *Primal ice.* "Kenaz." *Primal fire.* The word came out in a staccato burst. "Raidho." *Traveling.* Jenny's throat closed and she lifted her head, looking at the last rune in the circle. A long moment passed.

This is it. This is really it. After I say it, it can't be unsaid. No turning back.

Almost in a whisper she said, "Uruz."

For piercing the veil between the worlds.

With the last word the door began to flash like a strobe light. Black, white, black, white, black, white.

"God!" Audrey said. Everyone jumped a step back. But there was nowhere to go—they were up against the hallway wall. Michael barged into the telephone table and the handset fell off and struck the floor.

In the last month Jenny had seen plenty of bizarre things happen. Julian specialized in the bizarre. But this was different— maybe because the setting was so ordinary, a normal house, a normal door. Or maybe because they'd done it themselves.

And this wasn't just chills-up-the-spine bizarre. This was running-and-screaming bizarre. On Beyond Zebra bizarre.

Within the flashes the circle of runes began to glow like a wheel of fire. Then it started spinning.

Bright as fireworks at midnight—spinning like a Catherine wheel. It was dizzying to look at. Jenny's neck seemed to be frozen, but she looked out of the corner of her eye at the others.

Dee had taken up the Horse stance, in balance without effort, ready for anything. Audrey was flattened against the wall, the fiery light dancing crazily on her auburn hair. Michael's eyes were huge.

A dull roaring began. It seemed to come from the earth itself, vibrating the floor against Jenny's feet.

Oh, God, we did this to ourselves.

Jenny's heart was pounding wildly, out of control. The light was like needles stabbing into her eyes. She was light-headed, half blinded, but she could no longer look away from the wheel.

One final explosion of light—and the roaring became a tearing sound, like a huge tarpaulin ripping in giant hands. It made Jenny want to fall down, curl up, cover her ears.

And then it stopped.

Just like that. One moment agonizing light and deafening, screaming sound—the next moment perfect calm. The door was an oak door again. The wheel of runes was no longer spinning.

But, Jenny saw, it wasn't exactly the way it had been. Dagaz, the rune Jenny had drawn at the top, was now at two o'clock. As if the spinning wheel had overshot slightly before stopping. And the runes burned like sullen coals in the wood.

Jenny was breathing as hard as if she'd just run a race.

"We did it," Dee whispered. Her lips were drawn back from her teeth.

"Did we?" Michael asked huskily.

There was only one way to tell. Jenny gave herself a moment, then slowly reached for the doorknob.

She could feel her pulse in her hand as she grasped the knob. The metal wasn't even warm.

She turned the knob and pulled the door open.

Oh.

Through the open door she could see, not the stairs down to her grandfather's basement, but utter blackness, like a night without stars.

CHAPTER 4

Switching on her flashlight, Jenny stepped forward.

There was a resistance as she crossed the threshold. Not like anything solid, more like the g-force she'd felt when the plane accelerated to take off. It made her stumble, not hit the ground quite right.

And the ground seemed to be asphalt. Jenny's flashlight beam made a white circle on it, catching something that looked like a small yellow flower. A smashed flower.

No, not a flower, Jenny realized slowly. The shape was familiar but so far from what she expected to see that she didn't recognize it at first. It was a piece of squashed popcorn.

Popcorn?

Flashlights were switching on behind her, beams crossing

and recrossing in the darkness. Dee and Audrey and Michael moved up beside her.

"What the *hell* . . . ?" Dee said.

There was a sound like a door slamming. Jenny swung her flashlight around just in time to see that it *was* a door slamming, it was the door to her grandfather's basement. She saw it for one instant standing shut, a door with no walls around it, and then it disappeared.

Completely. It was simply gone, leaving them—where they were.

"I don't believe this," Audrey said. The flashlight beams were almost pathetic in the darkness, but they showed Jenny enough.

It was Michael who said it, in tones of shock and indignation.

"It didn't work! After all that—and it's not the Shadow World at all!"

They were in Joyland Park.

It *was* Joyland, exactly as Jenny had seen it that afternoon—except now it was dark and deserted.

The same wrought-iron benches painted green, with smooth wooden planks for backs and seats. The same fences (also green) caging in the same manicured bushes—"poodle bushes," Michael called them. The same pink-and-white begonias Jenny had noticed before—she always noticed flowers. Now their petals were folded tight.

Jenny's flashlight beam caught a heavy-duty brown trash can, an old-fashioned signpost, CANDY CORNER, the signpost read.

The candy store had metal shutters rolled down over its windows and the tiny lights around the signs advertising HOMEMADE FUDGE and CARAMEL APPLES were off.

Jenny just couldn't accept it.

That afternoon the park had been filled with sound: babbling, yelling, ride noises, laughing, music. Now the only sound was her own breath. The motion was the gentle fluttering of pennants at the top of a roller coaster.

Then she noticed something else moving.

On a huge billboard the pirate chest was slowly opening and shutting like a clamshell.

"Nobody's here—not even maintenance people," Dee was saying in dissatisfaction.

"It's too late," Michael said. "They've all gone home."

"But *somebody* should still be here. Look!" Dee's beam flashed across to a little orange cart, nosed up against a fence ahead of them. The cart looked a lot like something a maintenance person might use.

But we didn't see it until after Dee mentioned maintenance people, Jenny thought.

Not just her little fingers but the sides of her hands were beginning to tingle.

There was something wrong here. It *looked* just like Joyland—

from the artificial lagoon down to the refreshment cart with the red-and-yellow wheels. But it felt—wrong.

As if something in the darkness was awake and watching them. As if the deserted park around her could come to life at any moment.

"This place is creepy," Audrey announced suddenly.

"Yeah, well." Michael laughed. "Nothing creepier than a closed amusement park."

Words flashed through Jenny's mind. *Did I ever tell you about this amusement park nightmare I had when I was a kid—?"*

"Listen." She turned around abruptly. "Besides Michael, has anybody else had amusement park nightmares?"

Audrey stopped, flashlight drooping. After a moment she said in a subdued voice, "I have."

Dee said quietly, "Me, too."

"And so have I," Jenny said. "Maybe it's one of those universal things—"

"An archetype," Michael interrupted pugnaciously, his voice wobbling slightly. "But so what? That doesn't mean anything. . . ."

Jenny realized then just how bad his dreams must have been.

"Don't be silly, Michael," Audrey said, very gently. She reached out and Michael snuck a finger into her hand. "You think?" she said to Jenny.

"I don't know. It's nothing like I expected. It looks like Joyland, but—"

"But Julian can make anything look like anything," Audrey finished crisply.

Dee looked around, then chuckled. "All right! Listen, you idiots," she said, turning back to them. "This is *good*. If it *is* the Shadow World—or part of it—it's a place we've been. We'll have an advantage, because we know the terrain. And it's better than blue-and-green blizzards, or whatever Jenny saw out that window last time, right?"

Audrey nodded without enthusiasm. Michael didn't move.

"And if it's *not* the Shadow World, we're in real trouble. Because it means we've blown our chance to find Tom and Zach. Maybe our only chance."

"*C'est juste,*" Audrey said. "I forgot."

Jenny hadn't forgotten. "We'd better check around. See if this is the real Joyland or—" She didn't need to finish the sentence.

She didn't know exactly how they were supposed to tell. The place certainly looked authentic. They crept through the silent park, heading automatically for the front gates, passing a restaurant, dark and still.

"What's that?" Audrey hissed. "I hear something."

It was the sound of water. Faint, coming from up ahead.

"It's the Fish Pond," Jenny said.

She recognized the booth with its red-shingle roof. It was

dark, like the other attractions. But when they reached it, she saw that the opaque water was swirling around its circular channel.

"They wouldn't leave that on all night," Audrey said, needle-sharp. "Would they? Would they?"

Jenny's pulse, which had been beating erratically, settled into a slow, heavy thumping.

"You know what, Toto? I don't think we're in Kansas any-more," she whispered.

"Well, well," Dee said, stepping forward. "How about this?"

There was a fishing pole leaning against the booth. Dee hooked an index finger around it.

"Ah. Now. I have a *very* bad feeling about that," Michael said. It was the first time he'd spoken in minutes.

Jenny understood what he meant. It was too obvious, too *inviting*. But they didn't *know* they weren't in Joyland. It was possible that the park might leave the water going at night. Maybe it kept algae from growing or something.

"Shall I?" Dee said, twirling the pole. "Or shall I?"

"You're enjoying yourself, aren't you?" Michael said, and there was something flatly resentful about his voice. "But there's other people here, you know. Whatever trouble you make affects us, too. . . ."

"Oh, come on, you guys. It's the only way to find out, isn't it?"

Jenny chewed her lip. Sometimes Dee's recklessness went

out-of-bounds, and nobody but Jenny could stop her. If Jenny didn't say anything, Dee would do it.

Jenny hesitated.

Dee lowered the line into the dark, rushing water.

Jenny realized that she and Audrey and Michael were all braced. None of them was stupid. If this was the Shadow World, something bad would happen. Something *bad.*

The line dangled in the water, slack. Dee jiggled the pole while Jenny thought of all the things that might come up. Dead kittens. Severed hands. Mutant marine life.

Julian knew what you were thinking. He *took* things from your mind and made them real. So if they were in the Shadow World, then the worst thing—the worst thing that any of them was thinking—

"A bite," Dee said. "No, maybe it's just caught." She leaned over to look, catching the thick yarnlike line in her bare hand and tugging.

"Dee—"

"Come on, come on." Dee tugged, then reached into the water to grope. "What's wrong with—"

"Dee, *don't*—"

Audrey screamed.

The water erupted.

Jenny had seen a geyser once, not Old Faithful, but a smaller one. This looked just the same. There was an explosion of mud-colored water, straight up. It splattered across Jenny's face and beaded on her windbreaker. Then it just *stayed* there, until Jenny suddenly realized that it wasn't water at all, it was something that had come out of the water. Something that had come out and grabbed hold of Dee.

A man—it had hands like a man that were around Dee's throat. But something kept Jenny's brain from recognizing it as a man. In another instant she saw what it was.

The thing had no head.

Its body ended at the shoulders with the stump of a neck. The thing had volition, though, even if it didn't have a brain. It was trying to drag Dee under the water.

All this passed through Jenny's mind in less than a second. Plenty long enough, though, for the thing to wrestle Dee almost to the water's surface.

I'm not brave. I don't know how to fight. But she was grabbing at the thing's arm with both hands. To her horror, her fingernails sank *in,* penetrating the arm beneath the tatter of a sleeve.

It smelled. It smelled *incredibly.* Something terrible had happened to the flesh, turning it into a kind of white, waxy stuff that quivered loosely on its bones.

Like—like that clammy clinging stuff novelty stores use for flesh. Jenny's little brother Joey had a fake snake made out of it. But this creature's flesh was nothing fake. When Jenny involuntarily snatched her hand back, she saw that her nails were full of it.

Everyone was shouting. Somebody was screaming, and

after another second Jenny recognized her own voice. With both legs trapped up against the booth and Michael and Audrey hanging on to her, Dee didn't have room to kick. She was fumbling with the knife at her belt.

She got it free and her arm went up—and then Michael yanked her and the wicked-looking river knife fell into the swirling water.

"Her shirt! Her shirt! Her shirt!" Michael was yelling. The body now had Dee by the collar. Michael was trying to pull Dee out of the shirt, but the buttons in front were holding.

Jenny didn't want to touch the headless thing with her bare hands again. She didn't, she didn't—but then the thing wrestled Dee's head almost into the water, and Jenny found herself grabbing its rubbery arm again. It was bent over, dunking Dee's head like someone dunking wash in a river, and Jenny stared directly into its neck-stump. Nothing about its body was nice to look at. What flesh could be seen through the rags of clothes was grotesque—bloated and swollen until it looked like a Kewpie doll that had been boiled and then inflated with a bicycle pump.

The screaming and shouting were still going on. None of their pulling was doing any good. Without conscious thought, Jenny found herself scrambling *over* the wall of the booth, over the channel. One leg dangled in the rushing water, then she was standing in the booth behind the headless thing.

"Pull, Michael! Pull!" Jenny grabbed the thing from behind,

arms closing around its waist just above the water level. The waist squashed, like an overripe peach. She could feel things shifting inside the dripping clothes. Her cheek was pressed up against the back of its wet shirt. She locked one of her hands around the opposite wrist and pulled harder.

Oh, God—the *smell*. She opened her mouth to scream again at Michael and gagged instead. She couldn't see anything that was going on in front. All she could do was hang on and keep pulling backward.

The thing seemed to be rooted in the water. She couldn't drag it out. It was a ghastly tug-of-war, with her pulling at the body and Michael and Audrey pulling at Dee. But suddenly she felt something give. The body lurched backward, the tension was gone. Dee was free.

Jenny let go and staggered into the wall of prizes behind her. The thing's arms flailed for a moment, coming in contact with nothing but air. Then, as if something had grabbed its feet and jerked it sharply downward, it disappeared into the dark water.

Everything was silent again.

Jenny was sitting in a litter of plastic whistles, cellophane leis, Matchbox cars, and stuffed koalas. She picked herself up, swaying, and looked over the water channel.

Dee was sprawled almost on Michael's lap. Audrey was half kneeling, half crouching beside them. Everyone was breathing hard.

Dee looked up first. "Jump over quick," she said in the voice of someone who's had strep throat for a week. "I don't think it can see, but it can *feel* when you touch the water."

Jenny jumped over quick, discovering in the process that she'd hurt her ankle sometime, and then all four of them just sat on the asphalt for a while. They were too tired and stunned to talk.

"Whatever it was, it wasn't human," Audrey said at last. "I mean—apart from the head—a human body couldn't look like that."

"Adipocere," Michael got out. "It's what human flesh turns to after a while under water. It's almost like soap. My dad had a mask like that once—he got rid of it because it freaked me out." Michael's father wrote science fiction and had a collection of masks and costumes.

"Then that whole thing was your fault," Dee said unkindly, voice still hoarse. "*Your* nightmare."

Michael, surprisingly, looked hopeful. "You think so? Then maybe I don't have to worry anymore. Maybe the worst's over—for me."

"If your dad had a mask, it wasn't headless, was it?" Jenny said.

"No. What?" Michael looked confused.

"I mean that monster wasn't *exactly* what you had night-mares about. I think Julian is putting his own little twist on things this time. Besides . . ." Something had been nagging at

Jenny since the figure had come shooting up out of the water. A feeling of familiarity. But how could she be familiar with something as monstrous and repulsive as that? Audrey was right, it hadn't even looked human, except that it had two legs and two arms and wore clothes. . . .

Wore *clothes* . . . dank and stinking . . . tattered and dark with water . . . but familiar. A long flannel shirt, black-and-blue plaid, unbuttoned.

"Oh, my *God*. Oh, my God, oh, my God—" Jenny had gotten to her knees, her voice shrill. "Oh, my God, no, it was Slug! Don't you see? It was Slug, it was *Slug* . . ."

She was almost screaming. The others were staring at her with sick horror in their eyes. Slug Martell and P.C. Serrani were the two tough guys who had stolen the paper house from Jenny's living room—and disappeared into the Shadow World. None of Jenny's friends had much sympathy for them, but this . . . nobody deserved this.

"It wasn't Slug," Audrey whispered.

"It was. It *was!*"

"Okay." Dee, eyes wide, scrambled on her knees over to Jenny. She put her arms, slim but hard as a boy's, around Jenny. "Just stay cool."

"No, don't you see?" Jenny's voice was wild and keening. "Don't you *see*? That was Slug, without a head. In Michael's dream he saw Summer's head. What if we find Summer's body, like that? What if we find *Summer*?"

"Damn." Dee pulled back and looked at Jenny. "I know you think it's somehow your fault that Summer died—"

"But what if she's not dead? What if she's wandering around here—" Jenny could feel herself spiraling out of control. She was hyperventilating, hands frozen into claws at chest level.

Dee slapped her.

It was clearly meant to be restorative and it worked, mainly because Jenny was utterly shocked. Dee often threatened physical violence but never, ever used it except in self-defense. Never. Jenny gave a sort of hiccup and stopped having hysterics.

"It's bad," Dee said, her dark eyes with their slightly amber-tinted pupils close to Jenny's and unwavering. "It's really bad, and nobody's saying it isn't." She fingered her throat. "But we have to stay calm, because otherwise we're dead. Obviously we're in the Shadow World—I guess nobody is going to argue about *that*"—she glanced behind her at Audrey and Michael—"and this is some new Game Julian has dreamed up for us. We don't know what to expect, we don't even know the rules. But one thing we do know: If we let it get to us, we're dead before we start. Right?" She shook Jenny a little. "Right?"

Jenny looked into those eyes with their lashes thick as spring grass and black as soot. It was true. Jenny had to get a grip, for the sake of the rest of them. For Tom's sake. She couldn't afford to go crazy right now.

She hiccuped again and unsteadily said, "Right."

"We *all* have to stay calm," Dee said, with another glance

at Michael and Audrey. "And we need some weapons. I lost my knife, and if there are any more of those things around . . ."

Jenny realized suddenly that she'd never even thought of getting Tom's Swiss Army knife out of her fanny pack. She wasn't used to fighting. She quickly unzipped the pack and reached in to make sure the knife was safe.

"I've got this," she said, holding it out to Dee.

"Okay, but it's too small. We need something *big* to fight those suckers."

Audrey spoke up in a small, controlled voice. "There were picks and things in the mine ride today. I saw them this afternoon."

"She's right!" Michael said, excited. "They had all those scenes with miners—with axes and shovels and all sorts of stuff. Let's go."

Jenny got up slowly. "I need to get cleaned up first. There's got to be a bathroom around here somewhere." Her jeans were wet from the channel water, but even worse was the stinking ooze on her windbreaker and hands.

There was a bathroom beside the restaurant, and it was open. Jenny washed her jeans as best she could. The windbreaker she threw in the trash, along with her damp sweater. She washed her hands and face over and over and then stood under the blower trying to dry her shirt and jeans.

She and Dee guarded the rest room entrance while Michael and Audrey took their turn washing, and Jenny noticed a squashed cigarette butt on the ground. She stared at it for several minutes, the night breeze cool on her damp jeans. Every detail, she thought. Julian must have re-created everything in the real park, making it realistic down to the tiniest detail.

Which didn't mean there weren't nasty, unrealistic surprises around any given corner. They'd only been here half an hour, and already one of them had nearly died. On his own ground Julian's illusions were real—or real enough that no amount of disbelief would shake them. In the Shadow World he was the master. Jenny had the feeling that all her worst amusement park nightmares were about to come true.

And we haven't even *seen* Julian yet, she thought. He's got to be here, somewhere, laughing himself sick at us.

As they set off for the mine ride, Audrey said, "I hear music."

CHAPTER 5

The music seemed to be coming from a distant corner of the park—somewhere in back, maybe near the arcade. For an instant Jenny saw lights glimmering through the trees. But the rides they passed were dark and still. The bumper cars were motionless humps like frozen cattle, and Jenny got a whiff of the graphite that kept the metal floor slippery.

What is it about amusement parks? she wondered as the bulk of a roller coaster blotted out the stars. What makes them give people nightmares?

It's because there's something mystical about them, she thought. About some of them, anyway—not the really new, totally sanitized, Hallmark-Pepsi-Colgate kind, but some of the older ones, or the ones that had older sections. In some of those there was something mystical, ancient—significant. Something more than met the eye.

The lights twinkled like will-o'-the-wisps up ahead, but Jenny and the others never seemed to get any closer to them. The music was so faint that she couldn't make out the tune.

Then she heard a new sound, a *slap-pad, slap-pad* like quick bare footsteps. Dee whirled instantly to face it. Jenny clutched Tom's knife. An hour ago she would have been afraid to walk around with it open—it was *sharp*—and now she was afraid to close it.

Four flashlights swept the manicured shrubbery, illuminating nothing more sinister than a clock made of flowers. Then Michael shouted, "There!"

Something was scampering across a path on the other side of the shrubbery. The flashlights picked out a slate-colored figure. It was moving too fast for Jenny to get a good look at it, but her impression was of something very small and impossibly deformed. Something like a withered gray fetus.

It disappeared behind—or into—the Whip.

"Should we go after it?" Dee asked.

Dee was *asking*? She must be half dead, Jenny thought. She said, "No. It's not bothering us, and we're not armed yet." It gave her a vaguely military and important feeling to say *armed*. "Let's get to the mine ride first."

"But what was it?" Audrey said.

"It looked like a monkey," said Michael.

"It was little," Jenny said—and then she thought of something. Her dream. The little man in the elevator, the man with the mask.

Can we take you? We can carry you.

The Shadow Men might ask something like that—but that wizened thing couldn't have been a Shadow Man. The Shadow Men were beautiful, frighteningly and heartbreakingly beautiful.

"Whatever it was, we'd better watch our backs," Dee said. "There might be more of them."

The mine ride was as dark as everything else. Jenny shined her flashlight on the freestanding control box with its little lights and switches.

"We don't have to *use* that, do we?" Michael said.

"No, I don't think so," said Jenny. She glanced behind her at the miniature train that stood waiting by the loading platform, then turned her flashlight on the track. "I think the train runs on its own power—see how the track looks just like a regular train track?—but it doesn't matter. I think we should walk."

Audrey opened her mouth as if to protest, then shut it again. All four flashlights converged on the mouth of the "cave" where the track disappeared. In the ordinary park this cave was a dark and fanciful gold mine full of ghostly miners, flooded shafts, skeletons, bats, and dynamite. In the Shadow Park, it might hold anything.

"Let's do it," Jenny said.

Going into the cave was like being swallowed. As they walked slowly along the track, Jenny glanced back and saw a circle of lighter black behind them—the outside world, getting smaller and smaller.

At about this point in the ordinary ride there had been colored lights and mist around the train, probably meant to show you were going back in time to gold mining days. Tonight, there was just a musty damp smell.

There were no lights to illuminate the scenes in the cave, either, and it gave Jenny a jolt when her flashlight caught a figure in the shadows. It was a mustached miner with rolled-up sleeves, loading dynamite into a hole in the rock while two other miners watched.

"That one's holding a sledgehammer," Dee said.

"Yeah, but it's way too heavy. None of us could even pick it up," Jenny said. "We'd better see what's farther down. I do remember pickaxes and things."

"We can't get lost as long as we follow the track," Michael added. Jenny noticed he seemed almost cheerful now.

Dee shrugged and they went on. The next scene showed what happened after the dynamite went off—a cave-in that left the three miners trapped beneath a wall of boulders. In the ordinary ride there had been screams and moans of "Let me out!" and "Help me!" It was almost scarier without the sound effects, Jenny thought. The figures in the boulders were scary as waxworks, while the flashlights made shadows leap on the cave wall behind them. Jenny found herself staring at one clawed hand reaching above the tumbled rocks.

"Are they moving?"

"It's your hand shaking," Audrey said in an edged voice.

"It's all just papier-mâché," Michael said and thumped the cave wall. It sounded like hitting a surfboard. "Ow. I lied. It's fiberglass."

There were more scenes: a flooded shaft with real water, a hanging, even a wilderness saloon with skeletons as patrons. They climbed up to examine the saloon.

"These bottles might work," Dee said, taking one from a bony hand. Strange, Jenny realized—the bottle didn't look like modern glass. It was thick and milky with age and it said CROWN DISTILLERIES CO. on the front.

All the bottles looked old. They were brown, dark blue, green, even pink, and they bore imprints like AVEN HOBOKEN & CO. and PEARSON'S SODAWORKS.

"Very authentic," she said. "I didn't think Joyland took so much trouble."

The others exchanged glances, but said nothing.

"We'd better keep looking," Jenny added.

They passed another trapped miner, this one with thousands of small black ants crawling over his face. Jenny was liking the figures less and less—the feeling that they might start moving at any minute was almost unbearable. They passed strange waterfalls where purple water flowed like glass down broad steps of rock into a colored pool.

"There!" Dee said as they rounded a corner. "Picks!"

Miners were standing around a stream, leaning on shovels or holding pickaxes. Several had Bowie knives or pistols thrust through their belts.

Dee was already boosting herself up into the scene. "Look at this, it's great!" It was a tool with a wooden handle as long as a yardstick and an iron head. Neither side of the head was very sharp. One ended in a sort of blunt spike as long as Jenny's little finger, the other was flat and triangular. For scooping? Jenny wondered.

Dee was moving the tool up and down, trying to get it out of the miner's loose grasp. The miner, hat brim drooping wearily, stood impassive.

"Here's one I like," Audrey said grimly. She'd found a pick that was sharp on both sides.

Dee shook her head. "Too flimsy. See how the head's just tied on to the handle with rawhide? It might not hold." She succeeded in prying the tall pick loose and held it up triumphantly. "Now *this* is a weapon."

Michael was holding up an iron forklike thing with six heavy, curved tines. *"Nightmare on Elm Street,"* he said.

Jenny put the Swiss Army knife in her pocket, gripped her flashlight in her teeth, and wrestled free a tool of her own. It had a short wooden handle and an iron head with a five-inch-long projection. She couldn't tell if it was a hammer or a pick, but it felt good in her hand, and she swung it once or twice for practice.

That was why she wasn't sure if the ground really moved a moment later, or if she was just off balance. She stopped swinging.

"Did anybody feel that?"

Dee was looking at the platform they were all standing on. "I don't think this thing is too stable."

"I didn't feel anything," Michael said.

Jenny felt a flicker of apprehension. Maybe it was just the platform—or maybe she was just dizzy—but she thought it was time to get out of there.

"Let's go back."

"You got it, Sunshine," Dee said, swinging the pick onto her shoulder. They all scrambled down, knocking ornamental gravel onto the track with a sound like popcorn in a pan.

"Follow the yellow brick road," Michael said, waving his flashlight beam along the track.

And we can't get lost, Jenny completed the thought in her mind. We can't. We'll be fine.

So why did she have a cold knot in her stomach?

Michael, at the front, was now humming "I've been working on the railroad." Suddenly his flashlight stopped swinging.

"Hey. What the—*hey!"*

Jenny sucked in her breath, feeling her chest tighten even as she pushed her way past Audrey.

Michael was sputtering indignantly, staring down at his feet. Jenny saw the problem immediately.

The railroad tracks split.

"Did they do this before?" Jenny swept her flashlight beam first one way, then the other. Both sides were the same: metal rails laid over thick wooden boards. But they went in different directions.

"No. They never split. I would have noticed," Dee said positively.

Audrey let her pick down with a solid thump. "But it wouldn't have looked like a split from our direction. It would have been two tracks joining."

"Splitting, joining, it doesn't matter. I'd have noticed."

"But it would have been behind us. In the dark—"

"I would have noticed!"

"Hey, guys, guys—" Michael began, making the time-out sign with his fork and flashlight. It was completely ineffectual. "Guys—"

"I am not a guy," Audrey snapped and turned back on Dee. It didn't matter what the argument was about anymore, it was turning into another Dee-Audrey jihad.

"Oh, fine, yell at me, too—" Michael began.

"Shut the hell up—*all of you!*" Jenny shouted.

Startled, everyone shut up.

"Are you people crazy! We don't have time to argue. We don't have time for anything. Maybe the track split before and maybe it didn't, but we came up by *that* wall." She pointed to her right. "We'll go that way and it should take us out."

Except, she thought, that nothing is what it should be when Julian's involved. And that tremor she'd felt before—maybe the ground really had moved.

The others, looking as if a summer thunderstorm had come and gone in their midst, meekly set out in the direction she'd indicated. But Dee said quietly, "If we *are* going the right way, we should see that miner with the ants all over him pretty soon."

They didn't.

The knot in Jenny's stomach pulled tighter and tighter. The right-hand wall was blank—and it seemed to be closing in. This place was looking less like a tunnel for a train ride and more like a real mine shaft all the time.

It was almost a relief to finally run into the proof. She rounded a slight curve and saw an ore car sitting squarely on the track in front of her.

A real ore car—at least as far as Jenny could tell. It was four or five feet long with rounded corners and solid wheels set close together under its center. It smelled like rusty iron—like a witch's cauldron, Jenny thought—and echoed slightly when she spoke while bending over it.

"This isn't part of the ride," she said.

"It would be stupid of a park to leave it here," Dee said and tried to pull it by the hitch in front. It clanged, but didn't move far.

Jenny had a wild impulse to jump into it and stay there.

She looked up slowly at the others.

Michael's flashlight lit up Audrey's hair from behind, giving her a copper halo. Dee was just a slim black shadow at Jenny's side. Jenny didn't need to see their faces to know what they were feeling.

"Okay, so we're in trouble," she said. "We should have known, really. So whose nightmare is this?"

The slim black shadow showed a glimmer of white teeth. "Mine, I guess. I'm not in love with enclosed spaces."

Jenny was surprised. The last time they'd been down in a cavern, she hadn't noticed Dee having any problems—but then, the last time her attention had been focused pretty exclusively on Audrey.

"I'm just a *little* claustrophobic. I mean, I don't remember having any dreams about this kind of thing. But"—Dee let out a breath—"I guess if you asked me what's the worst way to die, I'd have to say a cave-in would rank right up there."

"God, do we have to worry about *that*? Horrible ways to die?" Michael exploded. "I could fill a book."

"What am I most afraid of, I wonder?" Audrey said, rather emotionlessly. "Pain? A lot of pain?"

Jenny didn't want to think about it. "We've got to go back

and follow the tracks the other way. It's our only chance."

They were headed deeper into the mine now. The hammer bounced bruisingly on Jenny's shoulder.

Since they were retracing their steps, the shaft should have opened up again. But it didn't. The walls closed in until Jenny could have touched irregular outcrops with her fingertips. The ceiling got lower and lower until it brushed Jenny's hair.

She gathered the flashlight and hammer in one hand so she could touch the cavern wall with the other. "Definitely not fiberglass," she murmured.

Not fiberglass but rock—and surprisingly beautiful rock. She could see veins of milky white and orange, the orange ranging from palest apricot to a rusty burnt sienna. It all sparkled with millions of infinitesimal pinpricks of quartz.

"Ore," Michael said. "You know, the kind gold comes in."

"This park was built on a coal mine," Jenny said. "They mined coal everywhere around here—but that was back in the eighteen hundreds."

"Different kind of mine," Michael said. "This is a real gold mine we're in."

Rock was everywhere—very rough, maybe carved but looking natural because it was so irregular. It was like being in a castle, Jenny decided.

And it was *cold*. She wished she hadn't thrown her sweater away.

Dee, a step ahead, was walking with her shoulders drawn in. Jenny could sympathize. She was beginning to feel the pressure of the rock around her—the solidity of it. They were in an endless buried shaft of orange and brown and black.

When the first junction came, everyone stopped.

"The tracks go straight," Jenny said. She knew perfectly well that that didn't mean anything. This wasn't the split in the tracks they'd seen before. A long corridor simply stretched out into the darkness on one side.

They followed the tracks straight ahead.

The stripes of white on the walls got bigger and bigger the farther they went. It was damp, now, and the walls felt icy and dirty. When Jenny touched them, her fingers came away black.

They came to a place where the roof opened into a sudden cavern—a horizontal shaft maybe thirty feet up. Jenny could see a vein of rust-colored rock at the top, and below that gray slate ridged and grooved as if water had flowed down it.

"That shaft or cavern or whatever goes back a way," Dee said. "We could maybe climb it. . . ."

"Or maybe not," Jenny said. She understood why Dee wanted to get out of the lower tunnel, but she didn't like the look of that black hole up there. "We'd break our necks, and there could be anything—or anybody—up there."

Audrey said, "Well, it's obvious that things are changing around us. I was wrong about the track, Dee."

Dee gave her a startled look. She wasn't used to apologies from Audrey.

Something cold struck Jenny's cheek. She touched it and felt wetness—and then another drop on her hair.

"Listen," Michael said.

At first Jenny didn't hear anything. Then it came, the loneliest sound in the world. Water dripping musically onto rock—slow drops that seemed to echo through the deserted shafts. It sounded far away.

"Oh, God," Jenny whispered illogically, "we really are lost." The lonely dripping brought it all home. They were trapped under tons of rock, in the dark, far from any help, and with no idea of where to go.

Dee said, "Uh-oh," and then stopped.

"What? *What?*"

"Well—I just remembered a nightmare I had once about a cave."

"It didn't flood, did it?" Jenny asked, thinking of the miners in the scene on the train ride.

"No. It just sort of collapsed."

Audrey said, "I don't think we should be *talking* about this. *Tu comprend?*"

She was right, of course. They shouldn't be talking, or thinking, or anything. Blank minds were what they needed. But Jenny's mind was out of control, following Dee's words like a spark running down a fuse.

"On you?" she said. "Did it collapse on you? Or were you just trapped—"

That was as far as she got before the ground started to rumble. Only it wasn't just the ground, it was the ceiling, the walls, everything.

"Which way?" Dee cried, as good in a pinch as always, even if this was her nightmare. She swung her flashlight around, looking up and down the shaft. "Where's it coming from?"

Jenny saw rocks falling from the vertical shaft behind them. Michael's flashlight was on the same thing.

"Come on!" he shouted, starting the other way. "Come on! Come on!"

"It's all coming down!" Audrey shouted.

"Come on! Come on!" Michael just kept yelling it, his voice higher and higher.

The floor was rocking—like the tremor Jenny had felt earlier, only much, much bigger. She couldn't see anything clearly. Flashlights were waving all over the place.

"We can't go that way—"

"Watch out—the *rock*—"

Above the shouting voices was the voice of the rock, a grinding, shuddering, smashing sound. Jenny was trying to run, bruising herself on outcrops that seemed to jump into her path. She was being thrown from side to side.

"The floor—!"

She heard Audrey's shriek, but was too late to stop herself.

There was a gap in the floor of the shaft, a vertical cavern down to another shaft. Small rocks were falling into it, and Jenny's flashlight illuminated dust particles swirling madly in the air. Then she was falling, too.

The first blow hurt, but after that she was in shock and just bounced off the outcrops numbly. She felt her fanny pack tear free. Her hammer and flashlight were already gone, along with the bota bag. Then she was rolling and sliding, part of an avalanche that carried her with it effortlessly.

Then the noise and confusion receded and her mind went blank.

She was alone, in complete darkness and utter silence. Her throat was full of choking dust. And she was terrified.

Jenny knew this before she remembered who she was or how she'd gotten there. It was one of those terrible awakenings—like the kind she used to have in the middle of the night, when she jerked out of sleep *knowing* that something was out there in the dark, and that it was bad. And that in the daytime she would forget all about it again.

The worst thing was that this wasn't a dream. There was no bedside light to turn on, no parents to run to. Instead there was only darkness and the sound of her own breathing.

"Dee!" The shout came out pathetically weak. And it didn't echo properly. Jenny turned her face up but couldn't feel the slightest air current.

She was in an enclosed place. The rock must have blocked up the entrance she'd fallen through.

"Dee! Audrey!" Oh, worse than pathetic. Her voice died out completely in the middle of "Michael!"

Then she sat perfectly still, listening.

If I don't move, it won't get me.

That was ridiculous, of course. It only worked for monsters under the bed. But all her muscles were locked, so tense they were shaking.

She couldn't hear a sound. Not even a faint after-rumble from the cave-in. The darkness folded on itself around her.

She felt herself begin to panic.

Oh, please, no . . . just keep calm, think of something . . . but I'm *scared*. There must be some way out . . . you can move around, see what this place is like.

But she couldn't. She couldn't move. It was too dark. She could feel her eyes widening and widening, useless as the blind bumps on white cave fish.

Anything could be out there—coming at me—from any direction . . .

The panic was now a riot. She was utterly terrified that she *would* hear a noise, a noise of something approaching in the blackness.

But I fell in alone. This is a small place; I can feel it. I'm alone. Nothing's here with me. Nothing can get in. Nothing—

Rock scraped lightly on rock.

Jenny twisted to face it, still kneeling. The faint sound was lost now because her heart was going like a trip-hammer and her ears were ringing with sheer terror.

Oh, God—

"Ragnarok," said a musical voice, "means both a rain of dust and the end of the world. To the people who discovered the runes, I mean. Don't you think that's interesting?"

CHAPTER 6

Julian . . ." The sensation was exactly like falling down the mine shaft.

Then she said sharply, "Where are you?"

"Here." Red light blossomed.

Jenny tried, in the moment before her eyes adjusted, to brace herself. But she could never brace for Julian—he was as much a shock to her senses as ever.

A beautiful shock, like a completely unexpected riff in a dull jazz piece. Like a picture you could pore over for hours and still find new and startling details in. Everything about him was so perfect and so perfectly outrageous that your eye darted from feature to feature in dazzled confusion.

Just now the red light glinted off his hair like fire on snow.

It turned his impossibly blue eyes to an equally impossible violet. It threw dancing shadows across the planes of his face, bringing into relief the sculpted beauty of his upper lip. It cast an unholy glow all around him—which was entirely appropriate, because Julian was as seductive as mortal sin and as haughty as the devil.

He was wearing black like a second skin, pants and vest without a shirt. The red light came from the torch he was holding.

Jenny, devastatingly aware that her jeans were crunchy from drying wrinkled and her denim shirt looked as if she'd crawled through a chimney, said, "You invited me to come—and here I am."

He answered as easily as if they'd been talking for hours. "Yes, and you're off to a bad start. Couldn't even avoid this simple trap. Don't even know what game you're playing."

"Whatever it is, it's the last Game," Jenny said.

It wasn't the same as it had been before, when she'd felt as if she were fighting him all the time in her mind—whether he was physically present or not. Fighting his sensuality, fighting his beauty, fighting the memory of his touch.

In those days part of her actually longed for the moment when she would stop fighting, for the final surrender. But now . . .

Jenny had changed. The fire she'd passed through in the last Game, the one he'd created to trap her, had changed her. It had burned away the part of her that had responded to Julian, that had craved his danger and wildness. Jenny had come through the fire alive—and purified. She might not be as powerful as Julian, but her will was as strong as his.

She would *never* give in to the shadows again. And that meant that everything was different between them.

She could see that he saw the difference. He said, "More light?" and made a gesture, like tracing a line in the air.

Kenaz, Jenny thought. The rune of the torch, one of the runes she'd carved on her grandfather's oak door. It was shaped like an acute angle, like a lesser-than sign in mathematics. When Julian's long fingers made the gesture, the light seemed to ripple, and with a magician's flourish he plucked a second burning torch from the air.

Jenny, stony-faced, clapped her hands two or three times.

Julian's glance was blue as a gas flame. "You don't want to get me angry. Not this early on," he said with dangerous quietness.

"I thought I was supposed to be impressed."

He studied her. "You *really* don't want to get me angry."

Oh, he was gorgeous, all right. Inhuman, incomprehensible, and so alive he looked as if he should be dripping fire or electricity from his fingertips. He brought a shine with him like diamonds in coal. But Jenny had a core of steel.

"Where's Tom?" she said.

"You haven't been thinking about him," said Julian.

It was true. Jenny hadn't. Not continuously, not constantly, the way she had in the old days when she'd never really regarded herself as a separate person, but as part of a unit: Tom-and-Jenny. It didn't matter.

"I came here for him," she said. "I don't need to think about him every minute to love him. I want him back."

"Then win the Game." Julian's voice was as cold and ominous as thin ice breaking.

He stuck one torch into a wide horizontal crack in the wall. Jenny hadn't really taken in her surroundings yet—when Julian was around it was very difficult to focus on anything except him—but she saw now that she'd been right in her guess earlier. This was an enclosed place, and a very small one, scarcely as big as her bedroom at home. Three of its walls were stone; the fourth was solidly packed boulders.

Below the crack with the torch was a sort of natural stairway, each step broader than the one above it. Like the fake waterfalls in the mine ride, Jenny thought, only without the water. She noticed her flashlight, apparently dead, lying by the bottom step.

There was no entrance or exit to the room. The ceiling was low. It had a very *trapped* feeling about it.

Jenny's heart sank a little.

No. Don't you dare let him frighten you. That's what he wants, that's what kicks him.

Besides, what's to be scared of? So you're buried alive

under tons of rock, alone with a demon prince who wants you body and soul and will literally do anything to have you. Who might kill you just to make sure no one *else* can have you. And you're pissing him off deliberately, but so what, why sweat the details?

She tried to make her voice quite steady and a little blasé as she said, "So just what is the Game this time?"

"The clue will cost you."

Icy fury swept over Jenny. "You're horrible. Do you know that?"

"I'm as cruel as life," Julian said. "As cruel as love."

The fury, and the steel at Jenny's core, gave her the courage to do something that astonished even her. She wanted to slap Julian. Instead, she kissed him.

It wasn't like the tender, cozy sort of kiss she gave Tom, and not like the terrified, half-wild kisses Julian had extorted from her in the old days, either. She jumped up and snatched his face between her palms before he could do anything with the torch. She kissed him hard, aggressively, and without the slightest vestige of maidenly shyness.

She felt his shock. His free hand came up around her, but he couldn't pull her any closer than she was already pressing herself. She ignored the danger of the torch completely—if it was close to her hair, that was Julian's problem. Let the great master of the elements figure it out.

Julian recovered fast. It was possible to take him off guard, but he didn't stay nonplussed long. Jenny felt him trying to take control of the situation, trying to soften the kiss.

But she knew the danger of softness. Julian could spin a web of shadows around you, with touches like the brush of moth's wings and kisses soft as twilight. He could turn your own senses against you until the kisses left you dizzy and breathless and the moth's-wing touches put you on slow burn. And by the time you realized what was underneath the softness, you were shivering and melting and lost.

So Jenny kept this kiss strictly business. A cheap and nasty sort of business she'd never had to do before because before Julian she'd only ever kissed Tom. She kissed him angrily, with a clinical coldness and all the expertise she could muster. At the end she realized she'd managed to startle him twice in just a matter of minutes. When she pulled away—which she did easily—she could see the shock in his eyes.

Didn't think I could resist, did you? she thought. She stepped back and with utter coldness said, "Now, what about my clue?"

Julian stared. Then he laughed mockingly, but she could see him losing his temper, see the blue eyes glitter with rage like exotic sapphires. She had struck at his pride—and hit dead center.

"Well, now, I'm not sure I got my money's worth," he said. "I've known icicles that were better kissers than that."

"And I've known dead fish that were better kissers than

you," Jenny said—untruthfully and with an insane disregard for danger. She *knew* it was insane, but she didn't care. The freedom of knowing that the shadows had no power over her was intoxicating. It made this encounter with Julian different from any other.

She'd struck home again. She saw the menacing fury well up in his eyes—and then his heavy lashes drooped, veiling them. A half smile curved his lips.

Jenny's stomach lurched.

He was evil, she knew. Cruel, capricious, and dangerous as a cobra. And she'd been stupid to goad him that way, because right now he was planning something bad—or her name wasn't Jenny Lint-for-Brains Thornton.

"I'll give you your clue," he said. He slid a hand into one skintight pocket and brought it out again, flipping something gold on his thumb and catching it again. The gold thing winked in the torchlight, up and down. "Heads I win, tails you lose," Julian said and gave her a smile of terrible sweetness.

Then he flicked the shining gold thing at her so quickly that she flinched. It hit the stone with a wonderful clear ringing clink. Jenny picked it up and found that it was cold and quite heavy. It was a coin, round but irregular, like a very thin home-baked cookie.

"A Spanish doubloon," Julian said, but even then she stared at him a moment before getting it.

Oh, God—of course. The game—the one the real Joyland

Park was holding. What had that kid said this afternoon? *"You get three tokens and they let you in free. . . ."* And the billboard: COLLECT THREE GOLD DOUBLOONS AND BE THE FIRST TO SET FOOT ON . . . TREASURE ISLAND.

And Julian had invited them to come on a treasure hunt. But Jenny hadn't made the connection, not even when that giant treasure chest had been the only thing moving in the park tonight.

"You modeled this whole place after Joyland because they were having a treasure hunt? Why? Because I used to go to the park when I was a kid?"

He laughed. "Don't flatter yourself. This whole—Shadow Park, if you like—already existed. It was created ten years ago and for a very different reason. A special reason . . . but you'll find out about that later." He gave a strange smile that sent a chill through Jenny. "It was built on an old coal mine, you know—a pit. The Shadow Men have been here a long time."

A pit. *Deep into the Pit,* Jenny remembered. That was a line from the poem she'd found on her grandfather's desk in Julian's first Game. Was that how her grandfather had found the Shadow Men in the first place? Had he taken a question deep into a pit, into some place where the worlds were connected?

She would probably never know—unless Julian told her, which didn't seem likely. But it cast a vaguely sinister light over the real Joyland Park.

Forget the conjectural crap, she told herself. Get down to business.

"Tom and Zach are on Treasure Island," she said.

She got a wolfish smile back. "Right. And don't even think about trying to swim there or anything. The bridge is the only way, and the toll is three gold doubloons. You'll find the coins hidden throughout the park."

"I've got one already," she reminded him, closing her fist on the coin.

His smile turned dreamy, which was even more frightening than the wolf look. "Yes, you do, don't you?" he said pleasantly. "Now all you have to do is get out with it."

On the word *it,* everything went dark.

It happened so fast that it took Jenny's breath away. One moment she was conversing by the light of two ruddy torches, the next she was in pitch blackness. Blackness so profound that it made her heart jump and her eyes fly open. She saw ghostly blue pinwheels, then nothing. It was like being struck blind.

Okay. Don't panic. He made a mistake—he got mad and screwed up. He left the flashlight.

I hope, her mind added, as she stuck the doubloon in her pocket and cautiously felt her way in the darkness.

Her hand closed around cold metal. She held her breath and thumbed the switch.

Light. Only a tiny light, a dull orange-ish glow. Either something had happened to the flashlight in the fall or the batteries were going dead. But it was enough to keep her from going crazy.

You shouldn't have made him mad, Jenny. That was really, really dumb.

Because, even with light, she was in trouble. By holding the flashlight very close she could see the rock walls of her prison quite clearly. She could examine every inch of it, from the low ceiling, to the uneven floor, to the solidly packed boulders that blocked the entrance.

There was no way in or out. She couldn't possibly shift those boulders by herself—and if she did move one, she'd probably bring the rest of them down on top of her.

Don't panic. Don't, don't, don't panic.

But the flashlight was already getting dimmer. She could see it, but not anything around it. And she was alone in the midst of solid rock and absolute silence. There was no sound, not even the drip of water.

Wait. You thought your way out of a fire in the last Game—why not a cave now? Come on, try. Just imagine the rock wall melting, imagine your hand moving through it. . . .

But it didn't work. As she'd suspected before, here in the Shadow World, Julian's illusions were too strong to be broken. He was the master here.

Which meant she was stuck, unless someone came to help her.

Okay, then. Yelling time.

She made herself shout. And again, and again. She even picked up a fist-size rock that lay at the bottom of the pile and banged on each stone wall, slowly and rhythmically. In between each burst of noise, she listened.

There was absolutely no sound in answer.

At last, with the flashlight nearly out, she sat down with her back against the boulders, drawing her arms and legs in like an anemone.

Then the whispering began.

It started so softly that at first she thought it might be the blood rushing in her ears. But it was real. The voices were distant and musical—and menacing. What they were saying was too indistinct to be made out.

Shoulders hunched, Jenny turned her head slowly, trying to locate the sound. And there, in the darkness, she saw eyes.

They glowed with their own light, like foxfire. They were cold, ravenous. She recognized them from her grandfather's closet.

The Shadow Men. The Shadow Men were here with her.

Their eyes seemed to stare out of the wall itself. They were *in* the rock, somehow. Jenny felt the hairs on her arms erect, felt a prickling that ran from her little fingers to her palms and all the way up to her elbows. A primitive reaction to what she saw in front of her.

Everyone, everywhere, knew about the eyes, she thought. Underneath, everybody really knew, even though people tried to suppress the knowledge in the daytime. At night sometimes the knowledge burst out—the sense of watching eyes that shared the world with humans. Eyes that were ancient and infinitely malevolent and that had no more concept of pity than a wasp or a T. Rex.

Except that they were gifted with intelligence—maybe more intelligence than humans. Which made them doubly terrifying.

And they want you terrified, Jenny. So just keep your head. They're here to scare you, but they won't do anything to you.

But they're whispering. . . .

Such a juvenile thing. They were whispering gibberish—and it frightened her sick. Distorted, unnatural sounds. Like records played backward, at low speed.

She couldn't help listening and trying to make sense of it—even while she was terrified of doing just that. She didn't *want* the gibberish to make sense.

Then, to her surprise and vast relief, the eyes went out.

They didn't fade away as much as seem to recede across some great distance. The voices lingered for a moment and then died.

Thank you, Jenny thought fervently, leaning her bent head on her knees. Oh, thank you. The silence seemed almost welcome now.

Then she heard another sound, a liquid rippling that the hissing voices had obscured. She turned the dying flashlight toward the wall with the steps, where the eyes had been. Then she jumped up with a gasp and brought it closer.

The steps—were moving. No. As she brought the flashlight right up to the wall she felt a splash of wetness against her hand. The steps weren't moving, they were just covered with water.

Water was flowing down the rock staircase, smooth as glass. Just like the waterfalls in the mine ride.

Only faster. It was pouring in a steady sheet all along the width of the crack—maybe three or four feet. It was flooding out like a hotel fountain.

Strangely, it seemed just an inconvenience at first, and not nearly as scary as the eyes had been. Jenny didn't recognize it as a danger until her feet were soaked.

It's not flowing out through the boulders, she realized slowly. Weird. They must be *really* packed to be sealed. Or maybe there's just a blank wall behind them and only the ceiling was open when I fell through. But now even the ceiling's blocked up.

And that water's still coming. . . .

It was coming, and faster every minute, and icy cold. Her feet were actually numb inside her hiking boots. Too bad I lost the fanny pack—I had those Baggies for wading, she thought, and then she realized that she was going to die.

This was a sealed cavern. Sealed. Smaller than her bedroom and filling up faster than her dad's swimming pool. The water was going to come in and in—

—and where will the air go? she wondered, stumped for a moment by this problem in physics. For a moment she thought she was saved. If the air couldn't get out, no more water could get in.

But there was probably room for the air to go out the ceiling, beyond the boulders somewhere. Up in some place Jenny couldn't find because the flashlight was completely dead now. She was standing in darkness, with water rising around her calves, and if she tried to climb those boulders blindly and pull at them, they would crush her. And if she didn't, she would eventually be left with her mouth up against the ceiling, gasping for the last tiny breath of air before the water took her.

She wasn't hysterical, but thoughts were rushing through her mind with dizzying speed. She was remembering the flooded-cavern scene in the mine ride above, and the clawed hand reaching above the boulders. And she thought she knew what some of the whispering voices had been saying.

"Die . . . die . . ."

So that had been the meaning of Julian's little smile. . . .

The oddest thing of all was that, even as the water rose higher and higher, she couldn't seem to bring herself to believe it.

Julian wanted her *dead*? Oh, it shouldn't be surprising—he was evil, wasn't he? Completely evil. And he'd been in a fury when he left.

But—*dead?*

The water was around her thighs now. It was cold—painfully cold. What a waste it had been to dry her jeans off earlier.

Without consciously knowing how she'd gotten there, she found herself kneeling on one of the waterfall's steps, pressing her hands against the crack, trying to stuff a rock inside. It did no good at all; she could feel the water gushing out in the dark, chilling her hands.

Maybe Julian just wanted to humiliate her—to frighten her until she begged for help. But, no, that didn't make sense. Julian knew she wouldn't beg. She wouldn't give in to him. He'd found that out when he'd set the bees on her in the first Game. Jenny had been willing to die then rather than surrender to him.

And so he must know she would be now, and so he must *want* her dead, really dead.

Unless—

Jenny wouldn't have thought it possible for her to become more frightened than she already was. She'd have thought there would be some limit, that her mind would go numb. But although her body was numbing with cold, her mind was suddenly reeling with a new idea that made sheer black horror sweep through her.

What if Julian didn't know? What if he weren't the one doing this?

Julian had stormed off in a rage—and then *they* had come. What if this water was *their* doing?

She'd be dead before he found out.

The thought resounded in her mind with a queer certainty. Julian had been at odds with the other Shadow Men once before—when five-year-old Jenny had first opened her grandfather's closet. The other Shadow Men had wanted to kill her, their lawful prey. But Julian had objected. He'd wanted her, wanted her alive.

And she'd stayed alive, because her grandfather had given himself up to them. But now . . .

Now, she thought, they're finishing the job. And Julian *doesn't* know.

It was odd, but she was suddenly sure of that. Julian might be evil, but the other Shadow Men were worse. More twisted, more malign. In the paper house, Julian had controlled everything—but she wasn't in the paper house now. She was in the Shadow World itself, and *all* the Shadow Men were masters.

The water was up to her neck. So cold, Jenny thought— and then the idea came.

What if it got more cold—ice cold? Julian had conjured up a torch with the torch rune, Kenaz. So, maybe—

She was so numb she hardly knew whether she was crawling or floating, but she found the top step and she found the rock she'd tried to stuff in the crack. She was blind, but she could feel the wall, and the rune she wanted was the simplest shape imaginable.

Just one stroke, up and down. A capital *I* without any bars. The ice rune, Isa.

She scratched it directly over the crack, directly in the flow of water. And then, blind and almost paralyzed, she waited.

It was too cold for her to tell at first if it worked. But then she felt jagged sharpness instead of the smooth numbing gusher.

The flow over the rune Isa had become a frozen waterfall. Although the water around Jenny remained liquid, it had stopped rising.

I did it! I stopped the water! It's ice, beautiful ice!

She sucked in deep breaths of air excitedly, not afraid to use it up any longer. Oh, God, it was good to breathe. And the rune, the rune had worked for her. She couldn't control the Shadow World with her mind, but the runes worked for anyone.

It was only after a few minutes that she realized she was going to die anyway.

Not by drowning—or at least not entirely, although that would come at the end. She was going to freeze to death.

It was too cold—had been too cold even before she had frozen the waterfall. Being here was like floating in the ocean the night the *Titanic* had sunk. She was going to die of hypothermia—lose consciousness and sink. And *then* drown.

601

And there was nothing at all she could do about it.

She was already too weak when her stupefied mind stumbled upon the idea of the torch rune. Kenaz. If she could remember it—if she could find her rock—or move her fingers . . .

But the rock was gone and her fingers were too anesthetized and her brain was fogging up. Blanking out gently, almost like the beginning of sleep. Kenaz . . . she waved the frozen lumps of flesh that were her hands vaguely under the water, but of course no torch appeared. Water could be frozen into ice, but not kindled into fire. She couldn't change the rules of the elements at her whim.

Disconnected scraps of thought drifted through her mind. It didn't hurt much anymore. Not so bad. And nothing seemed so urgent—whatever had been bothering her moments earlier wasn't as important now.

Help. She had a vague feeling that she might call for help. But it seemed—it seemed there was some reason not to.

Wouldn't hear me. That's it. Was that it? He wouldn't hear me anyway. Too far away.

It didn't matter now. Nothing mattered.

Gebo, she thought, one flash of coherence, of memory, just before her head slid under the water. Gebo, the rune of sacrifice.

CHAPTER 7

Oh, Tom.

Dying was painless—but sad. It hurt to think of the people she was leaving behind.

She kept picturing her parents, imagining what they would say when Dee and the others got home and told them. *If* Dee and the others got home and told them.

Her thoughts were very scattered, like dandelion fluff blowing erratically on the wind.

Mr. and Mrs. Parker-Pearson—Summer's parents—had been so hurt when they lost Summer. Jenny hated to think of her parents hurt that way.

And Tom . . . what would happen to Tom? Maybe Julian would let him go. No point in keeping him after Jenny was gone. But that didn't seem likely. Julian was a Shadow Man, he belonged to a race that didn't have gentle emotions. They weren't capable of pity.

Julian might take out his anger on Tom instead.

Please, no, Jenny thought . . . but it didn't seem to matter that much anymore. Even her sadness was fading now—breaking up and floating away. She was dead, and she couldn't change anything.

Strange, though, that a dead person could suddenly feel pain—physical pain. A burning. The frigid water had stopped hurting a long time ago, and since then she'd had no sense of her own body. Trapped in absolute darkness and utter silence, too numb to feel any sensation, she didn't seem to *have* a body. She was just a drifting collection of thoughts.

But now—this burning had started. At first it seemed very distant and easy to ignore. But it didn't stop. It got worse. She felt heat: a tingling, prickling heat that demanded her attention. And with the heat she began to have a body again.

Hands. She could feel her hands now. And feet, she had feet. She had a face, defined by thousands of tiny red-hot needles. And she was aware of a vague, fuzzy glow.

Open your eyes, she told herself.

She couldn't. They were too heavy, and everything hurt so much. She wanted to go back into the darkness where there wasn't any pain. She willed the light to go away.

"Jenny! Jenny!"

Her name, called in tones of love and desperation. Poor Tom, she thought dimly. Tom needed her—and he must be frantic with worry. She should go to Tom.

But it *hurt*.

"Jenny. Please, Jenny, come back—"

Oh, no. No, don't cry. It'll be all right.

There was only one way to make it all right, and that was to come back. Forget how much it hurt.

All right, *do* it, then. Jenny concentrated on the fuzzy glow, trying to make it come closer. Pulling herself toward it. The pain was terrible—her lungs hurt. But if she had lungs, she could breathe. Breathe, girl!

It hurt like hell, and darkness sucked at her, trying to drag her down again.

"That's it, Jenny. Keep fighting! Oh, Jenny . . ."

With a tremendous effort she opened her eyes. Golden light dazzled her. Someone was rubbing her hands.

I did it for you, Tom.

But it wasn't Tom. It was Julian.

Julian was the one rubbing her hands, calling out to her. Golden light danced on his hair, his face. It was a fire, Jenny realized slowly, and she was in another cavern, slightly bigger than the last. She was dry, somehow, and lying in a sort of nest of white fur, very soft, very comfortable. The heat of the fire was bringing her back to life.

The pain wasn't so bad now, although there was still an

unyielding knot of ice in her middle. And she felt weak—too weak and exhausted to think properly. It was Julian, not Tom—but she couldn't really take that in.

It didn't even *look* like Julian . . . because Jenny had never seen Julian look afraid. But now the blue eyes were dark with fear and as wide as a child's—the pupils huge and dilated with emotion. Julian's face, which had always seemed molded for arrogance and mockery, was white even in the firelight—and thinner somehow, as if the skin were drawn tight over bones. As for the dangerously beautiful smile that usually curved Julian's lips . . . there wasn't a trace of it.

Strangest of all, Julian seemed to be *shaking*. The hands that held Jenny's had stopped their rubbing, but a fine, continuous tremor ran through them. And Jenny could see how quickly he was breathing by the way his chest rose and fell.

"I thought you were dead," he said in a muted voice.

So did I. Jenny tried to say it, but only got as far as a hitching breath.

"Here. Drink this, it should help." And the next moment he was supporting her head, holding a steaming cup to her lips. The liquid was hot and sweet, and it sent warmth coursing into the cold, hard knot inside her, loosening it and chasing away the last of the pain. Jenny felt herself relaxing, lying still to absorb the fire's heat. A feeling of well-being crept through her as Julian laid her back down.

Gently. Julian was being gentle . . . but Julian was never

gentle. He belonged to a race that didn't have gentle emotions. They didn't feel tenderness, weren't capable of pity.

She probably shouldn't even accept help from him—but he looked so haunted, like someone who had been through a terrible fright.

"I thought I'd lost you," he said.

"Then you didn't send the water?"

He just looked at her.

It didn't seem to be the time for recriminations. Oh, she probably *ought* to say something—maybe list the kind of things he'd done to her in the past. He'd hunted her in every way imaginable.

But here, now, in this little cavern surrounded by rock, with no one present but the two of them, and no sound but the soft roar and crackle of the fire . . . all that seemed very far away. Part of a past life. Julian didn't seem like a Shadow Man, didn't seem like a hunter. After all, if he were a predator, he had his quarry right here, exhausted and helpless. He'd never have a better chance. If he wanted her, she wouldn't even be able to put up a fight.

Instead, he was looking at her with those queer dazed eyes, still black with emotion.

"You would have cared if I died," she said slowly.

The eyes searched hers a moment, then looked away.

"You really don't know, do you?" he said in an odd voice.

Jenny said nothing. She pulled herself up a little in the white nest, so she was sitting.

"I've told you how I feel about you."

"Yes. But . . ." Julian had always said that he was in love with her—but Jenny had never sensed much tenderness in the emotion. She might have said this, but for some reason it seemed—inappropriate—to say it to someone who looked so lost. Like a child waiting for a blow. "But I've never understood why."

"Haven't you." It wasn't even a question.

"We're so different." Madness to be talking about this. But they were both looking at each other, now, quietly, as they had never sat and looked before. Eyes unwavering—but without challenge. It meant something to look into someone's eyes this long, Jenny thought. She shouldn't be doing it.

But of course she had wondered, she had wondered from the beginning what he could possibly see in her. How he could want her—so much. Enough to watch over her since she was five years old, to pierce the veil between the worlds to come after her, to hunt her and stalk her as if he thought about nothing else.

"Why, Julian?" she said softly.

"Would you like a list?" His face was completely blank, his voice clipped and emotionless.

"A—what?"

"Hair like liquid amber, eyes green as the Nile," he said, seeming utterly dispassionate about it. He could have been reading a page of homework assignments. "But it's not the color, really, it's the expression. The way they go so deep and soft when you're thinking."

Jenny opened her mouth, but he was going on.

"Skin that *glows,* especially when you're excited. A golden sheen all over you."

"But—"

"But there are lots of beautiful girls. Of course. You're different. There's something inside you that makes you different, a certain kind of spirit. You're—innocent. Sweet, even after everything that's been thrown at you. Gentle, but with a spirit like flame."

"I'm *not,*" Jenny said, almost frightened. "Audrey sometimes says I'm too simple—"

"Simple as light and air—things people take for granted but that they'd die without. People really should think more about that."

Jenny did feel frightened now. This new Julian was dangerous—made her feel weak and dizzy.

"When I first saw you, you were like a flood of sunshine. All the others wanted to kill you. They thought I was crazy. They laughed. . . ."

He means the other Shadow Men, Jenny thought.

"But I knew, and I watched you. You grew up and got more beautiful. You were so different from anything in my world. The others just watched, but I *wanted* you. Not to kill or to use up the way—the way they do with humans sometimes here. I needed you."

There was something in his voice now besides clinical

dispassion. It was—hunger, Jenny thought, but not the cold, malicious hunger she'd seen in the ancient eyes and the whispering voices of the other Shadow Men. It was as if Julian was hungry for something he'd never had, filled with a crippling need even he didn't understand.

"I couldn't *see* anything else, couldn't *hear* anything else. All I could think about was you. I wouldn't let anyone else hurt you, ever. I knew I had to have you, no matter what happened. They said I was crazy with love."

He had gotten up and walked away to the edge of the firelight. As he stood there, Jenny seemed to see him for the first time, looking at him with new eyes. And he looked—small. Small and almost vulnerable.

Nothing in the universe was moving except her heart, and that was shaking her body.

She had never thought about what the other Shadow Men might say to Julian. She knew he was the youngest of a very old race, but she'd never thought about his life at all, or his point of view. She hadn't thought about him *having* a point of view.

"What's it like, being—" She hesitated.

"Being a Shadow Man? Watching from the dark places everything happening on the worlds that aren't full of shadows? Earth has colors, you know, that you never find here."

"But—you can make anything you want. You can create it."

"It's not the same. Things fade here. They don't last."

"But why do you *stay* here, then? Instead of just watching

us, you could—" Jenny stopped again. God, what was she saying? Inviting the Shadow Men to her own world? She took a deep breath. "If you could change—"

"I can't change what I am. None of us can. The rest of the nine worlds keep us out; they say our nature is destructive. We're not welcome anywhere—but we'll always be near Earth, watching. From the shadows."

There was something in his voice—too quiet and closed-off for bitterness. A—remoteness that was bleak beyond words.

"Forever," he finished.

"Forever? You never die?"

"Something that isn't born can't die. We have a—beginning, of course. Our names carved on a runestave, a special runestave." He said, almost mockingly, "The stave of life."

There had been something about staves in her grandfather's journal. A picture scrawled in ink, showing a sort of tall, flat branch with runes on it.

"Carve our names on the stave—and we come into existence," Julian said. "Cut them out—and we disappear."

It seemed very heartless to Jenny. Cold—but then the Shadow Men were cold. Not flesh and blood, but creatures that came into being through a carving in wood or stone.

How cold to *be* a Shadow Man, she thought. And how sad. Condemned by your own destructiveness to be what you were forever.

Julian was still standing at the edge of the firelight, face half in shadow, gazing at the darkness beyond. It gave Jenny a queer hollow feeling.

What would it have been like, she wondered suddenly, if he hadn't tried to force her?

From the beginning Julian had used force and trickery. He'd lured her into the More Games store and enticed her into buying the Game, knowing that when she put the paper house together it would suck her into the Shadow World. He'd *kidnapped* her. And then he'd appeared and bullied her: forced her to play his own demonic game to try and win her freedom. He'd threatened her, hurt her friends—*killed* Summer. He'd done everything to try and wring submission out of her.

"Couldn't you just have come and asked?" she murmured.

She'd said the same thing to him in the tower of the paper house. *Didn't that ever occur to you? That you could just appear at my front door, no games, no threats, and just* ask *me?* But in the tower the words had been part of a ruse to get free, and she hadn't really thought about them herself.

Now she did. What if Julian *had* come to her, appearing some night out of the shadows while she was walking home, say, and told her that he loved her? What would she have done?

She would have been afraid. Yes. But after the fear? If Julian had come, offering gifts, gentle, looking as vulnerable as he did now?

If she had accepted his gifts . . .

It was a strange future, too strange to visualize, really, but queerly thrilling. It was too foreign to imagine: herself as a sort of princess with a prince of darkness as consort. For just an instant Jenny got a rushing, heady glimpse; for a fraction of a second she could picture it.

Herself, wearing black silk and sable, sitting on a black marble throne in a big stone hall where it was always twilight. Growing paler and colder, maybe, as she forgot about the ordinary world she'd left behind—but happy, maybe, in her power and position. Would she have little Shadow World creatures to order around and look after? Servants? Would she be able to control the elements here the way Julian did?

Or maybe not a black gown—maybe white, with little icicles all over it, like Hans Christian Andersen's Snow Queen. And jewels like frostflowers around her neck and a blue-eyed white tiger crouching at her feet. What would Dee and Audrey think if they saw her like that? They might be afraid at first—but she'd serve them strange drinks, like the sweet, hot stuff in the mug, and after a while they'd get used to it. Audrey would envy the pretty things, and Dee would envy the power.

What else? Julian had said she could have anything—*anything.* If she could have anything in the world she wanted, with no limits, no restrictions on her imagination—if she could have *anything . . .*

I'd want Tom.

She'd forgotten him for a moment, because the picture of the big stone hall was so alien. Tom's warmth and strength and lazy smile didn't fit there at all—which of course made sense because Julian would never let him in. But any world without Tom was a world Jenny didn't want.

The vision of the white gown and the jewels disappeared, and she knew somehow that it would never come back, not the way it had for that one moment, when she could feel it and believe in it. She would never forget it, but she would never be able to recapture it, either.

Just as well, she thought unsteadily. She didn't want to think about this anymore; in fact, she thought it was high time that she got out of here. She was tingling all over with a sense of danger.

"I'm warm now," she said, pushing the white fur away. All she could think of was that she had to leave. She should thank him, maybe, for saving her life—although it wouldn't have been in danger in the first place if not for him.

He was looking at her. Jenny looked away, concentrated on getting her legs under her. When she stood, they were wobbly. She tried to step out of the white nest, and stumbled.

He was there in an instant.

She felt his warm hands close around her arms, steadying her. She stared at his chest, bare under the leather vest and lifting quickly with his breathing. The firelight touched everything with gold.

She didn't want to look up into his face, but somehow it happened anyway.

His eyes were still hugely dilated, the blue mere circles around pupils dark and bottomless as midnight. His pupils always sprang open for her, she realized, but just now there was something haunting about those lonely depths.

"I'm sorry," she whispered, hardly knowing what she meant. "I have to leave now. I'm sorry."

"I know."

In that instant he seemed to understand better than she did herself. He looked very young, and very tired, and heavy with some knowledge she didn't share. Face still solemn, he leaned in slightly.

Jenny shut her eyes.

It was different from any kiss they'd ever had. Not because it was softer—Julian's kisses were usually soft, at the beginning anyway. Not even because it was so slow—Julian's kisses were almost always slow. But it *was* different, in a way that sent Jenny's mind spinning into confusion.

Feeling . . . that was it. Not just sensation, but emotion. Emotion so strong that it left her shaking. It was such an innocent kiss, so—*chaste*. His warm mouth touching hers. His lips trembling against hers. How could something that simple move her so much?

Because she could sense his feelings, she realized. When she touched his lips, she could feel his pain, the almost unendurable pain of someone whose heart was breaking with sadness. What she tasted on those warm, soft lips was unbearable loss. If he'd been dying, or she had, she would have been able to understand such a kiss.

He's suffering like that—from losing *me*? Jenny had never been particularly modest, but she could hardly believe it. She might have rejected the idea outright—except for what she was feeling herself.

What she felt . . . was a shattering inside.

When he stepped back, Jenny was in something like a trance. She stood there, eyes shut, still *feeling* everything, unable to move. Tears welled up around her lashes.

But Tom.

The time in sixth grade when he'd broken his leg and sat in a tide pool, white but still wisecracking, holding on to Jenny's hand, not letting anybody else see how bad the pain was. All the many times he'd held Jenny for *her* sake, when she got scared at movies, or when she cried over the stray animals she took in. He'd stayed up all night when she thought Cosette, the kitten she'd rescued from a vacant lot, was dying. He had been part of her life since she was seven years old. He was a part of *her*.

And Julian had hurt him. Julian had blown his chance right at the very beginning, when he'd done that.

Jenny opened her eyes, the trance broken. She stepped back, and saw Julian's face change. As if he knew exactly what she was thinking.

"Tom needs me," she said.

Julian smiled then, grimly, in a way that chased the cobwebs out of Jenny's brain. The lost, haunted look was gone, as if it had never existed.

"Oh, yes. Tommy needs you like air. But I need you like—"

"What?" Jenny said when it was clear he wasn't going on.

"Like light," Julian said, with the same bitter smile. "You're light, all right—like a flame to a moth. I told you once that you shouldn't mess with forbidden things—I should have taken my own advice."

"Light shouldn't be *forbidden*," Jenny said.

"It is to me. It's deadly to a Shadow Man. Light kills shadows, don't you know? And of course the other way around."

He seemed to find this amusing. He'd done one of his quicksilver mood changes, and looking at his face now, Jenny almost wondered if the last half hour had been a dream.

"Don't think that just because I pulled you out of the water, the Game is over," he added. "You need three gold coins to get to your precious Tommy. And time's *tick, tick, ticking.* . . ."

"I've got one, remember. I—" Jenny broke off with an inarticulate noise, feeling in her jeans pocket. The Swiss Army knife was still there, but the gold doubloon he'd tossed her in the cavern was gone.

"But I *had* it. It must have fallen out—"

"Sorry. Only one turn to a customer. No replays. Do not pass Go, do not collect two hundred dollars."

"You—" Jenny broke off again. Her anger drained, but she felt something inside herself harden, ice over. All right, then. She must have been crazy, feeling sorry for Julian—*Julian!*—but now she knew better. They were opponents, as always, playing against each other in a Game that was as cutthroat and pitiless as Julian himself.

"I'll get the coins—if you give me the chance. I can't do much in here," she said.

"True. Exit doors are to the left. Please watch your step and keep moving. We hope you've enjoyed the ride."

Jenny turned and saw a rectangle of dim light. It hadn't been there before.

She took a breath and started toward it, careful to walk straight.

She didn't mean to look back. But as she got close to the door, close enough to see that it looked like an ordinary double door, like the kind that led out of Space Mountain at Disneyland, she threw a quick glance over her shoulder.

He was standing where she'd left him, a black silhouette in front of the fire. She couldn't tell anything by his posture.

She turned away and stepped through the door, blinking. She could see tiny distant lights, lots of them, sparkling and wheeling in a dazzling display.

"What—?" she whispered.

Something grabbed her.

CHAPTER 8

Thank *God*!" a voice shouted in Jenny's ear. Jenny relaxed against the slim but very strong arms holding her.

"Dee—you scared me to death. . . ." The lights were on the canopy of the merry-go-round across the lake. It was turning and Jenny could hear faint music from a Wurlitzer band organ.

"You scared *us* to death," Audrey said. "Where have you been for the last two hours? We ran down that shaft with the roof caving in right behind us all the way—and then when we finally got to the mouth of the cave, we realized you weren't with us. Then Dee went crazy and tried to go back while everything was still falling, but it almost killed us and we had to go out—and when we *got* out, it was just a ride again."

"The caving-in noise stopped," Michael explained, "and I looked back and the cave was fiberglass again."

"And empty," Dee said, giving Jenny a fierce hug before letting go. "We walked all through it, the three of us, and you weren't in it. It was just a mine ride."

"*That* is the Emergency Exit we just came out of," Audrey said, pointing a finger at Jenny's door. "So the question is, where have you been? You've seen him, haven't you?"

Jenny was looking down at herself by the light of a nearby fountain—a fountain which had been dark when they'd first gone into the ride. Her jeans were rumpled but dry, her hair was all ridges and waves, the way it got when it dried without her brushing it. The supplies she'd packed so carefully to help her face the Shadow World were gone. Even her flashlight was gone.

"I saw him," she told Audrey briefly without looking at her. "I found out what the new Game is." She explained what Julian had told her about finding the three doubloons to get to Zach and Tom. She didn't say anything about the other Shadow Men, or the rising water in the dark cave, or how it had felt to die. She wanted to; she wanted to talk about it in privacy, and maybe cry, and be comforted, safe with her friends. But she *wasn't* safe, and there wasn't any privacy, and what was the point of alarming everybody?

As for Julian and his bizarre mood swings—she didn't even want to get on the subject.

"So at least we got something out of that ride," Michael said. "I mean, it nearly killed us, and we lost most of our stuff, but we did get some weapons, and now we know what we're doing. What happens after we collect these doubloons?"

"I think we go to the bridge, just like that kid said in the regular park," Jenny said. She was grateful—and proud. They were all battered and tired, and there were only two flashlights left—but no one was even talking about giving up.

"The bridge must be on the other side of the lake, around back," she added. "When we get there, I guess Julian will let us across." She looked at the lake. The merry-go-round lights were reflected in it, and so were other lights, blue and green and gold, from the island itself. Shadows of trees broke them up.

In the center of the island, standing very tall and white, was the lighthouse. It looked the same as the one Jenny had seen that afternoon, in the real park, except that now it was illuminated like the Washington Monument. Like a tower for imprisoned princes.

"That's where Tom and Zach are," she said quietly.

"Where should we start looking?" Dee said, equally quiet.

The Emergency Exit door had brought Jenny out close to the front of the mine ride. "Well—we could go left to Kiddieland," she said, "or right, back the way we came from the Fish Pond. Or around the front of the lake, toward the merry-go-round."

Michael ran a hand through his rumpled dark hair. "Let's

621

go around the lake—it'll take us by the billboard about the contest. Maybe that'll give us a clue."

"That's where we came in tonight," Audrey said. "When we came through the door with the runes, I mean."

They walked past the dark ringtoss booth and around the gentle northern curve of the lake. There seemed to be no rhyme or reason as to which parts of the park were awake and which still slept.

They kept a close eye out for things like the one that had attacked Dee, but they saw nothing. Then, as they got closer to the billboard, Jenny heard a voice.

A low voice. It scared her—who else was in the park with them?

She rounded a clump of spruce trees and saw a car from a circus train, with a red roof and silver bars.

"I'm Leo the Paper-Eating Lion," the muzzle thrust between the bars said.

Only the voice—was wrong. It wasn't the peppy, friendly tenor of the Leo in the regular park. It had dropped two octaves and become distorted and almost machinelike. A thick, muddy cybervoice.

"Geez," Michael whispered.

Jenny moved cautiously closer, following Dee. The circus car was lighted, very bright and gay against a dark background of bushes. The animal *looked* like the Leo of the ordinary park, with a shiny caramel-colored face, dark mane, and painted body. Jenny's eyes were drawn to the muzzle, spread in a permanent smiling *O* so it could suck up trash. It looked as if it were calling "Yoohoo!"

"I eat all kinds of things," the growling, guttural voice said.

"I bet," breathed Michael.

"What's it doing here? Is it just to scare us?" Audrey said, circling the cart at a safe distance. Dee was playing her flashlight into the plastic muzzle.

"I think there's something in there," she said.

"You're kidding. You *are* kidding, aren't you?" Jenny edged along beside Audrey. She didn't want to get any closer to the lion than she had to—the asphalt path wasn't nearly wide enough in her opinion.

Dee knelt and squinted. "Something gold," she said. "No, really, I'm serious. Look way back in there, in the throat."

Unhappily Jenny took the flashlight and aimed it at the dark hole. It did look as if there might be something shining inside, but gold or silver, she couldn't tell.

"It might just be a gum wrapper," she said.

Dee leaned a casual arm on her shoulder. "Don't tell me, you've had Leo the Lion nightmares."

Jenny hadn't, that she could remember. But the lion had looked sinister even this afternoon, and it looked doubly sinister now.

"I am not putting my hand in there," Michael said positively.

Dee flashed her most barbaric smile. "No, Audrey can do it; she's got nice long nails. How about it, Aud?"

"Don't tease her," Jenny said absently. "Now, what we need is something long—but a fishing pole wouldn't work because it wouldn't catch a coin. Maybe if we put something sticky on the end . . ."

"Nothing's as good as a hand. Audrey could—"

"Dee, quit it!" Jenny cast a sharp look at the girl beside her. She didn't know why Dee and Audrey seemed to be having problems today—maybe it was a reaction to all the tension—but this was no time for Dee's skewed sense of humor. Audrey was standing a little apart from the others, head tilted back, chestnut eyes narrowed in disdain, cherry-colored lips pursed. She looked very cool and superior.

"Leo's *always* hungry. So feed me," the distorted, bestial voice said. Every time it spoke, Jenny's heart jumped. She was terrified that the caramel-colored muzzle might *move,* that she'd look up and Leo's head would swing toward her.

It can't. It's plastic, she thought. But she was afraid her heart would simply stop if it did. The quietness of the park around them, the darkness, made this one animated trash can even more eerie.

Dee sat back on her heels. "It looks like there's more to this than just finding the coins. We have to actually *get* them, which may be the hardest part. It's a quest game."

"Quest?" Jenny said.

"Yeah. Remember how I told you about the different kinds of games, once? Games fall into certain categories. The first one Julian played with us, where we had to get to the top of the house by dawn, that was a race game."

"Right, and the second one, where the animals were chasing us, was a hunting game. Like hide-and-seek," Jenny said.

"Yeah, well, there's another type of game, where you have to find things in order to win—like in a treasure hunt or a scavenger hunt. Or hot and cold. A quest game. It's as old as the other kinds of games."

"Naturally," Michael said. "Humans are terrific questers—they love to look for things. The Holy Grail, or the truth, or the treasures in Zork, or whatever."

"Surely you can find something to feed Leo the Paper-Eating Lion. I'm *starving*."

Jenny looked up, jerked out of the pleasant hypothetical discussion. Audrey was standing by the circus car, examining her nails. The usually perfect polish had been slightly chipped in the mine ride. She looked thoughtful.

"Go on, princess. I dare you," Dee said, her black eyes flashing in amusement.

"Don't be silly, Audrey," Jenny said automatically. The concept was so ridiculous, though, that she said it unhurriedly. Audrey never did anything reckless—not physically reckless, at least.

So Jenny didn't say the warning with urgency, and therefore

she was, in some way, responsible for what happened next.

Audrey put her hand in.

Michael was the one who shouted. Jenny jumped up. But for a moment it looked as if it was going to be all right.

Audrey, her face set, was fishing around in the hole. Her hand was in it to the wrist.

"I feel something," she said.

Jenny's heart was thudding. "Oh, Audrey . . ."

Audrey's lips curved in a triumphant smile that brought out her beauty mark. "It's cold—I've got it!"

Then everything happened very fast.

The caramel-colored plastic face was flowing, melting, like a very good morphing effect in a movie. In a movie it would have been fascinating—but here it was real. It was *real,* and so awful that it froze Jenny to the spot.

The colors bled and changed, going olive green, then a dreadful grayish cemetery tone with steely streaks. The eyes sank, becoming hollow pits. The mouth seemed to snarl, lips pulling back to reveal long teeth that had grown to trap Audrey's wrist.

It happened so fast that even Dee didn't have time to move. Audrey started to gasp, and then screamed instead. Her entire body snapped forward.

The thing had sucked her arm in to the elbow.

"Audrey!" Michael shouted. He covered the distance to her in two steps. Dee was right behind him with her pick.

No good, Jenny thought dazedly. It's not flesh, like that thing—like Slug. It's stone or metal or something.

"Don't hit it, Dee. That won't help—that won't help. We have to pull her out!"

The thing—it wasn't a lion anymore, but some sort of hideous cyberbeast—was now the color of an old statue coated with moss.

Audrey screamed again, breathlessly, and her body jerked. The nylon jacket was skinned up to her shoulder now, bunched like an inner tube as her arm was dragged farther in.

"It's taking my arm off!"

Jenny gasped, almost sobbing. Michael was yanking at Audrey.

"No, don't pull! Don't pull! It hurts!"

Vaseline, Jenny was thinking. Or soap—something to make it slippery. But they didn't have anything.

"Dee!" she said. "Use the pick—try to pry its teeth apart. Michael, wait until she gets it in—*then* pull."

Audrey was still screaming and Michael was crying. Vaguely, in shock, Jenny noticed that the stone beast was still changing, becoming more deformed. Dee wedged the tip of the heavy pick upside down between the gray, mossy teeth and pulled back on the handle. Jenny grabbed it to help her.

"Hard!"

Dee threw her weight down. Jenny prayed the wooden handle wouldn't break off from the iron head.

She felt something shift—the upper jaw lifting just a fraction, like a car lifting on a jack.

"Pull, Michael!"

Michael pulled. Audrey's arm came out.

She screamed on a new note—a shriek that pierced Jenny's chest. But her arm came out.

They all fell backward, the pick clattering down. With a common impulse they scrabbled back away from the circus car, still sitting, still holding on to one another.

It was only then that Jenny looked at Audrey's arm.

There were toothmarks. Or—some kind of marks, as if sharp rocks had been scraped over the skin. Long, raw gouges, just starting to bleed.

"Audrey—oh, God, are you okay?" Michael was gasping.

A gurgling, maniacal voice said, "I bet I'll have a tummy-ache tomorrow."

Jenny looked. The cyberbeast had stopped changing, its features frozen in a long-toothed snarl.

Dee raised a clenched fist, tendons cording in her slender arm. Then she dropped it. "I don't think it can move toward us," she said in a curiously quenched voice. Jenny glanced at her, but Dee turned and Jenny found herself looking at the back of her close-cropped head, where velvety nubs of hair glistened like mica.

"Does anybody have aspirin?" Jenny said. "I lost mine."

Michael, who had taken off his sweatshirt and was trying

to wrap Audrey's arm in his undershirt, thrust a hand in his pocket. "I've got some . . . here."

Audrey's left hand was trembling as she took them, washing them down with a gulp of water from the canteen Dee silently offered.

"*Are* you okay?" Jenny asked hesitantly.

Audrey took another drink of water. Her spiky lashes were dark against her cheek as she leaned back against Michael. She looked as white as porcelain, and as fragile. But she nodded.

"Really? You can move your arm and everything?" Michael's cotton undershirt was showing signs of pink, but it wasn't the cuts that worried Jenny. She was afraid Audrey's shoulder might be dislocated.

Audrey nodded again. A faint smile appeared on her lips. She lifted her right arm, the bandaged one, and turned it over. Then, slowly, she unclenched her fist.

On her palm, gold as a buttercup, was a coin.

Michael gave a shout of laughter.

"You got it! You wouldn't let go, you little—" He seized Audrey in a bear hug.

"You may kiss me," Audrey said. "Just don't squish my arm." She twisted her head toward Dee. "Good thing your pick wasn't flimsy. No rawhide there!"

It was an extraordinarily generous gesture, but Dee seemed to take it as an insult. At least, when Jenny looked at Dee, she could only see the fine curve of a dark cheekbone.

"If everybody can move, we'd better go," Dee said. "We're right in the open here; anything could be sneaking up on us."

Jenny helped Audrey up as Michael put his sweatshirt back on. The lion-thing in the painted cage watched them like a gargoyle.

"What should we do with the coin?" Audrey said.

"I'll take it." Jenny put this one in the pocket of her pale blue denim shirt and buttoned the pocket. "If we can get to the merry-go-round, we can rest. There's an arbor thing beside it."

The merry-go-round had gone dark, but across the shimmering water of the lake Jenny could see the shining lighthouse. Tom was there—and Zach. Jenny had to get to them, no matter what happened on the way.

Audrey didn't want to rest long. "If I don't get up now, I never will. But where do we go?"

"That lion was lit-up—working," Michael said. "And it had a doubloon."

"So we just look for something else that's working?"

"I don't like the idea of being led," Dee said, but she said it without her usual confidence.

Jenny was worried about Dee. Of course she hadn't meant for anybody to get hurt. She'd just been trying to get a rise out of Audrey. But the way it had turned out—

"What are those lights way down there?" Michael said.

Beyond the merry-go-round, beyond a stretch of greenery, tiny white lights twinkled between dark trees.

"I think—I think it may be the arcade," Jenny said.

"Well, it's working," said Michael.

"Allons-y," Audrey said, settling things.

They passed the dark merry-go-round and a rocket ride with all the rockets landed, down. As they rounded a slight turn in the path, a building came into view.

Hundreds of tiny white lights flashed, running along the borders of a sign reading: PENNY ARCADE. Jenny stopped in her tracks.

"But—it's different. It's not like it was this afternoon. It's like—" Suddenly she knew. "It's like it *used* to be. This is the way the arcade looked when I was a kid. I remember!"

"Well, it's open," Michael said.

The doors gaped invitingly. Jenny felt a qualm as they cautiously stepped over the threshold. She didn't know why Julian had made the arcade this way, but she couldn't imagine it meant anything good.

Still, it gave her a strange pang of pleasure to see what was inside the building. Not the gleaming, spotless, high-tech wonderland she'd seen in the real park that day. Now it was a dim, rather dingy room, crowded with old-fashioned wooden cabinets.

Automata, Jenny remembered. That's what her grandfather had called the machines with moving figures inside them. She remembered him taking her here, putting dimes in the slots, watching the mechanical action scenes.

Her grandfather had always seemed to have time for her. All she knew as a kid was that he was a professor of this, that, and the other, but he never seemed to go to work anywhere. He was always home when Jenny and Zach came to visit—unless he was traveling. He did a lot of traveling, and always brought back presents.

"What was that? There—at the back," Michael said.

Jenny looked, but only saw more cabinets.

"It's gone now. I thought it was one of those little critters—the scuttling ones." He spotted something. "Hey, you want some candy peanuts? I found lots of change in with the aspirin."

The machine dispensed black candy-coated peanuts, very stale, and square multicolored gum. Jenny felt a little better while chewing it, comforted somehow.

And the machines were interesting, in the absurd, picturesque way of times gone by. There were peep shows and nickelodeons and all sorts of mechanized figures.

"The Ole Barn Dance," Jenny read on one cabinet. "See 'em Whoop It Up! Watch 'em Swing! Drop two bits in the box."

The little figures were made of blocks of wood, dangling from wires. Their wooden jaws hung open grotesquely.

"Do you think we should try the things?" Audrey said doubtfully. Jenny knew what she meant—after what had happened with Leo, she didn't relish the thought of activating anything mechanical.

"I guess we have to," she said slowly. "In case the coin's

inside one of them. Just stay back from them—and if anything goes on by itself, run."

"And check the coin slots," Audrey said sensibly. "What better place to hide a doubloon?"

They moved carefully around the dim room, staying together, checking the tops and bottoms of cabinets for a gleam of gold.

Michael found a mutoscope and began cranking it, leaning gingerly to look in the goggle-type viewer and watch the flip-card film, SEE NAUGHTY MARIETTA SUN BATHING, the sign on the brass-trimmed machine read, PASSED BY NY CENSORS, OCT. 12, 1897.

"M'arm hurts," he said afterward. "And it's just some lady wrapped in a sheet."

Audrey paused in front of an elaborately carved machine with gold paint that was much faded and rubbed off. Dee found a cabinet that looked like a grandfather clock, labeled: SEE HORRIBLE MONSTER. TERRIFYING—SHOCKING—ONLY 5 CENTS. Jenny knew that machine: You put your money in and saw a mirror.

Jenny ventured a little farther down the corridor. Not that grip tester—she didn't want to touch it. She didn't want to step on the foot vitalizer, either.

There—a rather shabby wood box with dark glass. The sign read: ASK THE WIZARD, DEPOSIT 10¢ IN SLOT AND THE WIZARD WILL PERFORM FOR YOU. Below was a strip of plastic tape: RECEIVE PREDICTION HERE.

Jenny had always liked the kind of fortune-teller that gave you a card. She loved the outrageous predictions about whether you were going to get married and what your career would be. She picked out a dime.

The coin slot was shaped like a sphinx. Jenny hesitated an instant with the dime resting against cool metal. A flash of foreboding went through her, as if telling her to stop and think before she did anything rash.

But what was rash about turning on a mechanized wizard? And they *had* to search this place.

She slipped the dime in.

CHAPTER 9

As the coin clunked somewhere in the machine's innards, Jenny heard a faint buzzing, then a mechanical ticking. The glass brightened, and Jenny could see that two bare lightbulbs had gone on inside.

They illuminated a wizard, maybe two feet high and wearing a surprisingly mournful and pained expression. As Jenny watched, it began to move jerkily, like clockwork.

Its eyes opened and shut, and its eyebrows lifted and fell. Its lower lip seemed to be jointed and moved below a surprisingly fine and lifelike beard, as if it were mumbling to itself. Its face was ruddy plastic, with carmine lips and deep shadows under the eyes. Jenny could see layers of caked-up paint on the cheeks.

Poor thing, she thought. Absurd as it was, she felt sorry for the mechanical figure. It showed much finer workmanship than the barn dancers, but it was undeniably in a state of disrepair. Its paintbrush eyelashes were matted, its black velveteen robe dusted with red lint.

A strange feeling was coming over Jenny. A squeezing in her chest. It was ridiculous to feel this way about an automaton. But it looked so pathetic—so *trapped* there in that box, in front of a stapled-on backdrop of shabby red velveteen. . . .

And something about the figure . . . something about its face . . .

The wizard held a chipped and peeling wand in one clenched fist. He raised the wand and struck it on the table in front of him—Jenny could see the indentation where he'd done it many times before.

His eyes opened and shut, rolled around, moving back and forth. They didn't look at the wand.

His lower lip moved, showing white painted teeth, but there was no sound. He seemed to be talking to himself.

Jenny was mesmerized by the wizard's jerky, almost violent movements—but she didn't know why, and she was getting more and more frightened. It's because he looks like one of those homeless guys at the shelter, she told herself. That's why he's familiar.

No. It was more than that. Something about the plastic face, a face frozen in an expression of ineffable sadness.

The glass eyes rolled, staring straight out at Jenny. Dark as marbles, strangely tired, strangely kind.

She knew.

She really did know then, but it was such an impossible, intolerable concept that she pushed it away. Slam-dunked it back into her subconscious. Too insane to even think about.

She heard a click at the bottom of the machine and saw that a card had appeared. She reached for it reflexively—then stopped for just an instant, again feeling as if her mind was shouting a warning.

Her fingers closed on the card. She turned it over and stared at the writing on the other side.

Then she felt herself begin to faint.

The cramped lines of type were faded but perfectly readable. Not a prediction or a personality chart.

The entire card was covered with two words typed over and over.

HELP ME HELP ME HELP ME HELP ME HELP ME HELP ME HELP ME HELP ME HELP ME HELP ME HELP ME HELP ME HELP ME HELP ME HELP ME . . .

The letters swam in front of Jenny's eyes, merging into a scintillating black-and-white pattern. She couldn't control her trembling or the shuddering in her stomach. She couldn't feel her legs. And she couldn't scream—even though there was a screaming inside her.

She felt the floor bang her palms and rump as her legs gave way.

"What happened? Did it do something to you?" The others were around her. Jenny could only look up at the glass box, the card creasing as her fingers tightened on it.

Those tired dark eyes, oh, yes, they were familiar. But they didn't belong with a shabby velveteen robe and a long angel-hair beard. They belonged with a slight, stooped body, a cardigan sweater, and thinning white hair. And a smell of peppermint, because that was what he always carried in his pockets.

"It's my grandfather," Jenny whispered. "Oh, Dee, it's my *grandfather*, it's my *grandfather*. . . ."

Dee cut a glance at the box. When she looked back at Jenny, her face was composed. "Okay, now, you take it easy. Let's get you some water here."

"No!" Jenny screamed. She was completely out of control. She hit Dee, beating at her feebly with her fists. "Don't *humor* me! It's my grandfather in there—they've done it to him. Oh, God!" Tears were flying as she whipped her head. "It's a joke, don't you see? He was a sorcerer—now he's a wizard. I thought he was dead—but this is so much worse—"

Dee simply grabbed the flailing hands so Jenny couldn't do any harm. Jenny could see Michael's brown eyes, and Audrey's chestnut-colored ones, looking over Dee's shoulder.

"It's true," she gasped, quieting. "Look at the card. He wants help. *He wants out!*"

Michael picked up the card silently, showed it to Dee and Audrey. They all looked at the box.

The wizard was still moving, staring straight ahead with his tragic expression, hitting the table with his wand. His hands were all in one piece, Jenny noticed with wild precision. She could see beads of paint in the slight grooves between the fingers.

She'd thought the Shadow Men would eat him. That was what the hungry eyes in the closet had wanted.

But whatever they'd done with his body, his soul was here.

They'd put it in this—thing. Stuck it in a plastic body, so that he could stand forever, moving like clockwork when the machine was activated, endlessly banging his wand.

Julian had said the Shadow Park had been created ten years ago, and for a special reason. It was ten years ago that her grandfather had disappeared.

"They did it to punish him," she whispered. "They put him here so he could never die—they trapped him the way he trapped them in the closet. . . ." Her voice was rising.

Michael swallowed, looking sick. Dee's nostrils flared.

There was a click and another card appeared in the slot.

Dee reached for it, letting go of Jenny's hands. Jenny scrambled to her knees to see it over Dee's arm.

LOOK IN THE BLACK CABINET.

"There," Michael said. Jenny twisted. Behind her was a

shiny black machine with a wide, darkened oval window. It looked relatively new, and a plaque read: SPEAK TO THE SPIRITS. ASK ANY YES OR NO QUESTION, 10¢.

Jenny knew the type of game. The window lit up and a skull nodded or shook its head to answer you.

A wave of icy cold swept over her, as cold as the water in the mine ride.

"Do it, Michael," she whispered and held her breath.

Michael wiped his mouth with the back of his hand. He glanced uncertainly at Jenny, then put a coin in.

The glass brightened. There wasn't a skull inside—there were two heads with closed eyes. They were illuminated from below with a ghastly blue light which clearly showed there was nothing below either neck. At the sight of them, Audrey screamed thinly and Michael retched. Dee grabbed hold of Jenny hard enough to hurt.

"Now do you believe me?" Jenny said, her voice rising again. "They're here, they're all here!"

Michael was pressing his hand to his mouth. Dee was holding on to Jenny. Audrey was still making a thin wheezing noise.

Nobody answered Jenny, but in the cabinet the heads of Slug and P.C. bobbed.

The blue light shone on their chapped, loose-hanging lips. They looked unconscious—as if unseen hands were wagging them by the hair, making them nod.

You guys were so tough, Jenny thought, unable to look away from the cadaverous faces. Such bad boys. Breaking into my house, stealing the Game. Barging into the Shadow World uninvited. Now you're both here and you don't look so tough. And—

"Summer," Jenny whimpered. "If Summer—if Summer—"

"Jenny—"

"If we find Summer like *that*—"

There was a click. Dee snatched the card before Jenny could get to it. She read it, holding Jenny away.

"What does it say?"

Slowly Dee turned the card.

LOOK IN THE FUN HOUSE.

"At least it's not another cabinet," Dee said.

Michael said, "You mean, you think it's about Summer?"

"I—maybe. Or"—Dee's face relaxed—"it could be a clue for a doubloon."

Audrey shielded her eyes. "I can't stand those things— make them *stop,*" she said in a ragged voice.

The heads were bobbing slowly up and down, nodding again.

"I think that's our answer," Michael said.

"Yeah, but which is it—Summer or a doubloon?"

"I don't care, I just want to get out of here," Audrey said.

"We can't *go,*" Jenny said to Dee. "We can't leave him, we can't go anywhere." She pulled herself up using the wizard's cabinet as a support, and leaned a hand on it, looking into the glass. "I have to help him."

"Jenny." Dee touched her elbow gently. "There's nothing you can do for him." Then, as Jenny held on to the glass: "All right, what *are* you going to do for him?"

Jenny didn't know. Stay here with him—if she could keep from screaming. Break the cabinet to pieces.

But then what? Could she stand to hold the thing that was in there, cuddle it like a stiff, oversize doll? If she broke the doll, would it kill her grandfather? Or would he still be alive inside his pieces?

He'd rather be dead than be like this, she knew. But how did you kill something that wasn't alive, only trapped?

"Oh, I'm so sorry," she whispered, pressing her hand to the glass. "I'm so sorry, I'm so sorry. . . ."

It was her fault—he'd gone in her place. Given himself to the Shadow Men for her.

But Dee was right. Jenny couldn't do anything for him now.

Her hands trailed down the glass. "We'll go to the fun house."

On their way out she turned back to face the wizard's cabinet, looked into the dark, staring eyes. "I'm coming back," she said. "And when I do, I'll help you."

The heads were bobbing in their case as she left.

Out into the night again. Jenny wished she had a map. Her memory for some parts of the park was sketchy.

"The fun house is up near the very front," she said, "so it's got to be somewhere that way." She pointed the way they'd come.

"Yeah, but more to the left. We can cut across there." Dee was more talkative than she had been since Audrey's accident, but her voice was still not quite itself.

They passed rest rooms, trees, a large refreshment stand. The Tilt-a-Whirl was dark; so was the Enterprise. And so, as they approached it, was the fun house.

Then an uncanny sound began. Two slow, rising notes, repeated over and over. Jenny recognized it.

"The foghorn on the ark."

Lights were going on in the large boat, first outlining the roof, then illuminating the windows of the house on deck. Jenny could see animals in the windows: an elephant, an ostrich, a hippopotamus, and at the very top Father Noah, with an expression more like a leer than a grin.

The ark began to rock visibly.

"Looks like they've got the welcome mat out," Michael said.

They entered through the whale's mouth, walking on the spongy pink tongue. Inside, the doors were slanted, exacerbating the rocking feeling. Jenny began to feel giddy immediately.

She couldn't see much inside. Black lights made Audrey's white nylon jacket glow and Dee's eyes flash. We should have looked for controls, Jenny thought. There must be some way to turn on the lights in these places.

But when she looked back, the door she'd just come through was gone. Instead, there was a glass booth, with a human figure silhouetted inside.

Summer! Jenny's heart gave a terrible jolt. She took a step toward the booth, then stopped. She couldn't tell anything about the figure. She took another step, one hand out toward the glass.

Oh, God, I don't want to see this. . . .

A light in the booth went on.

Wild laughter assaulted Jenny's ears. It was the sound of somebody going insane, and at first it frightened her so much that she couldn't take in what she was seeing.

Then she focused on the figure. It was a hugely fat woman, bucktoothed, with freckles like birthmarks and scraggly hair. Her hands waved in front of her as she cackled and guffawed.

I remember that! Laughing—oh, *what* was her name? Laughing Lizzie. She used to be in the arcade, and she always scared me.

Jenny scanned the florid face, looking for something familiar in the empty eyes.

Could Summer—be in there?

Summer had been tiny, dimpled, with thistledown blond

hair and dark blue eyes. She'd been as light as a flower petal stirred by the wind. Could *they* have destroyed her body and put her in this bloated plastic thing?

Or maybe she was like P.C. and Slug. Maybe there was a table somewhere in here with a piece of Summer's old body on it.

But Jenny couldn't see anything she recognized in the fat woman's eyes. Nothing to make her want to look any closer, especially since the demented laughter was going on and on.

She glanced at the others. "Let's keep moving."

They stumbled through twisted corridors and across shifting floors. A blue Day-Glo hippo gaped at Jenny, a snake dropped from the ceiling in front of her. From all around came panting, growling, weird music—a cacophony of strange sounds. It made it hard for Jenny to hear even Dee and the others right next to her.

And it was hard to examine the exhibits. Chain-link fencing was strung in front of many of them and had to be pulled away. Every figure that looked even vaguely human had to be studied, and anything that looked like gold had to be scrutinized.

"*Everything* in here looks suspicious," Michael said as they stared at a laughing man with three faces that rotated slowly on his neck.

Jenny was most disconcerted by the mirrors. On the floor

they mimicked endless drops, reflecting lights down into infinity. On the walls they confused her, duplicating her own wide green eyes, Audrey's copper hair, Michael's pale, set face. It reflected Dee's supple movements, making it seem as if there were dozens of camouflage jackets all going in different directions.

Zach always hated these mirrors, too, Jenny remembered, turning a sharp zigzag corner. Enough that Julian put them in the paper house as part of his nightmare. She suddenly realized that she hadn't thought about her cousin in quite a while. She'd been too busy worrying over Tom—and over how to survive.

But she *did* miss Zach. She missed his winter-gray eyes, and his sharp-featured face, and his dry intelligence. Even if Tom had been safe, she would have come to the Shadow World questing for Zach.

"Ugh," Dee said. "What's *this?*"

They had come out of the mirror maze and were now in dark, windy corridors with very unsteady floorboards. There were displays every few feet—much like museum displays, except that Jenny had never seen this kind of thing in any museum.

"Disgusting," Michael said under his breath. "Replogle, disgusting . . ." Replogle was really the name of a map company, but Michael thought it made a much better adjective.

He was trying to cheer himself up. Because, Jenny thought, the displays really were gruesome. They were torture scenes.

Wax figures were set up as victims and torturers. Some of the equipment Jenny recognized. The rack. The Iron Maiden. The stocks.

And some of it was dreadfully and harrowingly unfamiliar. Boots with handles like the vise Tom's father had in his garage workshop. To break bones, Jenny supposed. Grotesque metal helmets with iron tongues that gagged the victim. Cages too small to stand or lie down in. Every kind of device to burn, or cut, or maim.

"This was *not* here this afternoon," Audrey said.

"It's my fault, I guess," Dee said after a moment. "I went up to San Francisco once with my mom, and there was a place at Fisherman's Wharf—like a chamber of horrors, you know? It gave me nightmares for *years*."

Abruptly she turned away from the nearest scene and leaned against the wall, head down. She was breathing hard.

Jenny peered through the darkness. "Dee?"

"Yeah. Just give me a minute."

"What are you *mumbling*?"

"It's—it's, uh, this thing for when you get upset. I got it out of—" She paused. "Ancient Chinese manuscripts."

"In what dialect?" Audrey demanded. "Mandarin? Cantonese?"

"All right, it was from a kung fu movie. But it works. It's pretty long, but the end goes 'I am as strong as I need to be. I am my only master.'"

"I am my only master," Jenny repeated. She liked that. Julian and his people might be the masters of this world, but not of *her*. No one was her master if she wouldn't let them be. "Is it helping?" she asked Dee.

"Enough. I don't think I'm going to faint or puke right this moment."

Shock tingled in Jenny's palms. The very idea of Dee fainting was so outrageous—so frightening—she couldn't cope with it. Dee was *never* that scared.

Only maybe she was, especially when confronted with things that physical courage couldn't do anything about. The stuff around them here was history—and who could change that?

"I'm gonna join Amnesty International if I ever get out of here," Dee muttered. "I swear, I swear."

"Mother and I already belong," Audrey said.

Mrs. Myers? thought Jenny, and Dee said, "Your *mom*?" Audrey's mother was a society matron, good at making finger sandwiches and arranging charity fashion shows. She and Dee didn't get along.

"Maybe all that organization is good for something after all," Dee murmured.

Jenny still had a very bad feeling about the place. She wanted to hurry through it, to not see as much as possible.

And they couldn't. They had to check every figure, staring into faces the color of peach crayons, with teeth that were a little *too* shiny in the spotlights. The skin of the wax figures had an unreal inner glow, as if the outer layers were translucent and the color buried somewhere inside.

But none of the glassy eyes looked like Summer's. And nothing moved, although Jenny was in constant dread that an eyelid would flicker or a chest would rise.

If they start coming to life, I'll go crazy, she thought almost with detachment. Just screaming, staring crazy. It would be a relief to go crazy at this point.

"Jenny—" Michael's voice was choked.

Jenny turned.

"Blue," Michael said, and Jenny saw what he meant.

It was on a table. Above it, suspended by a rusty chain, was a huge wooden disk with bloody iron spikes. It was a little pool of china blue precisely the color of Summer's shirtdress.

Something was inside the dress.

Funny that Jenny could remember that outfit so exactly. Summer had appeared on the doorstep wearing it the night of Tom's birthday party, looking fresh, sweet, and completely inappropriate, since it was freezing outside.

Now it was lying on a table, encasing a body. Although the figure's face was turned away from Jenny, she could glimpse sandaled feet curled up at one end and soft light curls at the other.

Jenny stood frozen.

It had happened too suddenly, she wasn't prepared. She'd

seen that dying in the Shadow World didn't mean you got buried and disappeared. She'd known they were looking for Summer, however transformed, however *defiled* Summer might be.

Ever since Michael's dream she'd allowed herself thoughts that Summer might not be lost completely.

But now that she was face to face with the possibility, she couldn't cope with it. She didn't want to go and look, didn't want to *know*. She glanced at the others, saw them standing paralyzed, too.

You have to look. You can take it. It's probably just a normal wax figure with nobody inside. And that's not blood on those spikes, it's red paint.

She knew this was completely irrational. She knew very well that it probably *wasn't* just a normal wax figure, and that there was no reason for the blood on the spikes to be anything but blood. After everything she'd seen in the Shadow World, after what had happened to Slug and P.C. and her grandfather, she knew that.

But her mind needed to say *something* to get her legs going. To keep away the pictures of Summer's head falling off when Jenny took her by the shoulder, or of some *Rosemary's Baby*-type monster looking up with crafty, glee-filled eyes.

The huge log disk swung on its chain above the table.

I can take it. I can take it. I'm strong enough.

Jenny inched closer. She could see the spun-sugar curls,

just the color of Summer's hair, and the little hands lying folded like rose petals. She couldn't see the face.

The log swung, creaking.

With sudden inspiration Jenny thought, *I am my only master.* She reached for the figure's shoulder.

"Look out!" Dee shouted.

CHAPTER 10

There was a clatter above Jenny—the sound of a chain racketing along wood. She reacted instinctively, before rational thought could interfere. She seized the body in the china blue dress and pulled it off the table.

Not fast enough. The huge disk came straight down—and then veered sideways, knocked out of line by something that leaped up by Jenny like black lightning.

Dee hit the disk with both heels, one after the other, so fast that the blows looked simultaneous. The disk swerved, crashing down beside the table. Then the table crashed into Dee, who'd just regained her feet. Dee sprawled on the floor beside Jenny.

The bundle in Jenny's arms stirred.

Shock had wiped all the dreadful thoughts out of her mind, all the pictures of what might be wearing that blue dress. All the fanged, deformed, decayed, or decomposing faces that might have looked up at her from under Summer's fluff of curls.

So it seemed quite natural to see Summer's own small face looking up, with cheeks like rain-washed roses and blinking, sleep-encrusted blue eyes.

Summer yawned and rubbed at her lashes.

"I'm so *tired*—what was the crash?"

Dee had picked herself up and was approaching gingerly. So were Audrey and Michael.

"Is it dead?" Michael said huskily.

Jenny knew what he meant. Just because Summer could talk, that didn't mean she wasn't dead—not here in the Shadow World.

But Summer's weight was warm in Jenny's arms, and Summer's flesh looked like real flesh, not like plastic or that hideous goo that Slug's body had been wearing. Summer looked—alive. Summer looked—all right.

Jenny felt very dizzy.

She couldn't say anything. None of them could. They all just stared at Summer.

Summer's eyes grew large and timid.

"What's wrong?" she said faintly. "What's . . . how long was I asleep?"

Audrey leaned over slowly.

653

"Summer . . . ?" she whispered, as if she found the word more foreign than any in all the languages she knew.

"What's *wrong*?" Summer wailed.

"How long do you *think* you were asleep?" Michael croaked. "What's the last thing you remember?"

"Well, I was . . . We were all . . ." Summer looked confused. "Well, I was in that hallway . . . and then you found me . . . and then we went into my bedroom. Only it wasn't my bedroom. And then . . ."

She stopped, her mouth open like a baby bird's.

"Kiddo," Dee said and waved a hand helplessly.

"Something bad happened."

"Yeah, but you don't have to think about it."

"I don't *remember* it. Just that it was bad. Did I get hurt? Did I faint?"

Dee looked at Jenny. Jenny looked at Audrey and Michael.

"I think it's really her," Michael said.

"It's her," Dee said. She reached for Summer briskly—almost feverishly, examining Summer's arms and legs. "Are you okay? *Really* okay? Does everything work?"

"Ow."

"*Summer,*" Jenny said abruptly, with a hysterical laugh. She put two fingers to her lips and began crying just as hysterically.

It was catching. Audrey began laughing and crying at the same time. Michael sniffled.

Jenny didn't know what was happening to her. Her heart was skipping—but then it had been skipping all night. She felt dizzy—but she'd been feeling dizzy on and off ever since she'd stepped into the Shadow World.

This was different. It was *like* pain, but it wasn't pain. It coursed through her, flooding up from her toes in an irresistible skyward rush. She actually felt lighter, as if she were lifting toward the ceiling.

All she could think was *oh, thank you.*

Her mind still couldn't get around the concept that Summer was here, in her own body, talking and moving and apparently well and strong. Not even bruised.

Oh, thank you, thank you.

She had an urge to bundle Summer up and hustle her away somewhere, pack her in tissue paper, keep her safe. Get her to sanctuary before anything else could happen to her.

But there *wasn't* any sanctuary, not here. Summer was alive, but still in danger. She'd have to take her chances like the rest of them.

And anything might happen before they got home.

This thought actually helped Jenny, stopped the giddiness and the trembling inside her. She'd been trying to picture Summer's little brother, Cam, with his tough face and his wistful blue eyes, and what he'd look like when he saw his sister again. The picture wouldn't come; it was *too* good, scary good. But now that she realized it might very well never happen, she felt calmer. It seemed more possible now that it was only a possibility.

"I'll *try* to get you out, though," she said, and only realized she'd said it aloud when Summer looked up at her.

"I know you will," Summer said, like a trusting child. "I hate this paper house. Do we look for Zach now? Isn't he next?"

Jenny felt another jolt of improbability as she realized how much they needed to explain to Summer. Wherever Summer had been since they'd last seen her, she obviously didn't remember anything about it.

"Uh, maybe we should talk about that later. Like when we get outside," Michael said, shooting a pointed glance at Jenny. "This place gives me the creeps."

Yes. They had to get out of this chamber of horrors before any other logs fell on them. The shift to ordinary concerns stopped the last of the trembling inside Jenny. It wasn't that she was less happy—she was *more* happy, now that she was getting over her disbelief. The first joy had been painful, but now a great quietness came over her. Whatever else happened, she could get Summer out of the fun house, to a place where they could rest and talk.

As she stood, helping Dee help Summer up, she saw eyes in the shadows.

Eyes like the ones she'd seen in the mine shaft. They burned with a pale fire. They were watching from the corridor behind Jenny, and they were full of malice.

Jenny slung an arm around Summer's shoulders, turning Summer so she wouldn't see them. "This way."

They won't touch you. I promise. I won't let them.

She meant it. Her happiness wrapped her in a cloak of protection. The Shadow Men could stare all they wanted, but they wouldn't get near Summer.

To her relief, the torture chamber part of the fun house ended with Summer's scene. The narrow corridor wound back and forth a few turns and then opened into a small room with a revolving door and a neon sign that read: EXIT.

"Made it," Dee breathed. Jenny wondered if she had seen the eyes, too.

Summer wriggled out from under Jenny's arm. "Wait, look at this." Her voice was just as it had always been, light and childish, eager. Jenny could hardly believe she was hearing it again.

Summer was standing in front of a candy machine like the ones Jenny had seen in the arcade. She thrust her small fingers into the one pocket of her shirtdress. "Do any of you guys have a quarter? I'm dying for some chocolate."

"Uh." Michael looked at Jenny. "I don't know if we better . . ."

"We should get out of here," Dee said positively.

"But I'm *starving*. And it'll only take one second—"

Michael looked at Jenny again, and Jenny said, "Oh, give it to her so we can get out," and looked back into the black corridor for the eyes. The candy peanuts had been okay; she supposed this would be. She could hear the sound of Summer putting the quarter in and turning the handle, and then the patter of falling M&M's.

"I hope I didn't get a lot of green ones," Summer said.

Dee said, "I'll open it. Never mind why, Summer."

"Just don't put your hand in," Audrey said, and Jenny turned around in time to see the look Dee gave Audrey.

Then the candies were spilling into Dee's hand—and Dee gave a kind of yelp that made Jenny forget everything and run to her.

Her mind had plenty of time to instantaneously flash over all the horrible things that might have come out of that machine. Dead bugs, red-hot pennies, blobs of acid. Why hadn't she *thought*—? But she was still a step away when she saw the answer gleaming in the pile of candy on Dee's palm.

"Five brown ones, four yellows, two greens, one red, and a gold coin," Michael said coolly, assessing the pile. "Not bad."

Jenny just beat Dee gently on the back.

"Put it somewhere safe," Dee said, and Jenny plucked it from the mound and held it tightly, feeling its coolness before it warmed in her hand. She rubbed her thumb against the engraving. When she opened her hand again, the coin was as rich and shiny as molten gold straight from the forge.

Then she put it in her shirt pocket and buttoned the flap. "Come on, let's go. We did it, we did everything we could here.

Summer *and* a coin." She smiled at Summer, who was looking utterly mystified. "We'll explain outside."

Summer accepted the pile of M&M's from Dee and looked somewhat comforted. They all began to go through the revolving door.

It would only take one at a time, and Jenny pushed Summer in front of her. Then she stepped into the next segment of the iron cage and pushed briskly on the thick metal arms, to get out of the fun house as soon as possible. Between the moving arms she could see only darkness—it was pitch black outside, and she couldn't even glimpse Summer's hair. . . .

She knew something was wrong even before she stepped out.

This wasn't the outside. It was a room. And the others weren't with her, because she couldn't see any flashlights.

God, where am I now?

She reached behind her and wasn't at all surprised not to find the iron arms of the revolving door. She was somewhere with no light and no exit.

And now I suppose I see the eyes.

Instead, a small shimmering light went on, and she saw a boy in a black duster jacket.

"Julian?" He looked so different. "Julian!"

Jenny ran toward him, joining him in the shadows. He didn't move an inch to come toward her.

It was the first time she'd ever been glad to see him. But she *was* glad: Happiness was blossoming like a flower inside her, petals opening frantically. She stopped in front of him, breathless and triumphant.

"It was you, wasn't it? You gave us Summer back."

"I gave *you* Summer back." His voice was subdued, moody. He was more modestly dressed than Jenny had ever seen him. The black duster jacket wrapped him in shadows.

"Thank you. You don't know—" She paused. Julian probably *did* know. He'd watched Jenny for years; he knew what Summer meant to her. He probably even knew she'd always felt that Summer's death was her fault.

"Is she—okay? Like, really, underneath?" Jenny asked, afraid to say the words, afraid of the answer.

"She's okay. She's been asleep. Just like the princess who pricked her finger on a spindle. Good as new, now." But Julian spoke flatly and he still looked moody. Almost—distrustful.

Jenny ignored it and met the shadowed blue gaze directly.

"Thank you," she said again, very quietly and looking at him so that he could see everything she was feeling.

Julian's heavy lashes drooped, as if he couldn't hold her eyes.

"Julian." Jenny touched both arms of the duster jacket, just below the shoulders. "You did a good thing. You shouldn't act as if you were ashamed."

"I did it for my own reasons." He glanced at her, one quick flash of blue fire, then looked away again.

"Why are you trying to ruin it? You did it, that's what matters." Why couldn't he ever stay the same person twice running? Jenny was thinking. The last time she'd seen Julian he had been subdued and sad—vulnerable. She'd almost felt sorry for him. Now he was cold and sullen—resentful. She wanted to *shake* him.

But she was too scared. You didn't do that to Julian.

"You know," she said, moving in even closer, knowing she was taking a risk, "there was a time when I thought you were completely evil. Completely. But now I don't believe that. I don't think you're as bad as you say you are."

He looked up then, and the blue fire burned steadily. "That's where you're wrong. Don't count on it, Jenny. Don't count on it."

Threads of fear went through her at his voice. It was as musical and cold as she'd ever heard it. The pitiless music of a clear mountain stream that could suddenly rise in a flood and kill everyone in its path.

"I still don't believe it," Jenny breathed. She wouldn't look away from him and she was very close.

"I told you, you're wrong. I am what I am, and nothing can change it." He simply stood there, immovable as rock, which wasn't like Julian at all.

Jenny's fingers clenched on the sleeves of his jacket. "You didn't kill Summer before, in the paper house. You saved her." She rapped out the words as if she were angry.

"Yes." He spoke just as coldly.

"And you *could* have killed her, the rules said you could."

"Yes."

"What about Slug and P.C.?"

He just looked at her.

"Don't play stupid, Julian!" She could have shaken him now, she was angry enough, but instead she stood as rigid and unmoving as he was, their faces inches apart. "Did you kill Slug and P.C.? Make them into what they are now?"

He stared at her a moment, blue eyes unfathomable. Then he said, "Yes."

"You're a damn liar!"

He just looked back at her. His eyes were absolutely bottomless, glacier pools that went down and down forever. Jenny wouldn't look away. She could feel warmth in her own eyes, tears of anger that wouldn't spill.

"Did you do it to Slug and P.C.?" she said, like a TV lawyer prepared to repeat a question endlessly.

Head slightly tilted back, he returned her gaze. Then, face still cold, eyes like blue ice, he said, "No."

His voice was hard and dangerous. Jenny heard her own voice, relentless and just as hard.

"What happened to them?"

"They opened the door to the closet and let me out. But when I *came* out"—a slight and very unsettling smile touched Julian's lips—"they ran. They ran out of the paper house and right into the arms of the other Shadow Men."

Jenny could feel something in her relax slightly, a mystery solved. She wasn't even sure *why* she'd thought Julian hadn't killed P.C. and Slug. He'd always said he had—there was no reason not to believe him. He was a Shadow Man.

But still.

"And they did that?" she asked.

"It was their right. Nobody comes here uninvited."

"And my grandfather. They did that, too." It wasn't a question.

"A long time ago. I didn't pay much attention; I wasn't interested in him. They would never let me touch him. I could keep Summer alive because she was *mine,* my prey that I'd caught myself. And I kept her for a reason, Jenny. To use her against you." His voice was harder than ever, his face like an ice carving.

"But you didn't," Jenny said.

"No. But don't let yourself think that means anything. Next time I will."

"I don't believe you, Julian."

"Then you're making a bad mistake."

There was still no kindness in the midnight blue eyes, nothing to encourage Jenny. Some part of her had the sense to be frightened, but recklessness was flowing through her blood.

There were two sides to Julian, she thought, and she remembered a line from something she'd read—Emily Brontë, maybe. Different as a moonbeam and lightning.

She wanted to reach the moonbeam part, but she didn't know how.

Very softly she said again, "I don't believe you. You're not like the other Shadow Men. You could change—if you wanted to."

"No," he said bleakly.

"Julian . . ." It was the bleakness that got her. She could see herself reflected in his eyes.

Without thinking, she moved even closer. And closer. Her upper lip touched his lower lip.

"You can change," she whispered.

The kiss began before she knew it. Everything was very sweet. Warmth flowed between the two of them.

Then Julian pulled back. A lock of hair had fallen into his eyes, white as the dogwood blossoms Jenny had seen by the highway. The mask of icy control was broken, but there was something frightening in its place. A kind of shattering.

Like what Jenny had felt herself the last time they kissed, in the cavern with the fire.

She was too excited to dwell on it. She wasn't thinking anymore, only feeling—and she felt hot and victorious. The conqueror. "You're not evil. You *can* change, you can be whatever you want—"

Something ugly sparked in Julian's eyes, the danger and wildness flaming up to overwhelm the shattered light.

"I *am* what I want to be," he said. "You forgot that—and that was your mistake."

"Julian—"

He was flushed, overwrought, his eyes blazing. "You want to see what I really am? I'll show you, Jenny. I'll *prove* it to you. I'll enjoy that."

He spun her around roughly. The revolving door had reappeared, and the neon Exit sign was over it.

"Julian, listen to me—"

From behind, he pushed her toward the door. "Go on, try a little more of the park. See what I've got waiting. *Then* we can talk."

"*Julian*—" She was frightened, but she turned around as soon as he let go of her.

And of course he wasn't there.

The room was empty. Jenny stood a moment, perfectly still, breathing hard.

He was—he was the most impossible—the most infuriating—

She had never met anyone as—as—

And he *scared* her. She didn't want to try to imagine what he might do next.

Something to prove he was evil, anyway. Something she wouldn't enjoy.

Gradually Jenny's breathing slowed. Summer, she thought. What's important is that I find Summer and get her out of here. No matter what happens, no matter *what*, I have to get Summer out.

Forget about Julian. There's nothing you can do for him. Concentrate on playing his Game and getting out.

Think about *Tom.*

She quashed the guilt that tried to well up then. She *was* thinking about Tom; she wasn't neglecting him. He was in her thoughts all the time, running like an undercurrent beneath whatever else was happening. He was the reason she was still on her feet, still fighting.

She wasn't going to stop until he was safe. Which meant she'd better get moving again right now.

She straightened her shirt, smoothed her hair. Then she stepped into the revolving door's embrace.

CHAPTER 11

They were all four waiting for her when she got out.

Summer said, "Where've you *been*?"

Audrey said, "Did you—"

Jenny nodded over Summer's head. Audrey hiked up a copper eyebrow.

"Just a little unscheduled detour," Jenny murmured to Dee and Michael. She said to Summer, "I'm okay. Everything's okay."

Summer's M&M's were lying scattered on the ground. "I don't like people disappearing," she said.

"Aw, honey, it's gonna be all right," Michael said and patted her awkwardly. "We told her where we are and sort of basically what's going on," he said to Jenny.

Jenny's buoyancy at finding Summer was gone; the effervescence had fizzled out of her blood. Julian was going to do something nasty—but what could be worse than what he'd already done? Since she'd known Julian, he'd chased her with UFOs, dark elves, and giant insects—not to mention a Shadow Wolf and Snake. He'd lurked in the shadows of her room and hissed terrifying messages at her in the dark. He'd caught her in a cave-in, left her alone to drown, and menaced her with a cyber-lion. He'd kidnapped her and hunted her throughout two worlds. What could he do to top all that?

"Where do we go next?" Audrey said.

They looked around. Nothing in the immediate vicinity was lit up. The park was completely dark and dead silent around them.

"Here, hold this," Dee said to Jenny.

Jenny took the flashlight and said, "Oh, be *careful*." Dee was shinning up one of the old-fashioned green-painted lampposts.

"I can see the lighthouse on the island," she said at the top with one long leg hooked over the crosspiece which supported a lantern. "And there're a lot of trees everywhere. . . . The Ferris wheel looks cool, it's sort of rising out of them like a mountain rising out of clouds."

"Is it lit up?"

"The only thing that's lit is something toward the back—it's got a big waterwheel and some boats shaped like swans."

"The Tunnel of Love," Jenny said.

Dee came down and they started toward the Tunnel of Love, Jenny guiding them. It was another ride she'd loved as a kid—not because it had anything to do with love, but because it was dark, and cool, and she'd loved the swan boats. Now, the thought of going into that tunnel was—well, it was better *not* to think about it.

They were skirting the lake when they saw the shape among the trees.

"It's a critter!" Michael said. "Only a big one!"

The flashlight beams caught it briefly, even as it moved back into the trees. It *was* big, and Jenny had a glimpse of reddish skin like tanned leather.

"It's got a head, so it can't be P.C. or Slug," Audrey said.

"Who or who?" asked Summer.

"Never mind. We'd better just watch out for it," Jenny said, and they did, keeping their backs to the water and watching the trees.

I should have asked Julian about them, she thought. Aloud, she said, "What *are* they, d'you think? And how come they're running around loose?"

"Other people the Shadow Men have caught," said Dee.

"Pets," said Michael.

"Or maybe just part of the general *ambiance*," Audrey said grimly.

Whatever the thing had been, Jenny felt an instinctive

horror and revulsion for it, just as she'd felt for the little gray one that had looked like a withered fetus.

Summer didn't join the conversation at all. She just hurried lightly along, one hand gripping Jenny's sleeve, staring at everything they passed. She was like a large blue butterfly skimming in their midst.

They were a motley group, Jenny thought—Summer in her springtime dress and Dee's camouflage jacket, Audrey with her arm tied up in a sling made of Michael's undershirt, Jenny herself carrying Dee's flashlight. Michael was carrying his own flashlight, while Dee carried Audrey's pick. The other weapons had all gotten lost along the way.

Jenny noticed that Dee kept her distance from Audrey.

Things still weren't right with Dee. She was too quiet, too un-exuberant. Sure they were in danger, but Dee *loved* danger, she got up and ate it for breakfast, breathed it, went looking for it whenever she could. Dee should be enjoying this.

Jenny edged closer and said softly, "You know, Audrey didn't mean anything by that—when she said not to put your hand in the M&M's machine."

Dee shrugged. "I know." She went on looking straight ahead.

"*Really* she didn't. She's just like my mom, sometimes she's got to say things for your own good."

"Sure. I know."

Jenny gave up.

They passed a food stand just before they got to the Tunnel of Love. Jenny had an urge to break in—even a cold hot dog would be good right now, even a bun—but she didn't say anything. They had two gold coins. They were so close. They couldn't stop for anything now.

Blue and red and purple lights shone on the waterwheel in front of the Tunnel of Love. There was a rustic old mill behind the waterwheel, and a sign on the tunnel. In the afternoon, in the real park, the sign had read: TUNNEL OF LOVE. Now it read: TUNNEL OF LOVE AND D—.

The last word was obscured by clusters of ivy. "I can't read it," Jenny said.

"Death, probably. As in 'Love and death are the only two things that really matter.' *N'est-ce pas?*" Audrey said.

"Oh, spiffy," said Michael. Summer got a firmer grip on Jenny's sleeve.

A swan boat was waiting at the loading dock, its white wings arched gracefully by its sides, its neck a supple curve. Beads of water glistened on the plastic. Jenny didn't want to get into it.

If that head turns around—

But they didn't have any choice. This was obviously the right place, awake and waiting for them. If Jenny wanted the third gold coin, she had to get on the ride.

"Come on, people," she said.

671

The boat tilted as they got in—Jenny and Dee on the front seat with Summer between them, Audrey and Michael in the back. They sat on wooden boards. As soon as they were all in, the swan began to move.

"Did you notice that cave looking like a face this afternoon?" Michael said as they approached the tunnel.

Jenny hadn't. The fiberglass rock *did* look like a face now, with crags and shadows forming the eyes and nose. The gaping mouth was the tunnel itself.

Inside, it was dank and dark, with a musty smell. And quiet. That afternoon there had been the sounds of people talking, the occasional echoing laugh. Now all Jenny could hear was the quiet lapping of water around the boat.

She was still holding the flashlight Dee had given her, and she trained it on the water, the walls, the swan's head. All unexciting. The water was dark green and murky, the walls were damp and trickly, the swan's head was staying put.

"Where's the stuff—the scenes and everything?" Michael whispered. It was a whispering kind of place.

"I don't know," Jenny said, just as softly. That afternoon there had been illuminated dioramas—silly things like Stone Age people playing cards and painting dinosaurs on the cave walls. Now there was nothing. The swan boat went on gliding smoothly into darkness.

That was when Jenny noticed something wrong with the flashlight. The light was getting dimmer.

"Hey," she said and turned it toward her. Orange. The white beam was receding into a sullen orange glow.

She banged it on the swan's neck and immediately wished she hadn't. It made a startlingly loud sound, and the light got even dimmer.

"Oh, criminy—mine, too," Michael said. She could hear the jingle of metal as he shook it.

"We should have kept just one on, to save the batteries," Dee muttered. "I *thought* of that before, and then I forgot. I'm *stupid*."

Even in the midst of her worry Jenny was shocked at this. Dee didn't talk that way. "Look, Dee, if anybody should have thought of it—"

"There it goes," Michael said. There was now complete darkness from the backseat. Jenny had been thumbing the switch of her flashlight and screwing and unscrewing the top, but it didn't make any difference. She could barely see the dim orange bulb. When she shook it, it went out altogether.

"Spiffy, spiffy, spiffy," Michael said.

Audrey said sharply, "Does anybody feel like we're slowing down?"

It was hard to tell in the dark. Jenny was thoroughly sick of darkness—it seemed as if she'd spent all night blind, wondering what might be coming at her from which direction.

But she thought Audrey could be right. The lapping water

was quieter. The only motion she could feel was the gentle swaying of the boat from side to side.

There was a quiet splash. "We're not moving," Dee said.

"Dee, get your hand out of the water!"

Dee muttered something inaudible, but Jenny heard the drip as she took her hand out.

"I don't *like* this," Summer said.

Jenny didn't, either—and she especially didn't like the thought of getting out of the boat and sloshing around trying to find their way.

"So we're stranded," she murmured. Everyone else was very still and tense.

Wondering what's coming at us, and from which direction. . . .

She could think of lots of things, all of them nasty. And she had time to think, because for a long while they just sat there, the swan boat rocking gently in the darkness.

"Just don't imagine anything," Audrey said through her teeth from the backseat.

"I'm *trying* not to," Michael answered defensively.

But of course it was impossible, like trying *not* to think of a pink elephant. The harder Jenny tried not to imagine what Julian might do to them, the quicker the images crowded into her mind. Every nightmare she'd ever had was suddenly clamoring for her attention.

"I can't take this anymore," Summer breathed.

Dee exhaled sharply. "No. Look, I'm gonna—"

Light.

It started as a fuzzy blue patch in Jenny's peripheral vision, and brightened when she turned to look at it. Like a spotlight in some overly dramatic stage show. Two other spotlights went on, one red, one purple. The colors of the floodlights outside—and the colors of the stained-glass lamps in the More Games shop, Jenny thought. The place where she'd first seen Julian.

"It all comes down to this, doesn't it?" Julian's voice said.

He moved out of the darkness, into the circle where the spotlights mingled. He was wearing a T-shirt with rolled-up sleeves, a black vest, and neat black boots. There was some kind of bangle around his upper arm. He looked urban and barbaric, like somebody you might find wandering the bad parts of town at night. Some street kid with no place to go and too much knowledge behind his blue eyes.

Summer took one look at him and crouched behind Dee.

Jenny felt at a disadvantage. Julian was in the place where the diorama should be—but she felt as if the five of them in the flimsy plastic boat were the show. Julian was in a perfect position to watch whatever happened to them—and they couldn't even stand without risking an upset.

"You were wrong about the sign on this ride," Julian said casually. He stood easily, seeming to enjoy their reactions as they stared at him. "It's not the Tunnel of Love and Death. It's the Tunnel of Love—and Despair."

The five in the boat just looked at him. Finally Dee said, "So what?"

"Just thought you'd like to know." He flipped something in the air, caught it. Jenny couldn't tell what color the thing was because of the lights, but it gleamed.

"What, this? Oh, yes, it's a doubloon," Julian said, looking into his palm as if only just then noticing it.

Everyone in the boat exchanged glances. The boat rocked gently.

"Don't you want to know what you have to do to get it?"

Jenny didn't, but she felt sure he was going to tell them anyway.

"You just have to listen, that's all. We'll have a little conversation. A chat."

It was up to Jenny to answer, and she knew it. "About what?" she said tensely, leaning back to look at him around Dee.

"This and that. The weather. Nuclear disarmament. You."

"Us?" Michael squeaked, startled into speech.

"Sure. Look at you—all of you. What a pathetic bunch. And *you're* trying to storm the Shadow World?"

"Right," Dee muttered and started to get up.

"You never learn, do you?" Julian said and took a step toward her.

That was all he did, but Dee sat down, only partly because Jenny had grabbed her arm and pulled her back. Julian was scaring Jenny right now—not with any overt display of power, but just with *himself.* What he was. Julian picked up moods and put them on like clothes, and right now the brightness in his eyes, the quick rise of his breathing, the way his lips were slightly skinned back from his teeth—they all scared Jenny. He was in the mood to destroy things, to bring down some ultimate disaster, she thought. Not just to hunt, but to kill.

"Please, let's all just be calm," she said.

Julian was still looking at Dee, with bright sickness shining in his eyes. "Maybe you're just too *stupid* to learn," he said. "That's the real reason you don't want to go to college, isn't it? You know you'll never be as smart as your mother."

"Don't rise to him," Jenny said. "Dee, turn around—just don't listen."

Dee didn't turn. Jenny could only see her silhouette, and the blue light glistening on the velvet nubs of hair on her head, but she could *feel* the stress in Dee's body.

"All this athletic stuff is just a front because you know you've disappointed her," Julian said. "You're inferior where it counts most."

"Dee, you *know* that's not true. . . ."

"She knows she doesn't know *anything.* She's been wrong about so many things recently—like about Audrey and the lion. Like about Audrey's mother. Imagine *Mrs. Myers* having done something Dee always meant to do."

"You leave her alone!" Jenny said.

"And she's nothing without her confidence. Haven't you noticed?"

"Shut up!" Dee shouted. It was a bad place for shouting, there were distant echoes. What frightened Jenny was the note of desperation in Dee's voice. Dee never cried, but just now Dee's voice sounded on the verge of tears.

"Despair," Jenny whispered suddenly. She reached around Dee to grip her arm. "Don't you see what he's trying to do? The Tunnel of Love and Despair—and he wants *you* to despair. To give up, to stop fighting."

"She should give up," Julian agreed. He was breathless now, the queer wild look in his eyes brighter than ever. "She's all talk. Hot air. Strutting around, building her muscles, saying 'Everybody look at me.' But there's nothing underneath."

Jenny thought of something. She leaned in toward Dee, her fingers biting into Dee's arm, and said, *"I am my only master."*

Dee's head turned slightly, like a startled bird.

"I am my only master," Jenny whispered urgently, prompting her. "Go on, Dee. You said it, and it's true. He can't do anything to you. He doesn't count. You are your only master."

She felt Dee's breath go out.

"Gets her philosophy from kung fu movies," Julian said. "Thinks fortune cookies are great literature."

"I am my only master!" Dee said.

"That's right." Jenny's throat hurt. She kept holding on to Dee's arm. Dee's neck twisted like a black swan's, to look at

Jenny just for a moment. Jenny got a glimpse of tear tracks on the dark skin, shining blue and purple in the light, then Dee turned back.

"I am my only master," she said clearly, to Julian.

There was a stirring in the backseat. "She's smart, too," Audrey said, astonishing Jenny. "And brave. She's done all sorts of brave things since I got hurt. She didn't mean to hurt me, and I never thought she did."

Dee turned and gave Audrey one sloe-eyed look of gratitude, and her shoulders straightened. She sat as proud and tall as Nefertiti.

"Besides, college and books aren't everything," Michael said, amazing Jenny further.

"I thought they were—to *you*," Julian said. He was looking at Michael now, and his voice was beautiful, like ebony and silver.

Michael seemed to get smaller.

"You're the one who reads about things because you're afraid to actually do them. You talk about your books—or make jokes. The class clown. But people are laughing *at* you, not with you, you know."

"No, they're not," Michael said, which was another surprise for Jenny. She wouldn't have thought Michael would speak up for himself.

"You're a nothing. Just a funny little fat boy that people laugh at. You're a joke."

"No, I'm not," Michael said doggedly. Jenny felt a surge of admiration. Michael was holding out—maybe *because* he'd gotten teased and stomped on at school. He'd heard it all before.

But Julian's face was more confident than ever—and more cruel. He flashed a smile that sent chills up Jenny's arms.

"We won't talk about the little rituals you had when you were a kid," he told Michael. "Like how you had to tear the toilet paper up into tiny pieces, exactly even. Or if you saw the word *death*, you had to count to eighteen. To *chai*—'life' in Hebrew."

Michael's chest was heaving. Jenny opened her mouth, outraged, but Julian went urbanely on.

"We'll just cut to the chase. Ask your girlfriend if she's ever called you 'Tubby' behind your back."

Michael turned on Audrey. Jenny could see that his defenses had torn; his face had that rumpled, not-ready-for-company look that meant he was about to cry. "Did you say that?"

Audrey looked pale in the blue and purple lights, her lipstick garish. She seemed ready to cry, too.

"Did you say that?"

"Of course she did," Julian said. "She said lots of other things, too. About how her dream boy was six feet tall and blond and a surfer. About how she only took up with you to fill in the time until she found someone better."

Michael was looking at Audrey. "Did you say that?" he repeated, his voice an anguished plea.

Jenny willed Audrey to say no. Audrey looked back at Michael for a long, horrible moment, then said, "Yes."

Michael turned away.

"Because you were good for a laugh," Julian put in helpfully. "Don't you want to laugh now?"

"Shut up, you bastard!" Jenny shouted furiously. She was sick with her own impotence—she'd helped Dee, but there was nothing she could do to help Michael. Not with this.

"I told you in the very beginning about the Game," Julian said. "Desires unveiled. Secrets revealed. Don't you remember?"

Audrey wasn't listening, she was looking only at Michael, her whole being focused on him. "I did say that," she said fiercely. "A long time ago. I didn't even really mean it then, I was just showing off."

"You still said it," Michael said dully, not turning.

"I said it *before*, Michael. Before you showed me that what people look like isn't important. Before I found out I loved you." She dissolved in sobs.

Michael turned halfway. His dark eyes were wide open.

"Oh—look," he said. "Don't. It's okay."

"It's *not* okay," Audrey stormed. "Michael Allen Cohen— you're an idiot!"

"That's what *he* said—" Michael muttered. Audrey shook him, turning him the rest of the way around.

"I *love* you," she said. "You made me fall in love with you.

I don't care how tall you are or what color your hair is—I care about *you*. You make me laugh. You're smart. You're gentle. And you're *real*, you're a real person, not some jock with a facade that's going to fall apart when I get to know him. I know you already, and I love you, you idiot. I don't care what you do with toilet paper."

"When I was *seven*," Michael said. Audrey was still crying, and he reached out a stubby thumb to wipe the tears off her cheeks.

"You're a good kisser, too," Audrey said, sniffling. She put her arm around him and laid her head on his shoulder.

"Hey, I'm a *great* kisser," Michael whispered. "As I will demonstrate when we get out of this freakin' freak show." He cradled her protectively.

Jenny felt a flush of pride and joy—in their strength, in the tenderness in Michael's face and the way Audrey clung to him.

She looked at Julian defiantly.

Julian wasn't happy. He obviously didn't like the way things were going. Then he smiled, sharp as a sword.

"That's right, cry, you whining baby," he said, his eyes fixed on Audrey's auburn head. "But make sure you don't smear your mascara. You're nothing but a painted mannequin." His voice was venomous.

"We're not listening!" Michael said. He began talking to Audrey, softly and rapidly, right in her ear.

"You're going to turn out like your mother, you know—a shrill and contentious bitch. Your father's words, I believe. You're afraid that you're not capable of having real feelings like other people."

Audrey didn't even lift her head. Michael went on talking to her.

"I'd say she's doing a pretty good imitation of having feelings," Dee said dryly. "Why don't you just back off, creep?"

Instead, Julian whirled on her—no, not on her. He was looking behind her, at Summer. "And as for the brainless bit of fluff in front—"

Summer collapsed onto the floor of the boat. "I know I'm stupid," she whispered.

Jenny's fury lifted her to her feet, making the swan boat rock.

"Oh, no, you don't," she said. "If you have something to say, say it to *me*."

And then she was doing what she'd *least* wanted to do all this time. She was getting out of the boat, splashing down into the water.

It was cool, but it only came up to her knees. She splashed through it without letting herself think what might be swimming in it. Waves churned up, wetting her thighs.

She reached the diorama in a few steps and scrambled up on it. Then she was facing Julian.

"Say it to *me*," she said. "If you have the guts."

CHAPTER 12

I'm the one all this is for," Jenny said. "It's me you want to despair. So talk to *me*. Let's get personal."

"No, let's get general," Julian said. "Want to talk about life?"

There was a kind of soft triumph in his voice. A cat-pouncing-on-a-mouse tone. As if he knew he had her.

"Did you know," he went on, "that in the Congo there's a kind of fly that lays its eggs in human flesh? They develop into little white worms that live inside you forever. Sometimes the worms surface and you can watch them crawling inside the skin of your arm. They say that when they crawl inside your eyeball it's quite painful."

Jenny stood where she was, appalled.

"That's Nature for you," Julian said and laughed. The laugh didn't sound quite sane.

Jenny got her voice back. "We're not worms."

"No. Humans are a lot more inventive. Mustard gas, for instance. It touches you, your skin comes rolling off. Happened to thousands of soldiers in World War I. Some man invented that for the benefit of his brothers."

Jenny wanted to look away from Julian, but she couldn't. The spotlights threw swaths of red and purple on his hair. His eyes were mirror-brilliant.

"It's the same all down through history. Two million years ago your hominid ancestors were eating each other. In thirteenth-century Peru they used to crack little boys' ribs wide open so the priests could take their hearts out still beating. These days it's drive-by shootings. People never change."

Jenny could feel her breath catch. "Okay . . ."

The soft, insidious voice went on. "So Nature is cruel and ruthless."

"Okay . . ."

"And life is fragile and bewildering. And death—death is inevitable and worse than anything you can imagine."

From the boat Dee said defiantly, "Who cares?"

Julian spoke without turning toward Dee. "*She* cares," he said. "Don't you, Jenny? You care if it's a cruel and pointless universe. You care if you're surrounded by evil."

There was something almost mesmeric about his gaze now. His voice was reasonable, flowing. "So why not despair? There's nothing wrong with that. Things will be so much easier once you've given up. Why not just relax and give in. . . ."

He was coming toward her, and Jenny knew she couldn't resist. He was coming to put a warm palm on the back of her neck, maybe, or press her hand. And whatever he did, she wouldn't be able to resist, because at that moment his beauty was so unearthly it was frightening.

"I believe you!" she said, speaking before he got to her. He stopped, head tilted slightly, quizzically. Then suddenly she was speaking in a rush. "You wanted to prove how much evil there is—well, fine; I believe you. And I don't know all the answers. I don't even know the stupid *questions*. But not everything is evil, like you say. There are good people. Like Aba. Like my grandfather. He died to save me, and he's not the only person who's died for somebody else. I can't explain the evil that's out there, but that doesn't mean I ought to *join* it. It doesn't mean I should give in."

The smiling victory had drained out of Julian's face, and something cold and ugly was rising in his eyes instead. But Jenny went on before he could speak, her words tumbling over one another. "You said I cared about whether it was a cruel and pointless universe, and I do. But you want to know something else I care about? I care about you, Julian."

He was startled now. He looked as if he might almost take

a step backward. Because Jenny was moving forward, deliberately, holding his eyes and speaking.

"You wanted to show me how it's all right to be evil, because everything else is that way. But I'm not buying it. And you wanted to prove to me how bad you are, but I'm not buying that, either. I care about *you*, Julian. I—"

He disappeared just as she reached him.

The gold coin fell spinning to the ground.

Jenny picked it up a moment or so later, after standing quite still and watching it spin on its side for a while and finally land flat. Looking toward the boat, she saw that they were all looking at *her*: Dee, and Audrey, and Michael—and Summer, who was just poking her head out. Nobody seemed to know what to say.

It's not what you think, Jenny thought, but she didn't know how to explain it to them. She *did* care about Julian. She'd seen the moonbeam side of him, the vulnerable side that was so badly hurt it made him strike out. She even . . . loved Julian . . . in a way she was just discovering. But that didn't mean she didn't love Tom. Tom was a part of her life, a part of *her*. She could never betray him.

But putting all that in words was beyond her. They'd just have to think whatever they wanted.

"You know," Michael said at last, running a hand through his rumpled dark hair, "I think we just won this Game." He smiled, a weak and wry smile, but a real one nevertheless.

"And I think we should get out of here on foot," Dee said. "My guess is this boat isn't moving."

Nobody talked much as they sloshed through the tunnel. Dee went first, one hand on the dank wall to guide her. Jenny followed with Summer, and Audrey and Michael brought up the rear, holding hands. Jenny had the feeling that they were all sore from Julian's last and most terrible attack—but they were stronger for it, too. In the end it had pulled them together. Julian had revealed their secrets—and Jenny had never felt so close to her friends before.

She was relieved to see Dee's form silhouetted against lighter blackness and to feel fresh air on her face. They had found the end of the tunnel. Now she could see the loading dock.

"Will you look at this!" Michael exclaimed when they reached it and climbed up. "Will you just look, please?"

The park was awake.

All the lights that had been off were on, and all the rides were going. Fairy lights twinkled and glimmered in the trees, white lights played on a fountain below them. To the left, the Turnpike was illuminated, with lines of sports cars standing ready to race. Straight ahead, the rocket ride was already in motion, red-lit rockets up and whizzing. The structure of the March Hare roller coaster was picked out in flashing neon, and Jenny could hear the clatter of a car on the wooden tracks.

Everything was going, all at once. It looked exactly like

a normal amusement park at night—except that it was still deserted. The rides were operating by themselves.

Beautiful, Jenny thought, but scary. As if the whole park was inhabited by ghosts. The merry-go-round music was distant but eerily distinct, and she could hear the Noah's Ark foghorn in the pauses.

On the central island of the lake, the lighthouse rose white and slender and silent.

"Now we find the bridge, I suppose," Audrey said quietly from behind Jenny.

Jenny unbuttoned her shirt pocket, reached in. She looked at the three doubloons on her palm, felt their satisfying weight. Then she closed her hand and heard them clink softly.

"There's something we have to do first," she said. "Follow me."

The arcade was only a short distance away. Its sign was lighted, too, but the inside was dim and quiet. Jenny went straight to the cabinet with the mechanical wizard.

She tried not to look at the black cabinet that stood opposite, but she got a glimpse of the heads anyway. They were as blue and ghastly as ever, their eyes still shut. Jenny turned her back on them firmly and faced the wizard.

He was moving just the tiniest bit. As if some battery were running down. His hand lifted the wand and dropped it slightly, lifted and dropped, a sad repetitive motion. His head bobbed just as slightly, the dark marble eyes staring out into nothingness. Every so often his lower lip moved.

"Grandfather," Jenny said.

It was a formal moment, and *Grandpa* didn't seem quite right. He was Grandfather, like all the Grandfathers in fairy tales, a mystical, archetypical figure. Someone who belonged in a story.

Dee had said there was nothing Jenny could do for him, and it was true. She'd accepted it before, really, and she was even more certain now. There was no way to put his soul back into his body—if he even had a body anymore, which Jenny doubted. No way to fix him or undo what the Shadow Men had done.

But there was one thing she might be able to do. It had come to her while she was talking to Julian, surging up in the back of her mind when she had said that her grandfather had died for her. He hadn't—exactly—but he'd meant to. And she was sure he'd rather be dead than be like this.

The only question was whether her idea would work.

"Grandfather, I thought of something, something from your journal. A way to help you. But I need to know if it will work—and if it's what you want."

The matted-paintbrush eyelashes seemed to droop, then lift. The glass eyes didn't look at her, and the ruddy plastic face couldn't change expression. But she had the feeling he was listening.

"I saw the runes in your journal, and I know that runes can do things here, they can change reality. They can make things happen. And the rune I'm thinking of is Gebo, Grandfather, do you understand? Gebo."

"What's she *talking* about?" Summer whispered, from several steps away, where the others waited.

"I don't know. Gebo—which was that?" Dee said, and Michael said, "Shush, okay?"

Jenny stood watching the mechanical figure in the black velveteen robe, and waiting.

Suddenly the glass eyes rolled. The whole figure moved jerkily, banging the wand up and down. The carmine lips opened and shut, and the head bobbed.

It was a perfect frenzy of motion, like a mute person in a straitjacket trying desperately to convey agreement. At least, that was what Jenny hoped it was. If she was wrong, it was going to be a terrible mistake.

"All right," she whispered. "I love you, Grandpa." She could feel tears starting in her eyes, but she wasn't going to cry, she wasn't. She wasn't really sad. She was happy and a little scared. Beyond all hope, she'd gotten to see her grandfather again. It had helped her remember him, how kind he'd been to her, how much he'd loved her—whatever his other faults. She'd gotten the chance to say she was sorry, and now she had the chance to say goodbye. It was more than a lot of people got, more than Jenny could ever have expected.

She reached into her back pocket for the Swiss Army knife.

It had been there all along, almost forgotten since she'd tucked it away in the mine ride. It had survived the cave-in and the flood and everything else. She was glad, because it was Tom's, and now because it was very useful.

She held it in her hand a moment, then thumbed open the large blade. She set the blade against the old-fashioned wooden cabinet, just above the glass, and, bearing down hard, carved a diagonal stroke. Then she made another that crossed the first in the middle, forming an *X*. Making Gebo, the rune of sacrifice. It was funny, how she'd had a premonition about that when they were carving it on the door. She'd felt that it had been important somehow—but she'd never imagined this.

She stepped back.

Pinching her left index finger between middle finger and thumb, she watched the end go purple with blood. Then, without hesitation, she jabbed once with the knife.

She didn't really know whether she needed blood for this. Isa, the ice rune she'd used to stop the flooding waterfall, had worked without it. But she wanted to do this just right, and make absolutely sure.

Squeezing the finger, she painted the *X* with blood. Then she stepped back again.

The mechanical figure was perfectly still, as if waiting. Everything seemed to be waiting, the universe holding its breath around Jenny. For a moment she was afraid she couldn't speak, but the dark eyes were at last looking straight at her. There was a silent encouragement in them, almost a plea. And a gentle trust.

The third step is to say the name of the rune out loud.

Jenny took a deep breath and clearly and quietly said, "Gebo."

Rune of sacrifice, of death. Of yielding up the spirit.

It happened immediately, startling her. The figure in the cabinet, the mechanical thing dressed in black velveteen and gold sequins, spasmed as if a jolt of electricity had gone through it. Both arms jerked up, the head rolled wildly. Cracks ran along the caked paint on its face, flaking off in pieces. Every part of the figure that could move thrashed frantically.

And then the clenched fist with the wand fell. The entire figure sagged, its head falling back. It was as if some mainspring had been sprung, or the wires to a marionette cut. The carmine lips were slightly open.

Jenny, scarcely breathing, stared at the face.

It—had changed. It was still plastic—cracked and peeling plastic. It was clearly a broken doll.

But—the pain was gone. The look that had wrenched Jenny's heart in the beginning, the look of ineffable sadness, wasn't there anymore. The carmine lips seemed to be smiling slightly, and the glass eyes, though open, seemed at peace.

There was an odd dignity that went with the peace. The face was patient and almost noble, for all that it was a doll's face. Whatever her grandfather had done, whatever secrets he'd meddled in, he'd paid the price—and this doll seemed to know it. Its expression was that of somebody who'd waited a long time to get to the end of a journey, and was home at last.

"You can rest now," Jenny said, and then she had to wipe her eyes on her denim sleeve.

A click made her look down. A fortune-telling card was in the slot.

Jenny took it, turned it over. There were only two words in the middle.

THANK YOU.

Then she really did cry, looking around as if her grandfather's soul might be floating somewhere in the room where she could see it. Wherever it had gone, it was free.

"What about *them*?" Dee said. Jenny looked at the others and saw that they were sniffling, too—and Dee was looking at the black cabinet.

Jenny wiped her eyes again, and her nose, and then she made herself look. Slug and P.C. were more hideous than ever because they were awake.

Their eyes followed her with the desperate longing of dogs that wanted to go out on a walk. Neither of them had been particularly handsome when they were alive, and in death they were grotesque. Jenny swallowed.

"Can you hear me?"

The two grisly objects bobbed.

"Did you see what I did?"

Bob. Bob.

"Do you—do you want me to do it for you?"

Bob, bob, bob, bob, bob, bob, bob . . .

Jenny burst into tears and went on crying as she lifted the knife. She *needed* to cry. She had never liked either of these guys; they'd stalked her on an empty street, they'd meant to do her harm, they'd broken into her house and stolen from her. And now they looked like those little dogs with nodding heads that people put in the back of their cars, and Jenny was going to kill them.

She went on sobbing as she carved the two *X*s, one over each head, and stabbed her middle finger. She was still crying as she began to stain the first *X* red.

So she didn't notice the attack until Dee started shouting.

Jenny looked up and froze. It was another body like the one that had grabbed Dee at the Fish Pond, and it had the same ghastly emptiness above its shoulders. The only difference was that it wasn't white and bloated, and it was wearing a black T-shirt and leather vest. It was P.C.

In the cabinet the head with the black bandanna was shaking violently—as if to disassociate itself with the lumbering body that Dee was fighting. Its eyes were terrified, straining sideways to try and watch.

"I think the Shadow Men must control the bodies!" Michael shouted, pulling Summer out of the way. Audrey had stumbled back, too, and Dee was fighting the thing alone, swinging Audrey's pick. Cabinets on both sides were smashing.

Jenny, caught completely unprepared, was still frozen.

"Come on, hurry!" Michael shouted. He grabbed the knife from her hand and stabbed his own finger. The next thing she knew he was staining the other rune, making sharp, slashing motions on the cabinet.

"Come on, Jenny!"

Trancelike, Jenny raised her finger, smearing pale red across the second stroke of the *X*. The headless body had gotten hold of Dee's pick and was jerking it away from her, pulling her within range.

Jenny whirled back to the cabinet, energized. The blue-lit heads gazed at her, looking imploring and stupid and more pathetic than anything she'd ever seen.

"Gebo!" she shouted.

Michael shouted it, too, maybe because his blood was in the runes. Then several things happened in quick succession.

Both the heads in the box jerked. Their jaws fell open, impossibly far open, revealing blue-stained teeth. Their eyes rolled up. And there was a noise—an inhuman howling that seemed to come from all around Jenny rather than from the open jaws. Down the corridor there was a terrible crashing.

P.C.'s body was flailing with the pick, breaking glass and splintering wood. As Jenny watched he flailed more and more jerkily, then stopped. His body flopped backward, collapsing like a pricked balloon.

Meanwhile, from every side, there was clicking and whirring

and plinking music. The entire arcade had come to life at once. The foot vitalizer was vibrating. In a shattered cabinet a mechanical ballerina was twirling. The figures in the Ole Barn Dance were clacking their wooden jaws.

"Let's get the hell out of here!" Dee shouted over the music of a nickelodeon.

Jenny cast one last glance at the black cabinet. The heads were still now, and she supposed their blank and empty expressions were peaceful. Certainly nobody was *in* there anymore.

Then she was moving, stepping over glass shards and P.C.'s motionless body, while the arcade gibbered and screeched around her. A minute later she was in the open air.

It was an unspeakable relief to get away from the noise. The outside seemed clean somehow, even if it was in the Shadow World.

She looked at Dee. "Are you okay?"

"Yeah." Dee was gripping her thigh with both hands, pulling bits of glass out of her jeans. "I got some shrapnel here, but I'm all right."

Jenny looked at Summer, who was huddling and hugging her own elbows. "Are *you* all right?"

Summer managed an extremely watery smile.

"I got splinters," Michael offered, holding up his finger.

"That was brave of you," Jenny said. She was remembering the way he'd looked in her grandfather's house when she had first explained that they needed to stain the runes with blood.

Michael just looked at her. "Huh?"

"Never mind. Summer, give Dee back her jacket. Audrey, are you okay to walk? Because I have the feeling we'd better keep moving. I think they're mad."

She squeezed her shirt pocket and felt the reassuring heaviness there. She felt the need to hurry, as if a storm were gathering behind her. The Shadow Men weren't happy with what she'd done to their prisoners.

"Wait, but how do we find the bridge?" Michael said.

"We'll just walk around the lake until we see it."

They saw it as soon as they cleared the trees by the Penny Arcade. It started somewhere in between the March Hare roller coaster and the Log Ride, rising in a beautiful arch like a rainbow that ended on the island.

"I don't *think* that was there before," Audrey said.

"Maybe it just wasn't lit," Dee said.

Michael said, "It's going to be like climbing the St. Louis Arch."

Everybody looked at Jenny.

"We'll do it," she said stoutly. "We *have* to. We have to get to Tom and Zach—and *quick,* because they may try to stop us or something. We've got to actually get to them to win the Game."

"I don't see how the coins fit in," Dee muttered.

But when they reached the nearer base of the arch, Jenny saw. There was a neat little tollbooth in front of it, and a fence with barbed wire that kept you from climbing up the sides. After the first ten feet it was so high in the air that you couldn't have reached the side if you had wanted to.

"What holds it up?" Summer whispered, and Jenny said, "Don't ask."

Attached to the white tollbooth was a coin receiver with a flat tray—like the kind you see in airports for getting luggage carts. Instead of four spaces for quarters there were three spaces for irregularly shaped coins in the tray. With a little twisting and exchanging, Jenny got all three gold pieces to fit neatly. They lay there and gleamed at her.

She looked at the others.

It was a momentous moment, a serious, *profound* moment. They'd finished the treasure hunt and they were about to go collect the prize. She felt as if somebody ought to make a significant gesture.

"Dee? You want to push it? Or Audrey?"

"You earned it, Sunshine. Go on and make it happen," Dee said.

Jenny was happy.

She pushed the tray in and felt it lock in place. The white-and-yellow striped turnstile lifted.

"After you," she said and gestured the others through.

CHAPTER 13

Dee took the lead, with Summer following her lightly and Michael and Audrey after that.

Jenny wanted the others to go ahead of her partly because she was afraid, and partly because she didn't want any of them trying to save her if she fell off.

Heights. She had always hated heights. But she was *damned* if she was going to let this bridge stop her from getting to Tom.

It wasn't all that bad at the beginning. Steep, yes, and narrow, yes. And there were no handrails. If the whole structure had been six inches off the ground, Jenny could have walked it easily, without a chance of slipping. The problem was doing it twenty feet off the ground.

But if she looked straight down and concentrated on her own feet, she couldn't see how they were climbing.

Just then, though, something drifted past her feet—a wisp of mist. Alarmed, she looked to one side.

No, they weren't cloud-height. They really were only twenty feet off the ground. But mist was rising around them.

"Oh, *spiffy*," Michael said from somewhere ahead, and Summer's voice said, "I can't *see*."

Dee's voice floated back from even farther ahead. "Reach back and hold hands with each other. I can feel my way along."

Jenny reached forward and took a handful of Audrey's nylon jacket—Audrey only had one good arm to use. She shuffled forward, gritting her teeth. Everything around her was white. She could barely see her own hiking boots.

In a few minutes, though, her head broke through the mist. She went on shuffling upward, inching out of it. Her legs were aching, and she hoped they were getting near the top.

It was only when Audrey stopped short in front of her, and gasped, that she looked around.

The mist was gone. What she saw beneath the bridge now was—unearthly.

It was dark, and arching through the darkness were other bridges, delicate and airy, some fiery, some that looked like ice. They led to clumps of land that looked like islands floating in space.

"Like Neverland," Jenny whispered. "A bunch of Neverlands. What *are* they? And where are *we*?"

"Oh, I don't believe this," Audrey said just as softly.

"I do," Dee said from the very top of the arch. Her head was thrown back on the slim dark column of her neck. Faint light from the bridges shifted on the planes of her cheekbones, and her eyes glowed. "I do."

Some of the islands were brighter and more substantial-looking than any landscape Jenny had seen on Earth—sharper in detail, more exquisite in clarity. Others were dim and vague—as if they had been partly formed and then abandoned.

Between the clumps of land Jenny could see stars—but not normal stars. These stars rippled and waved as if she were looking at them through a clear stream, or as if they were studded on a flowing length of black silk. There was something incredibly lost and lonely about them.

"But what *are* those things? Those other islands?" she said again.

Audrey gave herself a little shake and seemed to focus. "I think—those are the nine worlds. From Norse mythology—Norse, like the runes. I told you about them once."

"You mean—we're *above* the Shadow World somehow?"

"I guess. Now that—that's probably Asgard, the one way up there. It's got to be."

Jenny tilted her head back. Far above them—the farthest away of any of the clumps—was an island world that seemed all silver and gold. She could just glimpse something like a shining mountain rising into a golden cloud on it. The bridge to it was very narrow and seemed to be on fire.

"That's where the gods live."

"The gods?" Jenny spoke to Audrey without looking down from the shining island.

"So the myths say. Hmm, and I'll bet *that's* Vanaheim. World of primal water and plenty, where some of the less important gods live." Audrey pointed to an island painted in jewel-like colors, dark blue and dark green.

"Vanaheim—any relation to Anaheim?" Michael murmured. Audrey pinched her mouth on a smile, but ignored him.

"And that's Alfheim, world of light and air," she said, nodding at an island that was much closer to them, shimmering in the colors of sunrise: yellow, pale blue, light green. "Home of light elves—like good spirits. I'm remembering all this, isn't that amazing? I must have been about eight when I learned it."

"What about those?" Dee said, pointing straight outward. Two island worlds were floating at about the same level as the bridge they stood on: one rocky and lashed by what looked like tornadoes, and the other so bright with orange fire that Jenny couldn't make out any details.

"The rocky one's Jotunheim—the world of primal storms. And the other one has to be Muspelheim, the world of primal fire. Nothing lives there but killer giants."

"What's *that*?" Michael said, staring downward and to the left.

Audrey looked. "Hel," she said simply.

"I always thought hell would be hot," Summer said, her eyes widening like cornflowers blooming.

"Hel, with one *l*. It's the underworld, where everything sinks in the end. Ruled by Hella, queen of the dead."

It looked like a frozen lake, colder and blacker than the empty space between the worlds. Jenny had never seen such a lightless, joyless place.

The bridge to it was like a slide, broad and frosty.

"We *definitely* wouldn't want to go there. Or to that one—the one that looks like a cavern. That's Svartalfheim, the subterranean world."

"No more caves, thank you," Michael said.

There was only one island left. It was the one directly below them, and both ends of the bridge they stood on seemed connected to it. From here, the surface was obscured by dark mist and shadows.

Audrey said, "Niflheim, land of ice and shadows. The Shadow World." She shook her head. "I still don't believe this."

"Why not? It's no weirder than anything else we've seen today," Dee said. "But I only count eight worlds. Where's Earth?"

Audrey looked around, then shrugged. "Maybe we don't get to see that bridge until we finish the Game."

"Who cares? Look, we wanted to walk between the worlds, right?" Dee said, her eyes shining. "And now we're doing it. So—shall we?"

Jenny nodded. She felt very tiny and insignificant standing here, and her throat was tight. And she had the feeling that it was going to be harder going down than going up—because now the fall was so much longer.

They started moving. It was hard to walk in the place between the worlds—physically hard. After two or three steps Jenny began to feel muscle-burn in her calves and thigh muscles. She could hear Audrey panting in front of her.

And the barest glimpse of the fall on either side made Jenny's internal organs feel as if they were plunging out of her body.

Her legs wanted to freeze. She wanted to get down on her rump and scoot the rest of the way—no, get down on her stomach and *slither*. But that wasn't the worst.

She was afraid she would faint.

If I faint up here, I'll fall. Of course I'll fall. Nobody faints neatly forward. I'll slide off the side.

The moment the thought of fainting occurred to her, it blocked everything else out. She *was* going to faint. Just thinking about it made her dizzy. She was so scared of fainting, she felt like jumping.

Hysteria began to bubble up inside her. She shouldn't have thought about jumping. Now she was afraid she *would* jump, just because the idea had occurred to her. She had to try not to think about it.

Think of anything else. Think of Tom, think of getting to Tom. But the idea of jumping was now stuck in her mind. She started to picture it. She could get it all over with, turn to the side and just let go. God, no—she didn't want to, but she was afraid she'd go crazy and do it. . . .

The voice came from her own brain, but it was so harsh it seemed alien. *You keep on moving, girl!*

Jenny realized she was stopped, frozen. Staring down at her own feet in their brown leather hiking boots, and the white ribbon of bridge, and the formless darkness on either side.

Just put one foot in front of the other. The right foot. Put out your right foot.

I can't, she thought.

Yes, you can!

But if I faint—or jump—

You expect everybody else to face their fears, and you can't face yours? You're not your only master if you can't even control your own feet! You're just a coward!

The right boot jerked a little and stepped forward.

That's right. Now the other one.

The other boot came forward. Jenny was walking again.

She could do it—command her own feet. Just put one foot in front of the other. And one more step. And one more.

Don't look to the side. One more step. And one more.

There were only a few body-lengths of bridge in front of her. She could see where it ended. Ten feet. Five feet.

On legs that had suddenly gone weak as angel-hair pasta, Jenny stumbled and fell onto safe ground.

Dee bent over her. "You okay?"

Weakly Jenny patted one of Dee's hightops. "I'm terrific, thanks."

"I shouldn't have let you be last. I forgot."

Jenny sat up and wiped her forehead. "I did fine by myself."

"Yeah, you did. You seem to be doing a lot of that these days."

Jenny was very happy.

Then it hit her. They were across. They'd made it.

Tom.

She looked up so fast her vision swam.

After the alien grandeur of the place between the worlds, it was something of a comedown. They were on the central island in the artificial lake at Joyland Park. The lighthouse looked the same as it had all night, white and shining. The park around them was a riot of lights—but ordinary lights, illuminating ordinary rides like the SuperLooper and the Tumble-bug. Everything looked very ordinary.

Behind her, the bridge arched gracefully over the lake water, and the water reflected a wavering arch back. There was no mist, and no sign of any other worlds. The top of the arch wasn't more than forty feet high.

"A hallucination, I guess," Audrey said slowly. "One of Julian's things. And I suppose it must have been from me, since I'm the only one who knew about those other worlds."

Jenny opened her mouth, then shut it again. She thought Audrey must be right—but she wasn't sure. And the truth was that they would probably never be sure.

She looked back at the lighthouse. "Come on, people. This is it."

When she got up her legs were shaky, but she took the lead and Dee let her.

The lighthouse looked bigger as they got closer. It was life-size, with a widow's walk around the top and a weathercock. And it was attached to some broad dark building that Jenny hadn't seen before because it wasn't lit up. A restaurant, maybe, she thought.

There was a wooden door in the lighthouse's side, with a large iron handle.

"Monster positions," Dee reminded Jenny as she reached for the handle. Then Dee stood ready to kick the door shut if anything unfriendly was behind it.

"Tom and Zach will be at the top, of course," Michael said, resting with his hands on his thighs in anticipation.

But they weren't.

It was funny, how the end began. Jenny had been waiting for so long, working and fighting, and all the time *waiting* for the moment that she would see Tom. She was so used to waiting she wasn't really ready for it to end. She wasn't—prepared.

She almost couldn't deal with it.

But when it started happening, it happened fast, and prepared or not, she was thrown into it.

She pulled on the iron handle, and the wooden door swung open. There was no need for Dee to kick it shut. Everything inside was illuminated, and nothing came rushing toward them.

Black metal stairs curved up on Jenny's left, circling upward toward the top of the lighthouse. But straight in front of her she could see the interior of the broad building. The lighthouse had no back wall, and opened right into it.

It was a wonderful place, with a huge diorama two stories high as a backdrop. It looked like a movie set of a wharf scene, but the numbered flags on poles betrayed its real purpose. It was an indoor miniature golf course.

"Treasure Island," Michael said, peering around her shoulder. "Pirates, see?"

It was pirates. The diorama featured a mural painted on the far wall of the broad building, a marvelously realistic mural with a volcano in the background. Painted smoke and little neon lights for sparks showed that it was erupting. There was also a mammoth storm in the painted sky, and forked lightning that really flashed.

At the bottom of the mural, just behind the golf course itself, two dinghies were landing on some fiberglass rocks. One boat was painted, with a pirate in an eye patch and hat, a lace cravat, and boots.

The other boat was real, with Tom and Zach.

Jenny touched her mouth. Then she was running.

There weren't any words for what she felt next. When she'd been separated from Tom in the paper house, it had been for hours. This time it had been days. She was exhausted, over-stressed, starving, on the verge of collapse—and she'd never been so happy in her life.

Just the sight of him brought back everything that was good and homelike to her mind. It was like coming back to her own room after being away a long time with strangers.

It was where she belonged.

She threw her arms around him. And then she just held on, her heart pounding and pounding.

"Watch out, Jenny. He was here just a minute ago."

And Jenny, who had for so long associated Tom with pro-tection, with safety and security and coziness, found herself feeling passionately protective of Tom. As if he were Summer. Looking into his dear face, handsome and rather brooding just now, and his wonderful green-flecked eyes, she said, "Don't worry. I'll take care of you."

"Just let me *out*, please," Tom said sharply, and then gave up and kissed her back. Jenny's solicitous feelings had thrown her into a perfect spasm of love for him, and it felt *so good* to kiss him again.

"If you two could tear yourself apart for just a minute . . ." Zach's voice said.

Jenny looked up. Her cousin was in the back of the dinghy, yes, the same cousin she'd lost, she thought a little deliriously. Exactly the same, with his wonderful beaky nose and his ash-blond hair pulled back in a casual ponytail and his keen gray eyes.

"I missed you, too," she said and scrambled back to hug him.

"We're tied up," Tom said briskly.

Jenny saw that his brown wrists were tied behind his back with some kind of thick cord. "No problem," she said, just as briskly, and pulled out the Swiss Army knife. I'll never go anywhere without one again, she thought, and, crouching by Zach's feet, she began carefully sawing at the cord.

"Hi, Dee," Tom said, calm as if he were meeting her Saturday at the ball game. "Hey, Audrey, Mi—" He broke off and bolted upright, and Jenny cut his hand.

"Sit down," she said.

He didn't seem to notice. *"Summer?"*

"Hi, Tom," Summer said shyly.

"Summer?"

"She wasn't dead, just asleep," Audrey said.

Jenny said, "Sit *down,* will you? We'll explain later."

"Yeah—sure," Tom said weakly. He sat down. Jenny finished cutting the cord enough so that he could pull out of it.

Then, while he was rubbing his hands, she turned to Zach.

"Are you both okay?" she added. "I mean—not hurt or anything?"

"We're fine," Tom said absently. "He just put us here a little while ago. We were in the lighthouse, before, and it wasn't too bad—except I was afraid you'd come."

"You *knew* I'd come. I hope."

"I hoped you wouldn't. I was afraid you would."

"Tom"—a strand on Zach's cord sprang apart—"you don't have to worry about me." She looked up to find him looking down at her, in that new way, the way he had since the end of Julian's first Game. As if she were something infinitely precious, something that bewildered him, but amazed him—something he didn't deserve, but trusted.

"Sure I have to worry about you, Thorny," he said simply. "Just like you worry about me."

Jenny smiled.

"Nobody needs to worry right now. We've won the Game, Tom. We went on the treasure hunt and now we've found you. It's all over."

"I'll still be happier out of here," he said, and Zach said, "That goes for me doubled, tripled, and quadrupled."

Jenny glanced around. She supposed it was a spooky place in a way—if you were sitting and anticipating trouble. There were real cave entrances below the mural, leading to other parts of the miniature golf range. There were mock buildings holding the same thing—golf holes—with names like Lafitte's Black Powder Works. It was dark inside all these places.

"Don't tell me. You guys were afraid of the parrot," Michael said. Jenny followed his gaze to a section of the building beside the golf course, apparently an area for eating, because there were orange plastic tables and stools bolted to the ground. There was also a small stage with a sign that read: CAP'N BILL AND SEBASTIAN, THE WONDER PARROT. Also a mounted TV showing Woody Woodpecker cartoons, mercifully silent.

"No, we were afraid of the eyes," Tom said, stepping out of the dinghy and over a length of thick rope that sagged between two wharf pillars.

Jenny's head snapped up. "The eyes?"

"The ones that sit in the shadows and look at you. And the whispering."

Jaw squared, Jenny sawed through the last of Zach's cord and rubbed his wrists. So the other Shadow Men were around.

Tom was staring at Audrey's arm. "What happened to *you*?"

"Believe me, you're happier not knowing."

"You guys all look like you've been playing with the Raiders—and losing," Tom said.

It was true, Jenny thought, following Zach over the rope. The prisoners they'd come to rescue looked fine, just as they had when they'd disappeared behind Julian's wall of fire. A little crumpled and stained about the clothes, but otherwise fine. Zach still had his 35 millimeter camera around his neck.

It was the rescuers who were bloody and battered. Even Summer looked wounded, like a broken-stemmed flower. Audrey, usually the picture of elegance, looked more like a young hiker who'd been in a bad accident. Dee's jeans were stained dark at the thigh. Michael looked as if he'd been dunked in swamp water and then tumble-dried.

"You've been through a lot," Zach said, and for once his gray eyes weren't cool or unreadable. "Thanks, Jenny."

Jenny waved dismissively, but she felt a glow inside. "What happened back there in the fire, anyway? One minute I was holding your hand, the next . . ."

"I fell," Zach said. "Pure dumb luck. I tripped, and when I got up, I didn't know which way to go. I stumbled around and ended up back in Julian's base."

"Out of the fire, into the frying pan," Michael said.

"And then Tom came back for me." Zach looked at Tom, and something passed between them without words. The introverted photographer and the star athlete had never been particularly close before, but Jenny had the feeling that that had changed now. She was pleased.

"Aww," Michael said.

Audrey said, "Shut up—*mon cher.*"

Dee interrupted. "Here's a map of the park." The map was wood, painted to look like parchment, with iron chains around it.

"It *is* an amusement park, then. We could see some of it out the lighthouse window," Tom said. "Okay, look, here's my plan. . . ."

His voice trailed off. Audrey, Michael, Dee, and Summer weren't looking at him. Instead, they were looking at Jenny expectantly.

Tom looked at Zach, who was standing with his arms folded, something like amusement in his sharp-featured face.

"Okay, uh—why don't you tell us *your* plan?" Tom said to Jenny.

Jenny was fighting amusement, too. "I don't have one. We don't *need* one. We've won, and we ought to be able to just walk out of here. The only thing I don't understand is why Julian hasn't shown up."

They all looked at the various dark doorways and crevices.

"Do you think maybe—he's watching us?" Summer said.

"Of course I'm watching; that's what I do," a weary voice said.

CHAPTER 14

Jenny spun. Julian was standing beside a ticket booth with a brass telescope on top. He was surrounded by ferns and fake palms. And he looked—tired?

He was wearing the duster jacket again, and he had his hands in his pockets. His hair was as white as a winter moon.

It was up to her to face him, Jenny knew. She was the only one who could do this.

She stepped forward. She tried to look him directly in the eyes, but it was hard. His gaze seemed curiously veiled—as if he wasn't exactly looking at her, but through her.

"We've won," she said with more confidence than she felt. "Finally. It's the last Game, and this time there's no way you can bend the rules. You have to let us go."

What *was* the look in those eyes? They were midnight-colored and full of shadows—but there was something else, something Jenny only recognized when she felt a presence beside her. Tom was there, looking devilishly handsome and full of cold, protective fury. He wasn't going to let her face Julian alone. His hand rested on her shoulder, lightly, not possessively. As if to say he was there to back her up, whatever happened.

"I ought to try to kill you," he said to Julian. "I can't, but I sure ought to try. I will, if you pull anything this time."

Julian ignored him completely.

Wistfulness, Jenny thought. That was it. Julian wasn't exactly looking at Tom, but for a moment he'd glanced at Tom's hand on her shoulder—and there was wistfulness in his eyes.

The Shadow Man seeing the one thing he could never have, she thought. Human love.

"*Are* you going to pull anything?" Tom asked tightly.

It was a good question. Jenny was braced for some kind of a trick, too—ready to fight Julian, to argue him out of it. Every other time they'd won a Game, Julian had unveiled some weird twist at the last minute, had found some way to crush them and laugh at them.

Jenny had fully expected him to try it again this time—so why hadn't he? Why hadn't he appeared before they got Tom and Zach untied? Why wasn't he dressed as a pirate, fending them off with a cutlass, smiling and pointing out that they had to *get* to Tom and Zach to rescue them? Why wasn't he playing the Game?

Probably because he has something worse up his sleeve, she told herself. That painted volcano will erupt. Real lightning will strike. Or maybe—

—or maybe he was just tired of playing.

"We *have* won, haven't we?" she said, suddenly uncertain. She would have thought she would enjoy announcing her victory more than this.

"You've won," Julian said, and there was no emotion in his voice. He still wasn't really looking at her. And he did seem tired—his whole body looked tired.

He looked—defeated.

"So—I can leave."

"Yes."

Jenny was still looking for the catch. "And take everyone with me."

"Yes."

"Even Tom. I can take Tom with me."

"Let's go," Tom said abruptly, his fingers closing around her upper arm. Jenny almost—not quite—shook him off. This wasn't like Julian at all.

"I can go and I can take Tom," she persisted. "And everyone. It's the last Game, and it's over now."

For the first time Julian looked at her. His eyes were fully dilated, with the look Jenny had seen in the cave. An inward look, as if nothing mattered. It was too brittle to be bitter. A look like blue ice about to break up and fall into dark water.

A—shattering.

"It's the last Game," he said. "It's over now. I won't bother you again."

The corner of his mouth jerked as if he were about to say something more—or maybe it was involuntary. Then, without speaking, he whirled around.

"Get out. Get her out." Without looking at Tom, he spoke in a distorted voice, thick with restraint. "Get her out of here! Before I do—something—"

"Julian—" Jenny said.

"—we'll all be sorry for—"

He gave a shudder of suppressed emotion.

Tom grabbed Jenny's other arm and wheeled her in the opposite direction.

There was a rough wooden door standing on the far side of the building. It was set between two enormous stones, like a gate. But there was no fence or wall, just the door standing in space and looking tremendously solid, as if it had always been there.

It was partly open, and inside Jenny could see her grandfather's hallway, including the small telephone table with the white doily on it. The phone was lying on the floor where it had fallen, receiver off the hook.

"Home," Audrey said, in a voice of such startled longing

that Jenny almost yielded to Tom's steering hands. But then she twisted away.

Insanely, inexplicably, she wanted to stay and talk to Julian.

Julian didn't want to talk to her.

"Leave. Just *go*—now!"

Even without seeing his face, she could tell that his control was breaking. She tried to turn him around.

"Jenny, are you *crazy*?" Dee said. Dee and Tom were both pulling at Jenny now, trying to get her away from Julian.

"Just give me one minute!"

"Will you get her *out* of here!" Julian snarled.

Everyone was shouting. Summer was crying. And Jenny was having to fight off the two people she loved best—Tom and Dee—for a reason she couldn't even explain clearly to herself.

She knew the risk; she understood why Summer was crying. She could feel the storm building in Julian. The air was hot and electric, as if heat lightning were about to explode. He could do *anything* to them.

But she couldn't let it go.

"Julian, please listen—"

He turned, then, whirling so fast that Jenny stepped back. She was frightened by what she saw in his face.

"You cannot save me from myself," he hissed, saying each word distinctly, biting it off. Then he looked Tom straight in the face. "Get her out of here. I am trying to play this Game by the rules. But if you don't have her out in thirty seconds, all bets are off."

"I'm sorry, Thorny," Tom said and picked her up.

"No!" Jenny was furious at the indignity, at being made to go where she didn't want to go, like a child. And she was furious because she had just discovered the reason that she wanted to stay. Julian had said it for her. She wanted to save him.

It was like the sign on Aba's mirror. *Do no harm. Help when you can. Return good for evil.* That was what she wanted, to help if she could. To return good for evil where it had the chance of making a difference.

But Tom wasn't the only one she'd have to fight. Dee was marching along beside him, eyes fixed grimly on Jenny. And Michael and Audrey, Zach and Summer were surrounding them, forming a tight little knot to escort Jenny home.

"We're gonna drag you through that door by your hair, if we have to, Sunshine," Dee said, just in case this wasn't sufficiently clear.

"There are times when you can be *too good,* and this is one of them," Audrey added.

They all started for the door—but they never got there.

The mist was different from the fog that had risen around Jenny on the bridge. It was thick, interspersed with dark tendrils, and it moved *fast.*

Ice and shadows. A whirling, seething mixture of white and black.

Jenny remembered it very well—she'd seen it twice before. Once when she was five years old, in a memory so terrible that she had repressed it completely, giving herself amnesia. And once a month ago, when she'd relived the memory in Julian's paper house.

Tom was turning, enraged, to shout at Julian. Jenny slid from his arms. She could see by Julian's face that he had nothing to do with this.

Looking around was like being plunged into a nightmare—a recurring nightmare. Frost was forming on every surface. It was creeping up the wooden poles with rusty lanterns that stood throughout the golf course. It was coating the barrels labeled xxx and the boxes labeled BLACK POWDER. Icicles were growing on the tarred ropes linking the wharf pillars.

Freezing wind blew Jenny's hair straight back from her face, then whipped it stingingly across her cheeks.

"What's happening?" Audrey screamed. "What's happening?" Summer was just screaming.

It was so *cold*—as cold as the water that had drowned her in the mine shaft. So cold that it hurt. It hurt to breathe and it hurt to stand still.

Tom was shouting in her ear, trying to lift her and stagger toward the door. He'd made it through the fire. . . .

But not now. The ice storm was blinding. The white light was painfully brilliant, and the dark tendrils lashed through it like whips, like supple reaching arms.

They were holding Tom still. They were trapping everyone.

Slowly the wind died down. The blinding brightness faded. Jenny could see again, and she saw that the dark mist was gathering itself, coalescing. Forming figures.

Figures with malevolent, ancient eyes.

The other Shadow Men had come.

"Oh, God," Audrey whispered. She drew in closer to Jenny. There were ice crystals in her spiky copper bangs. "Oh, God—I didn't *know.* . . ."

Jenny hadn't known, either. She didn't understand. She recognized the cruel and ravenous eyes—she couldn't be wrong about them. But the forms that went with the eyes . . .

Michael wiped his mouth with the back of his hand, placing himself in front of Audrey. Summer was making small clotted sounds of fear. Zach's eyes glazed, then he shook his head and pulled Summer nearer to the group.

Those—things—can't be Shadow Men, Jenny thought. The Shadow Men are beautiful. Heartbreakingly beautiful.

These creatures were terrible.

They were hideously twisted and deformed. It would have been easier if they hadn't looked at all like humans, but they did. They were like dreadful, obscene parodies of human people.

Some of them had skin like leather—real leather, like something that had been smoked and cured. Yellowish-brown, so hard that their faces could never change expression. Others had skin like toadstool flesh—corpse-white and frilled, with dangling wattles.

It wasn't just the skin. Their bodies were distorted and maimed, and their faces were terrible. One had no nose, just an empty black hole. Another had no facial orifices of any kind. Nothing—only blank, stretched skin where eyes and nose and mouth should be. Another had a horn growing out of the back of its head.

And the *smell*—they smelled like decay, and like brimstone. Jenny's nostrils stung, and she felt bile rise in her throat.

Beside her, Tom was breathing hard. She looked at him, saw the open horror in his green-flecked eyes. Dee's nostrils were flared, and she was holding herself ready for an attack.

It came suddenly—one of the creatures scuttling across the tiled floor, to stop right in front of Jenny. Jenny gasped—and recognized it. It was the gray and withered fetus they'd seen in the park, the one that had scampered into the Whip. Now that she saw it more closely, it didn't look young like a fetus at all. It looked old, impossibly old, so old that it had shrunk and caved in on itself.

"Oh, God . . ." Audrey whispered again. Summer was keening.

Dee had fallen into the Cat stance, perfectly balanced, ready to initiate any action.

"Should I do it?" she said through clenched teeth.

Jenny opened her mouth, but before she could say anything, the withered fetus spoke.

"Can we take you? We can carry you," it said, looking at Jenny with eyes that glowed like a tiger's.

Then it giggled, wildly and obscenely, and scuttled away.

I never asked Julian what the little creatures were, Jenny remembered. She had been certain they weren't Shadow Men because they were so hideous. Now she looked toward him, hoping that he would have some explanation, that he would tell her what she was thinking was wrong.

He had stepped forward. There was a dusting of ice on his black jacket, and his hair glimmered as if it were made from frost. His beautifully sculpted face and mouth had never looked more perfect.

"What are they?" Jenny whispered.

"My ancestors," he said, introducing them to her, and destroying her last hope.

"Those—things?" She still couldn't connect them to Julian.

Without any emotion that she could discern he said, "That's what we become. That's what I'll become. It's inevitable."

Jenny shook her head.

"How?" Zach said sharply. He was probably the least repulsed, Jenny thought vaguely—that photographer's mind of his. He found grotesque things interesting.

But Jenny didn't. Not things like this, oh, never things like this.

"Is that—what they *really* look like? Or is it to scare us?" she heard her own voice saying.

Julian's strangely veiled gaze met hers. "Those are their true forms." He looked them over expressionlessly. "We're born in perfection," he said, without either modesty or arrogance— without *any* feeling that Jenny could see. "But as we age, we become grotesque. It's inevitable—the outer form changes to reflect our inner nature." He shrugged. "We become monsters."

The poem. The poem on her grandfather's desk, Jenny thought. She understood it at last, the line about them fingering old bones. These were the kind of creatures who would sit in a pit and do that. From Julian's beauty she would never have guessed, could never have pictured him that way.

Now she tried to keep it out of her mind, the picture of Julian looking like *them,* so distorted, so debased. It *couldn't* happen to him—but he'd said it was inevitable.

"But I don't know what they're doing here now," Julian continued, as if unaware of her reaction. "This isn't their Game; they have nothing to do with it."

"You're wrong," a tall Shadow Man said. It had the eyes of a crocodile. Its voice, though, was shockingly beautiful, distant and lonely as wind chimes of ice.

"It became our Game when she stole our prey," said another one, this one in the voice of somebody who'd eaten ground glass and fishhooks.

"*Who* stole your prey?" Tom shouted. But Jenny felt as if

the floor had suddenly dropped away beneath her.

Her little fingers and the sides of her hands were prickling as if small shocks were going through them. She looked at Julian.

Julian had frozen, hands in pockets, staring hard at the other Shadow Men. Then his eyebrows lifted minutely and his head tilted back slightly. He'd got it.

His eyes, still expressionless, shifted to Jenny.

"She took the old man," a third Shadow Man explained, in a whispering voice like snow blowing. "And the two boys, those were our prey, too. We hunted them. They belonged to us."

Suddenly voices joined in from all around Jenny.

"The old man was ours by right," a voice like a brass gong said.

"Blood right," a thick and muddy voice croaked.

"He made the bargain—his life was ours," a voice like a cat-o'-nine-tails added.

Julian looked the way Audrey's mother had once, when she had suggested Michael give his filthy sneakers to Goodwill. "But you were done with the old man—surely," he said fastidiously.

"We hadn't finished enjoying him."

"He was ours—forever."

"And the boys," a voice like cold wind put in, "we'd just started with the boys."

"Never got a tooth in them. . . ."

I'm glad, Jenny thought fiercely. She was glad she'd saved her grandfather, too, saved him from an eternity with these monsters. But she was still frightened.

The tall Shadow Man was moving forward. It looked down at Jenny with its crocodile eyes: ancient, pitiless, and endlessly malevolent.

"She stole their souls from us," it said formally, making the claim. "And now her life is forfeit. She is our rightful prey."

There was a burst of noise, rising and swelling from every corner of the room. It got louder and louder. It was composed of beautiful sounds and strident ones intermixed, wailing and yelping and pure tones like music.

The Shadow Men were laughing.

"Get out of here, you crazy bastards! Go away!" Dee shouted over the cacophony. She ran toward the assembled monsters, punching straight out from the shoulder, snapping her arm forward to hit with a flattened hand. She kicked, her legs flashing out too fast for the eye to follow, striking with devastating force.

"No!" Jenny screamed, plunging after her. "Dee!"

She did it without thinking, and Tom was beside her, ready to stop Dee or help her fight, depending on what the Shadow Men did.

Jenny was afraid they'd *kill* Dee. Julian had been able to throw Dee across the room without effort. But the Shadow Men just laughed more and more uproariously—and faded wherever Dee kicked. Dee's hands and feet never struck anything solid;

the monsters melted like shadows whenever she touched them.

She was panting and exhausted when Jenny and Tom reached her.

The action had cleared Jenny's head. She glanced at Julian, who was still standing where he had been, apparently unaffected by the sight of Dee going crazy. He looked—remote. Not tired, as he had before, but—disconnected. As if this were all a moderately interesting play. Maybe he was sympathizing with the other Shadow Men.

Jenny looked at the one with the crocodile eyes. She nerved herself to speak to it.

"You're saying that because I released my grandfather's soul, you have some right to me."

"By law, you're now ours," the tall Shadow Man said. "We can take you—embrace you—do what we like with you." Unexpectedly it looked at Julian. "The law can't be changed."

"I know the law can't be changed," Julian said flatly.

"She cheated us ten years ago—kept us from tasting her flesh—but now she belongs to us," the chilling, musical voice said.

And then, as quickly as that, it was happening. The dark mist was closing around Jenny, separating her from Tom and Dee. She heard Tom cry out. The mist was like cold hands touching her body. The freezing wind was howling in her ears. She was being dragged away, just as they had dragged her grandfather into the closet years ago.

CHAPTER 15

What came next was not a verbal shout—if it had been, Jenny would have thought it was Tom. It wasn't even a word exactly, more a wave of energy. And the energy was sheer negation, opposition. *No! No!*

Stop.

The mist uncoiled. Jenny's vision unblurred. She was standing, gasping, a little closer to one of the cave entrances. Tom and Dee were shaking their heads, wiping their faces, as if to get rid of some blinding haze. They were panting, too. Everyone seemed on the verge of hysteria. But the shout had come from Julian.

He was standing in the middle of the room. Desperate hope

leaped inside Jenny—maybe there was something he could do. But the next moment the hope folded and collapsed.

"You know the law," the tall Shadow Man repeated blandly. And Julian's eyes fell.

They're playing with us, Jenny realized dimly. With Julian, too; they like to see anybody suffer. They didn't stop because he yelled at them, they stopped so they could draw it out a little longer.

Another Shadow Man spoke. This one had liver-colored skin, with splotches here and there as if he'd been burned by acid. The white of one of his eyes wasn't white at all, it was red, red as rubies, red as blood.

"Nothing can stop us from taking her—unless someone else is willing to go in her place."

It took Jenny several heartbeats to get her mind around that. She wasn't thinking properly anymore. Then she remembered—her grandfather. They'd said exactly the same thing to him. *A life for a life. Someone must go in her place.* And her grandfather had, and now Jenny had rescued him and broken the bargain, and brought everything back to the starting place.

And meanwhile the terrible silence went on and on and on.

Then she heard a voice, a voice that was quite calm and devil-may-care—and human.

"I'll go."

Tom had stepped forward. His dark brown hair was neat

and short and his smile was rakish. He said it as if he were offering to go out and get pizza for the baseball team.

And he looked *wonderful.* Somehow he managed to make his rumpled and frost-touched clothes look like the latest fashion. He stood casually, and there wasn't a trace of fear in his expression.

For a moment, without thinking of anything else, Jenny was simply proud of him. Fiercely, *passionately* proud that a human, a seventeen-year-old who hadn't even heard of the Shadow Men until a month ago, could stand up to them like this. Could conceal his terror and smile that way and offer to die.

That's how I want to die, Jenny thought, and a strange serenity came over her. I want to do it *well*—since it has to be done. And I hope I have the courage, and I think—I really do think—that I just might. We'll see.

Because of course there was no possibility of letting them take Tom. She would never allow that.

Before she could say so, though, there was a short, wild laugh. Dee was beside Tom, her head thrown back, her eyes flashing like a jaguar's. She was as beautiful as some goddess of the night—some *warrior* goddess who'd just sprung up to defend her people. And she was grinning, the old barbaric grin that contrasted so oddly with her delicate features. The grin that Jenny hadn't seen since Audrey had gotten hurt.

"No," she said to Tom. "*You* won't go. I will." She was breathing very quickly, and laughing—she seemed almost exuberant. "Jenny needs you, you jerk. She'd never let you do it. *I'll* go."

"Just back off, Dee," Tom said softly. His eyes were oddly tranquil, even dreamy, but there was something frightening in his voice. At any other time, Jenny thought, Dee would have backed off.

Now she just laughed. She looked like Dee—reckless, war-like, and unconditionally loyal—but she looked like *more* than herself, too. A greater Dee.

"It's my choice," she said. "I know what I'm getting into."

And then, as Jenny listened in disbelief, other voices joined in.

"She's my cousin," Zach said. His face was sharp as a blade, and there was an intense, clear light in his gray eyes. He moved to stand sword-straight beside Dee. "I'm her blood relative. If anyone goes, it should be me."

Audrey and Michael had been whispering hastily together, now they stepped forward. Audrey's burnished copper hair was loose on her shoulders, and with her white clothing she looked like some kind of virgin sacrifice. Not elegant but exquisite, and holding herself with pride. Her skin was camellia-pale, and her voice was cool and steady.

"If everybody else is going to be a hero, then we can, too," she said. "The truth is that Jenny's worth more than any of us, and we all know it. So, now. You can take your pick." She looked at the Shadow Men. She very nearly, Jenny thought, tossed her head.

"Yeah," Michael said. "The only thing is, we figure we'll go

733

together, her and me. You know, for company, right?" He gave a No Big Deal shrug, and then his mouth trembled violently, and he grabbed for Audrey's hand. He looked for a moment as if he were going to be sick, but then he wiped his mouth and stood facing the Shadow Men squarely. There was a curious dignity about his stocky little figure.

Jenny's throat was so swollen that she could barely breathe. She was opening her mouth, though, when something like a small blue thunderbolt shot into the clear space in the middle of the room.

"Oh, please don't take Jenny," Summer gasped. She was looking utterly terrified and as fragile as spun glass, and there was a wild blankness in her eyes. Her words came in an incoherent rush. "Please—please—you *can't* take her. I'm not brave or smart—I should have been dead in the paper house. I—"

That was as far as she got. She collapsed like a bird shot out of the sky, and lay in a pool of blue until Zach picked her up. He held her—Zach, who never paid attention to any girl.

The Shadow Men were pleased. Jenny could tell. This was probably turning out to be a much better game than they ever could have hoped—much better *sport*. They had seven mice to play with, and they were clearly loving it.

"Are you sure you know what you're offering?" the one with the crocodile eyes asked gravely.

"We could explain to them," the one with the bloodred eye suggested.

"Tell them exactly what they're in for."

"How we mean to enjoy them." Other voices joined in, and the Shadow Men moved in closer. A wave of revulsion went through Jenny at the sight of them, as if she were seeing them for the first time. They were old as spiders, old as stone. They were—abominations. And the thought of them touching any of her friends was insufferable.

It was time somebody put a stop to this.

"That's enough," she said in a voice as sharp and dictatorial as Audrey's. "You've had your fun, but the game's over. I'm the one you want, the one that cheated you. So forget everybody else. Let's go."

That was *good,* she thought and a little wave of serenity came back. She was glad she could be as brave as the others. She was going to do this well, and that was all that counted now.

The Shadow Men seemed to know it was over, too. The red-eyed one held out a hand to her almost gently. It had fingers like a gorilla's—black, padded, thick as sausages and coming to a point at the ends.

Jenny put her hand in his.

The Shadow Man lifted his lips to show long, blunt teeth like tusks.

Something knocked them apart.

Jenny was knocked breathless, too, startled and confused. She thought it was some sort of attack.

It was Julian.

His hair was shining like lightning, like quicksilver. His whole being seemed full of elemental energy—of frightening intensity. And his eyes were the unbelievable, luminous blue of the precise moment before dawn.

He looked at Jenny for just one second, and then he turned and she could only see the clean purity of his profile.

"Go through the door!" he said. "That's your way home. They won't come after you."

He was between her and the Shadow Men. And apparently, unlike Dee, he could interact with them physically. At any rate, they were keeping back.

"Go on!" he shouted.

"We must have blood," the crocodile-eyed Shadow Man said. "We *will* have blood."

"Hurry!" Julian shouted.

Through the open door Jenny could see her grandfather's hallway.

"We have a right to a kill," the crocodile-eyed Shadow Man said. From the air he snatched up something long and flat and incredibly ancient-looking. His fingers were covered in scaly skin like a dinosaur's, Jenny saw. Then she realized what the long, flat branch must be.

A runestave. Like the picture in her grandfather's journal, except that this one was real—was *more* real than any object Jenny had ever seen. It was like some of the island worlds—the ones that were brighter and more substantial-looking than Earth. This stave was so real that it looked *alive,* throbbing with raw power.

There were not just single runes carved on it, but lines and lines of them, tall and needle-thin. Even though they were delicately inscribed, each stroke stood out clearly. It was as if the cuts were filled with liquid diamond that shone against the background of wood.

Jenny couldn't keep looking at the runes. It was like trying to read in a dream—first the details were sharp, and then the whole stave seemed to be swarming with changes. The runes seemed to move before she could identify them.

That's the stave of life. If anything ever was, that's the stave of life, she thought.

The voice like faraway ice bells said, "Give her to us."

"No," Julian said.

Jenny felt movement behind her. Tom. And Dee, and Zach supporting Summer, and Audrey and Michael together. They were all gathering near her, and their way was clear to the door. But nobody started for it.

"What's happening?" Audrey whispered.

"You know what we can do," the tall Shadow Man with the crocodile eyes said to Julian, and he held the runestave higher.

"Go through the door," Julian said, without turning.

"We can unmake you!" the tall one shrieked, and in that moment his voice wasn't beautiful. It was like an ice floe breaking, a cracking, smashing sound of destruction.

"What are they talking about?" Tom said.

His quiet, level voice helped Jenny. "They can cut out his name. If they cut out his name, he dies." Then she said, "Julian—"

"Go on!" he said.

The Shadow Men were very, very angry.

"We have a right to a kill!"

"Then take it!" Julian shouted. "But you won't get past me!"

The thin, scaly fingers of the Shadow Man's other hand were holding a knife. It looked like bone. It glittered like frost.

"Come on, Jenny," Tom said, not moving.

"Julian—"

"Go on!" Julian said.

The knife rose and fell.

Jenny heard herself scream. She saw the slash of the blade, the way the liquid diamond spilled like blood. There was a terrible gash in the stave now, a hideous blank space. A wound. They had carved out Julian's name.

Julian staggered.

Jenny wrenched herself away from something that was trying to hold her and fell on her knees beside him. Her thoughts were wheeling and spinning, with no order to them. There must be something to do, some way to help. . . .

Really, she knew by his face that it was too late.

The other Shadow Men were coming in a rush of darkness and freezing wind. Jenny looked up into the maelstrom and tried to lift Julian to his feet.

Then hands pulled at her. Human hands, helping her get Julian up. And then Jenny was running, they were all running, half carrying Julian with them, and the door was right in front of them.

Ice lashed at Jenny's back. A freezing tendril grabbed her ankle. But Michael was pushing the door open and Summer and Zach were falling through it—and then Audrey was through, and then she and Tom and Dee were, with Julian. She felt the resistance as she crossed the threshold, the g-force that threw her off balance and made her stumble and land on her knees.

The hallway was too small. There wasn't room for all of them, especially with Julian a dead weight. The telephone table went crashing sideways. People were falling on one another. Jenny was kneeling on somebody's leg.

"Get out of the way! We need to close the door!" Dee was shouting.

Everything was confusion. The leg under Jenny moved and she saw Audrey crawling away. She tried to crawl, too, dragging Julian. Tom picked up the telephone table and threw it over her head toward the living room.

Dee kicked the door shut just as the storm reached it.

"What about the circle?" Michael screamed. "Where's a knife? Where's a knife?"

Jenny knew she had a knife, but she couldn't move fast enough. Michael grabbed up something from the floor. It was a felt pen, the pen Jenny had used to sketch the rune circle. With a slashing motion, he crossed the circle out. The cross looked like a slanting *X,* like the rune Nauthiz. The rune of restraint.

"You don't need to do that," Julian said, and his voice was very distant. Powerless. "They won't come after you. They don't have a claim anymore."

He was lying on his back, eyes looking at the ceiling. He was holding his chest, as if the Shadow Men had cut out his heart instead of his name.

Jenny took his cold hands in hers.

So cold. As if he were a figure carved out of ice. His face was that pale, too, and his beauty was like a distant fire reflected in an icicle.

And it was strange, but at that moment Jenny seemed to see in him all the different ways he had looked before. All his many guises.

The boy in the More Games shop playing acid house music too loud. The Erlking, in white leather tunic and breeches. The Cyber-Hunter, in sleek body armor, with a blue triangle tattooed on his cheek. The masked dancer at the prom, in a black tuxedo and shirt.

It was as if each were a facet of a crystal reflecting back at her—and only now could she see the entire crystal for what it was.

Julian stepping out of the shadows, soft as a shadow himself. Julian wearing Zach's clothing, threatening her with the bees. Julian slipping the gold ring on her finger, sealing the bargain with a kiss. Julian leaning over her as she slept. Julian in the mining cave, his eyes dilated, his gaze shattering.

And she had never really found the right description for the color of those eyes. At times it had seemed close to this color or that color, but when you got down to it, words really failed. It wasn't like anything except itself.

Right now she thought she could see something flickering far back in his eyes, like a twisting blue flame in their depths.

"You can't die," she said, and she was surprised by how calm and matter-of-fact her voice was.

And Julian, although his eyes were looking somewhere past her, and his voice was weak, was equally calm. He almost seemed to be smiling.

"The law can't be changed," he said.

"You can't *die*," Jenny said. Her fingers were very tight on his, but they only seemed to be getting colder.

Everyone else had moved away. Jenny wanted to tell them that they didn't need to, that everything was going to be all right. But somehow she knew better.

"Did you know that Gebo isn't just the rune of sacrifice?" Julian said.

"I don't care."

"It means a gift, too. You gave me a gift, you know."

"*I don't care,*" Jenny said and began to cry.

"You showed me what it was like to love. What the universe could be like, *if.*"

Jenny put her free hand to her mouth. She was sobbing without a sound.

"This is my gift to you now, and you can't help but take it. You're free, Jenny. They won't come after you again."

"You can't die," Jenny whispered raggedly around the tears. "There must be something to do. You can't just *go out*—"

Julian was smiling.

"No, I'll dream another dream," he said. "I've made up so many things, now I'll just go into one. I'll be part of it."

"All right," Jenny whispered. She suddenly knew that there was nothing to be done, nothing except to help him all she could. There was something in his face that told her—a peace that was already gathering. She wouldn't disturb that peace now. "You go into the dream, Julian."

"You don't blame me?"

"I don't blame you for anything."

"Whatever else I did, I loved you," he said. He stirred, and then added, "Maybe you'll dream about me sometime, and that will help get me there."

"I will. I'll dream you into a place without any shadows, only light."

He looked at her then, and she could see he wasn't afraid.

"Nothing really dies as long as it's not forgotten," he said.

And then blue mist seemed to gather in his eyes and obscure the flame.

"Go to the dream," Jenny whispered. "Go quick, now."

His chest was still, and she didn't think he heard her. But she caught the faintest breath of sound—not with her ears, but with her mind.

"Your ring . . ."

The hand that had been on his chest slipped, and Jenny saw the gold ring there. Jenny picked it up.

The inscription on the inside had changed. The words were no longer a spell to bind Jenny.

Before, it had said: *All I refuse & thee I chuse.*

Now it said simply: *I am my only master.*

CHAPTER 16

The elemental energy, the quicksilver brightness, was gone from Julian's figure. Jenny was still holding his hand, but it suddenly seemed less substantial. She held tighter—and her fingers met.

Julian's body was dissolving into mist and shadows. In a moment even those had disappeared.

Just like that. Like smoke up a chimney.

Jenny sat back on her heels.

Then, slowly at first, but more quickly with each step, her friends gathered around her. Jenny felt Tom's arms, and felt that he was shaking.

She buried her head in his shoulder and held him as he held her.

* * *

It was Audrey and Michael who were the most helpful in what had to be done next. There were a lot of practical things to be handled.

Here in Pennsylvania the sun was just rising, and home in California it was 3:00 in the morning. Audrey and Michael went next door and woke the neighbors up and asked if they could use a phone.

Then Audrey called her parents and woke *them* up, and asked if they could please wire some money. And Michael called his father and woke *him* up, and asked him to explain to everybody else's parents that all the kids were safe.

That was something for Jenny to hang on to, once Audrey and Michael had reported back. The thought that Michael's father would be calling Mr. and Mrs. Parker-Pearson and telling them Summer was coming home. Michael's father was a writer and slightly odd, but an adult, and therefore somewhat credible. Maybe they would even believe him.

Jenny really couldn't wait to see Summer's little brother's face.

And she wanted to see her parents, too, and her own little brother.

There were other things. Angela, P.C.'s almost-girlfriend, who would have to be told that P.C. was really and truly dead. And there would be the police to deal with again, and impossible questions to answer.

But she couldn't think about all that now. She was still thinking about Julian.

Nothing died if it wasn't forgotten—and she would never forget him. There would always be some part of him in her mind. Because of him, all her life she'd be more sensitive to the beauty of the world. To its—sensuality and immediacy. Julian had been a very *immediate* person.

The most extraordinary person she would ever meet, Jenny thought. Whimsical, quixotic, wild—*impossible.*

He had been so many things. Seductive as silver and deadly as a cobra. And vulnerable like a hurt child underneath it all.

Like a hurt child who could strike out with lethal accuracy, Jenny thought as she watched Audrey moving slowly around the living room, tidying things. He'd hurt Audrey badly, and if he hadn't quite killed Summer, it had been close. He'd let his Shadow Animals kill Gordie Wilson, who'd only been guilty of skipping school and killing rabbits.

The truth was that Julian had probably been too dangerous to live. The universe would be a much safer place without him.

But poorer. And more boring, definitely more boring.

It was Summer who said the astonishing thing.

"You know," she said, after twisting around on the living room couch to see if the cab was coming, "Julian said the world was evil and horrible—remember? But then he proved himself that it wasn't."

Jenny came out of her own thoughts and looked at Summer,

amazed. That was it, exactly, of course. And that was why she could go on living, and even look forward to things. In a universe where *that* could happen, you *had* to go on living and hoping and doing your best. In a universe where that could happen, anything was possible.

That was Julian's real gift, she thought.

But there was another one, too, and she saw it as she looked at the others. They had all changed—Julian had changed them. Like the rune Dagaz, the catalyst, he'd transformed everyone who met him.

Audrey and Michael—look at them. They were walking around holding hands. Audrey hadn't even bothered to put her hair up. Michael was patting her shoulder protectively.

And Dee and Audrey had been enemies a month ago. After tonight, Jenny didn't think they could ever be that way again.

Zach, now—Zach was looking at Summer with puzzled interest in his keen gray eyes. Like a scientist who finds himself unexpectedly fascinated by a new form of flower.

Won't last a week, Jenny thought. But it was good for Zach to notice girls, just the same. To have a human interest, something besides his own imagination and his photographs.

Julian had taught Zach that imagination wasn't always better than reality.

Summer is different, too, Jenny thought. She's not half as muddled as she used to be. That's why Zach's staring.

Now, Dee . . .

Jenny turned to look at her friend.

Dee was sitting instead of pacing, with one long leg stretched in front of her. She was looking very thoughtful, her head bent, her thickly lashed eyes narrowed.

Well, Dee was Dee, and would never change, Jenny thought lovingly.

But she was wrong. As she watched, Dee looked up at her and smiled.

"You know, I've been thinking. And I was thinking—it would mean a major change of plans, you see. It would mean a lot of studying, and I hate studying."

She stopped, and Jenny blinked, then leaned forward.

"Dee?"

"I'm thinking of maybe going to college after all. Maybe. I'm just barely entertaining the idea."

Dee had changed, too.

"Aba would be happy," Jenny said, and then she dropped it, because she was afraid that Dee would turn balky. Dee really hated being pushed.

"It's your own choice," was all she added.

"Yes, it is. Everything really is, isn't it? Our own choice."

Jenny looked down at the gold ring on her finger, then clasped her other hand over it. "A lot is."

And Tom was different—the fact that Jenny was wearing that ring showed how different. He hadn't said a word about it; she didn't even think he minded.

He *understood.*

If he hadn't, Jenny could never have been happy. As it was, she knew he wouldn't hate her if she tried to dream Julian into a wonderful dream. He might not want to hear about it, but he wouldn't be upset.

He didn't take her for granted anymore, and he didn't need to be possessive, either. Jenny thought that maybe he had changed the most of all.

Or maybe she had.

"The cab's here," Michael said. "Okay, so first we have to go to the doctor. . . ." He stared at a scribbled list.

"No, first we go to the Western Union office, *then* the doctor," Audrey said, taking the list from him. "Then—"

"Then we *eat,*" Michael said.

"*Après vous,*" Dee said, gesturing them through the door. When Audrey hiked a copper eyebrow at her, she grinned. "I can throw those fancy words around, too. *Bonjour. O solo mìo. Gesundheit.*"

"*D'accord,*" Audrey said and grinned back at her.

Zach and Summer went out. Jenny stopped for just an instant on the threshold, long enough to look back.

The hallway was empty, the door to the basement was shut. That was good. If any adults would listen to Jenny, she would have them make sure that door was never opened again.

She turned and went outside.

As they headed for the cab, Michael said the kind of thing

that only Michael could say. The kind of thing that came from having a science fiction author as a dad.

"Look. What if—someday—somebody carved Julian's name *back* onto that runestave?" he said.

Tom stopped dead on the lush green grass for a moment. Then he started walking again, as Jenny put an arm through his. "Don't even talk about it," he said. "It'll never happen."

"No, I guess not. Just as well."

And Jenny, her arm entwined with Tom's, agreed—but, deep inside, some tiny part of her wondered.

She couldn't give in to the twinge of wistful sorrow she felt—she had a life to build. Things to consider. She couldn't just follow Tom to college now. She had to find out what she wanted to *do* with herself.

What do I like? she thought. Swimming. Computers. Cats. Helping people. Kids. Flowers.

She didn't know how she was going to put all those together—she'd have to find a way. After all, she was Jenny Thornton, her only master.

But just before she got into the cab, she looked up at the Pennsylvania sky. It was so blue—a bluer blue than California skies ever were in the morning. A beautiful, luminous color that seemed filled with promise.

If, someday, Julian should be reborn, she wished him well.

Not all vampires are out for blood. . . .

Don't miss L.J. Smith's
dark visions

You don't invite the local witch to parties. No matter
how beautiful she is. That was the basic problem.

I don't care, Kaitlyn thought. *I don't need anyone.*

She was sitting in history class, listening to Marcy Huang
and Pam Sasseen plan a party for that weekend. She couldn't
help but hear them: Mr. Flynn's gentle, apologetic voice was
no competition for their excited whispers. Kait was listening,
pretending not to listen, and fiercely wishing she could get
away. She couldn't, so she doodled on the blue-lined page of
her history notebook.

She was full of contradictory feelings. She hated Pam and
Marcy, and wanted them to die, or at least to have some gory
accident that left them utterly broken and defeated and miserable. At the same time there was a terrible longing inside her. If
they would only let her *in*—it wasn't as if she insisted on being
the most popular, the most admired, girl at school. She'd settle

for a place in the group that was securely her own. They could shake their heads and say, "Oh, that Kaitlyn—she's odd, but what would we do without her?" And that would be fine, as long as she was a *part*.

But it wouldn't happen, ever. Marcy would never think of inviting Kaitlyn to her party because she wouldn't think of doing something that had never been done before. No one ever invited the witch; no one thought that Kaitlyn, the lovely, spooky girl with the strange eyes, would *want* to go.

And I don't care, Kaitlyn thought, her reflections coming around full circle. This is my last year. One semester to go. After that, I'm out of high school and I hope I never see anyone from this place again.

But that was the other problem, of course. In a little town like Thoroughfare she was bound to see them, and their parents, every day for the next year. And the year after that, and the year after that. . . .

There was no escape. If she could have gone away to college, it might have been different. But she'd screwed up her art scholarship . . . and anyway, there was her father. He needed her—and there wasn't any money. Dad needed her. It was junior college or nothing.

The years stretched out in front of Kaitlyn, bleak as the Ohio winter outside the window, filled with endless cold classrooms. Endless sitting and listening to girls planning parties that she wasn't invited to. Endless exclusion. Endless aching and wishing that she *were* a witch so she could put the most hideous, painful, debilitating curse on all of them.

All the while she was thinking, she was doodling. Or rather her hand was doodling—her brain didn't seem to be involved at all. Now she looked down and for the first time saw what she'd drawn.

A spiderweb.

But what was strange was what was *underneath* the web, so close it was almost touching. A pair of eyes.

Wide, round, heavy-lashed eyes. Bambi eyes. The eyes of a child.

As Kaitlyn stared at it, she suddenly felt dizzy, as if she were falling. As if the picture were opening to let her in. It was a horrible sensation—and a familiar one. It happened every time she drew one of *those* pictures, the kind they called her a witch for.

The kind that came true.

She pulled herself back with a jerk. There was a sick, sinking feeling inside her.

Oh, *please,* no, she thought. Not today—and not here, not at school. It's just a doodle; it doesn't mean anything.

Please let it be just a doodle.

But she could feel her body bracing, ignoring her mind, going ice-cold in order to meet what was coming.

A child. She'd drawn a child's eyes, so some child was in danger.

But *what* child? Staring at the space under the eyes, Kait

felt a tugging, almost a twitch, in her hand. Her fingers telling her the shape that *needed* to go there. Little half circle, with smaller curves at the edges. A snub nose. Large circle, filled in solid. A mouth, open in fear or surprise or pain. Big curve to indicate a round chin.

A series of long wriggles for hair—and then the itch, the urge, the *need* in Kait's hand ebbed away.

She let out her breath.

That was all. The child in the picture must be a girl, with all that hair. Wavy hair. A pretty little girl with wavy hair and a spiderweb on top of her face.

Something was going to happen, involving a child and a spider. But where—and to what child? And *when?*

Today? Next week? Next year?

It wasn't enough.

It never was. That was the most terrible part of Kaitlyn's terrible gift. Her drawings were always accurate—they always, always came true. She always ended up seeing in real life what she'd drawn on paper.

But not in time.

Right now, what could she do? Run through town with a megaphone telling all kids to beware of spiders? Go down to the elementary school looking for girls with wavy hair?

Even if she tried to tell them, they'd run away from her. As if Kaitlyn brought on the things she drew. As if she *made* them happen instead of just predicting them.

The lines of the picture were getting crooked. Kaitlyn blinked to straighten them. The one thing she wouldn't do was cry—because Kaitlyn never cried.

Never. Not once, not since her mother had died when Kait was eight. Since then, Kait had learned how to make the tears go inside.

There was a disturbance at the front of the room. Mr. Flynn's voice, usually so soft and melodious that students could comfortably go to sleep to it, had stopped.

Chris Barnable, a boy who worked sixth period as a student aide, had brought a piece of pink paper. A call slip.

Kaitlyn watched Mr. Flynn take it, read it, then look mildly at the class, wrinkling his nose to push his glasses back up.

"Kaitlyn, the office wants you."

Kaitlyn was already reaching for her books. She kept her back very straight, her head very high, as she walked up the aisle to take the slip. KAITLYN FAIRCHILD TO THE PRINCIPAL'S OFFICE—AT ONCE! it read. Somehow when the "at once" box was checked, the whole slip assumed an air of urgency and malice.

"In trouble again?" a voice from the first row asked snidely. Kaitlyn couldn't tell who it was, and she wouldn't turn around to look. She went out the door with Chris.

In trouble again, yes, she thought as she walked down the stairs to the main office. What did they have on her this time? Those excuses "signed by her father" last fall?

Kaitlyn missed a lot of school, because there were times

when she just couldn't stand it. Whenever it got too bad, she went down Piqua Road to where the farms were, and drew. Nobody bothered her there.

"I'm sorry you're in trouble," Chris Barnable said as they reached the office. "I mean . . . I'm sorry *if* you're in trouble."

Kaitlyn glanced at him sharply. He was an okay-looking guy: shiny hair, soft eyes—a lot like Hello Sailor, the cocker spaniel she'd had years ago. Still, she wasn't fooled for a minute.

Boys—boys were no good. Kait knew exactly why they were nice to her. She'd inherited her mother's creamy Irish skin and autumn-fire hair. She'd inherited her mother's supple, willow-slim figure.

But her eyes were her own, and just now she used them without mercy. She turned an icy gaze on Chris, looking at him in a way she was usually careful to avoid. She looked him straight in the face.

He went white.

It was typical of the way people around here reacted when they had to meet Kaitlyn's eyes. No one else had eyes like Kaitlyn. They were smoky blue, and at the outside of each iris, as well as in the middle, were darker rings.

Her father said they were beautiful and that Kaitlyn had been marked by the fairies. But other people said other things. Ever since she could remember, Kaitlyn had heard the whispers—that she had strange eyes, evil eyes. Eyes that saw what wasn't meant to be seen.

Sometimes, like now, Kaitlyn used them as a weapon. She stared at Chris Barnable until the poor jerk actually stepped backward. Then she lowered her lashes demurely and walked into the office.

It gave her only a sick, momentary feeling of triumph. Scaring cocker spaniels was hardly an achievement. But Kaitlyn was too frightened and miserable herself to care. A secretary waved her toward the principal's office, and Kaitlyn steeled herself. She opened the door.

Ms. McCasslan, the principal, was there—but she wasn't alone. Sitting beside the desk was a tanned, trim young woman with short blond hair.

"Congratulations," the blond woman said, coming out of the chair with one quick, graceful movement.

Kaitlyn stood motionless, head high. She didn't know what to think. But all at once she had a rush of feeling, like a premonition.

This is it. What you've been waiting for.

She hadn't known she was waiting for anything.

Of course you have. And this is it.

The next few minutes are going to change your life.

"I'm Joyce," the blond woman said. "Joyce Piper. Don't you remember me?"

About the Author

L.J. Smith has written more than twenty-five books for young adults, and is the *New York Times* bestselling author of the Night World series, the Vampire Diaries series, and *Dark Visions*. She lives in the Bay Area of California, where she enjoys reading, hiking, and traveling. Her favorite place is a cabin in Point Reyes National Seashore. Visit her at ljanesmith.net.

Vampires, werewolves, witches, and shapeshifters:
They live among us. How much do *you* know
about the Night World?

L.J. Smith shares her inspiration for the series and answers the
questions you've been asking!

Also includes information about the clans, trivia from all nine
books, and two quizzes to see how *you* fit into the Night World.

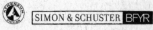

SIMON TEEN

Simon & Schuster's **Simon Teen**
e-newsletter delivers current updates on
the hottest titles, exciting sweepstakes, and
exclusive content from your favorite authors.

Visit **TEEN.SimonandSchuster.com** to
sign up, post your thoughts, and find out what
every avid reader is talking about!